THE ROOT

OF

FEY

MAGIC

Callie Pey

BY CALLIE PEY

The Root of Fey Magic

Copyright © May 8th, 2023, by Jennifer Cote

Cover Design by D Arte Oriel
Editing by Corbeaux Editorial Services

Dedication

To those who seek answers when all hope seems lost, knowing that love will find a way.

Special Dedication to Steve for your support while I pursue this dream, Kat B. & Allie H. for your help making this story all that it could be.

Table of Contents

Helpful Terms Guide

Artemesia – The planet that all the races settled on after leaving Earth during the great migration.

Vasilissa – Mother tree of a grove. A dryad with the specific magic tied to the designated elemental direction. There are four groves on Artemesia: Voreios, Anatoli, Notos, & Dytika.

Druwid – a bonded mate to the vasilissa. Powerful magic users that protect the grove.

Contessa – daughters of the vasilissa with the magical alignment for the element of the grove with the capability of becoming a mother tree.

Ryne – protector designated to watch over the contessa. If bonded with the contessa who becomes the vasilissa, they will become a druwid.

Watchtower – a powerful elemental warrior, usually a dryad, that protected the guardian before the fall of the shadow god, Cholios.

Chapter 1 – Lorsan

The trees in this forest always whispered silent horrors, but now they were screaming. An omen perhaps? Fey magic tied with the land in a way that would be considered turbulent by most, almost deadly to the inexperienced user. Our magic rippled across the atmosphere, each pulse coursing in my veins. The way the magic moved differently, as if numerous explosions went off across the kingdom, unsettled my nerves, though my trained facial features would never reveal that.

I stood on the balcony overlook, the highest point of the court, to watch the chaos. Echoes of screams many miles away poured into my mind. There was very little I could do for any of them, especially when we didn't know what was wrong. Without blocking the magic from everyone, I'd have to let some of the consequences play out. And with fey magic, there were always consequences.

Down the stairs, I could already hear the concerned bellowing of the upper court. I released a sigh, resigned to the forced company I was about to receive. In nearly a century I'd had no peace, why would I expect that to change this morning?

Banging on my door interrupted the rest of my thoughts. I'd never get a moment to myself ever again. Only by escaping to the liminal realm could I hide from the cluster of advisors and responsibilities, but eventually they would find me. The true reality was that once you were king, death would be your only escape. I counted down from three, then let out the breath I'd been holding as my door swung open with a heavy creak.

"King Lorsan! Are you hearing this? There have been 124 deaths just this morning." My aunt, Prinna, shouted hysterically like this somehow afflicted her personally. She wore a dazzling dress of gold, her favorite color after I'd been named king, that reflected the sunlight, nearly blinding me in the process. "What are we going to do about this?"

"Your Majesty! The fey are rushing the court gates demanding that you act immediately," my senior adviser and the last remaining person from my father's court, Vesstan, chimed in. Decked out from head to toe in the finest of linens, he'd spared no expense to establish himself as the elite in the court after the war was over. The monocle he wore in his left eye was unnecessary, but he deemed it dignified. His short dark hair left his bedazzled ears out for open display in overstated embellishment.

I covered my eyes. Barely a moment in and I already wanted to scream in fury. I'd never wanted to be king. It was my first thought every morning as I woke up in a room I'd never wanted, playing a part I hadn't asked for. I didn't want to follow in the footsteps of my father and grandfather, especially after their embarrassing losses against the other kingdoms on Artemesia. The seelie court needed to be ruled, however. The fey citizens would run amok without an authority figure in place, as evidenced by their display at the gates, but the fae were also a greedy people.

If asked what I had wanted to be, I'd have said a scholar. Not that it mattered. The goddess, Aine, had marked me at my birth a quarter of a millennia ago to ascend after my father. It wasn't supposed to happen for a long while as we can live for what feels like forever. Helio was power hungry and eager to make a name for himself. He became obsessed with the wrong nymph, and her druwids killed him for it, leaving me in this unfortunate position. He should have expected it, given that druwids were the bonded lovers of mother trees in the neighboring groves, but he made very little sense in his last few years.

Now, instead of pursuing knowledge and insight on the workings of the universe, I was plagued with a constant headache.

"Your Majesty?" Vesstan asked again as he waved a hand in my direction. "Are you paying attention to what I'm saying?"

"Death, fluctuations in magic, fey riots to speak with me personally. Yeah, I think I got the gist of it." I rubbed my brow in agitation. The last thing I wanted to do was request Ferox's presence. The older dryad was a bastion of power in the world beyond our realm, a former watchtower to the guardian before the fight against the shadow god attacking our planet. Unfortunately, he resided in Voreios, and those were the last people I wanted to know about this issue.

"I guess that is most of it, however, there's new information we have received. Prinna, you need to stop panicking or he won't listen."

"Well, he should listen to me! The stars tell me of great chaos if this isn't resolved. We could lose everything!" My aunt used her fake ominous voice that she pulled out when she pretended that she was a powerful seer.

I walked a few paces to my desk and turned the chair around so I could slide in easily. Leaning back, I kicked my feet up on the polished wood. "Aren't we already in great chaos? The lesser fey can't use their magic without destroying the surrounding area. This has been problematic for generations. Sure, the explosions have been larger and brighter in the past few weeks, but it's hardly worth the doom and gloom you are spouting."

"It will be worse! Mark my words, Lorsan. You need to listen to me. I've never steered you wrong before." Prinna leveled her exasperated gaze on me as if I'd missed everything she'd said.

I'd take the bait. If I was going to have an aching brow, why not let her do all the talking. "All right. I hear you. Do the stars tell us how to fix it? Do any of you know what this new variation even is?"

"We aren't sure what is wrong." Vesstan shook his head at Prinna before she could reply. "At least, not in a way that is different from the original imbalance. There is no way the stars can reveal an answer to this problem. The side effects of our magic being used by those who can't handle it is escalating rapidly out of control."

"Then why are you bothering me?" I knew it was harsh to speak to them this way, but I was tired of being brought problems. None of the esteemed members of the court wanted to do anything besides be near me as I came up with the solution to whatever ailed them. With a deep breath, I continued, "We need to cancel solstice events and bring all of our people home. Has anyone reached out to our scientists in Aramore to see if this is affecting them? The last thing we need is another war with the elves because we caused an explosion in their new research facilities."

"I didn't think to . . ."

"Get someone on it now," I snarled at my adviser. Our last bloody war had raged for over a century, and my people were proud. They wouldn't back down in a fight, even if we were in the wrong or severely outnumbered. Best to avoid the situation entirely. "Also put out an edict to restrict the use of magic. I want the well capped and locked down with double the guard."

"That could cause panic," Vesstan protested with a firm upper lip.

The door swung open behind him and my cousin, Trevan, strode in. He wore a decorated suit like mine, only his colors were red to denote his position as commander of the guard. The decorative sword tied to his waistband had never seen action but had been passed down in our family for millennia. His long blond hair fell down in waves over his shoulders. He had a sneaky smile on his face, playing that he knew something the rest of us didn't, but he'd always been a smug asshole like that. There wasn't anyone I trusted more.

"I'm not asking. Get it done. No—" I cut my aunt off before she could interrupt me. Some days I understood why my father had been so ruthless. No one talked back to him for fear of immediate execution. Ever. It was like they believed I wasn't a grown man because of how young I was when I took the throne. "When they are smart enough to control the magic and not kill themselves, then they can have it back."

The problem with how our magic worked was nuanced. Fae, like myself and the rest of the elite in our kingdom, received a bigger share of the magical resource. In my youth, I'd been taught that it was due to our lineage deriving from the goddess herself. As a grown man, I found this preposterous.

The other fey included all the other creatures in our kingdom. Many of the stronger races broke off many generations ago, like the elves, dwarves, and merfolk. Then a war with the forest folk before we'd left Earth split the remaining portion of our kingdom in half and created the four groves that lived outside of our borders currently. The lingering fey weren't able to control as much of our power, and when they did, it usually came with horrible side effects to the user and all those around them.

"I think it's more complicated than a matter of the general population's intelligence." Trevan leaned over the rail, his face reflecting the blue hues of the newest explosion in the forest. "Our guard will need to have access to their magic. That's what keeps us safe here in the court."

I nearly rolled my eyes that he was joining in on their side. "I will create a smaller well for them to pull from, but even they will need to scale back. We don't know how fast this chaos is spreading or who it is targeting. They have weapons, make them use those."

A messenger fluttered up with his translucent wings and landed beside my cousin. Trevan unrolled the message and read it quietly. The furrow in his brow indicated that the news wasn't good, but when he crumpled the letter and put it in his pocket, I realized he wasn't going to share.

Before I could demand that he read it aloud, Prinna grabbed my arm and held her head as if a growing pain ailed her. She fell to her knees beside my seat. "The visions are getting more intense. This is going to put us back into conflict with Voreios. The flames are so high!"

Clear trauma still lay with most of the higher court. The vasilissa of Voreios hadn't even fought any of them, she'd just set fire to the court on her way out from being held prisoner, controlling it so that everyone inside could escape as she did. Vasilissa was the term used for the mother trees in the grove, and although Aurinia could have destroyed everything here that day, she'd continued to argue with her druwids about the cost of life even when the shadows were closing in. I remembered our first conversation, on the day I became king, well.

The way we used to treat women in this court had been appalling, but none of the older generation could see that. Aurinia had only seen a glimpse of the horror Helio had planned for her, and after what happened to my mother, I never begrudged the way she chose to leave. Powerful fae, myself included, still liked to dabble with fear in our couplings when we fed. It was part of the thrill, but holding unwilling women hostage was a line I drew.

"There is not going to be any war with Voreios." The only grove I let visit us at the court was Anatoli. They'd been our allies throughout the war with the elves. Celeste, the vasilissa of Anatoli, was the daughter of a past fae druwid, so we knew we could trust them. Now with this issue, the chances that we would invite anyone else into our territory were even less. I snapped to get Trevan's attention. "Read the letter."

"The healers believe it is venenatio luteus that is ailing the population." Trevan paused, apparently processing that information. We'd not seen this type of poisoning in our environment for many centuries. It was curious to have it pop up again now, but it would take more research to discover the origin. "Our guards may have found one other discrepancy with the fey magic. The dru have not been impacted in their access to magic."

The dru? Those hollowed-out trees barely moved, so I didn't think about them often. "How did they even discover that?"

More explosions rippled through the forest behind me, sending out an unnerving wave of winds in our direction. While my aunt cowered at the display of turbulent magic, I wasn't alarmed in the slightest. With my position as king, I had the most powerful access to fey magic at this point. Very few could rival my pull to the source, and as such, none of these currents of chaos could touch me.

"According to this message, Macendil was talking to a guard at the entrance of the labyrinth. Really, we need to see if he will relocate." Trevan glanced in the direction of our world-renowned landmark. "I'd prefer to keep the entryway clear."

"Why do you think they are unaffected by the poison?" I rose from my chair and offered a hand to my aunt for her to get on her feet as well.

"It might be the wind elemental magic that Aurinia enchanted them with." Prinna spat out the words in disgust. "After their aid for Voreios led to the king's death, they should have been removed from our lands."

This wasn't the first time that fae members of the court had asked to exile the ancient trees. I always dismissed it quickly. Even if I did banish them from the lands, it would take decades for them to actually relocate, and I had other things to worry about that were far more important. The poisoning plague, for example.

"If that's the case, then perhaps the venenatio luteus won't spread to beings that have mixed magic?" Trevan rubbed his chin as if lost in that thought. The sound of bells chiming on the other side of the court seemed to confirm the train of their thoughts.

"They helped with the last poisoning, and as long as we don't imprison any dryads, they will not be called to move against us." If this was true, then the illness wouldn't spread around the world. This meant that the issue was limited to only my people and potentially one other.

"Do you think this will impact the dryad in Voreios?" I asked casually. In our court, you could never act too interested in anything, or there would be consequences.

16

"Oh." Trevan's eyes lit up at the mention. "You mean Aurinia's daughter born with fey magic. What was her name again?"

I moved to my bar to pour a drink for myself and raised the glass so that they could partake with me. My cousin agreed, but my aunt declined. "Aralia."

He took the glass from the bar once I filled it. "That's right. She'd be all grown up now. Why haven't we invited her to court?"

"Because she's one of them." Prinna wagged her finger at us both. "Do not start bringing any of Voreios back over here again, Lorsan."

"Don't forget whom you are speaking to." I leveled her with a glare, and she had the graciousness to look chastised. "No one said anything about inviting her to my court. If she's surrounded by elemental magic, she could be a good control measure to see if this illness is truly impacting all with access to only fey magic."

My cousin didn't reply immediately, and the calculation in his eyes only meant future trouble for me. "I'll send a message to Voreios. It doesn't hurt to prepare them and see if there is any insight to be gained. I can even take it myself."

"Don't do anything just yet. I'd rather have more information before we go around stirring up concern." As soon as he mentioned the message, my guard went back up. I was determined not to involve them in my affairs any longer, and I

17

would never choose Trevan to deliver a message of that nature to them. A little more than a century into my reign and I had two things my father didn't: my head and the start of a new world vision that didn't involve conquering the rest of Artemesia.

"Lorsan." My aunt fussed with the trim of my collar before I could wave her hands away. "Do you remember what begins today?"

"I hardly think this is a time for the trials while people are dying." I'd forgotten about issuing the edict to postpone the whole thing.

"You don't have any more time!" she insisted, while going for that blasted book again. Flipping through the pages fiercely, she stopped on the one that outlined my exact fate. "You must have a queen selected in the next two full moons. That is our law, and even you cannot erase that, despite how you have put nearly all your efforts into avoiding it. Any other young king would be glad to have a partner to share the burden with."

If I'd been a smart man, I would have asked Aurinia and Ferox to change that particular law with a contract, but I'd been young and irrational. Now I was stuck having to marry the next queen of the fae. Given how young my father had been when he died, I understood the push, but it didn't mean I had to like it. I didn't even get to pick her. The magic did.

18

"I can't recall the scrolls saying what happens if we don't run the trials. Helio didn't run them, and nothing all that bad happened to him until he picked the wrong kingdom to war against." I might find a way out of this if I were smart enough.

"Helio's elven bride had been accepted by rites to the magic as the queen, and you had already been born. You know how many potential heirs you have running around in this court?"

It was a rhetorical question. I had zero heirs at this time; there were no children for the magic to choose from.

"But Helio never married her," I argued as I leaned over to take the book from her hands and look for the information myself.

"Your father made a deal with Aine that he would rectify the situation after the war was won and the broken contract paid for. The goddess accepted his terms and didn't seek to enforce the bindings of our magic due to his continuous blood offerings." Prinna rubbed her hands together in discomfort. "He played a dangerous game and lost."

"Would I be able to make a deal with our divine lady, Aine?" I flipped a few pages, but I already knew this book inside and out. The only contract more dangerous to sign in the Feylands than one with the fae was one with the goddess of the fae.

"Only if the power you would receive from the delay in her will would be greater than the one that she intended to give you." When my aunt looked at me, her face had aged with wary

19

distress. "Do you know of a source on this world that could be stronger than any found here?"

Of course, there wasn't one. With the guardian, Aurinia, and her triad off our planet, there wasn't a person or tool around that could compare to what was in my lands. I shook my head and accepted my fate. To refuse Aine would bring destruction upon my kingdom.

The screaming trees echoed my forlorn thoughts as I straightened my back to do what needed to be done. "Then the decision has been made. Summon the volunteers."

Chapter 2 — Aralia

No one warned me that stepping out of my mother's shadow would be damn near impossible. It didn't matter what I did, or what any of my other siblings did, it wouldn't hold a candle to the light my mother had turned on. She'd been born to a destiny that I couldn't comprehend, and the mark of my mother's time on Artemesia spread into everything I could touch. What happened to the child of a hero, then? I was determined to find out once I resolved my own despair at the bland future potential.

The unicorns that pranced across the worn gravel path I walked on reminded me of my elven father, Kelan. Growing up with him had been the treasure of my existence. Quick to smile and teach, he shared everything he could with all of his girls. I cherished every lesson, every moment we spent  together, and I always wanted more. Even when I distracted him from his responsibilities, he'd always just give me a smile and show me what he was working on.

But my father had a special smile just for her. You could always tell when my mother was nearby because he would practically glow. As I got older, I knew that no one would come close to loving me like he loved her. Yet, I decided that I wouldn't settle for anything less. As I was determined for that to be the case, naturally, I was alone currently.

When Nylisa approached me with the twinkle of a secret in her eye, I gave her my most troublesome smile. Pillow talk and night secrets were supposed to be reserved for lovers, but who needed that when you had a twin?

"What's the dirt?" I asked teasingly before wrapping my arm in hers. I followed along the trail as she worked the roots the way Mom had shown us all those years ago. I liked to do this task with her, so we could spend a little time together every day. Just us.

"Evidone has just returned from Notos." Nylisa's mischievous smirk was all the clue I needed for what she was about to say.

"Did she find her mates?" As much as I would be happy to hear the speculation, it also rubbed in the fact that one of my youngest sisters was further ahead than I was at finding the loves of her life.

"She did. One of their border leaders and the messenger we sent over with her."

"Wait, didn't you send her with the one who just got back from Aramore?" When she nodded her head, I continued. "He'd been over there for years. How unfortunate for Notos, then. Losing a border leader is a hard pill to swallow. We don't really have the need for him here, though."

"Well, that's the thing. He didn't return with them this morning. Veon is furious with her request."

"Oh?" Now I was entirely invested despite my own self-pity. My sister's druwid, Veon, didn't display rash emotions like many satyrs could, so for him to be angry, there had to be a cause for it.

"She's asked to relocate her tree." Nylisa couldn't stop smiling as her attention was drawn to something I couldn't see before she spoke again. "Didn't even say hi, just burst out with the desperate need to return at once. Her new mate was a bit more respectful to the changing situation."

"She wants to move to the southern grove? Why?" My upper lip curled a bit in mock disgust, and my twin laughed heartily. Evidone had been born with fire magic, so it wasn't too much of a stretch to think she'd find the temperate desert comforting. With all the volcanoes and dry air, I had to say I'd not been impressed the last time I'd gone for a visit.

"Like all of us, I think she's trying to find her place. Notos seems exotic compared to the familiar forests of Voreios." Nylisa spoke this way for my sake. She'd always known her place was here and what her role would be, but she knew how hard I'd struggled. "I believe she has found a place that fits the vision she has for herself."

I could understand where Evidone was coming from. Our parents had prepared us for all the possibilities they could think of that life might throw our way. Our satyr father, Graak, had made sure that we were all well equipped to defend ourselves, with or without mates. Our mother, Aurinia, trained us in our magical and nymph abilities. Kelan made sure that we knew how to take moments to ourselves and celebrate life as it is. They wanted us to be well-rounded, but in a world void of conflict, most of those skills went to waste.

Nylisa took over the reins as vasilissa of Voreios like a bright beacon in the sky. She'd trained diligently, determined to make our parents proud as they embarked on the next phase of their hero adventure. She smashed all of their expectations, and now as a mother herself, she ran the grove with the same grace I'd only before associated with our mom. As happy as I was for my sister, I bemoaned my own lack of purpose.

"What's the real reason that you think Veon is mad?"

Nylisa sighed with a gentle demeanor that reminded me too much of mother. "That is harder to say. I think he's trying to keep our family together. We've already had two sisters leave, and then Petris went to the academy."

"Yeah, but he's talked about going since he was old enough to speak the words. He's going to come back." Our brother venerated our grandfather, who helped him through the subtleties of being a male nymph, so of course he'd always planned to go to follow as many of Ferox's footsteps as possible.

"We know that. Veon is taking it personally and thinks that he's letting everyone down. He believes that is the reason they are leaving."

"You have to know that's not what it is," I insisted with a turn in her direction.

She smiled a bit sadly and shrugged. "I know we aren't the same."

I quickly shook my head and blond strands of hair fell into my face, obscuring my sight before I could push them back. "Mom didn't want you to run this grove the same way she did. She wanted you to be yourself."

"I'm just worried that one day you will leave me too."

"That will never happen." I dismissed the statement immediately. Sure, I might be bored, with no real goals or motivations of my own, but a world without Nylisa would never satisfy me.

The library by the sea was my favorite place to spend the day. My father Graak had built it on the coast as an act of love for my mother. A century after it had been built, it was still one of the largest in our world, rivaling even the ones in Aramore. There was always something new to learn or uncover here. It allowed me to get lost in new knowledge, and maybe somewhere in these pages was a hint at what the future could hold for me.

"That's not even the worst part of Evidone's request. She is adamant that she shouldn't have to wait until after the elves leave."

"She does know that not just anyone can do the spell, right?" I shook my head, frustrated on Nylisa's behalf. "I don't think Aunt Cassie is even here."

My sister ran her hand along some of the books and looked thoughtful for a moment before she spoke again. "She says she can't bear to be apart from her new mate. That her soul just might break, and with me being so close to flowering again, the delay could be longer than intended."

"Spoiled seedling," I muttered. My younger siblings shared the smallest amount of pressure and responsibility. They'd not seen the demands that our parents had gone through to transform the grove. They did understand the burden that Nylisa carried with keeping us all safe, but they'd never carry that weight. "She can wait a few days, or he can come here and wait with her. Who knows, they may like it here better."

"He's a border leader. You know it's not that easy."

"You act as if any of them have a real role now that the infernals are gone. He could take a few days to be with his mate. As a matter of fact, groves normally automatically give those when you find your mate."

"You didn't listen to that message from Dad at the last meeting of the guard, did you?" There was a warning in her voice that gave me pause. Could something more than the perfect peace my parents left behind truly be going on?

"I may have tuned out for the later part," I admitted, rubbing my neck.

"Mages are gathering in scattered parts of the world. They told us to stay extra vigilant in all our dealings with outsiders, particularly fae."

"I never understood why the focus always seems to be around the fae when mages are brought up."

"It's because fey magic is the source of power for the mages. I don't know why, but perhaps our brother could fill us in when he returns."

Of course, my form of magic would be the best magical tool for acolytes of Cholios. The shadow god had been dead a few years over a century, but that didn't stop his followers from trying to embed his will across the universe.

"Perhaps I can go out and help with the borders then. Might give me a sense of purpose."

"Not today, you aren't!" she exclaimed. "I need you for diplomacy with the elves. Plus, you know Rux doesn't really love when you are on the border."

"He thinks it means that he has to watch me more. Really, I don't understand why he has to watch me at all. Veon needs him more than I do."

"Let's not start that conversation again." She sighed and turned back to me with a beautiful smile. "What do you think you will study today?"

"I started working on my Draconic last week, but I can't tell if I am pronouncing the consonants right without hearing it. Perhaps I should travel to Notos with Evidone to see if they can get me into the forbidden land of the dragons." I was mostly teasing; I didn't have much inclination to travel anywhere when Nylisa couldn't go.

"That would be a grand adventure!" My twin beamed brightly at the thought of the journey. "Could you imagine finding out one of your mates is a dragon?"

"Too much fire for my liking." I stuck my tongue out at her playfully.

"Honestly, Lia. I think you are too picky."

"Says the woman who still only has one druwid. Where are your other mates?"

"It could take years to find them, you know that. Plus it's hard to think of anyone beyond Veon. I'm pretty sure it's no one in the grove, but how will destiny bring us together?" She sighed wistfully. She loved the idea of meeting her matches. Part of me was just terrified over the prospect.

"Speaking of border leaders, you haven't seen some of ours recently . . . maybe a little detour now and again wouldn't hurt."

"I see what you did. You spun this back on me!"

She tsked and wagged a finger at me before she pulled out a book on Draconic and set it on the table. "I think you should travel. Just make sure to bring any lovestruck stragglers back to Voreios. Your tree would be here so we could still talk every day. What better way to learn than through immersion?"

"I think I'll wait another year. I still want to try to get as much vocabulary under my belt as I can before I start traipsing through their lands."

Nylisa's voice lowered, and she leaned in closer to me. "Have you been to the fey pools recently?"

"Sure. I feel like I was just there." I waved off her concern with a quick hand gesture and an easy smile.

"Mom said you need to go every season, but I don't think you have left for at least the past year." Her eyebrow raised as she waited for me to fight against her innate knowledge on this topic.

"You worry too much. I will make it a point to go next week. Honestly, I don't understand why I have to do it. Nothing ever changes."

"It's a good place to run into . . . you know."

I laughed in disbelief as she attempted to call me out on my childhood crush on the neighboring fae king. I'd long gotten over him, but it didn't stop any of my sisters from teasing me about it. "Stop trying to play matchmaker! The gods implied that something would come up for my destiny at some point. I just need to patiently wait it out."

"I think you need to experience more life before it comes to you. How can destiny reveal itself if you never leave the grove's borders?" Nylisa pressed, and I hated the wisdom in her words.

Chapter 3 — Aralia

When Veon appeared in the doorway of the library, I knew my time with my sister before the elven ambassadors arrived had drawn to a close. Running a grove was time consumingly complicated, and I was glad that I didn't have anything to do with it.

Nylisa radiated light immediately when she noticed her druwid, love highlighting the soft curves of her face. They'd instantly fallen into step with one another when Nylisa matured. I would never admit it aloud, but I had been so jealous.

"My beautiful star," Veon purred as he took her into his arms, ignoring me. "The elves should be arriving within the hour, just in time for the fires. Can I steal you away for a few moments on my own?"

Veon's dark hair fell down past his shoulders. His tanned, curved horns rounded into an almost perfect circle around his ears on both sides. The shade of his black fur was striking and masked him when he moved through the forest. His muscles were thin and packed, almost disarmingly sending the message that he wasn't as dangerous as he was. Not to my sister, of course, but to anyone who even looked at her sideways. He and Rux trained hard with my fathers, and Graak was hard to please.

I hated that my mind trailed to Rux. The thorn in my side from the day I was old enough to understand why he was there.

When a mother tree had a daughter born with the elemental magic of the grove, they were differentiated by being labeled as a contessa. Our ties in Voreios ran with earth magic. In a rare turn of events, every single one of my siblings was gifted with one elemental magic or another, aside from me. When a contessa was born, trials for a ryne protector occurred, and thus the new seedling had a dedicated guard. When a contessa assumed the role of vasilissa, any of her bonded lovers, ryne or otherwise, would become druwids after a ceremony bonding them to the trees and the shield protecting the lands.

Being the twin of a contessa meant I had the pleasure of a ryne for protection and friendship. Once my magic was revealed, there was never a chance I could become a true contessa for Voreios, but my ties to Nylisa established the need for an extra set of eyes that I could never escape from. Almost every single contessa and ryne fell in love once the nymph matured, but I had to be broken because I couldn't stand the guy.

Rux trailed not too far behind Veon with a nereid named Rhenei. She'd attached herself to my ryne as soon as I made it clear to all the nymphs that anybody could have him. Why they hadn't gotten their fate marks was beyond me at this point. They were always together, even when he was babysitting me on trips around the grove.

"Aralia," Rux greeted me dutifully. I knew he took his job very seriously, even if I didn't want him to.

"Rux. Rhenei. I was just about to be off. You can count me not injured or dying, and I'll see you again at the top of the next hour." I waved at him with an eye roll and spun on my heels to walk the opposite way.

"Lia . . ." My sister hummed disapprovingly. She didn't enjoy the tension between us, but it couldn't be helped.

"I thought we would go over the protocol with the elven visit." Rux slid around Veon and Nylisa to catch up with me before I could slip away, down the stairs, and out of the library.

I didn't attempt to hide the annoyance in my sigh as I glowered at him. "There's no protocol needed between us anymore. I'm not a contessa. Never have been. I won't leave the grove with any elves, same as any of my younger sisters."

His shorter, choppy brown hair caught the wind, resting on his horns. His fur was a lighter brown than Veon's, and his packed muscles weren't hard to look at, if only he would treat me like he did all the other nymphs. I hated that the elders didn't seem to know what to do until we both found our true matches.

"Rux, I think she's good," Rhenei called to him. "We all know not to leave."

"Exactly," I agreed and waved him off. "Run along and have fun. I have better things to do."

He was giving me that look. The one that heated my skin like he was going to call my bluff. I was hungry and he knew it. Nymphs only fed from being pleasured, which is truly unfortunate when you have someone watching you all the time, and when you don't want to settle for anyone less than perfect.

Satyrs, on the other hand, fed from pleasuring their partners. A fact I hated to admit that he was very good at.

"Rhenei, I need to have a conversation with Lia. Let me catch up with you later." Rux turned his normal charm onto the nereid whose cheeks lit up with a rosy tint. It made me want to gag. Then he grabbed my wrist without a thought toward Veon and Nylisa, who didn't pay us any mind anyway, and he led me toward the back of the library.

"What do you want now?" I tried to pull my hand away, but he only tightened his grip.

The heated look he gave me sent shivers down my spine. "The elves will be here soon. I can tell that you are starving."

"Worried that I'll turn my glamour on an elven ambassador?" I snarked at him as he pulled us into one of the tiny alcoves.

"You can cast your glamour on anyone that you would like."

"Oh, right. Of course, because then you would be free of me."

"That's not wha—"

"Save it. I don't need or want your help right now," I
spat, making sure I kept my glare steady. In these moments of
hunger, I did want him. I wanted all of him. His broad
shoulders, the grooves in his muscular chest, even the way he
looked at me like this could be fire. That flame wasn't mine to
claim though. He'd made his decision long ago, and I'd never
forgive him for not waiting. I'd been silly as a sapling to think
that just because it was destiny for everyone else, it would work
out for me. If she were his mate like I suspected, then it worked
out how it should have, even if it hurt me at first. "I'm studying
Draconic now. You can either die of boredom watching me or
you can go do your other jobs as Veon's second and prepare for
the elves' arrival."

"Are you trying to imply that I am not doing my job?"

"That's what it looks like to me." I shrugged casually
before I moved past him back toward my books.

"Why are you studying the language of the dragons? They
don't ever come here to visit us." Rux rubbed the back of his
head. I felt his gaze trailing after me.

"I was discussing a trip out there in the next few seasons
with Nylisa."

"That's not a good idea."

"I don't care what you think about it."

"Lia, you know you aren't going by yourself. It's not safe."

"Then assign a guard."

"I *am* your guard," he growled out before he released an exhausted sigh. "Why must you continue fighting me on this?"

"Eventually you will get tired of this life, and you will beg to be released from this obligation. I'd thought it would have happened by now, but Veon is being quite stubborn."

"Your fathers both wanted this as well. This will not go the way you seem to think. You cannot chase me off. Maybe if you gave me a chance, things could be quite . . . pleasant."

"How about this? Please . . . please go away. I am asking nicely." I tried my sickly sweet, persuasive voice that I'd used on him all the time when I was a sapling. It always worked then, and now his shoulders sagged in defeat.

"Fine. We aren't done talking about the planned trips though. If I have to wait to talk with Nylisa and you at the same time, I will. Veon is suggesting locking us in a cave together until we sort this out, but I know how much you would hate that."

He turned and I couldn't help the appreciative glance down his chiseled back. His tail flicked a few times, expressing his annoyance.

It drove me crazy that I wanted him this way. I'd never admit it out loud, because my pickiness also extended to feeding partners. Unfortunately, he was the only one I trusted to get this close. I'd have to change that if I ever hoped to unbind our connection. With all the visitors coming to the grove, a new idea blossomed in my mind.

Tonight, I was going to woo an elf.

Chapter 4 — Lorsan

Everything in the newly built seelie court was opulent. I withheld no expense in the past century as I reclaimed the grand structure and made it a vision any king could dream about. The kings before me preferred the dreary, unwelcoming halls to avoid visitors. I loved to entertain when people weren't bringing me problems to fix. In my earlier years, I often sought to bring the vasilissa and druwids of Voreios here just so they could marvel at what I had built from the ashes they'd left behind.

Instead of the dark halls that haunted my youth, everything now was coated in white with gold accents and fixtures. There were splashes of blue for my mother, Calla, on the large entrance doors and again in the grand hall where most of the court would gather for meals and dancing. She always loved to dance and, before the war with the elves, had been the first one to greet any visitors to the court. My mother was always as bright as the sun. I'd had a sculpture of her commissioned for the grand hall where she now watched over all of our activities. I would have her honored in my court, the way she never was by my father.

I waited until half an hour past the time I'd told everyone to gather for the presenting of the women who sought to earn their title as queen. As much as I enjoyed some aspects of being king, I hated the long-winded nature of some of these formalities. Aristocratic families believed they were entitled to more of my time than they actually were, but good luck telling them that if I wouldn't follow it up with insane acts of cruelty. Yet another gift from my late father.

With long strides down the hall, my wings manifested behind me. Everyone sees our magic differently, but since I was a child, I would see it in ripples and splashes of gold, white, and black. The power I wielded could barely be contained, so the gold flickered off my wings in waves that the world around me could also see. It was why I could never hide as king. Those using our powers would identify me immediately.

"I can't wait for you to see them," Trevan teased as he came out from the ballroom to greet me. He seemed to always know where I was, a good trait in the captain of the guard.

"It doesn't matter if I see them. I don't get to pick," I reiterated for what felt like the hundredth time.

"Sure, but sampling is on the table."

"Perhaps," I conceded. We all needed to maintain our powers throughout the trial, so sampling might indeed become necessary. I didn't currently keep a mistress or a consort, the concept dragged up those complicated feelings about my mother's death and soured the notion.

The doors opened with a flick of my wrist, and I descended the stairs to where my throne sat elevated above the fae gathered in the center of the open ballroom. Some of them fell silent as they realized I'd walked in, and others hurried to get their last few sentences out. As I took everyone in, the families of the women began to disperse to leave the twenty-three contestants in the center on their own.

"Welcome, ladies." I kept my voice level and calm. Some of them would be here of their own ambition, and others would have been forced by families. That was another thing that I'd need to discover along the way. I was familiar with some of the daughters from more ambitious family names, and others I'd not seen since childhood.

The women were an enjoyable variety of sizes, tones, and confidence levels. Only three had the bravery to display their wings. Our wings displayed valuable information about us and our magic levels, but they also allowed our glamour to flow more readily. Lines were already drawn about those who came to play, and I might as well take note.

The first fae woman was tall and slender with a bronzed tone to her soft skin. Her bright gold eyes sparkled as she beamed under my gaze. Her wings were rounded, indicative of seelie lineage. Her black-and-pink hair was twisted into intricate braids that fell around her shoulders.

The second woman had wings that pointed at all four of the tips, unseelie fae, and her pale skin was accented by her shorter, dark locks of hair. She had no trouble displaying any of her assets based on the way her shirt pushed up her breasts and the strips of fabric barely concealed her thicker frame.

"You are going to have a very hard choice," my cousin whispered to me, also taking in his own eyeful of the selection.

"I don't get to decide anything. The magic does."

"I didn't mean about the queen, I meant about who to feed from first."

It was a crude point to make, but he wasn't wrong. The women were open game to any in this court before they were selected as my queen. Ultimately, they were here to sway my pull of the magic to their favor, but that didn't mean they were tied down—well, at this moment.

"Can you keep focused beyond the fucking?" I snarled at him so he'd drop the subject.

The last woman who displayed her wings proudly marked that she came from a blended court. Her wings were rounded at the top and pointed at the bottom. Her mother had been unseelie and her father seelie. This was the exact opposite of mine. Her blond-and-purple hair sat up in a fancy bun on the top of her head. She wore a simple, elegant dress, but it was the fire in her eyes that caught my attention. She was here to win. I could respect that.

The final woman who joined the group forced me to do a double take. It was the last fae woman I'd ever expected to end up at the trial for my queen. Though her wings weren't out on display to make a statement, her confident stride spoke volumes.

Tasi's family had been banned from my court after I ascended to the throne. I would usually never allow her to compete, but this was yet another reminder that I wasn't entirely in charge here. Aine was.

I waited a few minutes before I spoke again. Being king meant I could do things in my own time. The magic stilled, indicating no more late arrivals. I hated to be interrupted, so it would be a truly unfortunate start to the queen's trials if they appeared while I was speaking.

"It appears we have all of our contestants. Let's get the unpleasantness out of the way first."

Scrolls unfurled in front of each of the women as quills appeared to their left. We'd poured over these contracts for days prior, but I could only make minimal changes. I really should have called Ferox in, but I didn't.

"Signing this scroll means that you are willingly agreeing to the terms of the trial for the queen of the fae. The limits of your magical abilities will be trained and tested over the next few weeks. This can lead to severe consequences including, but not limited to, dismemberment, disenchantment, and death. If you are caught using magic enhancers or other forms of cheating, you will be disenchanted and left in the labyrinth."

I paused, not really wanting to vocalize the next part, but it had to be done. "Historically, there are only three outs from these trials. One is to become queen. In the past, the other survivors would be added to the harem for the king. I do not wish to have a harem, so that option is void for these trials. Think carefully before you sign because the final way out is death."

"You know I'm going to change your mind on that. These have been kept women . . . they want to be kept," my cousin whispered over my shoulder as the women reviewed the contract. Six of them didn't even read it before they signed, and the rest displayed varying levels of hesitancy. Two looked over their shoulders at what I could assume was family before they begrudgingly signed.

"I told you that the changes I made were permanent. When we dissolved the harem last time, I had no intention of rebuilding it. The women hated it."

"That's because they were forced into it. I bet some of the women here thought they only needed to survive. Now you've taken that hope."

"Then may they all try their hardest to be successful."

Walking through the library, I watched all of our scientists pouring over their books. Someone needed to come up with an answer quickly. Most of the fae were oblivious to this threat, and I did my best to keep the information from spreading. Because the illness impacted the lesser fey first, we had a limited window to resolve it before the elite families began breathing down my neck, especially with so many of them visiting for the trials.

"How does this differ from previous contaminations of fey magic?" I asked, leaning against the table behind me.

"One team checked the well today, and it is completely clear. There are no foreign contaminants in the water at all. The chemical balance is completely within normal ratios," Yerirn replied, turning his full attention to me for my position. He was the top scientist and mage in the land, and the person who would lose his head if he didn't come up with a solution in the timeframe that I deemed reasonable.

"We've only checked the well? We have another very large body of water that could also be the source of this sickness," I reminded him, though my wings fluttered with my annoyance at having to even say anything.

"We didn't have a team prepared to go through the labyrinth." My expression shifted, and he immediately amended his statement. "I am working on that as we speak."

"This should have been dealt with immediately. What is the purpose of the delay?" I sighed and ran my hand over my face. My people could be cowardly. "You don't need a team to collect samples from the pool."

"But the monsters . . ." Yerirn's face turned ghostly pale as he trailed off, clearly realizing that I would not accept this as a reasonable concern.

44

"Please tell me how a pregnant dryad and a faun made it through the labyrinth unscathed then," I growled. My voice made all the gathered scientists jump. "I will not settle for excuses. This is killing off our kind, and no one thought it was worth the risk? There may be monsters in there, but I promise you that inaction will force my hand. I will do much worse than those beasts."

Even with fear in his eyes and scent, Yerirn gathered his thoughts before he spoke next. "With the fey magic in this weakened state, there are scientific concerns that it could impact the monsters living in the labyrinth. We'd need some trained guards, you know, in case the magic fails."

"How many guards do you need for a scientist to feel confident about going to get the data that we need?" I tried to sound reasonable, but my temper was boiling and would spill over if they didn't pull together a tiny bit of spine among the twenty or so of them.

"Why do we need to go in there at all? Can't we wait for Ferox—"

Of course, they would bring up Ferox again. Three of the four retired watchtowers—elemental warriors—resided in Voreios. Now that Lilise, his mate and former water watchtower, had given up her extraordinary magical abilities during the fight to defeat the shadow god, Ferox was considered the most powerful magic user on our planet. Cassie almost never left the borders of Voreios anymore, but Ferox and Lilise would travel as often, both on world and off, as they wanted to. It was rumored that the fourth watchtower, Minithe, had vanished into the dragon lands.

"No," I growled again and glared at my head scientist. "We are not waiting on a watchtower to fix this for us again. I have not even reached out to him because these are our lands. If we involve Ferox, then we involve all of Voreios. If there isn't an issue at the well, then we need to find the source. Do you not understand that?"

"Ah . . . I see, sir."

"How many guards do you need?" I repeated my question.

"Six?"

I bit my tongue before I called the man a coward. Bravery wasn't a trait that ran in my people unfortunately. Too many in high places were given positions merely for the way that they'd haggled in the past. "Never mind. I'll do it myself."

"Sir? It's dangerous out there."

I leveled him with a glare that muted any additional protest he may have had. I was the king, but I was also the most powerful user of fey magic in our lands. After my father lost his life in a sword fight, I was determined to be competent in all forms of weaponry as well. Beasts and foul fey creatures did not frighten me. Nothing frightened me really. Unfortunately, I just lived in a state where nothing excited me either.

The entrance of the labyrinth was less than half an hour walk from the moat that separated the fae court from the rest of the Feylands. Convenient to throw people in when they displeased me, it was also almost too close for comfort for most of the fey that would live closer to me if given the choice. Blessing or curse? I wasn't sure yet.

Trevan flew in beside me as I knew he would. He always knew what I was up to, even if I just stormed out of the court without a word to anyone. His guards also kept tabs on me, but none of them had opted to join.

"Why are you going to the labyrinth?" he asked as he took to foot just a step behind me. "You are supposed to meet with the fae women individually."

"That is a waste of time. Most of them are going to die." I dismissed the reminder and kept my eyes focused forward.

"Prinna has been preparing for the last few hours. She's going to be pissed."

"I don't care. The fey magic is my only priority. I need it to achieve a new kingdom in the liminal realm that will tie to our own planet. The queen will be selected, and I can meet her then."

"You will need to play your role in both of these situations. You cannot be absent from the selection process, according to customs. Leave the magic issue to me and the scientists,"

Trevan offered, but that would never work. I needed to ensure this issue was addressed properly.

"Did they actually request guards to go with them to the labyrinth?"

"Not that I am aware of."

"You are captain of the guard. Where else would they have made that request?" I snapped at him. Sometimes these details slipped through, and I knew he was more focused on the new snacks in the court than his obligatory role.

"The pool is going to be fine, Lorsan. Ferox would have told us otherwise."

I felt the heat rise in my throat and stopped the fight before it could begin. I was really tired of not being self-reliant. They didn't want Voreios's involvement, and yet turned to the watchtower at every single chance.

"Then this will just be a good stretch of my legs. I can handle this alone. Why don't you go back and look over the women." I really needed some time to myself before a queen came along and I would never be alone again. That was an awful thought.

Macendil, the leader of the dru, was rooted into the ground next to the entrance of the labyrinth. He'd moved to this location almost a hundred years ago, and we couldn't get him to move elsewhere. He'd leave occasionally to go visit Aurinia and Ferox in Voreios as their grove grew, and we'd hoped he'd stay there, but he always came back.

The dru could be terrifying for new people to experience, especially in the night. The hollows in their bark would create monstrous faces for those experiencing drugs, alcohol, or fey hysteria. At the end of it all, however, they were just trees. Trees that moved slowly and would only fight with their magical abilities. Past kings would have used them as eyes on unsuspecting fey or criminals. The dru had taken sides with the dryads against us, so while their numbers were dwindling, I was content to let them fade to extinction.

"Macendil." I acknowledged the ancient tree as I walked by.

"King," was his only reply. He almost never spoke to me in more than one- or two-word sentences.

"You need to address His Majesty properly," Trevan spat in fury on my behalf.

I couldn't help the eye roll as I was once more halted when I hadn't wanted to be. "It's fine, Trevan. Macendil, are the dru experiencing any of the effects of the yellow poisoning?"

"No."

"Are there any dru in Voreios currently?"

"No." The tree seemed to hesitate when I asked, and I'd never heard that before. The dru were fond of all of Aurinia's seedlings, so I waited just a moment more, and he asked another question. "Why?"

"I was wondering if the nymphs were feeling any ill effects. It doesn't matter though."

"Dru will go to Voreios to check."

That was the longest sentence he'd ever said to me. Trees, once they gave their loyalty, never wavered. It was exhausting to me, but what could I do about it?

"I'd prefer you all stay out of it for now. There is likely no danger to any of them."

"We will check on seedlings," he repeated, emphasizing his intent to not listen to what I said anyway. The ground began to rumble as his roots shook free of the dirt.

I shook my head and crossed into the threshold of the labyrinth. It would take him weeks to get to Voreios and perhaps he'd stop bothering me while he was busy with his new quest.

"I agree that we should have banished them after the war. You said they'd die off, but in a century, we've only lost five." Trevan sped up to follow me down the path.

"You are still coming with me? Wouldn't the women be a lot more interesting?"

"Lorsan, you are still king. You really shouldn't be wandering all over the place by yourself. I'll protect you." He sounded like he genuinely believed that.

For the first time today, I wanted to laugh. My cousin was a certified ass-kisser, not a fighter. I didn't need protection, so it didn't matter. Instead, I kept my face from displaying any of my enjoyment at the thought of him fighting anything.

The labyrinth would change its pathways every few days according to the whims of our magical lands. People thrown in here from crimes to the kingdom would deal with the worst of the beasts: manticores, wraiths, chimeras, and more. If a creature were in the way of the stone and vine wall as it moved, they would be absorbed and stuck until it decided to move again. A lot of people didn't survive that alone.

I stepped over a cracked skull, and Trevan stopped to glance back at it.

"Should we leave this as a relic of the past when we move to the liminal realm?"

"Hadn't thought about it, really," I admitted. Most of the beasts would sense me coming and stay away, but honestly, I was hoping to get into a bit of a fight tonight.

"Well, if you asked my opinion—"

"I didn't," I stated, but I knew he wouldn't listen to me either. I really should behave more like my father.

"I think we should leave the labyrinth and most of the fey here."

"Leave the fey here to themselves? That won't work. They handle most of the day-to-day tasks that fae don't want to do." They were also the only variety that offered both chaos and fun, but I wouldn't say that out loud.

We turned a few times. The fey pool was the largest source of our magic. A few centuries ago, my great-grandfather had created the well to cap the magic available to the masses. Through some trickery with the old shadow god, we'd all forgotten that the pool existed until a century ago. Aine granted the kings and queens of the fae power directly from the pool and not the well.

Much to my dismay, outside of random screaming, nothing came to greet us on our stroll through the labyrinth. The fey pool existed in a place that was separate from both Artemesia and our liminal realm. The portal between our worlds had been stabilized in the center of the labyrinth with a detailed brick archway.

I stepped through the reflective glimmer. The plush grasses created a bounce in each of my steps. The lands around the pool were always beautiful, trapped in an eternal spring with fresh air that filled my lungs. Only to catch a whiff of something foul.

Trevan began to cough immediately as he followed me through the portal.

"We need to get out of here. I can barely breathe." He waved his hands to clear the stench from his nose.

"I am here to get samples. You can wait outside." I took a few steps farther in, and a yellow cloud billowed up into the air above the usually clear pastel waters. The barrier of the pool was made up of boulders of a variety of stones such as jade, tiger's eye, moldavite, and many more. The cloud rising from the pool was so thick that I couldn't even see the obsidian on the far side of the water.

Someone had to be poisoning our magic once again. The shadow god was dead. Why did this keep happening? Using my own magic, I quickly used two small containers to take samples of the water and air. I placed a shield over my mouth to purify the air that I breathed and moved along the tops of the boulders around the edge of the water.

A trail of a dark liquid pooled toward the center, but I'd never seen the water that dark before. I should get a sample of it before leaving the area. After passing from the hematite to the emerald, I paused as I noticed a hand sticking out from the cloud of smoke coming from the water by the opal.

Was it a woman?

"Who's there?" I called first. Very few people should have access to this space. Could this be someone who'd been thrown into the labyrinth and made their way to the center?

There was no reply to my question, so I continued forward. I willed my magic to blow the yellow gasses in another direction, and my jaw fell open at the sight of the naked woman who lay twisted in a position that should not have been possible, a broken leg dangling into the water. Dried blood was caked on her body, and the stench of decay hit me as I got closer.

She'd been here a while. Her blood washed away into the pool. Leaning forward to investigate further, I ran my hands across the blanket she'd been tossed upon. A gelatinous substance mixed with her blood and limbs. Her dark brunette hair ran down her length, but I couldn't take my eyes off the brown blanket I rubbed between my fingers.

Then I realized what I was looking at.

"Fuck," I cursed to myself before shouting across the pool. "Trevan! There's a selkie."

"What? I can't hear you," my cousin shouted from the entrance.

Using her fur, I pulled her back away from the pool. Her limbs groaned, her body struggling to stay in one piece because of the quantity of strange cuts. I used my magic to quickly isolate her into a funerary bubble; the smoke stopped bubbling up as soon as she'd been removed. I created another container of obsidian and removed the blood floating in the water.

Trevan watched me nervously from the other side of the pool as the air began to filter and clean itself. I may have just resolved the yellow poisoning, but my troubles were only beginning.

"Did you say that you found a selkie?"

"Yes. This is an emergency. We need to find all the selkies at once, they need to be brought to court or relocated to a grove until further notice."

"There's only twenty of them left, and they could be anywhere in the ocean. That will take a lot of resources."

"I'm not asking. Get guards on it immediately. The kelpies can find them rather quickly."

"You don't actually think it's . . . the mages, do you?" I didn't miss the way he gulped. His eyes danced around the pool nervously as if we'd see the mages right now and he'd have to actually do some work.

"It's not a chance I'm willing to take. Selkies were the first sign before his arrival last time, and we will not ignore their slaughter while I'm king." My grandfather had ignored it because the women were fey. Within months, the selkie numbers had dropped from over three hundred to one isle with thirty women. "If it isn't tied to him, I'd rather find out now."

"All right. I got it. You need to go spend time on your other tasks. I'll take the vials to the scientists and start the hunt for selkies. You find us the queen. I have a feeling we are going to need her." He held his hand out to me to take the samples, but he continued to scout the area for the danger.

The mages might have been lurking, but she'd been dead so long that I doubted they were still here. I would need to keep an eye on the pool a little more closely now.

One thing I couldn't deny was that having a queen would straighten out the balance of power, and if mages were coming . . . I'd need all the help I could get.

Chapter 5 — Aralia

When elves came to a grove there were a few things that would always happen. The first was that they would lead with pompous arrogance, titles and pleasantries that became quickly boring. After the third introduction I'd already lost attention, and now I didn't have names for at least three dozen elves standing around the fire this evening.

The next thing they would do when riding their unicorns through our grove was comment on our lack of proper buildings. They marveled at our beautiful temple to our gods and the library and then were mortified that we hadn't decided to continue building. Dytika, their closest ally, didn't have any buildings in their grove, but I guess they thought my father had shown us "the way."

"Would you allow me the honor of this dance?" a tall elven man asked as he slid up beside me from the trees. He had longer dark hair tied back in elegant braids. Polite brown eyes greeted me as he extended his hand toward mine.

"I'd love to," I answered honestly. So far, most of the elves had stayed away from me after the introductions. My plan was not going very well.

"Nymphs really do love to dance. I'll be honest, I wasn't quite sure what to expect coming out here."

"Is it your first time to Voreios?" I inquired politely as we stepped up to the cleared space around the fire.

"It is. You're all so lovely and a lot friendlier than I expected."

"Well, here we have a saying: if you're allowed through the border, then expect to have a memorable experience."

He laughed and I enjoyed the deep timbre of it, but I wasn't getting that feeling that my sisters always talked about. The one that said this was it, this was everything. Even his touch didn't scorch me the way I wanted it to. There I was, off being picky again. I just needed one random lover to get over the attachment to Rux. Just one and I could be free.

Of course, the mere thought of him brought him to the edge of the fire. His gaze met mine, but there was nothing. Nothing more than observation. Why would there be more? He was just making sure the elf didn't kill me, but beyond that, it didn't matter to him. Rhenei appeared at his side, whispering in his ear until he finally broke our eye contact.

Just one, Lia. You got this, I encouraged myself as I spun around to my dancing partner and wrapped my arms around his neck. I'd never purposely used my glamour before, but I was going to try.

His breathing hitched as I leaned in closer to push myself against him. I was hungry, but I didn't know him. I hadn't expected this to be so hard.

"You are so lovely. I'm still not quite sure how I can tell if you are mated or not." His arms wrapped around my body, and I began to feel trapped in a way I wasn't sure I liked.

"If I were bonded, my mates would likely be throwing you off of me right now."

At this, the handsome elf glanced around nervously, and it made me laugh. I probably shouldn't laugh at his expense, but our men could be a bit intimidating.

"Relax. I'm unattached. No one is going to attack you out of the blue."

"I'm surprised by that." He leaned in again and his nose brushed mine. "What happens next in this scenario?"

"Well—"

"Alosrin! Can you come over here this instant?"

"Ah." The elf slowly released me and took a few steps back. "I'll return in just a few."

"Of course." I gave him what I hoped was a glamour-filled smile that didn't reflect the disappointment racing in my veins. I didn't want him, but I also didn't want to be in a situation to need Rux.

The two elves spoke rapidly while I was walking back toward a group of my sisters. I could see them both turn to look at me, and my smooth dancer's face paled. What was that about? Were they specifically avoiding me?

Now that my dancing partner wouldn't be returning, I decided to cut my losses and go back to Nylisa. She sat on a wooden bench in front of Veon who chatted excitedly with the elven ambassador. I could tell it was his fake enthusiastic voice, but that was a twin secret I would take with me to the grave.

"Are you done dancing already?" Nylisa reached her hand out to me with concern on her face.

Our hands met and she scooted over to make room for me to sit beside her. Veon also shifted to include me in the space. I wasn't sure how he felt about me always third wheeling it with them, but he never complained aloud. Nylisa and I were pretty inseparable.

"Yeah. I don't think the elves want much to do with me tonight," I replied through our root network, so the ambassador wouldn't hear.

"Nonsense, he looked into you."

"Until he spoke to the other guy. I don't think I acted out the last time I was in Aramore with Lilise or Dad."

"Let me see what I can find out," Nylisa insisted before she turned to the ambassador with wide eyes. "Elaith, have you met my twin, Aralia?"

Veon cast his gaze down at her for the interruption in the conversation, but the way he stroked her hair was so gentle. The ambassador, though, looked unnerved.

"Yes, I do believe we have met." He offered a hand to me, which I gently shook.

"I was considering making her our ambassador to your people because she did get the most of our father's looks out of all of us. Look at her beautiful ears!" Nylisa exclaimed and pushed my hair back to show the group. Mine were nearly two inches longer than any of our other siblings. A fierce blush crossed my cheeks. "Her Elvish is also the most perfected. How would Queen Aiyana like that? The twin of the neighboring vasilissa as our ambassador?"

"Well, about that." He then gave a long pause as he seemed to consider his next words.

My twin glanced up at Veon, looking frustrated with the delay. "Is there something the matter with my choice?"

"If I'm not mistaken, Aralia, you were gifted with fey magic. Is that right?"

"Yes—"

"The queen just doesn't feel comfortable at this time associating with anything that is heavily influenced by the fae. I hope you can understand. We are still working on rebuilding our relationship with you after the long war."

"A relationship that will not improve easily by insul—" Nylisa moved to sit up and argue, but Veon caught her shoulder.

"That's a shame. Lia is our most skilled asset in Voreios, but if her talents won't be useful with the elves, she will find a place elsewhere." Veon placed a kiss on Nylisa's forehead. "Wherever she does end up is likely to have our favor."

I could appreciate them both for what they were trying to do, but yet again, I was being shielded. The elves here tonight didn't want to interact with me because I was too fey.

"I hope you don't take this as an insult," Elaith said to Veon, instead of addressing me. This only served to further fuel the embarrassment that I'd even bothered with them to begin with.

"There's no insult," I replied, clipping each of my words for emphasis. "The elves aren't near interesting enough to hold my attention. Excuse me."

Well, this whole evening had been a bust. Hungry, hurt, and exhausted, I decided it was time for me to call it a night.

Chapter 6 – Rux

I felt her pass in the tree beside me after the conversation with the ambassador. Lia was too proud to admit that she'd been hurt. I followed her easily to the one spot she thought would always be hers. She'd grow little fey flower rings in the area to practice her magic, and the pixies would keep her company on the days when she felt like she didn't belong. It happened more often than I liked, but she wouldn't talk to me about it.

"Lia," I called, not wanting to startle her.

"Ugh, I just want to be alone," she grumbled without any bite to her words.

"Don't let the elves chase you away from the fire. You love to dance." I took a few steps closer to where she sat on the grassy hill.

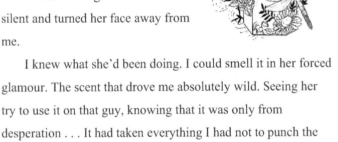

"I was looking for—" She fell silent and turned her face away from me.

I knew what she'd been doing. I could smell it in her forced glamour. The scent that drove me absolutely wild. Seeing her try to use it on that guy, knowing that it was only from desperation . . . It had taken everything I had not to punch the man. So much for diplomacy if I'd done that.

Now she just looked defeated. "I look like an elven dryad, but I am too fey. What chance do I stand on this side of the world? I guess you are going to have to find a guard to assign to me. I'm asking Nylisa to send me to the dragons next week. She'll have to send Evidone to Notos first, but as soon as she's ready, I'm out of here."

I held back my groan. Not about going to the land of the dragons. Getting out of the grove with Lia could be just what we needed to break this stalemate we were in. I wanted to groan because she still thought I would assign another person. No way in all the underworlds would anyone else be going with her.

"I hear it is chilly there even this early in the year, so I'll have to make sure to bring my best cloak."

She raised her eyebrow at me, her unamused face signaling that she was picking up on what I was declaring.

Her dark forest-green eyes studied me intensely. She was past the point of general hunger now. Slowly, I approached her. Her blond hair fell down past her shoulders, and today she'd braided it into a half bun with the rest of the strands flowing loosely. Her dress only modestly hinted at her breasts. She'd brought her A game to try and hook the prudish elves. They were all fools.

Aralia was easily the most beautiful woman on the planet.

"Rux . . ." she said softly, almost like she would fight me again.

When she let me caress her cheek, I knew that the barrier was down. Only when she was hungry could I touch her like I wanted too. Only when she'd damn near starved herself would

63

she let me hold her, pleasure her. Every bit of me knew that she was mine to claim, but I could do nothing about it. I played the part of the monster that she had cast me in, but I watched her like a hawk because only in these moments could my heart relish the passion of our fated connection.

I knew the day that I'd broken her trust. It sat between us like an open wound. I'd only been doing what I was supposed to do, but it hadn't mattered. I watched her little heart break before she could even comprehend the emotions that she experienced.

Not even two decades of friendship could repair what I tore apart that day. When she'd matured, she'd struggled with this part of her nymph needs. She wanted the love that she'd seen between her parents. Her elven father set expectations that no satyr could ever hope to meet. Driven insane from hunger, she'd practically pounced on me in frustrated fury when the need became too much. What I hoped was that somewhere deep down, she knew we were supposed to be together.

I knew every inch of her body from the decades that followed. Sometimes in deep heat, she'd ask me repeatedly for what I would never force on her. I'd never wanted anything more, but my heart needed her to truly want me in return. Knowing that my fated mate would never return my affection scorched the entirety of my soul.

Even as I felt her skin heat under my caresses, I knew I could never have more. I turned her around as I pulled her into my arms and felt her sink into me with a sigh.

"Don't you need to get back to—"

I pushed my fingers into her mouth and groaned when she closed her lips around them. "No talking."

She hated it when I gave her orders, but she whimpered as the fight left her again when my other hand caressed up her inner thigh. I really didn't have time to torture either of us today. Veon needed my help with the elves, and Nylisa was about to flower, which meant he would be gone for days in their cavern. All I could do was pray that it didn't happen tonight. Timing in a grove always seemed to be slightly off kilter, and healthy seedlings was the top priority.

The best part about nymph clothing was that it could be ripped with no harm being done. It was all an elaborate bit of magic. They could change what they wore with a mere thought. Catching one of the open lines in the bodice of her dress, I tore the fabric so that it hung loose out of my way. Leaves manifested around her, and the material vanished entirely, leaving her looking like my sweetest dreams and nightmares.

As I circled my little dryad's clit, she moaned around my fingers again and pressed that perfect ass back against me. I knew she was hungry, but her body language was begging already. Was Lia about to flower too? The fact that she hadn't flowered at all since she'd matured caused quite a commotion,

65

but the elders thought it had to do with her fey magic. If she was, I wouldn't be able to fight her glamour, but I also wouldn't be able to stand by and let another try to claim her.

"Are you going to be a good girl and be quiet?" I murmured in her ear as I dragged my fingers through her slit. All of my willpower was barely enough when I felt how wet she was already. I cursed silently as she nodded, her tongue caressing the side of my other pointer as I pulled those fingers out.

The ground softened with plush green grass. Intimacy in nature wasn't uncommon, but that didn't mean we didn't like to be comfortable. As young men, we were trained in the arts of pleasuring our nymphs through rigorous trial and error, and I knew how to make her crazy.

"Lie on your back," I commanded with a heavy rumble in my tone. Her gaze met mine briefly as she weighed out defiance or compliance. Her dilated pupils told me long before her movement did which way she was leaning.

I stood over her, enjoying the way her form moved in front of me as she rested back against the soft-textured grass. Her blond hair fanned around her. Lia's eyes swept down my bare chest and paused at my bulging erection before she bit her lip.

If that small action didn't make my cock painfully harder, the sight of her parting her legs for me did the trick.

I knelt down immediately and ran both hands over the top of her knees.

She never meant to use her glamour on me, but once a nymph was turned on, it came instinctually. Her scent of wildflowers and honey drove me wild as it did for all men when they met their mates. It was one of the biggest reasons I could tell what she was to me. Just a slight whiff of that and instant hard-on.

I needed to taste her. Planting kisses from her knee up the inside of her thigh, I felt her body tremble. She wanted me to go faster, and it took everything that I had not to dive straight into that glistening treasure.

I blew a hot huff of air over her sensitive, engorged clit, and her hands clamped over her mouth as my tongue stroked across her once, twice, and swirled around to make sure she was feeling me. I lapped lower to teasingly swipe through her slit, barely pushing those lips of hers apart, and she rose from the ground as I licked up the underside of her nub.

When I sucked her into my mouth, my name tumbled from her. There was nothing better than the sound of your mate saying your name in any context. Her thighs tightened around my shoulders, and as I dove my tongue into her pussy, her hands fell into my hair around my horns. I sank down lower on my elbows to make the most of her gyrations, pushing my tongue deeper into her. I'd always encouraged her to ride my face. I loved the mess she'd leave behind.

Her orgasm gushed and I ate her through it, lapping every bit of her, savoring the taste of her pure ecstasy. The next part had been tricky to discover, because while she loved oral, she needed to be penetrated to get full satisfaction. It was one thing for me to provide her with orgasms, but another entirely for her to let me satisfy myself when, as she came back to reality, she hated me.

Those green eyes haunted me as they opened with their beautiful glow. I knew mine were glowing as well because my hunger cramps subsided with her radiating pleasure. The need in her expression as I moved to hover above her while I changed our positions made my cock jump, but I couldn't. I lay beside her and pulled her back up against my chest.

I separated her legs farther and, using my stone magic, locked her into place with rock cuffs around her ankles. Her breathing hitched as she felt the familiar obsidian stone glide down her stomach. I'd matched it to the size of my erect cock. If she ever came to realize how much I felt for her, the last thing I wanted to do was hurt her. I wasn't a small man.

"Rux . . ." She whimpered as the head of the stone brushed against her clit and slid slowly into her soaked channel.

Aralia pressed her body back against mine as I thrust the obsidian fully in and out a few times slowly. Her thigh rubbed against my erection, and I bit back my own groan.

I couldn't help kissing her shoulder. Her skin was slick with the heat of my pleasure. Lia moaned as I moved the stone with my magic. I wrapped one hand in her hair to expose her neck to me and the other cupped her left breast. As I pinched her nipple and licked up her neck to her ear, her body shuddered again. I could do this every day for the rest of my life. How blissful she was right now, her features soft in ecstasy that I wanted to give her all the time.

I just didn't know how to be honest with her about how I felt. I feared her rejection even when I knew that I would love her to the depths of what she dreamed about, if only she would let me.

"Rux, please." Aralia pulled against my stone bindings, trying to turn around. When she couldn't break free, she twisted her body to rub her ass against my trapped cock. Sometimes the stone still couldn't alleviate the tension between her thighs. "I can feel you want this too."

I could only give her my most charming smile. *Someday, you might let yourself be mine, but that's not today.* Instead, I increased the tempo of the thrusting stone and moved my hand from her breast to her clit, massaging her into a panting mess.

"That's not what I'm asking for and you know it," she half moaned and half shouted at me. Her hands wrapped around my horns in a half-assed attempt to pull me around her body. She was so wound up that I felt her tighten in mere moments.

Aralia fell to pieces in front of me. Always the most beautiful light in my world but seeing what I could do to her made up for all the nights I went to bed alone. I took a deep inhale of her like the obsessed lunatic that she wouldn't notice I was in her current state. I wanted to remember every bit of this moment when I finally had a chance to wrap my hand around my cock. "You should be satiated now."

"Am I not good enough for you?" Aralia whispered as she rolled out from under my hold once all of the stones had vanished. Leaves appeared to dance in the world around her before she was cleaned and dressed in less than a moment. She wore a new light green dress, her blond hair tied back away from her perfect, flushed face. She sat up on her knees facing me with a flutter of hurt, fury, and confusion.

"What are you going on about now?" I stared at her dumbfounded. How could she take that away from what I was giving her? Did she have any idea how hard it was for me to not throw myself at her feet and beg her for affection?

"Why won't you . . . you know?"

Oh, that. We didn't talk about that.

Poor innocent little Lia wouldn't even admit to what she was actually asking me about. Back to putting the boundaries in place, the ones that protected her current narrative. "Are you still hungry?"

"No," she admitted begrudgingly.

"Then you should return to dancing. Ignore the elves and just go have a good time." I tried to reason with her before I lost my mind. "There will be fewer firepits in the land of the dragons, so enjoy the ones you get to have now."

"You can't know that. The dragons are very secretive about their culture. Besides, that's hardly the point. You're deflecting and you know it!" She balled her hands into fists at her side as she rose to her feet, not quite meeting my gaze.

"Then ask me directly," I pressed her. If she wanted to go all out on feelings tonight, well, then I'd have to own up to them. How would she respond? Could I handle outright rejection this evening? It wasn't what I'd been prepared for going into the day's events.

"Never mind. Ugh. You are so infuriating!" She didn't even give me another glance before she stormed up the trail going higher into the mountain.

Someday, my princess, you will be mine. I just have to wait for you to realize it. Or until I'm brave enough to admit how I feel.

Chapter 7 — Aralia

I couldn't run from Rux fast enough. I hated the way I became when I was hungry, and he knew it. He could see through me in a way that only served to further piss me off. In all groves, the sex was casual until it wasn't. Until you found your mates. Before then, everyone needed to feed, so why make it something more than that?

The fact that he'd put this barrier between us made the almost-sex feel taboo. He wouldn't touch me like I knew he did the other nymphs, like he did with Rhenei. Was I just that repulsive to him? It didn't have to mean anything if we didn't let it.

The only place I could go to be alone anymore was up in the mountains. The wild elf pack still resided here with the centaurs, but during the day they would all be out on the borders. Even more so with the hyped-up visitors from the elven kingdom. Their new queen had determined to make better alliances after she took the throne and wanted to try again with peace and harmony. This meant personal visits to each kingdom every few years.

I would rather negotiate with pixies than hang out with the elves. My father always took me with him when he went to Aramore on travel, but even he didn't seem to understand that it was spending time with him one-on-one that mattered more than anything I could find there.

Pulling on my magic, I created a few lightning sparks in the sky. They almost looked like the ones he would create for me, but I knew the truth. All my magic was good for was imitating. Fey magic was just an illusion. I'd never have any value here in Voreios. All my siblings could do true elemental magic. They connected with the world in a way that I never would be able to. I'd say my mom ran out of magic to give when she got to me, but I was the eldest. How could she run out before she'd even gotten started?

No one could ever want me for an ambassador or a lover, no matter what Nylisa tried to say. I was a dryad tainted by fey lineage that couldn't be hidden. Everyone in the world could see it. I let out another bit of magic that took the form of pixies dancing in the open field in front of me. More illusions of not being alone.

Rux complicated my life. When I was hungry, I wanted him to want me. Now, I could rationalize that he was only doing what he needed to do to keep me alive, since I hadn't found another to feed from. Begrudging protector until the end.

"It would just be easier if I vanished."

My head hurt and my throat hitched with the need to cough. Covering my mouth as I gave into the urge, a wet substance hit my palm. My eyes widened at the red color splattered against

73

my skin. A dull throbbing pulsed through my brain, but I couldn't get up on my feet to make my way back to my tree. Maybe just lying here for a minute would help.

Was I sick? I never got sick. What was happening to me? Everything felt wrong.

The black spots in my vision seemed to settle as soon as I closed my eyes. Perhaps I was just tired. I could rest here for a bit.

The fey pool reflected sparkles of all colors from the many gemstone boulders around the border. The plush green grass felt soft against my bare feet. I couldn't feel Voreios's roots from here, but this space still felt inviting to my subtle explorations.

"Come here, my little love," my mother said, encouraging me with her hand out to take mine.

My hand was smaller than hers, but I could hardly focus on that when she gave me that bright smile.

"Why isn't Nylisa here, Mama?" I asked her.

"Darling, as you get older you will find that while your twin bond is so very important to who you are, there is more to both of your journeys. Nylisa is going to run Voreios, but you are not her shadow. It's time you became familiar with your powers, and we are going to start that training." Mom ran her fingers through my hair and tucked the loose strands behind my ear. "Ferox will help

sometimes, but I want this to be something we do together. Just us. How does that sound?"

I had forty-one sisters and a brother. Getting alone time with any of my parents could be a challenge. "I'd like that."

"Oh good." She hummed approvingly and rose to her feet, turning to face the water. "Is there a stone that catches your attention?"

"I like the quartz," I replied as I pointed at the clear boulder on the left of the pool.

"What a lovely choice."

I followed her eagerly as she walked around the edge of the waters along the top of the other stones. Her magic enchanted the entire world around her with a grace and certainty I'd never seen from another in all of my young years. She was poised and confident. I knew that she'd never felt out of place like I always did, like she didn't belong. With more time like this, maybe I could find my place in the world, too.

"You know what's amazing about quartz?" she asked with a playful twinkle in her eye.

"What?"

"It is a universal stone. Sure, emeralds, diamonds, and the jasper over there have fantastic colors but quartz is powerful in healing, manifesting, and even protection. It's unassuming, but oftentimes the most beautiful things are."

"But isn't that what all the other stones can do too? Is it an imitation like my magic is?" That had to be the reason for this conversation.

"Your magic is so much more than imitation, and that's what I am going to show you." My mother watched me with those green eyes that I knew matched mine. The ones that told the world we were Voreios dryads. "Place your roots into the soil around the quartz. Anchor and center yourself. Do you feel the well of your magic here?"

Her hand pressed flat against the center of my chest, and the warmth filled me. She always looked at me with love, confidence, and unwavering support. I nodded my head once.

"Hold that feeling," she instructed while gliding around to stand behind me, and then I felt her roots burrow in. I wrapped one of mine around hers. She was our anchor even as much as the quartz was for this lesson.

I couldn't help the little smile that tweaked at the corner of my lips. A white glowing light spiraled up from the center of the pool, thin at first but the circumference grew with each twist.

"Follow my magic."

"But I can't sense what element you are using." I strained to see what to imitate, but there was no elemental flavor that I could pick up.

"This isn't elemental magic, little one. This is our shared magic. This is your destiny and your unique capability. You are not a shadow; you are not a reflection. Embrace who you are, Aralia."

The well in my chest poured out to meet her magic. For the first time, a new confidence rose inside that maybe the gift I had been born with wasn't absolutely meaningless.

Maybe there was something more that I could do.

Chapter 8 – Rux

How could I manage to make her feel better and then worse all in the same encounter? I was always the bad guy in her story, but I could hardly be faulted for not taking advantage of her in that state. I wanted Aralia badly, but I wanted her to genuinely want intimacy from me, not just out of hunger.

"Is Aralia okay?" Zrif asked from the tree beside me as I approached the main grounds to rejoin Veon's effort with the elves. "I noticed she stormed off after talking with the ambassador."

Zrif's small mate, Elura, sat on the stone not far from him rocking their first selkie pup, a beautiful little girl with the bright blue eyes of her mother. His other bond mate, Arbane, was tickling the squealing girl. Elura tensed when I moved closer to the group, a subconscious response that not even a century of healing had been able to remove.

"Back to hating me as usual, but I think she will be all right. She's never been a fan of the high elves." I waved dismissively.

"Who is?" Arbane added, agreeing with me. His pack of wild elves had moved in with our grove when I was a child, and they never once had any desire to return to the elven lands. Even after the change in elven leadership. Since he was an alpha, the pack chose to stay with him, even though he offered to settle them back with another alpha on the other side of the border. They'd always been a huge asset to Voreios, so I was grateful they stayed.

Zrif tossed an exasperated look at his lover before he met my gaze again. "I think you should stop parading around with Rhenei. You both have played these games long enough, and at some point, you will need to grow up."

"To what end, Zrif?" I sighed.

The pup hiccupped and turned into a little white seal on her mom's lap. It was stupid cute, and I couldn't help but smile at Elura's cooing to the tiny thing.

"Lia runs away any time the conversation turns in a way she doesn't approve of."

"She's not chasing anyone except you when she gets hungry. That's a sign. It may be a hard conversation, but you need to tell her how you really feel."

"You don't see the way she looks at me. I need more alcohol." I tried to keep the emotion from my voice. The last thing I needed was Lia's eldest brother pestering me to be honest about what would be a full-on disaster.

"We all see the way you look at her. Show her that."

"Someday. She's still working on her angst phase, I think."

Another hiccup and the seal fur slid down from the baby girl into Arbane's waiting hands. She squealed and patted his face excitedly.

"What are you going to do when she flowers?" Zrif dragged my attention back to him.

This was not a topic I wanted to think about at all. A nymph flowering meant that they were fertile and usually very hungry. I counted the small blessings every season that she didn't flower because we could keep avoiding what would be absolute devastation to my pride if she chose someone else to see her through it. "Let's talk about something else, please."

Screaming erupted from the main grounds, and all of us men jumped to attention. Nothing could get past the vasilissa's barrier. Without wasting any time, we took off toward the sound. Once we crossed the tree line separating us from the firepit, I noticed Nylisa convulsing violently. Veon's eyes met mine in what I knew to be his calm panic as he held his lover steady, protecting her head while she thrashed.

"What's going on with her?" I called to him as I gestured to a messenger to run for a healer.

"I don't think it's her."

What could he mean by tha— Oh no. Lia must be in trouble. My heart sank into my hooves. I'd only left her unsupervised for what felt like a few moments. This was how it happened, though, with troublesome contessas. "I'll find her."

"She's in the mountains." Nylisa pointed as the shaking subsided, then she passed out. Veon scooped her up and carried her into his cavern, but I didn't waste a moment.

The grove was connected by a series of portals so that each member could move across our vast lands fairly quickly. I passed by the centaur caverns swiftly. Aralia always tested the bounds of how fast I could run, and I practiced every morning, running a minimum of thirteen miles a day. The familiar burn sang through my muscles as I rounded every tree until I found her body collapsed among the brush. Pixies hovered in the air around her as fey magic leaked out in a stunning array of colors.

"Lia!" I yelled, and the pixies dodged out of my way.

"She who paints the sunrise from the pool."

"What are you saying?" I bit back the snarl at the pixie as I reached for my tiny charge.

They didn't answer me, however. I adjusted her body so that her face turned toward me, and her soft breath brushed against my skin, sending chills down my neck. She was alive, thank all the gods.

"Aralia. Wake up." I patted her face a few times gently while feeling for her pulse with my index and middle finger on her wrist. All rynes needed to have basic medical training for this reason. Especially when the twin of the vasilissa blacks out. A healer would be going to the main grounds for Nylisa. They could also see Aralia there. "I need to know that you are hearing me, Lia."

With one arm under her knees and the other behind her shoulders, I rested her head against my chest. Dryads, as with most nymphs, weighed practically nothing. Her tiny frame was only half the size of mine. Her soft breathing continued against my collarbone, and I would never admit how much that settled my racing nerves.

"I know you fight me on everything, but I will figure this out, Lia. You are going to be okay." I moved as quickly as I could without shaking her through the portals and back to the center of Voreios.

"What happened to her?" Zrif shouted as I appeared in the tree line. His water magic ran against her face. Water carried some of the strongest healing properties. "It's not a fever yet. Has Nylisa awoken?"

"Yes. She's stable, but she won't stop crying long enough to get out any words," Veon said from the front of the cavern.

"Bring Lia to her," Zrif directed as the nereid healer followed behind me closely, trying to get a glimpse of the dryad in my arms.

Nylisa quieted as I entered the cavern and set Aralia down beside her. In seconds, the two were tangled in a tight web of limbs. Nymph twins functioned much like I assumed a lot of twins did, but their roots could talk when their spirit forms couldn't. Lia's fingers tightened on her sister's arm.

"What is happening to her?" I asked the vasilissa quietly. I needed to know how to wake her up.

"I felt as though she were drowning, but she wasn't anywhere near the river at that height in the mountain. Now she feels so far away from me. Why is this happening? She's leaking fey magic."

"She was doing that when I found her."

"Ferox is on his way with Lilise. What are we going to do about the elves?" Nylisa asked. Her voice was still soft as she stroked Aralia's cheek and rubbed along her twin's back. "I can't leave her like this."

"Zrif and Arbane will handle them until Lilise arrives. Then she can take over. The elves have always like Lilise." Veon sank to the edge of the bed to rub Nylisa's feet. He and I had grown up in pretty close proximity to the twin sisters. I had no idea what they were going to do when they found Nylisa's second and potentially third mates. There would be no room for anyone in the bed with her unmated sister always at their side if she refused to accept our bond.

Nylisa sighed and turned her tearful eyes to Veon. "Can you tell them I will be there in a little while? I have to hear what

Ferox says. I can't lose her." Tears streamed down her dark skin before she whispered again, "I can't lose her."

"Aralia is stable, my star." Veon reached forward to grab her hand. "Once your grandparents arrive, they will know what to do."

"I'm here." The deep voice of the former watchtower echoed as he stepped swiftly into the cavern. I stepped to the side to make room for him as his eyes traveled along the fey magic that seeped out of Aralia. "I haven't seen anything like this in a very long time. When was the last time she visited the pool?"

I shifted uncomfortably as I knew he wouldn't like the answer. "It has been quite a while. Two—no—three years ago this summer."

"Well, that can never happen again. I know that she hasn't accepted you as a mate, but this is essential to her well-being." Ferox let out an exhausted sigh. He took Aralia's hand and trailed two of his fingers down the inside of her arm from elbow to wrist. The colors immediately began to recede.

"Did you fix her?" Nylisa sat up straight, and we all watched the magic disappear.

"Not quite." Ferox frowned and ran his hands along his forehead. "Call Maik in here. I need to confirm something."

Maik? The faun keeper of the dryad grove had come back with the girls' mother after the war between Voreios and the fae. What could he possibly know that Ferox didn't know?

"Actually, we will go to him. Nylisa, go take care of your guests. They are being overbearing to Lilise already. Rux, bring Aralia."

"I need to know she's okay." Nylisa spoke at the same time as I said, "Where are we taking her?" He gestured for me to pick Aralia back up again. Her fingers gripped her sister's while she still seemed to be out. "Lia, I got you. I promise you are safe."

"I will give you root updates as we learn more. If she takes a turn for the worst, we will call you to her side again. Okay?" Ferox encouraged the vasilissa, who frowned but nodded at him. The three elder watchtowers were the only ones who could force any of the dryads to do something they didn't wish to do. Nylisa had turned into a wonderful leader for Voreios in the absence of Aurinia, but her one defining weakness was her twin.

Once we'd left the company of Nylisa and Veon, I followed Ferox slowly as he made his way toward their trees. "Aralia will be okay, won't she?"

Ferox only gave me half a glance, followed by the longest silence I'd ever experienced. "I don't know. If it is what I suspect, then this illness hasn't been seen in centuries. Even I have only read about it. Without Lilise's healing abilities, we may not be able to reverse the contamination."

My breath caught as I thought over his words. Contamination? What the hell had she gotten into? "Is this because her magic is different?"

"Yes."

"Why now?" I growled at him. "Could Aura fix this? Graak has the ability to heal almost as efficiently as Lilise used to."

A frown tugged on his contemplative face. "Rux, I understand that your relationship is complicated with Lia. Aura and Graak are on another world right now in the trenches of battle. They can't come back. This is on all of us to fix if we can. First, let's see if Maik can help confirm my diagnosis."

"You will tell them though? If something happens to one of their daughters, they will want to know."

"Until we know what this is, I'm going to need you to trust me. Of course, they would all want to be made aware of her condition. It will do us no good to pull Graak away for his healing, though, if he wouldn't be able to do anything to help in this case."

The faun wasn't far from the dryad grove in his own tier of caverns to the north. He'd settled nicely in Voreios with an oread, Diomis, and a satyr messenger, Kreb. His sons did most of the work in his stead unless a particularly complicated matter came up. This would count.

"Ferox," the faun greeted from the stool outside his cavern. His youngest oread daughter played with rocks at his feet. His face grew somber as he took in my posture with Aralia passed out in my arms. "I'd hoped to never hear of this again."

"You can already confirm that this is it?" Ferox's shoulders sagged as if burdened with the heavy weight of the simple sentence.

"What is it?" I asked them both as they exchanged glances between themselves and Lia.

"There's nothing else it could be." Maik leaned in and pointed to a black mark growing along her dryad lines.

They were ignoring me, and I couldn't take it anymore. "Will one of you tell me what the fuck this is and how we fix it. Now!"

Both of the older men stopped talking and turned toward me. Maik cowered from my tone, but Ferox only raised an eyebrow. The man delayed his response once more to walk into the dryad grove that began only over the hill from Maik's cavern.

"Vitium sacer. A variant of this hit Voreios a little over three hundred years ago."

"I thought you just said you hadn't seen this before?" I could barely keep my frustration under control.

"This isn't impacting anyone but Aralia. If this were the same illness, we'd be dealing with more than thirty very sick nymphs already. By deduction, it is likely an ancient strain that hasn't been seen on Artemesia before."

Ferox and Maik walked between the cluster of dryad trees toward the center of the grove where Nylisa and Aralia's trees were. As the oldest daughters of Aurinia, they were the closest to the heart. What had been one dryad tree during my childhood had grown to sixty-five trees.

"How would she have even contracted this virus if no one else is sick?" I met the root base of her dryad tree, and her spirit form vanished to merge the two halves. I hated the emptiness in my arms, but if she was sick, she would heal faster as one with her tree.

"I am checking to confirm that no one else is sick." Ferox needed to only stand still and connect into the root network. Maik on the other hand was doing a visual inspection. He checked Nylisa first as she was the heart of Voreios.

"We are going to need to separate them," Maik said as he finished his inspection.

"They can't be separated though," I argued immediately. It would kill Lia if she had to be isolated.

"Nylisa could get a secondhand illness. We don't have a choice. She's not sick yet, but it will only be a matter of time with how tightly their roots are connected." Maik gestured me closer as he pointed to Lia's trunk. "Do you see the white etchings in her bark that are spreading from this point? These will turn black as they settle deeper. I can't believe we missed this, but I am guessing she hasn't mentioned anything about feeling ill to you?"

"No. Lia wouldn't admit anything to me." It was beginning to feel like I had failed her more thoroughly than I'd thought.

Maik gestured to his children to come over and quickly showed them what he had just discovered before he dug the dirt away to reveal her upper roots. "Every single dryad is going to need to be watched carefully, especially the ones closest to Aralia's location. It hasn't spread yet, but this is going to become life or death for every dryad impacted. If this is spotted, the dryad will need to be removed from the grove immediately. I need you all to watch this ritual closely in case we need to do it again."

I turned to Ferox hoping that he would disagree with the faun, but his grim face didn't give me any hope in that matter.

"Unfortunately, I agree. Aralia will need to be separated from the dryad grove."

"There must be another way. She already feels the weight of how different she is. If you separate her from her sister, I don't know if she'll recover. Where will she even go?"

"When this happened the last time, the only people who were able to help were the fae." Ferox summoned the winds and a bright quartz hovered along the breeze toward him. It was the size of my fist. "You will need to take her to Lorsan; she needs to be replanted with direct access to fey magic."

"Will he agree to this?" The fae weren't on bad terms with Voreios, but we weren't really friends either.

"We don't have any other options, or we risk losing all the nymphs in this grove. It will not only impact the dryads. How do you think she will feel if she hurts any of her siblings and her community? You will need to make him accept her. Just don't sign any contracts and don't let them separate you from her." Ferox patted my hand and offered the stone to me. "I will not leave you alone, but I need to head to the tower and get answers. We are in a race against time now. Can you do this to save her life?"

I would do anything to save her life, even if she would take it out on me when she woke up.

"Can you place the stone along her northern roots?" Ferox asked me and then turned his attention to Cassie as she appeared. The former earth watchtower kept an eye on all of Aura's children after the triad left to defend the universe.

"This was the last reroot I ever expected to have to do," she admitted sadly. "I agree with Rux that we need to advise them as soon as possible."

Good. Ferox had filled her in on the entire conversation, or she'd heard it from her tree.

"I appreciate how everyone feels. Aralia is my granddaughter, and you know I would never suggest this if I thought it would be worse for her. I would not do this if there were any other choice," Ferox replied to both of them and then gestured for me to put the stone down. "This is the only chance she has."

Cassie tossed me a knife that I caught by the handle. "We are going to bind the stone and her tree to your blood. Make sure the fae understand that you are a package deal. We will work with them on being friendlier and agree to more court visits to enhance the relationship between our people. You are going to have to walk on a narrow ledge with all the innate knowledge you both have of our grove but do what she needs first to survive."

"I understand." I nodded my head. I was Veon's second-in-command, and Lia shared everything with the vasilissa. It would be difficult to separate loyalties, but if they could save her, I would be respectful.

"Slice your palm and gather the blood in the center," Cassie ordered, and vines began to grow in the ground around us in a circle.

I followed her directive, feeling the slight pain as the blade caressed my skin.

"Seeds of time we now reverse. What's intertwined must be dispersed. Combined souls in nature must become distinct. A connection that can no longer be linked."

My blood began to glow with imprints of leaves. Sounds of Nylisa weeping came from her tree at my back, but I could not comfort her. I knew Aralia would be crying right now if she could.

"Next part." Ferox leaned closer to me and said, "Small graces that she will not be awake to experience this firsthand, it is quite painful for the dryad."

"Not helping." I glowered at him but kept my hand still.

"Stay focused," Cassie snapped at me as some of my blood trickled down the side of my hand.

I shifted my hooves into a rock so that I would be unfazed by the tremors in the world around me. If I needed to keep from moving, for her, I would do it. I would do anything.

"Petrified root, trunk, and bark, unanchor yourself from this mark. Place yourself into this stone until your name has been intone."

Aralia's tree exploded into thousands of little energy orbs that hovered for only a second before they crashed straight into the quartz. I almost had to avert my eyes, but I wouldn't miss a thing. I refused to be unaware of anything that she went through. After a few minutes, the light receded.

"Rux, pour your blood on her stone and then place your hand on the top, palm against the surface."

The quartz was a bit smaller than my head now as it swelled with magic, but even with the size, the blood ran down around the entire surface. I looked to Cassie for the next direction as there had to be more.

"Repeat after me: this stone is bound to me."

"This stone is bound to me." I didn't hesitate.

"Only I may release the life within."

"Only I may release the life within." I was okay with that, but what if the fae killed me for bringing her over? Then who could release her?

"This stone is my priority over everything else, and no harm shall come to it."

I raised an eyebrow at the woman, but it wasn't any different from the vow I'd taken after the ryne trials. "This stone is my priority over everything else, and no harm shall come to it."

"All right. You need to get ready to go immediately. The quartz will slow the illness to a crawl, but it will continue to spread until it consumes her." Cassie patted me on the shoulder. "When she is able to be replanted, draw a line on the top of it with your finger and then a circle going clockwise, starting and ending to the north. You will say her name nine times."

"I do have a question. Why are your spells in Druidic? At that academy, we learned everything in Latin."

Ferox fought back a laugh at my question, but Cassie didn't seem to share his amusement.

"Unlike all of you, I did not attend the academy. Latin is for stuck-up mages to show off that they went for the training.

Spells can be spoken in any language and are not any more powerful if they are spoken in Latin than in Druidic. Now get going, unless you need to pick up some belongings. You could be there a while."

"I will be there in a few days. I will follow you with your things," Ferox said as he waved me in the direction of our shared border with the fae.

With Aralia, I'd known we'd likely leave someday. This wasn't how I'd intended to have it happen though.

Carrying her this way felt unnatural. At least in my arms, I could tell she was there. Her skin pressed to mine or her bark under my fingertips let me know she was with me. The cold stone offered no comfort. My mind fought against the fact that I'd witnessed her tree disappear into the rock. My blood had sealed it.

"I heard you were leaving us. Figured you might not get a chance to say goodbye," Rhenei said as she walked up the path slowly before I approached the border. The pixies never took long to pass on the news of changes. "When will you be back?"

"I don't know," I admitted and rubbed the back of my head. Part of me felt a little bad as I realized I'd forgotten all about Rhenei after my dryad passed out. "Everything depends on Aralia's condition."

She glanced at the stone in my hand and frowned. "I'd hoped she would have found her mates at this point so you wouldn't have to chase after her all the time."

Everyone just assumed that because we hadn't been all over one another after she matured that I would never be matched to Lia. I'd played the game too. I continued to pretend that I could feed off others like I hadn't met my match, but I didn't. I just liked the feeling that came with being wanted. Aralia was hard to love because she wanted nothing to do with me and made sure that everyone knew it. It didn't change the fact that I feared the day she would fully reject me as a potential mate.

Unless they were the vasilissa, most nymphs wouldn't discover their mates until they found all of them, whether it was two or three. I knew that I was one, and I was pretty confident that Lia's second match wasn't in Voreios, so I watched every interaction that she had with others. I'm glad it hadn't been the elf, but now it was beginning to look a lot more likely that they might be fae.

"This is what I trained to do; this is my role here." I knew I sounded defensive, and it wasn't Rhenei's fault.

"I know. I just hoped that we'd be able to explore . . . our full potential soon, and now you are leaving."

As gently as I could, I pulled Rhenei into my open arm, and she hugged me tightly. Her fingers caressed down the front of my bare chest, and her lips turned to an adorable pout. When I brushed a kiss to her forehead, I steadied myself before continuing. "I think we both know that this wasn't ever going to be anything more. Your mates are looking for you now, and it's time you allowed yourself the opportunity to find them."

"I wasn't suggesting I wouldn't wait—" She looked as if I'd slapped her, and I felt a growing remorse that I'd not been honest with her sooner.

"I may not ever come back, Rhenei. Everything for me depends on what Aralia needs. I won the trials to be her ryne, and she will always come first, even if she isn't ever my mate."

Watching her eyes fill up with tears, I knew I was a jerk. She pulled out of my grip and ran back into the grove without another word.

Chapter 9 — Lorsan

I leaned over the balcony of my suite and furrowed my brow as the satyr walked across the bridge of the moat and straight into the court grounds. I could recognize him anywhere. He'd hit me enough times over the years to make me wary of going into Voreios. What was Rux doing here, and how had he gotten this far without a guard detail?

We'd gotten into fights over the little dryad with fey magic because I had barely been able to contain my curiosity about her light even as she grew up. What can I say? Fae kings were known for our obsession with power, and I hadn't turned out to be that different. Her parents always blocked my attempts to bring her to the court, but to find her ryne coming to me? What could this be about?

I made my way down to the main halls slowly. Commotion, naturally, followed him as he made his way past my interior guards. Rux was a burly satyr with a physique not found in the Feylands often. Our kind were usually slender framed, so my guards often avoided conflict with more muscular opponents, as they were clearly doing here.

Rux growled through clenched teeth as if restraining himself from reacting in fury. "I have already told you that I will only speak with Lorsan."

"The king is otherwise occupied. You will have to wait."

"She doesn't have time for this. Get him now!"

The guards backed up farther from the fury in his voice.

But my interest was locked onto what he'd said more than my incompetent guards. He had come alone, but his mention of her sent my thoughts to the nymph. "Does this have to do with Aralia?"

Rux locked eyes on me, and I kept my face emotionless even as he exhaled a relieved sigh. He held up the stone in his hand, and my guards put their hands on their weapons. The man didn't even appear fazed by the weapons pointed in his direction.

"She's very sick. Ferox told me to bring her here. She needs to be replanted closer to the source of fey magic. He said that you can save her."

Interesting. I didn't always trust Voreios, but Ferox wouldn't hurt us. The only time he'd gone against the fae was when we had his daughter. If he was sending his granddaughter to us, then it likely wasn't a trick. I eyed the stone with hesitation. "Is she in there?"

"Yes. I have the spell to get her out, but I need to know where to put her tree."

"Does Ferox know that we are having trouble with fey magic right now?" I asked, surprised at my unwillingness to put the dryad in any further danger.

Rux frowned. "He's returned to the tower to look for answers to her ailment. What do you mean trouble? She has vitium sacer. Is the trouble with the fey magic what is making her sick?"

The mention of this particular disease eased my worries that the yellow cloud had migrated. "No. Vitium sacer is a different illness that typically presents only in nymphs when it occurs."

"Can you help her then?" he asked. "You may be the only one who can save her . . ."

I could see how much that hurt him to say, so I wouldn't rub it in, even if my ego liked to see this man knocked down. A protector who couldn't save his woman.

"All right. We'll take her for a price. Voreios owes us a favor to be called in at a time of our choosing. Jot the spell down here and pass her over to me. You can return to Voreios with our terms."

"I'm not leaving her," Rux growled again, causing the guards to shift in their stances as if they would actually attack him. He pulled the stone back against his chest. It was either a very good act. or she was truly in the stone. "I will stay here, but you can send a messenger with those terms. However, the favor can only be something that Voreios alone can provide and must not include loss of life or autonomy."

"The invitation wasn't extended to you. I can make the space for a night before you travel, but you will not be moving into the court." I didn't bother negotiating the favor further. There was nothing we wanted from Voreios. I also was very curious to get a glimpse of the dryad. I hadn't seen her in a few decades.

"Then I will find a cave outside the court. I will not be returning to Voreios while she resides here. That's not how our customs work, and you know it."

Actually, I didn't fully understand how their society was structured. I never really cared to know. "I think you are getting rather pushy for someone coming in and asking for favors."

"The spell is attached to my blood, and I know how to care for dryad trees. I am not going to leave her, or she will die anyway."

I glowered at him but knew that he'd made some arguments that I couldn't dispute. The only one who could make the satyr go away was Aralia herself. Fine, he won this round. "Bring her out to the garden. We'll find you quarters near her so you can care for her tree."

Making my way down the rest of the steps, I took in the quartz in his hands as I gestured for a messenger to bring a healer. The irony of this situation wasn't lost to me.

My father had died for stealing a dryad to put in his garden, and now here I stood with one being handed to me for mine. Was she as sick as he claimed? The even bigger question was, why did I care?

In the center of the stone was an etching of what I could only imagine was her tree. I feigned disinterest because I could easily ask him these questions, but I didn't want to talk with him more than I had to. The tree didn't look any different from the ones that we had in the forest. How could one tell if they were dryad trees?

Rux gestured for me to show him the way, his fingers protectively holding the quartz like I would try to steal it from him. I wasn't interested in the stone though, just the nymph inside of it.

I took him to the garden that was closest to the entrance he'd charged in across the moat. It was the least developed, but it was also the one that I could see directly from my room above. What could be a better way to observe the new arrival. I'd get bored of it in a week, I was sure, but why not enjoy the week? The perimeter of the garden space had bushes and bundles of flower clusters along the gray-curtain walls to the exterior of the court. Other than that, it was a blank canvas with lots of grass. I assumed he would have enough room.

Rux waited for me to give him a nod that this was the place, and then he walked in a circle to the left, his hooves making clean tears in the ground. The satyr took a quick glance at those gathered around, and for the first time, he looked unnerved. She had to actually be in there. Inside their border, the Forest Folk never appeared to be out of place, but as he took in all the fae watching him, he seemed resigned to the situation.

He placed the stone on the ground, and I waited. How long had it been since anyone not from a grove had seen a dryad tree? Was this an honor or a plague on us? Nymphs never chose to come to the Feylands, even if the mates they selected were fae. There had to be a reason for this.

Rux spoke in Druidic to the stone, but the words were too quick for me to follow. I could have sworn he said her name, and my heart raced with a thrill I hadn't felt in a long while. This moment alone was something my past two predecessors hadn't been able to pull off. I wouldn't get cocky because all I'd done was agree to it, but still, this could alter the Feylands forever.

The stone began to pulse a white light as Rux continued to whisper to it. The quartz splintered into a thousand pieces, and the ground began to shake as a hole opened up in the soil. Leaves and branches grew from the empty space, and an oak tree manifested where there had not been one before. I still couldn't tell the difference, and as I watched Rux place his palm to the tree, I wanted nothing more than to do the same. I was king, I should be able to touch it, but out of respect for the potential nymph, I did not.

"Are you sure about doing this?" Trevan whispered to me as we all took in the tree. "There are so many problems with this. What if this is Voreios's attempt to take over our kingdom? She's the twin of their vasilissa. If that's not the intent, then what if she spreads the supposed illness?"

"Enough. I can handle one dryad. If it's an attempted attack, then they both will die here." I gestured for one of the scientists to go investigate for the illness.

Rux took in the man as he approached the tree and seemed to decide that he needed to be agreeable. The satyr pointed out something on the bark of the oak and the fae's hands lit up with magic to run his own tests. I didn't like the frown that formed on his face before he came back to me with the results.

"Sir. This isn't the normal variety of vitium sacer."

I waited for him to elaborate, but he stopped speaking. "What does that mean?"

"This strand hasn't been seen since before the migration. I'll get to work on producing the antidote. Should only take me a few hours."

I grabbed his arm before he continued on his way. "Is anyone else in danger from her being here?"

"Not at this time. The fae cannot be harmed by this illness, and even the other fey creatures we have should not be impacted. Some of the rose bushes may die, but we can replant

103

as needed," he replied smoothly and turned to give me his full attention. "Did you have other questions for me?"

"Is the nymph still in danger?"

"As of right now, yes. She won't survive three more sunsets at the rate of the spread." He turned to meet Rux's gaze. The satyr fought to keep the expression off his face, but he couldn't hide the full extent of his despair.

Rux didn't have the mate markings I'd become accustomed to seeing on our trips to Anatoli, so perhaps he felt a brotherly affection for the dryad he'd been tasked to protect. I would explore that dynamic further after she woke up.

"With a proper antidote, she should be well enough to come out from the tree in the early hours of the morning."

"How can you tell it's a dryad tree?" I asked. He'd just walked over there and immediately knew. Our scientist hadn't seen them in years, so how could he tell so easily?

"Context clues, sir. It can be very difficult to tell them apart. The first hint is the satyr's protective flexing, they can try to misdirect, but as more of us approach, it's harder to hide the fact that he doesn't feel comfortable with us around her tree. Your garden plants have taken on, effectively, their own glamour now that she is in the vicinity. This only happens with nymphs and some other plant fey creatures. The dark markings on her bark would not be present on an oak tree. Only a nymph can contract this illness." He bowed to me with a considerate lowering of his head. "May I?"

"Yes, go make the antidote."

Trevan and I exchanged thoughtful gazes as we pondered what he'd just said. The garden did seem to look a little brighter despite the shade her branches now cast on the space.

Rux rubbed along the trunk of her tree. There was an intimate tenderness in his expression and the way he moved his hand.

"Lia, please wake up." When he turned back to the fae still gathered around him, his frown grew. "Where do you keep your soil? Her roots are going to be shocked with the replanting, so I'll need to balance out the soil for that. I also need water."

One of the guards went off to collect everything he would need.

His fingers trailed along the marks in the bark, and I watched intently to study every gesture he made with the tree. I was no stranger to women, but how did one interact with an element of nature? So many questions. For now, I just needed to be patient until she woke up.

Chapter 10 — Aralia

Everything was silent. I couldn't feel anyone or hear them. My siblings, my cousins, Nylisa . . . everyone was gone. Our root radio channels, as my mom always called them, had gone quiet. Pushing out from my bark, my brain swayed with dizziness and pain as my spirit form manifested. I'd never been here before; the plants spoke differently in a mess of chaos and abstract thoughts.

Where was everyone? My heart raced, and I felt my breath come rapidly before I screamed. Clutching my hands over my ears, I sank down to my knees. Rux darted from around the corner of whatever castle this was, and though my first thought was relief at my safety, panic set back in.

He lifted me up to my feet and pulled me against him like he always did if I had a panic attack. "It's okay, Aralia. I promise, it's okay. You are okay." He gave a shaky laugh like he'd been worried about me. "I never thought I'd be so happy to hear you scream like that."

"Where are we?" My voice wavered. "Where's Nylisa? I can't hear them, Rux. I can't hear them."

"I know. I bet it is very quiet for you right now." He stroked my hair like I were a child, but it worked, I admitted begrudgingly. "We are at the seelie court—"

I shoved back against him before he could continue. "Why am I here? We were going to the land of the dragons, not the fae court. What have you done? Why can't I feel my sister!"

"Lia. I know this is scary but let me finish."

"What did you do?" I knew it had to be him. Who else would have taken me away from the grove?

"You are sick. We had to separate you from Voreios—"

"Nylisa . . ."

"She's safe. So are you. Look, I know it's not what you wanted in the moment, but the fae have resources we don't, and Lorsan has agreed to look after you—"

He was going to leave me here? Of course. My face fell. I'd never belonged there, and how could any of them truly move forward if I was dragging everything down. "What was the final straw?"

"What?" Rux's expression turned up in confusion. "Your illness hadn't spread yet, but your clump of roots was tied too closely to Nylisa."

I could accept that as a reason to turn me away. I would never want to do anything to endanger my sister. Rux tried to step closer, but I needed to break myself away from any comfort I used to expect from him. That much hadn't changed. How had this happened? My mind was just blank after the memories, my

107

roots didn't even remember being moved. I hated the silence more than anything, but my mom had been alone for decades, I could do it too. I just hadn't expected it to be this quiet in my head.

"Lia . . ."

"No, don't touch me. You've done enough."

He shrugged and shook his head at me. "Is the soil balanced for what you need? I tried—"

"Stop doing that," I replied curtly and straightened my spine. He was smothering me with this overprotective bullshit. "I just need to think."

"I just want to make sure you are comfortable."

"Well, I'm not. I can't feel my sister, I woke up a thousand miles away from my home, and I'm forced to accept that this is my new reality. Leave me be."

I heard him sigh, just like I had all of my life when I gave him this tone. "If there had been any other option, I would have done it. You have to believe me."

I rolled my eyes and gave my best fake smile to a few of the fae I caught watching me, lowering my voice so only he could hear. "I didn't even get to say goodbye. When will I be able to go back?"

"You were unconscious. I couldn't let you die. There weren't very many options."

"Why not let me die? Wouldn't that be easier than this? You don't have to pretend like this has turned out how either of us wanted. You would have been free."

"I would never want that, Lia" Rux retorted immediately as his fingers caressed down my arm.

Before I could make a reply of my own, the magic around me shifted. I felt the ethereal fae king long before the glow of him came out from the court. He walked the garden with poise and grace, with a slender build and confident strides. My eyes swept over every detail of defined muscle I could spot through his hardly practical shirt. His long, blond hair fell almost as low as mine did when I wore it down. Those dark wings, though, were unlike any of the other fae. Translucent, but I knew they were real. Each of the many points on both wings pulled to a tight point.

He hadn't always displayed his wings when I'd watched him from the border of Voreios, so this had to be intentional. Whatever the reason, I was transfixed by him. He'd not been this close to me in decades, and I was beginning to question if my little secret crush was as dead as I'd thought.

"Welcome to the fae court, Aralia." Lorsan took my hand and kissed the top of it.

I felt my cheeks grow hot with a flurry of sadness, attraction, and embarrassment for my reaction to ending up in his court.

Rux rolled his eyes as he stepped back to let us talk for a moment, something I was grateful for and also terrified of. Though we'd both been trained in diplomatic relations, I needed to tread a very careful boundary with limited information. All while I tried to mask my very base attraction to the man in front of me with a crowd of fae.

"Thank you for offering me hospitality and care. I apologize for the inconvenience this may have caused you."

A smirk twitched on the corner of Lorsan's lips. Those damn, beautiful lips. "I've been trying to invite you to the court for some time. I'd have fought harder if I'd known the land would respond this way to you."

Everything was lit up, and fey magic swirled in the air around the entire garden, centering around us both. The satyrs spoke of this in Voreios also, that the land would shimmer when a nymph was present. Being a nymph, I never saw anything except the world this way. What was different about these grounds were the plants, but if he liked what my presence could do here, then I would happily keep doing it.

When my gaze returned to him, he spoke again. "It looks as though the antidote is working. You should recover entirely in a few days as if it never happened."

"Oh, thank you so much for your help. I know that we likely had to negotiate something. I promise it will be paid," I replied graciously. The fae never did anything for free, but

I wasn't sure what else to say to him. Was he this handsome when I was younger? I knew I'd had a crush on him, but by trying to avert my eyes, I got a very good look at his chiseled chest through the gaps in his shirt.

"It was only for a favor. We don't have anything in particular that we need from Voreios at this time." Was that dismissal in his tone? There was just a slight inflection as the words came rapidly. Our people weren't close, and the fae had been rather isolated from the world after the war.

"I understand. Well, when you are ready to claim it, just let me know." I would ensure that my sister and Veon kept whatever promise we'd made. Maybe, if this encounter went well enough, I could return as an ambassador to the court. The fae wouldn't reject me for my magic. "What happens next? I'm not very familiar with this illness, do you know how long the recovery will take? When will I be permitted to return home?"

"This antidote will only hold if you remain in the Feylands." Though he offered the words as softly as he could, there wasn't any remorse in his eyes. "You can never return to Voreios, but please feel welcome to change the gardens as you would like to suit your needs and growth. We can discuss long-term arrangements once you are feeling well."

I didn't know how much I could believe him to tell me the truth of my condition, but Rux didn't dispute his words. I glanced around the garden, keeping my face pleasant even as a pit tightened in my gut. I could never go home.

"Given your status in Voreios, I will be extending a seat among the royal court to you. Rux will stay on as your guard for the time being. We don't often have fey members in the palace walls, so please forgive the learning curve the other members of the court will experience," Lorsan said graciously, but I did not miss the way he said *fey* as if it were dirty.

"Please do not put yourself in any unnecessary position. I can stay in the garden."

"Nonsense. We have the best libraries and hospitality of anyone on this planet. Your use of our language is well enunciated and clean. I would be honored to have you as part of our court."

"Thank you." I glanced down at my fingers trying to keep them still. I'd wanted to talk to him for so long, and now his intense gaze sent glorious waves of excitement all over my body.

"King Lorsan. You have important matters to attend to." A fussy woman in gold approached from behind him and leveled me with a glare. "If you are serious about having her in the court, then I am better versed at explaining the rules to her."

"I am serious." Lorsan shifted his attention to this older fae woman. "Aralia, this is my aunt, Prinna. I will leave you in her capable hands. The court gathers every night before dinner for announcements and festivities. I hope to become much better acquainted with you."

My cheeks burned at the possibilities tied to that statement. It might all be in my head, but the way his eyes drank me in told me he could feel a little heat between us too.

Prinna waited until he'd vanished back into the court before she leveled a new glare on me. "He is the king, and you will treat him more respectfully next time. Why he wants to add a fey to the court isn't beyond me, he's just a man in the end. But you will not distract the court with your presence. Do you hear me?"

"I have no intention of distracting anyone," I agreed with a glance at Rux. Per usual, he wasn't very far away and listened keenly to everything being said to me.

"Good. The king is holding the forum for our magic to select the queen of the fae. These proceedings must be done in a very specific manner. You will join us for dinner, but say nothing to anyone unless you are directly spoken to, do you understand?"

"Yes." That might be harder to follow through with. In my grove, we all spoke as we felt called to, but this wasn't Voreios, and I was going to have to work with their rules.

"Do you have anything but that rag to wear?" She gestured with distaste, and I glanced at the simple green dress I wore, which wrapped around my form and then tied at the back of my neck.

"I don't own clothing—"

"This is the problem with fey. Did you just expect that we would provide everything for you? How selfish." She was about to rattle on and only stopped when she noticed I shook my head.

"That's not what I meant. I can make whatever clothing I need."

"Oh, you can afford cashmere and silk then?"

I knew my face looked confused, but instead of explaining, I called the leaves and changed my outfit so that it matched her dress. I did a quick spin for her. "If there is a dress code, I can abide by it. I just . . . didn't know."

"You are not allowed to recklessly use fey magic that way!"

"It's not fey magic. This is my ability as a nymph." If this was how they treated my mother and the vasilissa of Anatoli, no wonder our relationship with them was strained. I could help fix that, it just seemed like I was going to need a whole lot of patience. Not a trait I was known for, but I could adapt.

Instead of appearing appeased by this answer, she curled her lip in further disgust. "Fine. You will also need to wear shoes moving forward."

My toes wiggled against the soil at the mention, and though I was limited to only sensing the garden, my anxiety shot up at not being able to connect to the earth. "I see."

"If you break these rules during the day, then you will not be allowed to join us for that evening. Let's see if you can manage to pull this off. I know he invited you to the court, but really, you might be more comfortable out here with . . . the rest on your level." Prinna's gaze flicked not only to my ryne but to the other guards standing on the perimeter. "There's no place for you in this court, and you will realize that soon enough."

I waited for her to storm off before changing my outfit back. I would need to change everything about who I was to fit in here. I just hated that I already knew I didn't belong, and I'd only been here a day.

Rux appeared at my side as the rest of the fae retreated back to the palace, and he frowned as he took in my sad expression. "It'll be okay, Lia. Let's take this one day at a time."

He cupped my cheek and then opened his other arm for the hug he somehow always knew I needed. I wouldn't cry, not until I went back into my tree, but the sadness washed over me as I melted into his embrace.

"Can I really not go home ever? Can I not leave?"

"I don't know. Ferox said he would join us in a few days. I really want him to look over everything the scientist has given you. If you can't go home, then we will stay here. We'll make the best of it." His grip tightened on me, offering the grounding that I needed beyond my roots. An anchor against what we would have to endure, but he was right. Maybe in a few days, this would look different.

If I was going to fit in, I couldn't just dress like them. I needed to look like them too. Manifesting a fey replicated mirror beside us, I faded the dryad lines that ran down my body until they didn't exist anymore. I turned my head to glance at my ears that were just a bit more pointed than any of the other fey. I shrank those down. The person in the mirror was almost foreign, but I could be that if I had to. I would find my place here. With the addition of the head circlet and a green silk dress and shoes, I could almost appear fae.

Rux frowned in the mirror as he took in all the changes, but there wasn't anything he could say. We both knew that my survival depended on giving up what made me different.

Chapter 11 — Lorsan

I wouldn't admit that I stared at her tree as often as I could while we waited for her to heal enough to manifest her spirit form. Now that she was here, it was all I could think about. Whether I was in my quarters, my office, or the adviser chambers, I hovered near the window so that I could keep her in my sight.

I could tell the moment that she woke up, not because she screamed. No, it was before that. The garden began to glow as it only did in the areas around the fey well. Each plant responded to her magical call as the land made her its centerpiece. Even the fey magic moved around her as if the goddess herself ordained this new arrival.

Whenever I'd gone to visit either of the neighboring groves, I'd always found the nymphs to be beautiful. I'd thought I was prepared to see her as she fought with the satyr in the garden. I was not. I'd never needed to touch anything more than I did in that moment, and yet, even as king, that was denied to me with all those eyes upon my every action. I wanted her closer, though. She was quickly becoming an obsession, and she'd only been up for a few hours.

Each time I glanced out the window, I nearly broke my clean composure to scowl. I hated how intimate Rux's touches were. The way he stroked her cheek or held her like he was doing now. He didn't seem to care what the others thought of his open displays of affection toward the nymph. Unfortunately, their interactions also revealed that this was not some brotherly dynamic like I'd initially hoped. Removing him would be more difficult than expected.

"Aralia really has grown up to be rather stunning," Trevan said as he noticed where I looked, and I knew he watched her as closely as I did. I hated that too, but unless I moved to make her a consort, I couldn't do anything about any of the men in my court. I'd dissolved my father's harem, and I didn't have any intention to bring it back, but there were few options in the fae world to prevent the open sexual practices of our cultures.

"Most nymphs are," I agreed, trying not to show too much interest.

"Yeah, but this one is special, and now she's ours."

Ours. I knew he meant that she was one of my subjects, but a possessiveness set in on hearing the claim. I had to take a queen from the fae women who were here, yet I'd never wanted something as much as I did watching the new dryad in my garden.

I'd never imagined being so enraptured by a nymph. Fae women were beautiful too. Hell, I had twenty-three of them in the room behind me. But her blond hair fell perfectly framing her face. Her smile felt sincere, and the ease with which she'd transitioned from Druidic to Fae while speaking caught my notice. The way she swayed her hips when she chatted animatedly with her satyr. I didn't like the affectionate way Rux looked at her, but I had to accept that they were a package deal until I could find a way around it.

Those piercing green eyes ignited something in my soul that I'd never experienced before. Even in the midst of hunger, I'd never craved to touch someone with this intensity, A thought came unbidden from the depths. Once I figured out what the mages' plans were and how they were attacking the magic, I would seize her to be mine. Was this what my father had felt for Aralia's mother? He'd become quite mad in his need to possess the dryad, and now, after only a few sentences, her daughter threatened to take my sanity.

When she'd asked about returning to Voreios, I'd misrepresented the cure she'd been given. Unintentional as that had been, I now knew my brain had been ahead of me. She'd never be allowed to leave. I had a rare opportunity to change the kingdom forever, and I wasn't about to let her slip through my fingers.

"Have the scientists found any remedies for the situation with the fey pool?"

"They are removing each stone right now and studying the magical effects. We've had forty-four more casualties so far

119

today." He filled me in as he moved toward my meads. He really did enjoy drinking more than he probably should. "The water has returned to the soft pastels, but the cloud of gas will not disperse, and they worry that it may impact the pool again."

"Can they confirm that this is what's causing the outbreak of venenatio luteus?" All other tests hadn't yielded definitive results. I needed answers before this turned into something more contagious, or worse, a disease that impacted all the fae gathered for the trials.

"They haven't run the tests on the smog yet." Trevan shrugged his shoulders. "I'll let you know when I hear something."

How had that not been done straight away? We get a solid clue and then nothing yet again. How was I surrounded by such incompetence? "Fine. I will stop by to see them later. Any word on the trail of the mages who murdered the selkie?"

"The shadow god is dead. It couldn't have been them. His mages have no power any longer. I think it may have just been a horrific accident. There haven't been any sightings of mages in decades."

"Accident?" I didn't bother to mask my surprise at his offhanded remark. "Did you look at how I found the body? That was done purposefully and intentionally. If you don't think it was the mages, then find out who it was. Immediately."

He paled a bit in response to my fury, but at least now I had his full attention.

The itch rose to look back at her tree again. I found the addition of her tree to the garden to be soothing in a way I'd not expected. The shrubbery had already begun to shift around as if directed by a new gardener. Whether that was Aralia's influence or Rux's, I couldn't be entirely sure.

"I'm not saying it couldn't be mages. He had acolytes spread all over the universe. Yerirn thinks that if the right conditions are met, the shadow god could be reborn," Trevan admitted uneasily as he took a seat in his favorite spot on the couch.

"Do we know what those conditions are?"

"I believe they have a book. There's nothing in our library that talks about it, but Salixa, the last mother of Cholios, reportedly had an ancient book. She brought it with her everywhere, supposedly."

I rubbed my chin while I mused on the prospect of an ancient tome carrying all of our answers. The first issue was even finding the mages, but once we found them, it might not be too hard to follow them to the information we needed.

"I think you should have Aralia join the classes under the tutor with the other women, so we can test her abilities." Trevan took another long sip.

With the mention of her name, I did glance out the window again. Her leaves rustled in the wind. It'd been interesting to experience a tree that did not scream. Growing up in the Feylands, I'd been accustomed to the horrifying sounds that nature would make. Her silence was almost eerie in its own way.

"That is a good idea. We should know what we are getting ourselves into. Rux doesn't seem to use fey magic, so we probably don't need to test him."

"He's a satyr. Of course, he doesn't use magic. He's nothing more than a generic guard."

I didn't believe that was true. What little I did know was that rynes went to the magical academy of their people. It was quite a big thing from what I'd gathered at the world meetings when the groves would discuss it occasionally. He had some type of magic, likely elemental. It'd be arrogant to dismiss him so easily.

"I'll let her know after my meeting with the women." I'd take any chance I could to speak with her.

Trevan leaned forward with a calculated expression, the one he only used when it came to chasing women. "I can handle all the communications with her if you'd like. You're far too busy to deal with a sick fey. Focus on the potential queens and let me take this off of your plate."

"Maybe in the future." I tried to sound agreeable, though I wanted to poke his eyes out for the lechery

122

embedded in their depths. "For now, I can spare a few minutes. The timing of these illnesses with the trials is suspicious, and I want to investigate it with my magic."

He couldn't argue with that, so he didn't. Being the most powerful holder of our gifts meant that I could see things even the brightest minds couldn't.

"King Lorsan, it's time! We have been waiting for long enough." Prinna shouted through my door before she knocked.

Without waiting for a response, she burst into the room and leveled me with a stare. I think they wanted me to step up with a firm hand, and if they kept pushing, I would do it.

"One of these women will be your queen! Show some interest in getting to know them. What could it hurt?"

"I am on my way to them now. Things will move in my time, no one else's. Even as queen, that fact will not change for them." I stood from my desk and smoothed my clothing down.

Fae, including me as the king, were not afraid to display our assets. My dark wings broke into points that flared out in multiple places. While not entirely bare of a shirt, most of my chest was available to peruse through the X in the leather that crossed my muscles.

I'd not missed the way the nymph beheld me for those few moments, unsure of where to put her eyes. There had been a scent of honey and wildflowers that was absolutely delectable to me. Nymphs had their own version of our glamour, but I'd never been on the receiving end of it. The implications laid bare perhaps an underlying attraction that I would need to unpack later. I pushed the thought away before I could become aroused. The fae women would notice my state and want to act.

"There is something that we need to discuss before you go." Prinna stepped in front of me before I made it to the door.

"Out with it. You are stalling me now."

"At first, we thought we found a guard with one of the women, but he was fae. It appears he snuck in to retrieve her. They don't have the council's blessing, but he is claiming they are mates. We have arrested him, and he's in the dungeon now."

"Once she signed the agreement for the trials, she became property of the king. Theft is a high crime." Trevan rose to his feet behind me. He glared at Prinna before he met my gaze with a heated look. "This needs to be dealt with straight away."

I didn't feel all that angry over the declaration, but what would this incident say about the start of the trials? What would my father have done? Now was the time to assert that I would not have everyone walking all over me. Apathy would not rule this kingdom anymore. I was king, and I would own that burden.

"Execute them both. I'll meet with the other women now."

"Them both?" Prinna paled, and as she raised her hand up to protest, I snarled in her direction.

"She has broken the pact with the magic that she agreed to. This is more egregious than him attempting to steal a woman. I was quite clear when I said there were only two ways out of this." I turned my attention to Trevan before I spoke next. "Can you handle this?"

"Yes, sir."

"Prinna, if you find any of the others harboring 'mates,' then they can follow. I will not unknowingly cuckold myself to a woman from a power-hungry family who plans to take the crown and keep her lover on the side."

The energy had shifted in the room as they realized I was serious. I knew the women would play with the members of my court, and even my guards, while they were going through the tests. I didn't begrudge them that experience as all but one of them would die. They all needed to feed to be at their most competent, and I wasn't about to go through the effort of keeping more than twenty women satisfied. It would stop if I took them as my queen though.

Mates weren't a thing with the fae unless agreed to by our council. In the days of the declining female population, my father would take all the women coming to ask for this blessing and execute the men. I had not continued that tradition, but my council had also never given the title to any that came in looking for it. I would not tolerate those claims from these women. They'd all chosen to sign up for these trials.

Trevan left the room silently, and as I met Prinna's expression, I found disappointment. But she did not voice her complaints. Nice to find out there was one way to shut her mouth.

I crossed the hall and opened the door to find the other twenty-two women sitting quietly, waiting for my arrival. Soleil's eyes met mine first. Her light wings fluttered with what I took to be excitement. The large space that we'd converted to a queen's waiting room had been intricately designed with those gold accents and bright, airy comforts, down to the cushions they all sat on. My mother would have enjoyed the way the light from the floor-to-ceiling windows along the back wall bounced around in here.

"How are you ladies doing?" I asked as kindly as I could to mask the fury that still raged underneath. How many of them were here for the right reason? From the eagerness on six of their faces, I could guess who I would get to spend the most time with. One contender appeared to be on the verge of tears, and I knew I needed to get to the bottom of that.

"We are well, Your Majesty," Soleil purred with a glowing smile. A fae's glamour usually created a radiant effect on their skin and wings. "You have provided for all of our needs."

I doubted that was true, but I'd let the pleasantry slide. My aunt slipped in the door silently behind me. Her mouth was set in a thin line that told me she still wasn't sure how to respond to my last declaration. I didn't care. She was right about one thing: one of these women would be my queen. I needed to take this a bit more seriously than I had been.

Prinna cleared her throat, and the women turned their attention from me to her. "Today we will be doing an experiment to test your magic. Using a bit of your own unique gifts, you will touch palms with the king. This will grant Aine the option to show him a glimpse of what your future together might look like based on your personalities. You will be unable to persuade this vision to be anything other than what Aine would like him to know."

This might be interesting and could provide some good insight into each of their intentions and driving motivators.

"He is a busy man, so gather around. Soleil, how about you demonstrate the process to the others. I'll walk you through it." She gestured for me to sit down, and after I did, the fae woman sat across from me.

She held her palm up and the white tint of fey magic danced along her hand. "I'm ready, my lord."

I placed my palm up against hers, igniting my own magic, and she gasped at the force as the world around us faded to nothing more than clouds. A woman's laughter rang in the back of my mind, but I knew her voice. The goddess, Aine, was not a

127

subtle lady. We'd spoken quite frequently over the course of my reign.

"Power," Aine said as a dark bubble rippled out in front of me. "The drive toward absolute success in everything you could want. That's what a life with her will offer you, and I have to admit, even I have been enthralled with her attempts at persuasion for my favor."

I saw myself standing with Soleil in front of a pair of dark thrones, lightning crashing outside. As the image zoomed out, representations of the fey held our platform on their backs. Underneath them were the other kingdoms on Artemesia. I'd succeeded where my father and grandfather had failed.

That wasn't my dream though. I'd grown up during the war with the elves, and during my short life I'd seen the turn of three kings. Aine wouldn't show me this without an intention. Perhaps I needed to look at the vision differently. What was the message behind what she could bring into my life? Soleil would bring the backing to achieve any goal I wanted. Ultimate supremacy.

The room with the other women came back into view, and Soleil smiled shyly as our eyes met.

"I hope it was to your liking," she whispered as Prinna shooed her out of the chair for Tasi to take her spot.

Tasi's family and mine had a long history that ended with them almost exiled from the Feylands altogether. I had been surprised to see her enter the trials at all. Even now, the expression on her face didn't show the same eagerness that some of the other contenders had to be my queen. The one thing I couldn't deny was that I knew she was skilled with our magic.

When my palm met hers, she shuddered and again the room vanished. In the last vision, there'd been an oppressive, heavy feeling that weighed down my shoulders. That didn't appear here now. Tasi's lighter energy gave way to visions of piles of precious stones and metals.

"Wealth. With a shrewd mind, this queen would open the fae world to soar to new financial heights. Her contracts are more layered in perceptive detail than most," Aine revealed to me.

Unlike Soleil, Tasi stood behind me, almost as if to hide in my shadow. I'd have to write the details down and decipher some of it later. As my mind returned back to the room, I pulled my communicator device out of my pocket and made a few notes about both of the visions. I never used the thing, but perhaps this could be a good purpose to start.

The women remained silent, waiting for me to finish. I glanced at Soleil, who watched me like a hawk, and Tasi, who stared at her hands. "Did you see the vision she showed me?"

"No, my lord," Soleil answered politely while Tasi shook her head.

"What do you see when our hands touch?"

129

"Well, it happened so quickly, but there is an intensity to experiencing your magic from the direct connection of the pool. I didn't see much of anything," Soleil admitted and then looked to Tasi.

"Agreed, it was as if there was an overload of magic in my veins."

I nodded my head and then turned to Dalila, who blushed a bright red as our hands met. Her raven-black hair was pulled into four tightly plaited buns. She didn't shy away from using her glamour to display her physical attraction, and her dark skin was radiant. I wasn't willing to show my hand just yet to these contenders, so I kept my own glamour in check as I mused on the thought of my first sample feed briefly.

The room transformed again as I'd expected, but instead of a white tint it was pink. A dozen small fae children ran around me and a very pregnant Dalila. The distance between us was notable as I didn't seem to interact with her or any of our children, but the proof of copulation was undeniable.

"Legacy. There'd be no shortage of heirs for the magic to select in this match."

Well, I could have figured that one out on my own. I wouldn't say that to the goddess.

The rest of the women went on with a variation of the concepts. Power, wealth, envy, some were stronger than

130

others. Experiencing Aine this way was exhausting, however. I was grateful that I now sat in front of the last one, Forsythia.

Dried tears had left stains down her cheeks on both sides even as she tried to smile at me now. She was on the frail side of thin, and every curve of her bones poked through her skin. Her shoulder-length blond hair was choppy in a way that I couldn't tell if it had been intentional. Fear that couldn't be hidden was layered in her big brown eyes.

"What is making you sad?" I asked cautiously. I really didn't want to deal with a hysterical woman right now.

"It's nothing, Your Majesty." She waved away the concern and attempted to offer her palm.

Instead, I waited until her head fell forward in shame.

"My cousin was in the trial until this morning. I am disappointed in her actions and distressed about the shame that it must have cast upon our family in your eyes." Another tear fell down her cheek, and her hand trembled.

If I'd paid more attention to the roster, I would have noticed that some of the women were related. I'd grown up knowing all of their families, but the women rarely came to court, even after I'd ascended, so I only knew a few of them personally. "You are not responsible for her actions. Do not carry the weight of that shame."

I thought that might alleviate her tears, but instead a few more fell, and I felt like I was missing something. When she held up her hand again, I didn't waste time and immediately gave into the surge of the vision shift.

There was nothing. It was dark and empty. The feeling was hollow and cold.

"I have marked this clan," Aine purred in a dark tone that sent goosebumps up my arm. "There will be no future for you here."

Chapter 12 — Aralia

The king's aunt, Prinna, had taken a few days to go over acceptable wardrobe with me from my outfit changes. I hated her scrutiny of every detail, but I couldn't settle into the court until I got her blessing. Finally, as she scowled at me from head to toe, I knew she would clear me.

"Tonight, you will attend dinner. What's your number one rule at the table?"

"Don't talk unless someone speaks to me directly," I repeated dutifully. Rux smiled but kept quiet. He knew I would never be able to follow that rule. Dinner was likely going to be a one-time experience.

"How long are you able to hold this appearance?"

I'd quickly learned that she didn't want to understand how nymph abilities worked, and she didn't need the details. "All day."

"Good. Without all your fey markings, you almost look like one of us, so visitors will not be distracted. Finally, stay away from the king."

I went to nod, but the fey magic rippled, letting me know he'd entered the garden. Prinna must have also noticed this and turned around immediately.

"King Lorsan, what are you doing here? You should be at the council meeting."

"I can be wherever I like." His eyes fell on me, and I offered him a soft smile in return.

"Avert your eyes," Prinna hissed, but I couldn't. My body wouldn't let me.

"Why are you fussing, Prinna? Leave our guest alone. I need to speak with her, since I'm assuming you are the reason she has not been coming to dinner."

"She's dressed appropriately now; she will be there this evening." Prinna's confirmation that I was good enough released some of the tension in my shoulders. The woman's rounded wings fluttered a couple of times. I knew that these movements likely meant something, but I needed some more time to figure that out.

"Wonderful, now leave us."

"King—"

"Leave, Prinna." Though his words could be considered harsh, his tone hadn't changed to reveal any type of anger or frustration. He simply waited until she'd left the garden on the path back to the court, but he didn't take his eyes off me. "I hope she isn't affecting your recovery."

"Not at all. She's trying to make sure I don't make a misstep in the presence of your court while you have such an important gathering going on. I appreciate the efforts she's

134

taking," I answered politely, but his expression told me he didn't believe that.

"You're being far too kind. I'm very familiar with how she behaves with guests." Lorsan assessed me from head to toe with a curious expression. My breath caught as I waited for him to speak again. "How did she do this? You look almost fae."

"She didn't. It's nymph magic. I can alter the appearance of my spirit form." I kept it simple. I didn't want him to get flustered with me the same way his aunt had.

"Ah. I see," he said as some indecision warred on his face. Maybe he didn't like it? "I have a few of the best teachers of fey magic arriving tomorrow. I would like it if you would train along with the women in the queen's trial to take advantage of their expertise." Lorsan twisted a piece of my hair in his fingers with a smile that seemed to imply he thought he was doing me a favor. That glow on his skin made my mouth go dry as he leaned closer into my space.

"Lia is already—" Rux spoke up behind me, but I waved him off quickly.

"I'm grateful for your interest in my continued education." Who was I kidding? I really liked this guy. If he thought I needed more training and continued to look at me like that, I could pretend. Maybe I'd actually learn some new tricks. Mom always said to look at lessons as an opportunity to further expand the mind.

Lorsan's eyes roamed all over my face before he took a step back. "They will meet in the northern gardens at first light. I'm looking forward to seeing you at dinner finally."

"I will be at both," I replied before he strode back to the court. Once he was out of sight, some type of giddy sound came out of my mouth before I caught Rux's bored expression. "What?"

"You don't need that training," he answered in Druidic.

"You can't know that. There could be parts of fey magic that Mom and Ferox didn't know about. You are hardly a fey magic expert. He's the king!" I pulled up every rationalization I could for why I might need this experience. Who was I to turn down Lorsan's suggestion? Even if there was a part of me that knew both of my mentors had been considered the strongest fey magic users in the past. There could still be more. There had to be more.

"Doubt it. I don't get why you are playing dumb." Rux gave me his arrogant, disapproving head tilt and crossed his arms. "You could just tell him that you've already trained with great teachers."

"Honestly, you are such a know-it-all for someone who doesn't have a lick of fey magic abilities." I spun on my heels and walked around my tree, determined to get away from his judgmental observations.

"You have literally cast every single thing you have ever learned at me one time or another. I've had to learn about it so I can protect you. That meant experiencing it entirely! Do you have any idea how many times you trapped me in horrific mental games or threw me through fey rings?"

He had a point. Ferox always insisted that Rux was the target of my lessons because he had to be able to withstand the magic even if it wasn't his gift. I still wouldn't let him have it though. "Cry me a river. You are a ryne. You are supposed to be able to handle it."

"Correct me if I'm wrong, but I'm still alive, so I'd say I've done pretty well, no thanks to you." Rux sighed in defeat. "All I'm saying is that I obviously have some understanding of powerful fey magic."

"What do you mean 'no thanks to me'?"

"Never mind. This is pointless. Attend your stupid lessons." Rux stormed off to sulk on the ledge of the boundary wall. Always close enough that he could keep an eye on me, but still far enough away that we couldn't speak anymore.

Rux hadn't spoken to me for the rest of the day. As I got ready for dinner, he came out of his cabin room with a jacket on that would allow him to blend in as well. His horns would give him away in a moment as a satyr, but I was glad that he couldn't hide them.

"I'm sorry," I started as he approached me. "I think I am being crabby about the whole situation, but it's selfish of me to continue to take it out on you."

He considered my words for a moment, and then the tension between us fell. "This isn't easy. I know you want to make a good impression, and they don't know you like I do. Let's get some food. I just hope it tastes better than the rations for the guards do."

"I hope for your sake that is true, too," I teased, and he gave me a dashing smirk. I didn't know how he was always able to let things go so quickly as if they never happened. Another lesson I could learn somewhere along the way.

The garden trail met the stonework of the bridge that continued up to the front doors of the fae court. I'd had no reason to go in so far, so I took smaller steps to enjoy the three-story arch that surrounded the massive doors, which I would not be able to open without magic. Everything inside the doors was white with accents of gold.

We'd never had anything so opulent in Voreios. From the way the stones were placed and the smooth markings, I could tell each stone had been individually carved. It was impressive.

Rux gestured to a door on the left, and from the sounds of the people inside, that was likely where we needed to go. As soon as we entered, an older fae man with a weird glass in front of his eye approached us.

"Ah, Prinna said you would be coming tonight. I will escort you to your seat. Rux is it?" He waited for Rux to nod. "You are not allowed to pass this blue line in the tile. It goes around the whole room, so you can stand as close as you'd like to her, or you can leave her here and come back after dinner."

"He can't sit with me?" I asked, wringing my hands as my anxiety rose at the thought of being separated.

"The king has made an exception for you as a member of the court despite your fey blood. That did not extend to him." The man pursed his lips ready for the argument.

"Lia, go with him. I'll stay back behind the line with the other guards."

"Okay." I frowned. Even as I followed the man to my seat, I kept looking back around for Rux as he dodged around the pillars and the other guard present. They were essentially making him jump through hoops.

"This will be your place for dinner every night." My escort gestured to a seat in the middle of a group of chattering fae.

The men continued to talk even as they both observed me from head to toe in a few seconds. Time to see if I could pass the test with the rest of the court. I was at the far end of the table across the room from where Lorsan would sit, so this could be a great chance to practice my fae banter.

"What clan is she from?"

"Didn't you see her come in with the satyr?"

"That means she's the dryad?"

"Sitting with us at the court table? How have we fallen so far from grace?"

"When Tasi wins the title of queen, we can be restored finally."

Were they talking about me when they knew that I could hear them?

Giving everyone around me a warm smile, I took my seat. Before I could try to strike up a polite conversation with either of my table mates, they both turned their backs to me. Wonderful. This was going about as well as it had with the elves.

Plates with massive amounts of food appeared in front of me as well as goblets of blue liquid. Everything in this room was immaculately kept, down to the polish on the crystal plates and the pressed white tablecloth. If I did eat, I would be terrified of leaving any type of mark on the fabric.

Once more, the magic shifted in the familiar way that told me the fae king had arrived. I located him immediately as he strode into the room. He was a beacon with the way he commanded the attention of everyone. Even without his wings, there would be no mistaking him in any crowd. He strode up to his massive chair and raised a glass to the room. I raised my glass to him after everyone else.

"A toast to welcome all the clans and visitors who've not yet had a chance to experience the new court. With the trials underway, make sure you get to know your neighbor, you don't know whose favor you would like to ensure that you have."

A toast or an omen? It was an interesting choice of words, and with the fae, each word mattered. The crowd murmured ominously, and a few people across the vast oval table glanced in my direction. The next time I looked up at Lorsan, he watched me as he took a drink. He was too far to make out any distinguishing details, but I could feel the intensity of his gaze. Taking a sip of mine, I almost spit it out. It was so sweet. What was it? It gave my chest a nice buzz as it went down as if it was a strong mead. I should not drink very much of that if I wanted to keep my wits about me.

When Lorsan turned to address a man sitting next to him, I looked over my shoulder at Rux. They'd not given him any food at all. I could change that as I wouldn't eat any of the food. I opened a small fey ring on the side of my goblet and the other side appeared next to Rux on the pillar. He glanced at it, and I moved my plate closer so he could pick a piece of meat.

I covered my mouth to stifle my laughter as I saw the face he made after he'd taken a bite. The food must have tasted as off-putting as the drink they'd given me. We'd have to adjust, but so far things weren't looking so good.

"It is considered rude to not eat." Prinna's harsh voice came over my shoulder, and I jumped in my seat.

"Dryads don't eat food like this. I get my nutrients from the soil and sun," I whispered, trying to not draw attention to myself from my neighbors.

"Yet another way you are inferior. You cannot give your guard food from this table. Do not let me catch you doing that again or it will be one strike. At three, you will be expelled from this court."

I frowned but nodded that I understood. If they expelled me from the court, would I have to leave the Feylands? I didn't like all of these new rules. Rux didn't like the food anyway, so we'd have to find something else.

There had to be a reason I was here, and I would find my place in this court. My throat itched with the need to cough. I took another drink of the sweet stuff to wash down the blood before it could come out. I didn't need Rux to see it. If I didn't figure out how to get along here, I was going to die. I needed to make this work.

Chapter 13 — Aralia

As the sun broke the horizon, shining warmth on my leaves, I pushed my way out of my bark and settled into a silk dress with heels. Every part of this felt unnatural, but I had to move past this part if I wanted to be permitted to explore the court more fully. Today I would find a way to connect with some members of the court and start building the community I desperately needed to survive here.

"I thought you were training today?" Rux shut his door and groaned as he stretched.

I definitely didn't watch the way his muscles flexed, or the easy way he strode over to me. We'd never shared such a close proximity to one another before, so I'd not noticed how in sync he was with my chaotic schedule.

"I am." I smoothed the dress over my curves. "How do I look? Fae enough?"

"Lia, you are always beautiful." Rux placated me before he hesitated, then said, "Shouldn't you wear something more suited to training?"

"Prinna told me I have to always wear dresses in the court, and they have to be silk or cashmere."

143

"Ugh, that's not practical." He rubbed circles against his forehead like the thought hurt him in some way. "I guess you will have to make friends with the new queen to change things around here."

I gave him a small laugh and shook my head. "Not doing so well there yet, but today is a new day. At least we all have the same magic. That's got to count for something."

The gardens wrapped around the entire castle, only separated by a few wrought iron fences. Which I thought was strange because the fae supposedly didn't like iron. It didn't bother me, though. I pushed open each of the gates easily, not quite understanding why these gardens needed to be isolated from one another. There were no other trees in these spaces, just bushes, vines, and flora. The ground of the gardens glowed as I walked through. Their messages were muted because of the shoes I had to wear, but I could feel the acceptance of my presence. Now I just needed to repeat that with the fae contestants.

I strode up confidently to the gathered group of women. It'd been shocking to me when I'd left Voreios's borders for the first time as a child and saw how few women there were in the elven and dwarven cities. So much testosterone. Even in the Feylands, the discrepancy was still evident. Last night at dinner, there was only one woman for every four men in the court.

The timing of my illness with the trials really could be perceived as fortuitous if spun in the right direction. How many of them would be here if it weren't for this event? I was ready to forge a new sisterhood with all these women, to create a community. After all, Rux was right. One of them would be queen, and it wouldn't hurt to make friends now.

Except what I thought was a very friendly smile on my face was only met with scowls of fury or resignation.

That's fine. I can turn this around. "Hi, everyone. I'm Aralia—"

"We know who you are. You shouldn't be in this class." A blond woman with a purple gown glared at me from the far corner. I'd only given her a passing glance at dinner the night before because she'd been hidden away behind the more boisterous contenders.

"Lorsan told me . . ."

I fell silent as the other women gasped, and I realized my error very quickly. My sisters and I often didn't use royalty honorifics when we talked about the other kingdoms, but this wasn't a casual event.

"Look at how familiar she is already, speaking about His Majesty. Look, nymph, stay in the back and out of the way. The trials aren't for lesser fey."

I'm not fey, I wanted to snarl back at her, but my mother had taught me better. Given the complexities of our cultural history, to them I was fey. With a deep breath, I continued. "I think we got off on the wrong foot. I'm new to the court and didn't mean to offend any of you. Seeing you all gathered here

145

like this just reminded me of my sisters at home. I hope that we can be friends."

"Why bother?" One of the darker-haired fae women turned from me and walked away. I glanced back at Rux. Not that he'd be much help, but could I really be this bad at meeting others? When he appeared to be just as confused from his place up on the wall, I had to guess that maybe it wasn't all me.

A hazel-skinned fae with bright purple eyes let out a sigh and then gave me the first smile. "Ignore them. I'm Tasi. Since you aren't competing against us, I think we can be cordial. What Sebille means to say is that only one of us will be here after the trials are complete, so there's not much meaning in building friendships."

"Oh." I nodded and rocked on my heels. Surely, they'd still want friends in the court even if they did return to their own manors. But emotions were obviously running high. I could be patient. "That makes sense. I'll be sure to stay out of your way, so I don't distract any of you from your training."

Moving quickly to the back of the gathered women, I waited patiently for something to happen. The women barely spoke to one another, but a few did turn around to offer me a smile here or there. They'd get used to me after a few days.

Four older men appeared in a fold of fey magic and took their places at the centerpiece of the gardens. They wore gray robes with accents of blue and black along the trim. All of them had long white beards except for the one standing in the center. His beard was still a rich black.

"Attention, ladies. We are going to breeze through the basics today so that you can begin to practice for your performance. Roles will be decided based on how you perform today." The man with the black hair still hadn't introduced himself, but a chart manifested out of the magic, and he began scribbling down what they would be covering.

"Most of you should already be familiar with pulling out a sphere of your essence," the man on the right said as he demonstrated a ball of white fey magic hovering over his open hand. He gestured for all of us to repeat the effort. I noticed the man in the middle took a seat and began to jot down furious notes without even looking at the book in his lap.

I kept my face neutral at the mundane task and matched the size of the ball that he had in his hand. Was it really necessary to go this far down to the basics? As I watched two of the women struggle with the task, I had to rethink my question.

A blond-and-purple haired fae at the front of the class continued to peek back at me, but her expression hadn't softened as she observed my ease of use with the magic. I'd watched her a bit more closely at the gathering last night because she'd left her wings out. Soleil was her name. Names were important for making friends, but the more eye contact we made, the less likely that seemed. I think some of the contenders were hoping I would suck with fey magic, but I wouldn't pretend to be entirely incompetent just to fit in.

He made us put the magic away and pull it back out quite a few times. The strain became more evident in two more of the contenders. Rux shot me a look that asked me why I was doing this again, and I rolled my eyes.

The teachers shifted positions and another one in the back on the left raised his hand to gather our attention. "Illusions are a core principle of the magic that is unique to us all. Whether creating an image or creating a world, it requires diligence and focus to maintain an illusion so that others cannot notice it for what it is."

I waited anxiously for this part. I remembered the illusion lessons I'd had. Rux's mention of them did bring to light that not all of it had been so wonderful. The infernal attack on Voreios had plagued me in these practices as I'd grown older. I'd seen monsters that day which haunted my mind's eye. Hopefully I wouldn't summon any of those.

"To keep it fair, we would like you all to summon a butterfly. Match them to the color of your dresses and features so we can keep track of whose butterfly is going where."

Oh. That was easier. I created the most realistic butterfly I could and layered in the blond and green accents throughout the wings. I caught Rux's smile from the corner of my eye. I guided my butterfly to go over to him, and he opened his palm for it to land.

Fourteen other butterflies hovered in the air. A far cry from the number of women here in the garden. I made mine vanish as I noticed some other eyes on me, pretending I might have run out of steam. I wasn't here to upstage them, but I did want to get to the advanced classes.

"Very good. We've made our notes. Now we head on to the next beginner technique." The man with the dark beard had resumed his position at the front of the group. "Imitating nature."

A ball of fire bounced between each of his hands, with the trails of flames following his jump. My mom said not to start with fire during our training, but I'd always wanted to copy Daddy's lightning first. In the end, I'd won.

Focusing on the flame, the element appeared in my hand instantly. Then my elbow was gripped at the same time I recognized a very familiar signature in the roots of the garden.

"Hey . . ." I complained quietly before I noticed Ferox's stern face looking down at me.

"What are you doing?" My grandfather didn't look pleased, the way he usually did during our training.

I glanced shyly at Lorsan standing only a few feet away. He didn't appear to be angry with me, just confused by the interaction. "Practicing my fey magic with the others."

"This is basics."

I didn't want our conversation to interrupt the class, and it sounded like he'd moved on to earth. "Ferox . . . unless you are here to tell me I can go home, I need to go back to class. They are going to move to advanced stuff tomorrow for those of us who do well enough."

He pinched his nose and let out a long exhale before he continued. "Aralia . . . you do not need any of this training."

"Is there something wrong?" Lorsan asked Ferox, interrupting his lecture. "If she's going to be part of my court, she will need to learn how to control her abilities."

"Has she displayed any lack of control?" Ferox ignored the young king and looked to Rux, who shook his head.

Lorsan replied as, apparently, he'd not seen the watchtower glance to my ryne instead of him. "Well, no, I've actually seen remarkably little of her magic at all."

With that answer, Ferox eyed me suspiciously. He turned my wrist over to look at my forearm, and I felt his mind brush along my roots. "You haven't been leaking more fey magic, have you?"

My mind raced at his question. What could that even mean? "No. What? When was I doing that?"

"Did Rux not tell you?" Ferox glanced back at Rux who only shrugged in reply. "This is going to be even more trouble if you won't communicate with each other. Why aren't you using your magic?"

"I just haven't wanted to, okay? I'm practicing it now if you'd let me get back to the class."

"Aralia, I know you are sick," he said gently.

I glanced down at my feet, hating the way that my toes moved against the shoes. "I'm better. They gave me the cure. Can I go home now?"

"We aren't sure how you were infected to begin with just yet. It is better that you remain here for the time being." Finally, his stern face broke into something much softer, perhaps sensing my grief. "Are they treating you well?"

He asked the question even with the king standing there as if my reply would be anything but polite. "He's welcomed me to his court, and they have been very gracious despite the inconvenience of my illness to their busy schedules. I couldn't have asked for better with these circumstances. Is Nylisa safe, at least?"

"She's safe, but she's heartbroken," my grandfather admitted with remorse. "We'd never intended to separate you, and certainly not this way. I will find a way to fix this, I promise. I just need you both to be brave."

"Okay." I fought back the tears that pulled at the corners of my eyes. I couldn't cry in front of the fae court. How pathetic would that look? I could be brave like he asked, even if my heart broke too. "I need to go back to class. I want to get to the advanced stuff."

"Aralia, advanced fey magic is dream walking, spatial illusions, and making fey rings and portals."

"Oh." I blew out an exhausted puff of air. I'd been doing that since my mom took me to the fey pool when I turned twenty. "There's really nothing else?"

"No. Your mom and I went to great lengths in your training. There is nothing that they can teach you beyond what we have."

"Wait." Lorsan looked between the two of us with a raised eyebrow. "She can already do all of that?"

"Are you really surprised?" Ferox shook his head. "Her mother is the guardian. You really should have joined Aura at the fey pool a few times. Aralia isn't limited by the constraints of the well. In the future, if there are any issues with her control, send a messenger for me immediately. I am going to work on syncing our roots to the fey pool. You won't be alone for much longer."

Those last words were for me, and they meant everything. I wrapped my arms around his neck and hugged him tightly. I wanted to cry from how securely he hugged me back. I was so used to the constant touch and affection shared by nymphs that this small touch almost shattered my carefully studied features. The fae were cautious and calculating, like I'd have to learn to be, but right now, I just held on for dear life.

He rubbed my back in soothing circles like he had done all of my life when I was upset. "Lia, I know this hurts, but I want to encourage you to truly look around and see who is beside you as an ally. Look beyond perceptions and ideals you have set in your mind. You have friends here, okay?"

"Yes, Ferox," I whispered into his neck as I hugged him tighter. I knew he was going to leave again, but he was right. I needed to find my way here.

Chapter 14 — Rux

I didn't sleep often, learning the rhythm of the fae court so that I could keep her safe. The nymphs would never understand the true scope of what we went through to protect them. In my case, I needed so much more than to just keep her alive. I wanted her to hear her laugh and follow her as she disregarded the rules that forced her to be silent amongst the court. I wanted her to get well and have the full life she deserved.

The words that scientist told Lorsan the day she arrived tore me apart from the inside. Lia would have died if I'd delayed even a few days. Had I missed some sign in this game that we played? Knowing she was protected would have to be enough for now, but I knew I was lying to myself.

The illness continued to recede, and I checked the black markings on her tree in the first morning light. Each day she would get stronger. I'd not been able to hide my disappointment when Ferox confirmed that, for now, she would need to stay here. They'd stayed up late into the night talking under her tree. He'd filled us both in on

Nylisa's new seedling on the way and stories from the chaos at the academy.

I liked seeing that version of Aralia best. Once he'd taken her from training, she'd let her hair down and stopped pretending to be fae. From the chair by my room, I'd watched and adored her little pink toes, which wiggled animatedly as she talked with her grandfather.

Aralia would sleep for a few more hours, leaving me a little time to myself. I hadn't run since our arrival, so I would use the opportunity to get in a really long run on the stone wall. My world had always been about her, and the Feylands had done what I thought traveling might. She looked for me often to share the experiences in this new land, and I would always be there. This was the way for us to change the course of our path to something new.

The breeze felt great as it raced through my fur on the high walls of the fortress that made up the fae court. My hooves struck consistently to the pace I'd set for my run.

The sound of metal clashing caught my attention as I turned the third bend. Upon a quick look over the edge of the wall, I could see the fae guard training. This I could watch. It'd be good to know how the defenses of the fae lined up with my training from Voreios. After all, there was no mother tree barrier protecting the citizens here. Aralia was left exposed. I'd need to make sure they met my expectations.

A gathering of forty men and women with their backs turned to me lined up in the open courtyard in front of me. A few of them had good strength in their strikes, but most of them had poor form. Across the way, Lorsan's second-in-command noticed that I was now watching them. He gestured for me to come over, so I did.

"Good day," I forced the words out of my mouth politely. "New recruit training? It's a never-ending process."

I tried to be relatable. I'd taken over training the newer guard from Kelan a few decades back and knew how tricky it could be with the enthusiastic young ones.

"Good day. Where is your ward? I figured you'd not be far from your dryad, yet I do not see her." Trevan glanced behind me.

"I'm well within my range to keep her safe," I replied shortly. Lia wasn't any of his concern. "Does your trainer not correct them in their stances?"

"These are skilled fighters. They are doing their daily stretches before they go out to their positions."

I raised an eyebrow at him. "We must have different definitions of *skilled*."

"Fae warriors primarily use magic, so any capability with weapons is just an added bonus."

"Sure, if they do it properly. They might as well not do it at all if this is the effort that they will put into honing their skill." I gestured to the front row where they were holding their swords by the hilt.

"What would you know about this? Satyrs are bred to be brutes, not to have the finesse of magic." Trevan waved his hand at me.

I couldn't stop the chuckle under my breath.

"Am I wrong?"

This interaction could go one of two ways. I knew I could be hotheaded, but I needed to always put Lia first. Getting into a pissing match with Trevan wouldn't help her position in the court any. "You know what, sure. Let's say you're right. Fey magic has drawbacks though. They should be prepared to fight with or without it."

"This is good enough," Trevan insisted, and turned away from me to continue his observations of the guards below.

"I disagree. If Aralia is going to live here, then we need to step up their training. You may feel comfortable defending your king and court this way, but I will not leave this to chance for her sake."

"What is the issue?"

I groaned as I heard Lorsan's voice. He walked along the path that I'd been running on. Well, I wasn't sure if he was walking or if he was gliding. His wings were out on display, and I wondered if he often took a stroll on this wall or if he was following me.

"Rux is just giving his opinion on the inadequacies of this guard if the little dryad princess is going to live here." I noted the heavy sarcasm dripping from his tone. "He thinks she needs more protection than the entire fae court."

The king eyed his cousin with a small bit of agitation. "What did you have in mind, Rux?"

"Since satyrs are known to rely more on physical strengths, I was thinking I could train them. Not enough to take them out of rotation, but at least enough that they know how to properly hold weapons." I winced as I looked back at them. That was going to be a lot of work. However, if I could convince Aralia to hang out nearby, then maybe we'd find her second partner out here in this mess. It'd be nice to have a second set of eyes on her. I'd long wondered if our triad would be completed by a fae because of her magic. This might be a good opportunity to find out.

Lorsan's forehead scrunched up as he thought over what I said. The calculations in his eyes expressed that he was listening very closely to how every sentence had been spoken. He seemed to know that I wasn't being entirely truthful about the realm of my skills. I was as gifted with earth magic as Aralia was with fey, but never show your whole hand to an enemy. I frowned again at the thought. I needed to stop considering them an enemy if we were going to live here.

"I think that could be arranged as long as it doesn't take up too much time. Never any harm in more training for guards."

Lorsan appeared thoughtful as he took a moment to watch the group gathered below.

"I will come up with an efficient system and present it to you both tomorrow," I agreed readily.

"How is Aralia feeling?" the king asked, not meeting my gaze. "I don't see her with you at this time, and she seemed quite sad seeing Ferox yesterday. I believe I can count on you to be truthful where she is polite."

"It's been a hard transition for her. She misses her twin. They've never been apart for this long. Physically, she's getting better every day. Whatever your healer is giving her seems to be helping." I answered as honestly as I could without giving away all of her feelings. "She stayed up with Ferox rather late, so she's still sleeping."

"You can tell that from here?" Trevan asked and gave me a strange look.

"I'm her ryne and can speak with the earth from my training. I can tell when she separates into her spirit form as long as I'm within the court walls. Outside I could do it farther, but the block you have in the moat is quite the dampener."

"I did have another question." Lorsan leaned against the railing, and his wings blew in the breeze. "I noticed most nights she attends dinner she does not eat. Prinna mentioned that she'd said that she gets nourishment from the soil and the sun. Is that the truth or does she just not like our food?"

"It's the truth."

159

"Is that all nymphs?" Hearing the king's questions, I took a new curiosity. I'd watch him closer during the interactions with Lia moving forward. There was a masked interest that I'd not expected with the king's current quest to find a queen.

"All nymphs. They feed through their element for primary nutrition and then in the same way that all of our races enjoy. They may sample food to see what the fuss is all about, but usually they aren't interested in it."

"Hmm. Thank you. Please let Trevan or me know if she needs anything. I doubt she will ask." Lorsan nodded his head and then continued on his way as if he'd never stopped, leaving me with his cousin.

"I'm the captain of this guard, and you'd do well to remember that in the future," he growled at me when we were alone.

"I don't want your role. I want to keep Aralia safe. That's it. You should want to keep your new queen safe too, because that's looking like it's going to be a rough pick."

"Mind your place. How dare you judge our women with this level of disrespect. You both don't belong here. We'll make space for the dryad if she stays, but for you, just wait until you piss off the king."

I must have made him look bad, and I knew I had more tact than that. Aralia was trying to make friends, why couldn't I? This was likely going to be home, might as well make the best of it. I didn't have to like the man to show him the respect that

160

his position entailed. "Captain, I hear you. You run this guard, I'll answer to you, but I'd like to help where I can."

"You can start with teaching them how to hold weapons properly."

"I'll look over your schedule for them and present you with an outline of a training regimen first thing in the morning."

Chapter 15 — Aralia

Only two days had passed since Ferox had come in and gone like the whirlwind he was. Every day, I prayed to each of our elemental gods that I could find a way home, but even they remained silent now. I couldn't train in the magic lessons with the other women because it was too basic, and they became embarrassed by my proficiency. After another fancy dinner where none of the food did anything for me, I knew I couldn't put it off any longer.

Lorsan again observed me through dinner. The people who I sat between no longer turned their backs to me, but they didn't want to speak with me either. Tasi was the only queen contestant who showed any kindness, so I told the fey magic whom I was rooting for. Every evening, the center of the room 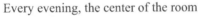 transformed from dining tables to an open floor for dancing to the lavish music that was played by a variety of fey bands on the far side of the hall. Once that began, it was easier for me to sneak out.

Rux's garden room was in sight of my tree, and I could be thankful for that little treasure. A small candle flickered in the window, telling me he'd likely still be up. Once I was settled at dinner, he'd often return to his quarters to eat and wait for the festivities to wrap up before he'd walk me back to my tree each night.

I used the back of my hand to knock on his door quietly a few times, and he opened it quickly. His eyes did that succinct scan of my face, and he knew what I needed. In one smooth motion, he drew me into the room and closed the door and then the curtain. "Finished dancing for the evening already?"

"It's not the same," I replied wistfully. It wasn't anything like the fires back home. Could I get used to it? Yeah. I had to. But it wasn't the same.

He didn't reply with anything other than gentle caresses down my curves and soft kisses along my neck as I exposed the skin to him by unbuttoning the top of my dress. When he pressed himself against my back, I could feel his cock grow hard. His fingers worked against the fine fabrics, a tease of his skill as he untied the remaining straps of my dress to let it fall between us.

"I heard that you were training the fae guard today?" I whispered as he corralled me toward his bed. It was smaller than the one he had at home, but we'd both still fit. A small whimper escaped me as he cupped one of my breasts.

"You need to be safe here. That's my only goal."

Was there something else layered in those words or was he still just doing his job? Of course, it couldn't be more. He'd left his mate in Voreios to bring me here. He was just trying to get

163

back to her sooner, but he hadn't once mentioned leaving. I didn't know what to think. His hand trailed lower down my stomach as his fingers fanned out to heat my skin. Before he arrived where I needed him, he twisted me in his arms and laid me out with a gentle dip onto the rough fabric of his blanket.

It infuriated me on some level that they treated him so poorly when he was practically Veon's second-in-command back in Voreios. Again, he was only here because he forced himself to come along with me so I wouldn't be alone. His eyes fell to my lips, and my heart skipped a beat, but then he pressed his mouth to the skin of my neck and trailed down, pushing my legs apart so he could settle between them. We didn't kiss like that, even though sometimes I wanted to. That was reserved for your lovers; this was just a meal, not destiny.

His wet kisses left a trail down my stomach. I was already ready for him, but I thought he enjoyed tasting what was between my legs. He was an enthusiastic eater. As his tongue split my lower lips, a moan tumbled out of my mouth. My fingers wrapped around his horn for support as my body trembled at the way he lapped my core. His mouth closed around me, sucking in my clit, and I thrust my body off the bed.

The satyr only used that as an opportunity to get deeper with that evil tongue of his. His hands gripped my ass and angled my body so that his oral penetration could stroke me repeatedly as he vibrated on my sensitive skin. I loved and hated that he was so good at this. I was ready to explode.

164

My mind screamed his name on repeat, or maybe I was saying it out loud, I didn't even know anymore. His fingers only dug in tighter as he was determined to have every drop of my enjoyment. He ate like a starved man, though he hadn't once pressured me since we'd arrived. When I released his horn, he set me down back on the bed, and as he stroked my clit with his tongue, two of his fingers pushed into me.

He set a lazy pace as he groaned in his own satisfaction at the way my body responded to his thrusts.

"Revelare te," Rux whispered as he kissed my pelvic bone. It was a Latin spell that undid all of my glamour. His fingers worked me steadily toward the next orgasm as he kissed his way very slowly up my body. I was panting and crying in need as his fingers pushed in and his thumb rubbed my pearl in the small circles that drove me mad.

"Rux," I crooned, and I heard him respond with a growl. It was possessive in a way that made me crave more of this aggressive sound. This time, as he stared at me hungrily, there was fire. He caged my body in as my fingers tugged on the fabric of his chiton. I didn't want his toys, I wanted him. I wrapped my hand around his cock and my fingers couldn't touch all the way around his girth.

There was an urgency as he used his knees to push my legs farther apart, something new and frenzied that I was shaking for.

"Move your hand," he groaned as I slid down his length again. He never let me touch him, so I disobeyed in order to take a few more strokes, memorizing the silky flesh in my palm.

I wanted to protest, but as soon as I moved, he was pushing into me and all I could see were stars as I stretched to welcome him. He went slowly and I quickly realized he was larger than his toy, which I'd thought was already pretty sizable. I was soaking, so that eased his efforts, but my body felt full to the brim as he bottomed out inside of me.

My toes curled as I locked my legs around him as best I could. I wrapped my arms around his biceps as he tested out some gentle rocking before he slammed into me. I got lost in the rhythm of his body gliding through mine, using mine, and all I could do was let go to the torrent of need washing over me.

"You're being such a good girl, taking my cock like you were made for me," he praised in my ear as he thrust roughly before he kissed along my neck.

I shuddered involuntarily, not used to the praise since his mouth was usually occupied. But now that I'd heard it, I liked it maybe a little too much. When he let loose and began to rocket in and out, I let my mind wander out to the depths of pleasure and surrendered to my next orgasm.

Chapter 16 — Rux

She was calling my name. I didn't even care if she was quiet anymore. I wanted him to hear what I did to her. I felt the change when he entered the room, but she was so lost in the pleasure that I was able to give her that she hadn't sensed him yet. I couldn't confirm his presence until I'd broken the spell of her glamour. The unintended side effect of the spell was that it revealed him as well.

Aralia rolled herself against me as I finally settled my full length deep in her. I wanted to shout out my thanks to the gods for how perfect she was. Instead, I was giving that fucking fae a scowl as I boxed her in from his view. He was supposed to be running trials for his own queen, not stalking the woman I knew to be my mate. And he was stalking her.

Thrusting was its own beautiful torture. She was so tight, but the way she was digging into my skin with her nails told me she wanted to hold on for dear life. I'd only tasted this bliss with her once before. I'd known that day she was mine, but I couldn't tell her that.

"Rux," she panted, and her legs tightened to trap me inside.

Oh, little nymph, I wouldn't want to be anywhere else, if you'd just let me stay. I kept her in a perpetual state of bliss, as she rolled from one orgasm into the next. I'd fuck her for days if she'd let me, and it still wouldn't be enough.

I hated that I knew he watched, but that asshole could be envious all he liked. Her breasts brushed against my chest each time I drove home, and I shifted my body to brush her very sensitive clit with each of my movements. Her cries filled my ego and stroked my pride as she clenched her core around me.

"Is this what you needed?" I taunted Lorsan as much as I enjoyed hearing her response.

"Yes, oh, Rux." She stumbled for words and settled into the most beautiful chant of her moans as I guided her toward the next hill. My body couldn't hold out any longer. She felt better than I ever imagined when I relived each of our encounters when I was alone in my cavern back home.

Lia's head fell back and her shout in open pleasure was my undoing. I released my seed inside of her, working her with slow and steady thrusts as we both came down from the high. Even pulling out of her almost made me hard again, and as I reached over to grab a linen to clean us both, I was careful to keep her covered. Her green eyes had returned to their bright color, and she watched me from under heavy lids as her breathing began to even out.

I pulled up the blanket and watched the room transform. Everything became soft and less scratchy; the room looked a little brighter from the cleanliness. Immediately, I grew insecure about bringing her into this space. Lorsan vanished when she began manipulating the magic, but still I covered her up. Nymphs didn't care about being naked, but that was a gift she could share, not one that he could just take from her.

"This room was a bit messy. Sorry about that. Once I adjust to your new feeding schedule, I can make sure it's up to par."

"This isn't your fault. I think it's another jab at us for not being fae. I can take care of us just fine, though I don't know what to do about the food. Can I stay?"

Aralia never stayed with me after she'd fed, so I knew I hesitated, but before she could think anything of it, I tried to play cool. "Sure."

"Okay. Seeing Ferox just really made me miss my sisters. I haven't slept alone since . . . I don't think ever."

"You haven't," I agreed easily. She'd always had Nylisa from the very beginning.

Aralia yawned and snuggled closer into my side, her eyes flickering shut. "I hope that this won't bring you more pain, missing Rhenei."

My heart sank. I'd never loved anyone but Aralia, however I'd never done anything to dissuade her assumptions that I could be mated with others. It was easier than addressing the pain of her continued rejections. Graak had told me this would come back to get me because trees really do remember everything. Zrif's point had also been made.

Eight decades ago, I'd become a man and had to start dealing with my own needs. As a ryne, you get put in a very precarious situation because the grove needs sons to protect her, but your potential fated mate is nowhere near maturity. Aralia had been only twenty when she'd found me flirting with Rhenei. As I stroked Aralia's hair to enjoy the sound of her sleeping, I could remember the sadness in her tiny face that day. Something she shouldn't have understood. I chased after her, but she hid in her tree for days, only talking with Nylisa. Her father Kelan coaxed her out eventually, but from that day on, she had decided that she didn't need me anymore.

Forty years I put everything else to the side. I had no sons while Veon had plenty. I was determined to wait Aralia out. I stayed away from flowering nymphs and only honed my craft so that I could please her when she finally decided to give me that chance. But when she matured alongside her sister, her anger did not lessen.

Each year that went by only made it harder to be honest.

"Aralia, I love you. Only you."

She hummed in her sleep, but otherwise didn't respond. I'd let another day pass without telling her how I felt.

Chapter 17 — Lorsan

I shouldn't have followed her last night. There was just something different in her gaze when she left the grand hall. I wanted to understand what each of her expressions meant, what her thoughts were as she took in the scenes of the court. She'd sat at the end of the table as a guest surrounded by people of little importance to me, and I wanted her closer. Much closer.

She'd not eaten again, yet there was a hunger in her expression. At first, I worried that it may be the soil, or had it been too cloudy that day? I followed her in the liminal state, needing answers, but I saw she headed straight to him. I watched her fall into an easy step with him without even an exchange of words about it. He just knew what she needed, and now I had to know how. The sounds she made as he pleasured her called to me like a siren.

Her beautiful breasts and bare skin out on display for me this way . . . Is this how he often saw her? In front of the court, she was so proper. Her dresses were more of an innocent tease than a blatant invitation like most of the fae women. Yet as he stripped her of the magic that made her appear as one of us, I only wanted to run my hands down every single one of those lines along her skin.

I knew the moment he sensed me, and he made sure that I was aware. We'd never gotten along, however with the way she tempted me now as a woman, I would have shared. He did not want to share. Rux claimed her. I could take the message this time, but I would snack on the energy of her pleasure.

Hours had passed, and still, I could only see her when I closed my eyes to the constant chatter of my advisers.

"Are any of the women pulling ahead in the competition yet? Any early signs of favor from Aine?" my aunt clattered as she looked over the photos of the remaining women.

"Nothing yet," my cousin replied as he strolled across the room to make another drink. "Lorsan's not even interested in any of them."

"That hardly matters." I draped my elbow over my eyes, wishing I could end this entire conversation. "I don't pick the queen, the magic does. It comes down to whomever survives, so why would I pick favorites?"

"You are allowed to make a request of Aine if you have a preference. After all, in the end this will produce an heir. Is this about the dryad?" Prinna chided, and I rolled my eyes.

I forced myself not to glance out the window at the top of her tree. "How could anything be about Aralia? She's not fae and isn't in the trials. The magic can't pick her."

Prinna turned away from my intense stare to pick at her nails. "She showed up at an awfully convenient time. You should send her away until the trials are complete, and the new

172

queen is in place. Some of the fae women think that she is impacting the selection process in an effort to seize your attention."

If only that were true. I wouldn't have had to watch her with the satyr if that were the case. "For fuck's sake, she's a tree. This is not something I am discussing any longer. Our garden needed some sprucing up after all the chaos lately. Let her accent the space."

"I don't like it. Voreios took everything from us, and here they are again messing up our grand traditions."

"They handed us back our kingdom a long time ago. This one nymph is not staging a direct takeover of our kingdom. She hasn't come storming in here making demands of me, or in any other way caused trouble. I will not approve anything regarding her departure from *my* hospitality. Drop it."

"All of the northern isles are vacant," Trevan cut in as he read the stacks of reports at the end of my desk.

"Why are they vacant?" This did catch my attention. Hundreds of our citizens lived on those isles, including some of the remaining selkies.

"There's a letter from the merqueen." He waved another letter at me as he continued to go through the stack instead of answering me.

"No, why are the isles vacant," I asked him again, and he instantly snapped to attention at my tone. "Where did those people relocate to?"

We had data tracking for everything, so he would have to know this answer. I didn't want to head out there myself tonight, but I would if I had to.

"It seems as though they just vanished." He frowned as he read the report again.

"What have your people discovered about the selkies? How many have you located?"

Trevan set the stack of papers down and rubbed the back of his head. "We haven't found any yet. That might be what the merqueen is writing about. Perhaps they moved there?"

"It's Voreios," Prinna added her thoughts to our conversation, and my fury rose. "They are seizing more of our lands."

"Stop it," I snapped at her. "The lands wouldn't be empty if another leader had taken them over. If it makes you feel better to think of it this way: we have collateral. The twin of the vasilissa is dependent on our court for survival. Voreios will not attack us, especially if you start treating her with even a shred of kindness."

"So, you are taking her prisoner?" Prinna asked with a wicked gleam in her eye as if that had been my intent all along.

My mind unhelpfully went to binding the beautiful woman to my bed like I'd seen some of the older fae do in my childhood. "No. But if it makes you feel better to think about it that way then stop your hysteria."

An explosion rocked the grounds of the court, shattering the glass in the room. My first thought went to the gardens before my mind caught up to the screaming around me. The court was under attack.

Prinna wildly screamed like a siren, and I shoved her through a portal to the liminal realm where she would be safest. The woman would be no help in a fight at all. My ears immediately felt the relief so I could focus.

With a running start, I leaped out of the window and hovered in the sky to survey the damage and get a measure on the scene. Small fires and big stacks of smoke billowed in the air, distorting most of my view. A large mound of earth sat where Aralia's tree should have been.

Guards shouted all around as smaller explosions went off in the combat that took place along the wall. As I flew closer, a familiar blond-headed nymph ran under a satyr on the wall. A mage jumped up on the wall beside her, and before I could do anything to him, she'd already run him through with a short sword I hadn't seen her holding.

The old mages of Cholios often wore these same gray cloaks with red-and-black designs along the back. The mage stumbled as he spat blood at her. Rux twirled her out of the way rapidly, before the man could touch her, and took off his head with a blade.

On the far side of the castle, I heard Trevan shouting orders about the breach. Half the guards split off, but I couldn't care about them as much. I landed on the perimeter wall and summoned all the fey magic back to me. If the mages couldn't wield that, then they wouldn't be a threat to any of my people.

Aralia dodged under another attacker to my left and small tremors of lightning rippled from her fingertips and jolted around the guy, giving Rux an opening to take that one out too. Where were all of my guards that should be over here? Why was this entire corner only being defended by a satyr and a nymph?

As the magic stripped out of the air to answer my call, I heard Aralia cry out in pain, and my fury blazed. Blood ran down her arm. I would murder them all. While Rux had already dispatched the one that hurt her, I wouldn't let this go on any longer.

Dark masses grew out of the ground, feeling for all the energy sources that should not be here. They carried the marking of an ancient god who was not Aine. Well, I wouldn't have that in my kingdom. As the masses attached to the mages' shadows, they would seep into their souls, tearing each one of them apart from the inside out.

All of the fae in my court felt the calling of my power as these souls shredded in front of them. Everything fell to silence with the exception of my magic humming across the land as it shredded the mages one by one.

"Aine, accept my offerings of your enemies." I couldn't help the sadistic smile that pulled on my lips. Their fear was palpable, and it fed me almost as much as Aralia's pleasure had. Just because I was a quiet king, didn't mean I wasn't everything that my father was before me.

But then there was only one thing I could focus on as I swept my glance over the people gathered below me. A set of green eyes watching only me in the midst of all the chaos.

Chapter 18 — Aralia

I wouldn't admit to myself what a rush it had been to fight beside Rux. We moved in sync, like an extension of the same being. Had everything changed the other night? I couldn't stop thinking about it. He'd caught me looking at him a few times afterward, but nothing seemed to shift in his expression. How could it? His mate was back in Voreios. He didn't seem to be angry with me either, just doing his normal routine.

Loneliness. That had to be what it was. I didn't have my sisters anymore, but that shouldn't allow me to move in on another's mate. It was just sex; it didn't have to mean anything. Right?

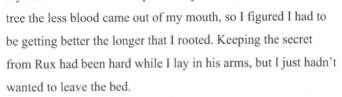

The court was on lockdown, so I spent most of the day around my tree. The more time I spent in my tree the less blood came out of my mouth, so I figured I had to be getting better the longer that I rooted. Keeping the secret from Rux had been hard while I lay in his arms, but I just hadn't wanted to leave the bed.

Stop thinking about him, it, whatever. I tightened my fists into little balls and closed my eyes. My magic brushed against Lorsan's as he entered the gardens. It was only a fraction of what I'd experienced the night before. Witnessing him in that state of fury and absolute control sent tingles all the way down my body. Here was yet another man I really shouldn't be thinking about. He was looking for his queen in a court full of fae women.

"I came to check on you after last night." Lorsan approached me like he would a nervous deer he'd found in the woods. His magnificent wings folded neatly into his back before they vanished. I wanted to touch them, but that would be much too forward of me.

"Checking on me, Your Majesty?" I asked sweetly before turning in his direction, confident that any rogue blushing was minimal. "That is kind of you to concern yourself. However, I am perfectly healthy."

"I want you to know that you are safe here." The insistence in his voice caught my attention.

I raised my brow at him, unable to hide my curiosity. Was he making the same appeal to all of his court? The intensity of his gaze once more on my face as I figured out my response caused me to blush, regardless of my intentions. Why were these unavailable men torturing me?

"I have absolutely no doubts about that. While the attack seemed to come out of nowhere, it was resolved. You acted so swiftly that I feel fortunate to be just outside your residence." I felt a lot of things being this close to him all the time, but this was one I could vocalize without showing my hand entirely.

There was a tension that eased from his shoulders as the words left me as if he had genuinely been concerned.

"You took a few hits yourself though. I really wish you wouldn't have been in the fray at all." Lorsan's golden eyes swept down my figure. "Is there any way to convince you to take a room in the court?"

"I recover as soon as I return to my tree, Your Majesty. This spirit form is easily mended as long as my tree is intact." He likely didn't know much about nymphs, and why should he? We were considered beneath him in the Feylands. "My true form wouldn't do so well being kept inside, but I promise that I feel safe enough." Electricity shot up my skin as he took my hand to inspect my elbow as if he didn't quite believe me. My breath caught in my throat.

"There isn't even a mark. And you didn't see a healer?"

"No need to waste their resources if my tree is nearby." I might as well have whispered the words for how quietly they came out. Forcing my racing heart to slow was difficult, but I had to get myself back under control. His proximity triggered my glamour response, and I knew we could both tell from the way he leaned in closer. "How fare the trials?"

An ever so slight scowl crossed his face. The step he took away from me was just enough so that I could breathe properly again. My mom had taught Nylisa and me all about schooling our faces when interacting with others, as a leader should. It was something he'd learned as well since he seamlessly corrected his expression.

A part of me wanted nothing more than to know what he was actually thinking. But I was in no position to offer him that. I was nothing more than a guest here for now, perhaps even an inconvenient one.

"It goes." Was that dismissal in his voice or just my hope to hear it? "The magic will begin making its selection in the next few hours. Should be quite the show. Will you be coming to dinner at the court tonight?"

"You know I really don't eat the way you all do." I twisted my fingers around each other in front of me as I fidgeted against the thought of making him upset.

"I enjoy seeing you in the grand hall."

Hard to argue with that. I enjoyed seeing him too. "I will be there this evening."

"Good. Is there anything else I can get you . . . and Rux?"

I didn't miss the hesitant way he mentioned my ryne. With a gentle touch to his arm, I shook my head. "I believe that is anyone's job but yours. I have it handled. You have so much more on your plate. I'd love to be able to assist with your burdens, as you have opened your home up to us with more grace than we could have hoped for."

"What would you like to assist with?"

His genuine question caught me off guard. Would he really be open to letting me do something of value here?

"Anything really. I speak most of the languages on Artemesia. I'm working on Draconic, but the rest I can speak with relative proficiency. I often traveled with my fathers and grandparents to the other kingdoms. I know most of their protocols and customs."

"Were you going to be an ambassador for Nylisa? Your ears are a little more pointed. I bet the elves liked that. We do a lot of work with their research facilities."

I frowned at my last memory with the elves. Lorsan pulled me straight out of the thought as the back of his finger trailed along my left earlobe. He'd moved back in closer, so I had to tilt my head up to meet his gaze. "Unfortunately, they found me a little too fey for their particular tastes. It may be best to send me anywhere but there."

Heat flared in his eyes at the implication I'd laid before him.

I knew I was playing with fire at this moment, it promised to scorch me alive, but having him look at me this way, I couldn't help it.

"That may not be a bad thing if you are going to represent my kingdom. I want them to have no doubt of where you belong."

Hmm. What a thought. To have no doubt of where I belonged felt like a dream. Even Voreios couldn't offer me that, but being with Nylisa made the unsettling feeling worth it. "I may have already burned that bridge with my fiery personality the last time I saw the ambassador."

"Considering how polite you have been while you've been staying in my court, I would say that any reaction from you was caused by disrespect from the elves." Lorsan paused for a moment to take in my tree behind me. "How does travel work for you with your tree? Rux brought you here in a stone, would you have to travel that way? I think the garden would miss you too much, so I'd have to consider the implications of travel with your recovery."

"Oh, my tree would stay here." I glanced at my oak and the bright lights floating around the garden. "I can move about the world freely now that I have rooted."

"I have a lot of questions about"—he hesitated as he gathered his words. I loved the way he perfectly pronounced each word he said—"nymphs. You know we have a fairly close relationship with Anatoli, but even with that, all of the couples tend to relocate to the grove rather than come back to the Feylands. How would you feel about working on improving that relationship and advising me? I'd like to discuss making the Feylands more hospitable to nymphs and nature in general."

"Wow. If you think that I could aid with those efforts, I would be honored," I replied with a soft smile as I turned my eyes away bashfully. My glamour was rampant again, but when his form began to radiate the fae's version of glamour, my desire for him became overwhelming. The king was returning my attraction! What could this possibly mean? He was so beautiful with this ethereal glow on his skin.

His fingers under my chin guided my eyes back to meet his, and I wet my lips when he leaned in closer.

"King Lorsan, you are needed at once in the meeting room. There's an update on the well." His cousin stood behind him on the bridge. Cold calculation sat in his firm brows before it vanished into his usual charm. I hated the way he scoped out my form, but sadly, that was the energy in the court. Women were nothing more than playthings. At least Lorsan wanted me to help him with something . . . I hoped.

"Let's discuss this further on the morrow." Lorsan ran his finger over my bottom lip as he stepped back again. Apparently lost in his own thoughts, he didn't wait for a reply before he vanished from the gardens.

Why was I torturing myself? Between Rux and the king, I was going to end up entirely alone, and I'd have no one but myself to blame.

"Something doesn't feel right about the energy," Rux whispered over my shoulder as we headed toward the hall for dinner. They still wouldn't let him eat at any of the tables, but he always came with me to keep an eye out. He'd decided that

184

he preferred to hunt for his own meals than eat their food anyway.

I bit my lip instead of responding. What could I say? I felt it too. The fey magic moved around like a viper poised to strike out. Something dangerous lurked inside the court this night, and even the haunting song of the trees outside couldn't compare to the turbulence I felt in each step.

Rux took a stride to catch up to me walking in front of him. His palm splayed out against my stomach, and he lowered his voice as I came to a halt. "I don't like it. Miss tonight and let this play out how it will. Let the fae have their traditions and we will stay by your tree, please."

I wanted to moan at how his breath rolled against my shoulder. Instead, I rubbed the top of his hand and shook my head. "I told the king that I would be there. I need to be a woman of my word if he is going to take me as an adviser. This could be a fresh start for me, and I can't ruin it by breaking my agreements on the first day. I promise I will leave if I feel that I am in danger."

"I don't believe that you will. Besides, it could be too late after you enter the hall. Please, for once, let me do my job to keep you safe."

"Aralia, Rux. So glad you could join us for dinner. I have your seat over here, my lady," Trevan cut in before I could cave to the distress I saw in Rux's expression. "Rux, I think the guard has some concerns about security for our big event tonight. I'd like to have you check the perimeter with them."

I met Rux's gaze and placed my hand on his arm. I would be fine. "Go, I will make sure they bring something for you to eat. I'll feel safer with you out there."

Those seemed to be the magic words. His gaze softened immediately, and affection rolled through my being at his determination to make me feel protected.

When Rux had left, I followed Trevan to my seat. The room was loud with excitement for the fae women's performances tonight. This ritual was said to enchant the magic to select the ones it would like to be commanded by. I noticed that Trevan didn't place me in my usual spot. Instead, I'd moved up closer to the king's advisers.

"King Lorsan insisted that I move your seat. Don't think I miss what game you are playing." He lowered his voice so only I could hear. "It caught me off guard, at first, seeing you attempt to snare him earlier. You know that you don't have to aim for the king to get the most power in this court."

"I'm not aiming for anything, sir." I smiled at him politely, trying not to be offended at what he was suggesting. "I merely relocated for survival, and if you recall, I was unconscious when I arrived. Expressing gratitude is my only motive. The king is charming in his concern, that is all."

"He is likely to forget about you and move on once he selects his queen." Trevan's words were harsh, but if I was

186

going to take a mate, I'd want them to forget about their other lovers too. "You do know that he is not keeping a harem, right?"

"Why would I know or care about that?" I frowned, not understanding what a harem had to do with this conversation.

"It means that he won't have a place for you to be protected. You might as well start looking for other options. You have been a bit prudish since your arrival. Don't think we all haven't taken note, and now you are glamouring the king. . ."

"I'm not sure that I particularly like what you are implying. And what exactly do I need protection from in this court? I have Rux. And the king showed last night that he can protect us all." I was thoroughly confused by the direction this had gone.

"Fey women tend to get into a lot of unfortunate circumstances in the wilds. Most of our women are kept, claimed."

That was what Lorsan was talking about when he said the couples preferred to move back to the groves. Back home, I didn't have to worry about any of the men. Everyone respected all the women. I was beginning to get the picture that that might not be the case here. "I'm merely getting my bearings. Best to not upset the wrong people when I don't even know who all the powerful motivators are."

Now he smiled at me with genuine interest. "I can promise you second hand to the king and captain of the guard is not a bad place to start."

Gross, I thought but then gave him my soft smile. "I will bear that in mind."

I cast a glance toward Lorsan and found him staring right at me. He'd been observing my interaction with his captain. I nodded my head as a sign of respect as I took my seat, and this seemed to please him. At least, now I was close enough in the hall to actually see his expressions. For better or worse, I enjoyed the tiny glimpses that I could see of him behind the shell.

Trevan wasn't wrong about one thing, I noted as all attention settled into the performance about to start. Lorsan wasn't in the market for a dryad. He was looking for his queen. At some point, I'd have to stop falling for the men who were already attached to a different destiny and find my own mates. Perhaps I did need to expand my horizon and explore other options. Just not tonight.

The twin doors behind Lorsan's chair burst open and the group of twenty-two women came in, each dressed in one of five colors. As they took choreographed places in the center of the dining tables, I leaned forward on my elbows to get a better view. A hazy gray smoke poured along the floor to cover the ground in the open circle between the tables.

Five were dressed in blue, green, red, and yellow, while only two were dressed in purple.

"Tonight, the ritual will be performed in honor of our newest guest to the courts, Aralia." Lorsan pronounced my name and shivers ran down my spine. He gave me a smug smile as if expecting me to be humbled by the mention, but instead my heart raced as pins and needles prickled down my spine. Perhaps I had gone too far this morning. Nothing could come from his attention. Plus, the energy in the room felt like a lightning storm about to go off. "Let's find out who the magic favors, shall we?"

I straightened my back and risked another glance at him as the women began to move. The colors must correspond to the magic they were attempting to imitate; the women in the red dresses each lighting a flame between their hands. Those in green dresses twirled as blossoms appeared to run down from the waist to the hem of their skirts.

I recognized the seasonal rituals from our shared culture, before the division of our people, in the hand gestures. Nylisa would do these same exact displays as she spoke during the spring ritual to welcome in the new growth. The women with the yellow performed graceful, elegant movements as the magic responded like a wind blowing up a torrent around all of their guests. When they took center stage, it wasn't hard to spot the women with the most control.

Blue magic flashed, and droplets of water fell from the sky above the guests gathered before it hardened into ice that sparkled like diamonds. These five women took over as the first group slid to the perimeter. The smoke rolling across the floor transformed into imitation of snow drifts that I could feel along my open-toed shoes. Shooting stars burst into delicate snowflakes that fell onto the table in front of me.

I was transfixed by the beautiful display as they wove their magical abilities together in practiced harmony. Even with that, I couldn't shake the unnerving sensation that a blade pressed against my back. Was everyone else as on edge as I was? I needed to calm myself before I triggered anything unexpected with all the power floating beside me in the atmosphere. I was surrounded by talented magic users; how bad could it be?

As the earth dancers moved to the center, the ground trembled, causing laughter from the onlookers as the fancy dinnerware rumbled into one another.

"Save the ambrosia!" the adviser next to me chuckled as he handed me my glass before the table could spill it all over us both.

A warm laugh slipped from my lips. There were many people talking quietly all around us, so perhaps I could ask this fae what to expect tonight. "Thank you for that. Definitely would be a waste."

"The closer you get to the king, the better the quality is. Trust me." He gave me a conspiratorial wink and leaned closer. Everything in me pushed like a magnet away from him, but that would hardly be polite to the first person who decided to talk with me at dinner. "My name is Tuimac. I'm the adviser to the king on behalf of the broonies."

Oh, so he wasn't fae after all. He was a fey like me to this court. "It's a pleasure. I'm—"

"We all know who you are, Aralia." Tuimac's long, spindly fingers nudged mine again, reminding me that he still hadn't let go of my goblet.

His hair was poofed out like a griffin's mane, and he had a button nose that somehow still worked on his elongated face. I removed my hand first and left him holding the ambrosia. I would not be drinking any of that tonight, and he took the open invitation to finish my portion.

Averting my gaze to the contenders, I tried to change the subject. "How do we know when the magic makes a selection? Will we know who the queen is tonight?"

"Oh no." He laughed heartily at my questions. "This is only the first night. The magic won't decide anything until the solstice."

"That's still weeks away," I commented with a frown. "Does the king get any say in it?"

"He can persuade Aine if he favors a queen, but so far, he has been rather silent on the matter. Aine would drive a hard bargain if he made a different choice than the one she is leaning toward."

Lorsan's dining throne sat at a higher elevation than the rest of us in the audience. Since Tuimac sat to my left, it was easy for me to catch a glimpse of the king behind him. I wondered if I could spot whom he may favor. It was one of my favorite

191

games with my sisters before we matured and after we'd started to develop crushes.

The neutral expression on his face didn't give away much about what he felt in regard to the ceremony going on in front of him. Beautiful flashes of light flickered across his features as the flames danced in an organized chaos. He seemed lost in his own thoughts, and I could only hope that someone on this stage could ease the burden he surely felt. I'd seen how much stress Nylisa had been under, we talked about it often, and she had Veon to share that with. Lorsan had been doing this for more than a century by himself.

His eyes met mine, and my cheeks flushed with embarrassment at being caught. I looked away with a new pit of shyness growing in my stomach.

"You don't have to look away from me, sweetheart," Tuimac whispered and threw an arm over the back of my chair. "Trevan mentioned you were timid."

Horror sank in as I realized how he had interpreted my actions. Why had I sent Rux away again? "Oh, I—"

"Here it comes." Tuimac gestured to the center of the room. "Can you feel the change in the magic?"

I could. The tension grew so thick I could cut it with the utensils that I hadn't used to eat dinner. Suddenly the tables in the room vanished, removing the barrier from between us and the show that played out. The women who wore the elemental dresses stood in a semicircle facing Lorsan. In their hands were electrical spheres matching the color that they wore.

The two women in purple strode to the center and held books open in their hands. The room fell silent, waiting for these women to speak. Breathing became difficult as it felt like the air was being sucked out from my lungs.

The first one dropped her purple cloak to reveal her gorgeous wings and her nearly naked form. I recognized her blond-and-purple hair. She was the woman who hadn't wanted me in the classes, yet she'd watched me like a hawk. Soleil. As her power brushed each of us, I could feel the true force of her gifts. This would be a woman to watch. As much as I wanted to gauge Lorsan's response to her, I didn't want to have him catch me again.

"When Aine granted us the magic of the fey, we had three tenants to uphold." Her voice was smooth like the silk I wore, with a sexy rumble underlaid in each word. "The first was to respect the magic. The second was to gift the magic to others wisely. The last was that the magic should only be wielded by those it chose."

The winds from earlier turned into a mighty squall, and I barely managed to anchor my chair into the ground with roots before sliding into Tuimac. I did not need to be any closer to him, but thankfully the wind seemed to move every one of us.

The second woman, Sebille, dropped her cape and her wings flared to life but not as brightly as the first. I didn't know much about a fae's wings, but I was sure there was something to that. This woman looked more nervous than her light-haired companion. When she also began to hover above the ground, the diamonds from the water demonstration turned back to rain that fell upon everyone. The crowd hissed in disapproval at the surprise, but then fell silent again aside from a few whispers.

A brief thought to Rux as the cold drips of water ran against my skin. He hated getting wet, and he would not have liked the sensations of this event. Yet, I wished that I had him close. He was right. He was always right. I wasn't sure I should be here, and now there was no way to get out without causing a scene.

The new woman's timid voice could barely be heard over the air howling in a circle around all of us. "The magic walks among us, beside us, calling in our mind. If we beckon it, we draw the risks of summoning its favor or its ire. Who among us is ready to rise above the rest in this test of queens?"

Lightning crackled along the room as the temperatures began to rise. The red dancers spun around the two hovering in the center of all those gathered, their spheres of flame growing larger with each moment that passed.

Out of the corner of my eye someone moved, but I couldn't make out any features. A lithe form that moved with even more grace than these women, if that were even possible. Goosebumps broke out along my arms as this figure glided through the smoke between the women dancing. Did no one else see her? The form sank to her knees underneath the two that were hovering and turned to face me. How I knew I wasn't sure, but a red crack where the face should have been smiled at me.

I was so distracted by this figure that I didn't see what happened until an explosion ripped through the grand hall. Sebille fell to the floor, the book skittering a few feet away from her. Blood poured out like an open waterfall as if she had a hole carved through her body. One of the dancing red women had also been struck, her skin boiling through layers of her flesh in only a few seconds as the flames consumed her. Ice shards protruded out from the lifeless body of a third woman.

The magic was tipping past the boiling point. This needed to be stopped immediately, before the magic impacted us all. Hadn't the teachers warned them about pushing their magic too far? Briefly, I remembered this was a trial and that the winner got the prize of the king. It really shouldn't be surprising that they'd push themselves to such lengths.

The dark form in the center vanished as the screaming began. No one else moved as these women scrambled for a way out of the center. My fingertips charged with the madness as the chaos began. I couldn't keep up with the blood and bursts of magic as the other women's spheres exploded in their faces. I'd only seen something like this once while I trained. My mom wanted me to know exactly what this was and how to walk back from it. Why was no one helping them? Seven women, at least, were dead, and no one moved a muscle.

Rooting my feet farther into the Feylands' soil after I kicked off my shoes, I held out my hands. The ripple of another explosion passed by my senses, and I caught it in time to inverse implode it, grounding the chaos into the earth. Time moved slowly as I followed the ripples in the world around me and pulled them back under control.

At some point I must have stood, because as soon as I opened my eyes to the silence that surrounded me, the men had slid away and the would-be queens sat on the ground covered in ash and gore, most of them crying. Only Soliel had her eyes on me, and they were not friendly.

A tug on my elbow made me trip on my feet, and I shrank back when I noticed Lorsan. He was clearly furious as his fingers dug into my skin. He dragged me from the room, and I could barely keep from stumbling with how quickly he moved. When he slammed me against a wall in a private hall a few turns away, I nearly shied away from his glare.

"I don't understand. How have I made you upset? The magic was killing those women." I spoke in a flurry of words as I tried to take a breath. "I had to stop it. Someone had to stop it."

"That is the ritual, Aralia!" Lorsan shouted at me and shook my shoulders. "You interrupted the entire process."

"I . . . what?" I couldn't apologize for saving them. The court just expected me to sit there and watch women get slaughtered?

196

"Eleven contenders were to be eliminated tonight, and your action changed the intent of the ritual for three of them." He tried to explain again as if that would make the situation any easier for me to understand.

Now, my own fire was lit. He had the audacity to come after me for doing what he should have done to begin with? That was not okay. "Fae women are still rare, Lorsan! You would stand by as eleven of them are sacrificed for a barbaric old ritual? This is a sadistic display of power, and for what purpose? How does this aid your people?"

His grip loosened but his glare did not. "This is only one phase of the trial, more of them will die as this continues."

Now it made sense why they'd not wanted to welcome me or get to know me. They knew that they were going to die. "There would only be one left" didn't mean in the court. It meant life. This was so much worse than I'd thought before. "Why would you invite me to this?"

"The world isn't just a perfect pretty rainbow like you nymphs seem to think it is. You are going to live here. There are things that you need to accept about our reality as fae."

"I will never accept that. If you want to kill women, you can do it without me in attendance." I shook loose from his grip and tried to duck under his arm, but his hand on my stomach pressed me back against the wall. "I will never accept this as appropriate. If this is how it truly is to be part of your kingdom, I'll take my chances elsewhere."

197

"The magic demands this." There was a slip in the confidence with which he said it that raised my ire.

"The magic does, or your arrogant male dominance? Those are two very different things. Those women should be cherished, not dragged out like show pieces to perform. You asked me why nymphs don't feel safe here? I think I have found the answer. Court those women, find your queen any other way. Please. I beg you. You're the king. Make a new deal with the magic."

I realized how close he was to me then. One of his hands slipped to my waist and the other tightened on my arm. The fury in his eyes had changed to something very different as they roved over my face. He closed the tiny distance, our lips crashing together. He took the opportunity I gave him with my slight gasp to brush his tongue against mine. There was urgency and need, a desperation to be seen and felt as he searched for something he would never find in me, something we could never have with each other.

My arm wrapped around his neck to pull him closer. How often had I thought about this? The fae king was kissing me. Everything else faded away as I melted to his body, the hand on my waist trailing down to cup my ass. His erection pressed into my stomach. He groaned into my mouth as I rubbed myself against him. He was long and thick, and everything in me wanted him.

"I should punish you for speaking to me this way." He warned with a slight part of our lips before I heard him rip my dress.

"Try it and see what happens," I quipped back and rubbed my free hand down his length between us when I kissed him again. He tasted like the sweetest drink I'd ever had on my lips. Like sunshine after weeks of snow.

The growl he gave as he hoisted my legs up around his waist before he slammed me back against the wall drove me wild. My breath hitched as he undid his pants and tossed the rest of my dress out of his way. Without any warning, he slammed into me like a man on a mission, swallowing down my pained cry. I was soaking and ready, but usually Rux treated me gently. Lorsan wasn't as thick as my protector, but his length felt like it pushed deep into my gut.

"This is why he didn't want to share." Lorsan sounded euphoric and gave me a moment to catch my breath before he pulled out and slammed back in, using gravity to bounce my body back down to the hilt each time.

Each deep thrust made my legs tremble, and I dug my nails into his shoulder to gain some stability, but he only picked up his speed.

"You will say my name," he commanded as he thrust in again.

"Ki—"

"No," he growled in my ear, and I whimpered. I couldn't help it. I wanted to please him, whatever would make this continue.

"Lorsan," I moaned as he sank in. My mind grew dizzy from spiraling pleasure when he shifted his angle so his pelvis could stroke my clit as he slid in and out of me. I closed my eyes and gave in to the supportive brick wall behind me.

Lorsan worked my body to his liking, and I was going along for the ride. His fingers dug into my pelvic bone and his breathing sped up. Stars grew behind my eyelids, and I let him take what he wanted from me. My orgasm crashed like a tidal wave sweeping me away out to sea.

"Lorsan!" I shouted, not caring if they could hear me back in the dining room. I didn't even know where we were, just some stupid hall.

He grunted, and with one final thrust, my ass crashed into the wall with his body pinning mine in place. His cock twitched inside of me as I felt him release his seed.

"Why couldn't you have been born fae," he murmured against my skin as I caught my breath. His tongue trailed up my neck as if getting in one final taste. "At least now I can finally get you out of my system."

And it was as if my heart broke all over again, even if I knew he was right.

Chapter 19 — Rux

When the screaming began in the hall, I knew I'd fucked up leaving her alone in there. Even if she'd said she felt safer with me guarding her tree. If anything happened to her, I would tear down this court myself. I threw the weighted bell that I'd been exercising with to the side in between the gathered guard. I spun on my hooves and leaped down to the ground to head for the dining hall.

Cirro clapped a hand on my shoulder to halt my forward movement. "Hang on a moment. You don't need to worry. Your dryad is safe. We can't go in there right now."

The lanky faun had quickly grown on me in his determination to train hard in the few mornings I'd had with the guard. Even the fae ones had begun to warm up to me once they realized that I wasn't there to put them down.

"How could you possibly know that she is safe?" I growled at him and brushed his hand off. I didn't appreciate the amusement in his expression.

"This is a scheduled event. Half of the queen contenders will die tonight as the magic winds through to reveal Aine's choice. No one else is in danger." He offered me a ration of the guard's food and gestured to a seat. "Why do you think the rest of us are so calm? We aren't that bad at being guards, regardless of how we hold our weapons."

Lia was going to be traumatized by this experience. I covered my mouth with my hand and disguised all my judgmental thoughts about the situation. Now I needed to focus on providing her with whatever she would need to process the horrors she was witnessing. What could even help with that?

"Is this going to happen again?" I asked, deciding I needed to know more about this if there were going to be more events. We'd be living here for the foreseeable future unless something drastically changed with Ferox. I needed to better manage life for us with the fae.

"Two or three more times and then the hunt. The hunt always terrifies the women. I'd recommend she stays in her tree that night," Cirro replied between bites of his own rations.

"When is the hunt?" I didn't like the sound of this hunt if the women were afraid of it. I needed to have all my plans in place with backups in case Aralia decided she wanted to do the opposite of my suggestions again. So far in the Feylands, she had been listening marginally better than back in Voreios. That could change at any moment.

"The king runs them during the winter solstice. If you can get your dryad to stay put, you should come out with us to watch. The fae are crazy that night, almost like possessed wild animals."

"Sounds like a great time." I scrunched my face in distaste that only made the other guards laugh.

Cirro took a seat beside me. The screaming had settled a bit inside, so my nerves were also evening out. I needed to leave to make sure I was back to the garden before she returned.

"Some of us are going out tomorrow night to the faun glades. Maybe you'd like to come with us?"

My first thought turned to Aralia. I couldn't leave her unguarded, but it didn't hurt to get more information. I really missed being able to gather with friends and let loose, even just a little. The fae were so regimented against what they considered their lesser-class citizens. "What happens at the faun glades?"

"They party like I think you do in the groves." He gave me a knowing smile and my heart lifted. I missed Voreios. More than I'd ever admit. This could be a chance for a little piece of home. Cirro seemed to notice my hesitant excitement, so he added, "You should try to bring your dryad. I think she'd like it too."

"It wouldn't be an open invitation to her if she came," I said firmly. Fauns had a reputation in the groves for tricking fey women into bad situations. Not that I'd let anything happen to her, I just didn't want to go on false pretenses.

"Nah, show up with her. Everyone's pretty respectful in the glade. Lose the fae dresses for a night and let her be herself. No one will mess with her unless she wants them to." Cirro smiled

203

broadly at me. "Not a man there would be opposed to her wanting to take a turn, however."

"We might come out," I replied, fighting my urge to declare her as mine. Her other partner was out here somewhere, but so far, she'd shown no inclination that they were among the guard ranks. How could she find her second mate if I fought against every single interested contender? That would only hurt my little nymph in the end.

A night out around a fire with music and dancing hit every note of what could soothe the ache of leaving Voreios. Part of me needed this experience. If she wouldn't go, well, I'd cross that bridge when I got there, but with a little convincing, I had no doubt she'd be interested.

As I walked back to my room, I noticed Aralia sitting in front of my door. It was still early for all of the dinner events to be over, but after what she may have witnessed, I shouldn't have been surprised that she found a way to sneak out early.

I could smell Lorsan on her as I got closer, and I grimaced until I saw the silent trail of tears rolling down her pretty cheeks. She glamoured them away when she noticed me walking toward her.

"Rux . . ." She rose to her feet, and when I offered her a smile, her features softened. I was still her safe place, and that fact meant everything to me.

I opened my door and gestured for her to come in. "I heard all the screaming inside. The guards said it was part of the trials, but are you all right?"

"I am not hurt. I . . . I messed everything up for them tonight." She let out a sigh that was too deep for one her age. "It doesn't matter. I snagged a few bottles of their stupid fancy mead. You want to share it?"

"Mead?" I laughed and took one of the bottles that she showed me. "How could I turn down an offer like that? I think I have glasses somewhere in here."

"Oh, let's just drink it out of the bottle. I'm over the proper protocol for the night." Lia popped the lid off the first one and took a long drink before she handed it over to me. The bed shook subtly as she climbed across the mattress to settle in. "Why do men have to be so awful?"

"Well, I was hoping that you may have noticed this about me, however, I'm not too proud to admit it in words." I leaned forward like I was going to offer her a secret, and she waited with a look of growing curiosity. "I am all man, so lumping us in together isn't accurate."

This earned me a coveted, genuine smile that almost showed her teeth. Her eyes trailed down my chest before she took another sip of mead. "I don't know, in light of this new evidence, I'm thinking my statement still stands."

"You wound me, princess," I teased her, and though she scowled at my old nickname for her, the smile kept pulling at the corner of her perfect lips. Why couldn't I just say those three little words. . .

"I can't with you tonight. Why did I come here again?" She moved to get up, and I easily stopped her by placing a hand on the bottle she brought. Her next words were so soft I almost missed them. "Do you miss Voreios?"

I took a long drink of the sickly-sweet honey liquor before I responded. Questions like these had a way of coming back to bite you. Honesty wasn't always the best policy when it might isolate the person you care for most. She might never be able to leave the Feylands, and I needed to come to the same terms that she was now. "There are things that I miss about it, sure. But there's a lot of excitement out here too."

She gave me a look that told me she didn't believe me. "I've had enough excitement and horror. I miss everything about Voreios. I wish I could go home."

I gestured for her to sit up so I could climb in behind her to rest my back on the wall. My heart raced as she pressed against my chest after taking another sip. "Maybe we just have to find things here to bridge the gap. You haven't had a chance to really make friends yet."

206

"That's hard to do with fae. Everyone thinks that every move I make is a play. That I'm scheming for power. Oh, that or if I do make any friends, then they are likely going to be murdered in a trial to become queen." Her voice dripped with sarcasm and fury. "I don't want to talk about that, though. How are you doing with the training?"

I didn't respond to the way her nails scratched against my arm or the sweet way she buried her toes into my fur. In the past, if I drew too much attention to it, she'd run away. I'd do anything to never have this end. "I think once they realized I was actually trying to help, things shifted. In a grove there just isn't so much ego. I have hope for a few friends."

"Can I come out to train with you tomorrow?"

"You are always welcome to spend time with me, no matter what I'm doing." I couldn't stop the kiss I placed on her forehead, but she didn't respond, just took another drink of mead. I wouldn't admit that I enjoyed her lack of negative responses to my affection more than I probably should. It would hurt if they returned, but there was something special about being able to interact tenderly with your mate. "So tomorrow night, and I understand if you'd prefer to go to dinner again, I may have something fun for us to do."

Her bright green eyes rose to meet mine, reminding me that she'd just been with Lorsan. I was prepared for her to find her second bond mate, but not this. The fact that Lorsan had found a way to tempt her pulled up a fire in my gut. She'd liked him for so long as a young sapling that I should have expected it to happen once. It didn't mean that I had to like it.

"What's that? I need a break from the court life and those dinners, maybe for the rest of my life. I'm up for just about anything." The exhaustion returned to her voice, and I really wanted to know what happened this evening. I'd not be talked into spending any more of these events apart from her.

"It seems like the fauns know how to party like we do back in the grove. You want to dress down and go dance?"

"Oh, to not have to wear silk! This sounds like it could be just what the healer ordered. If you think it will be safe, then I'm in." She put the bottle down on the ground and rested her head against me again. "Thank you, Rux."

"Always," I murmured and pulled her tighter against my chest. The covers were much softer now that she'd been checking in on my belongings, and I instantly felt her snuggle in. "Do you want to talk about it?"

I didn't really want to know about the situation with Lorsan, and I wasn't sure how I would feel once I had the knowledge of where those tears had come from. But even being king of the fae wouldn't save the man if he continued to torture my dryad.

"Not yet," she whispered, and I heard another small sniffle. "Doing my own thing away from court for a while seems like it will be the perfect remedy."

Chapter 20 — Aralia

Avoiding Lorsan hadn't been as difficult as I might have expected. He didn't seem to go around the guards all that often, and with the chaos I'd brought on the trials for the new fae queen, he had a full plate. I kept hearing those last words roll through my mind. Maybe it shouldn't have bothered me as much as it did. I knew that we couldn't have anything more, and yet my heart just felt crushed.

I'd often told myself that sex didn't have to mean anything. Tensions were running high after I'd interrupted their ritual, and he could have banished me from the Feylands. Instead, I felt like I was a box he was just marking off his list for the day. A silly part of me wished that our casual flirting and then passionate encounter would make him realize that I'd crushed on him for as long as I could remember. The real ending destroyed all those dreams.

Seeing how Rux trained all the guards throughout the day made for an enjoyable experience. He was a natural leader, and as I focused on his charming smile and the way his laugh tugged at my heart, I knew I'd been lying to myself. Sex must have changed everything. I'd missed it in the grove. I'd been running so fast away from him that I may have shoved him straight into the arms of another. All my prayers to our gods that he'd find a different mate came to haunt me, and I couldn't change any of it. I'd fucked up my own destiny.

With all of his diligent training, I almost felt inspired to get up and work out my lazy muscles, but then I would see glimpses of the fae women who'd died. Rux kept a close eye on me and eventually brought me a book to practice my Draconic, as if I'd still be going there any time soon. When the coughing fits would arise, I'd take a walk around the corner so he wouldn't hear me. I'd used a lot of magic to pull the chaos into order, and the consequences revealed themselves quickly with new black rashes along the tops of my legs. Only with glamour could I fade them, but how long could I keep up that ruse?

After a quick nap before what I hoped would be an all-night dance party, I felt Lorsan's magic brush my tree.

"Aralia? Are you here?"

There were no contextual clues in his tone to tell me what he might want. Was he still mad? Well, if he was, that would be fine with me. I was mad too, and heartbroken about all of those women who were dead.

"Where do you keep running off to?" he said in a frustrated growl that only served to turn me on yet again. How did he have this power over me?

Prinna appeared on the walkway above and scowled in the direction of my tree. "Why are you down there, my lord? We have more work to do on correcting the grievances from last night."

"Have you seen Aralia today?" he asked, completely dismissing her other comments.

"I haven't, and after that stunt, I hope she has the good sense to stay far away from all court proceedings. Come, the contenders have gathered."

I wished I could see his face, but his back was turned to my tree once his aunt arrived. What expression was he making? Outside of Prinna's growing dislike of me, I'd gained no additional insight into what he had come here for.

I remained absolutely silent until he flew back to his rooms. He didn't know that I could still see and talk with him even if I wasn't actually in my tree. I wouldn't tell him my secret, but I was curious as to what he'd wanted to talk to me about.

As the sun began to set, I emerged from my tree as a showered Rux stepped out from his garden quarters. He took my hand as we briskly walked through the gate with only a nod at the sentry on post at the entrance to the seelie court. I'd abandoned the fancy silk-style dresses of the court for flowy pieces that would move with me as I danced, left the vines in my hair instead of masking them away to fit in with the fae.

My bare feet caressed the ground, and the roots of trees all around sang their memories of when my mother had walked these lands. The trees greeted me with exuberance, and much like the gardens around the court, the land began to glow with balls of light rising from the soil. I liked that they didn't feel the need to scream their haunting hymns when I was nearby.

"I think those of us who live in a grove often forget just how close to nature all of the nymphs are." Rux broke the silence with a squeeze to my fingers. "It's beautiful to see how the world responds when you are in proximity. First the gardens, and now this."

"I wish I could connect with these trees when I am in the garden." My fingers caressed the bark of each tree I passed. The warmth I received was like the biggest hug to my heart. My mother had left a mark here too when she'd righted all their cycles back to alignment. There was a whisper of anticipation about what I could do now that I was here, and I had to admit, I asked myself the same question.

"I don't see why we can't address that the next time we see one of the king's advisers. That could help speed your recovery."

A rickety sign had some Fae words spelling out Faun's Glade, so it looked like we had arrived. Rux tensed a little at the sounds of laughter, music on flutes and drums, the smell of a bonfire. It did feel like home. Every night we had a fire just like this one, even at the peak of the summer. With an excited smile, I tugged on his hand to move him forward. This was just what I needed, maybe what we both needed.

I watched his muscles roll as he loosened up, and I took in my fill of secretly observing every crevasse of his defined back when he passed.

"This feels right." There was relief in his voice as he echoed my thoughts, and I failed to cover up my appreciative gaze fast enough when he pulled my body up to his. A playful mischievousness lit up in his eyes. "Ready to go make some more friends and then . . . dance?"

The way he said *dance* made my heart race. "I'll follow you. Lead the way."

Grass and branches brushed against my legs as I let him guide me through the trees toward the party ahead. Though the air was becoming frigid with the upcoming winter season, the warmth of the large bonfire beckoned me in. Memories of what had been while we were in Voreios transitioned to what could have been mine if I'd let go of my anger. Why couldn't I see then how right it felt to have him holding my hand?

The fire fell hush for a moment as the various fey men and women stopped to take us in. There were so many creatures among the fey that the crowd was a breathtaking contrast to the elite fae in the court. People that our kind used to be a part of, and at the core, there were a lot of similarities still. My unique features blended in with the flora fey, they were a merging of my two forms.

"We were wondering when you would find your way out here," a man replied and waved us over to where the mead filled

213

familiar oak barrels. The music started back up, and any awkwardness seemed to fade away.

"I wanted to freshen up after training today," Rux explained as he greeted the faun with a bump of their wrists. "From the looks of it, you must have just bolted over."

"We don't get to have these parties as often as you did back in Voreios, so we try to make up for it when they do happen." His laugh was infectious as he poured two wooden goblets of mead for us. "It's nice to meet you less formally, Aralia. I'm Cirro."

"Pleasure to meet you. I hope we get to spend more time out here moving forward. This looks wonderful." The sounds of this gathering soothed a hole I'd not known had been silently weeping. I'd thought I was fine outside of missing my sister, but that was simply not true. I couldn't deny it any longer.

"You're welcome here. Most of the women have been eager to meet you. We were surprised when he offered you a position in the court given your ranking." Cirro winced as he thought back on the words. "I probably shouldn't have said it like that."

"Please do not worry about that. I've seen how they treat Rux, and honestly, I just think my treatment is because of my grandfather," I admitted. Ferox was still a powerhouse in this part of the world. If he thought they were mistreating me, well, I couldn't promise that things between Voreios and the fae would remain neutral. "I didn't know that everyone knew I was here. I'd love to make friends."

214

"The trees have spoken of nothing else since your arrival. They do say that you are unwell."

I coughed at being caught off guard and then smiled with a dismissive wave as Rux's gaze fell back to me. "I *was* very unwell, but these lands have welcomed me. I am stronger every day and ready to dance. You have no idea how grateful I was when Rux mentioned you do this out here."

"It looked like you could both use it after the event at the trials. I'm surprised the king let you out of the court honestly."

Flashes of Lorsan pressed against me ran through my mind followed quickly by the images of the dead women. So much was tied up in that one evening that I had to shake myself to rid my mind of the visions. "The king has other things to attend to, and, well, I think we all know that nymphs do what we want."

"Well, that's true," Cirro admitted. He clanked mugs with Rux, and they exchanged a fond look before he waved at the fire. "Let loose out here. There are no court guidelines in this space."

"Thanks, Cirro." Rux wrapped an arm around my waist to guide me along with him before he leaned in closer. "Are you still feeling sick?"

"No. I promise. I feel better than I have since we left Voreios." When I ran my free hand up his abs, using the music to tease him, I could see that I was shifting the focus. I loved that satyrs preferred to wear minimal clothing and that my dress tonight would allow for a lot of skin-to-skin contact.

He pounded back his mead and then eyed me seductively while I chugged mine, albeit slower than he did.

"Good girl," he praised as I finished. Rux took my hand and we danced our way to the fire.

We'd both been dancing all of our lives, but never with each other. I wouldn't let him back in Voreios. What started slowly with our bodies separated quickly shifted as he twisted me into his chest. My back pressed against him as he trailed his hands down my exposed skin, only pausing to rock with my hips to the beat. He didn't bother hiding his erection just as I didn't stop to hide my glamour call. I would be the only one he saw tonight. I could pretend he was mine just this once. Tomorrow was a day for consequences.

He growled against my neck as I ground down on his cock with my ass. How many songs had it been? Only three? I wanted him driven so insane that he wouldn't make it past those trees on the outer rim before he claimed me again. To hell with whomever might watch. I loved the way his fur felt against my legs, the way his hand caressed over the top of my thigh as the other cupped my breast.

I bumped back to make enough room in his hold for me to turn and face him, and I wrapped my arms around his neck. He was so much taller than me usually, but he sank down to pull me in. His hands gripped my ass firmly, driving my body against his with his strong cock between us. I slid my knee up along his

216

side and he caught me immediately. His eyes took in my face and then moved down to my lips.

I promised to never kiss him, but now, I needed to. He held me tightly, offering the support he always had. My eyelids fluttered shut as my heart knew the way to go. His grip on me grew tighter, and I yelped in surprise as Rux spun and kicked someone square in the gut.

They hit the rock that Rux had raised presumably to avoid damaging any of the trees. My heart sank as I took in the person Rux had hit. The regal uniform could only indicate a member of the court, and others began to flee from the scene.

"I'm sorry. Normally he doesn't interfere," Cirro whispered behind us. I leveled my breath out as I wiggled to get down to the ground. My face was blazing hot at getting caught up in my own glamour.

Rux let out a string of curses once we separated, and he stalked over to Trevan as he came back to consciousness.

"Lia, are you okay?" Rux asked, only half paying attention to the fae man.

"I'm fine. I'm sorry, Rux . . . I was so lost in the moment. I didn't mean to . . ." Yes, I had. I meant to take him as mine tonight, knowing full well that he had a mate back in Voreios.

"You hit me!" Trevan snarled and shot to his feet with his wings flapping furiously.

"You were going to grab her. No one gets to touch her without her permission," Rux said with his arms crossed. "You

217

may have different policies out here for your women, but Aralia is exempt from that, and you will not try it again."

I'd never heard Rux so furious before. Sure, we'd fought all the time up until recently, but he always sounded more annoyed. I began to worry for Trevan's safety, but the fae man seemed to not notice.

"She should not be out here. Dangerous things lurk in these woods at night. None of the court is allowed to be out here."

"Then why are you?" I asked with a raised brow, but when he turned his glare on me, I slid a little closer to Rux. Easy to be brave when you hid behind a six-foot-something satyr. He didn't seem to mind as he wrapped an arm in front of me around my waist.

"Looking for you." He narrowed his eyes and rubbed his stomach where Rux had landed his kick. "Prinna saw you both leave the court before dinner. When you weren't present for the meal, she advised me where you had gone."

"Didn't think anyone would care." I shrugged and glanced at my protector who looked to be grounding his energy with a fast meditation. He was quick to respond, but it sometimes took a few beats to cool his anger. I scratched my nails softly against his strong arm as my own nerves settled the longer the conversation dragged on.

"King Lorsan immediately asked about you when he noticed you were missing." Trevan stood on shaky legs as he rose to his feet. "You could bring other energies with you when

218

you return to the court. It's safer for everyone if you remain inside. You may be a guest with us, but it looks like there may need to be some stricter rules."

Rux met my gaze for only a moment before he looked down at his hooves. I could only pray that he wasn't beating himself up for my actions. I was the one who hadn't been respectful of his mate.

"How about if we relocated outside of the court?" I asked hesitantly. "I understand a lot of exceptions have been made for me, and the last thing I'd want to do is put anyone in danger. I'm not fae, so perhaps we could move my tree again now that I am getting better."

"I don't think that's a good idea, Lia," Rux murmured to me.

Wouldn't it be better for us to be with the people who were more like us? I could actually make friends out here and have a life, but my protector still wouldn't look at me, so I couldn't begin to guess what he was thinking. The more I tossed this idea around in my mind, the more it felt like the better option.

"The only one who could approve of that is the king. You have put him in a difficult situation with Voreios, so he needs to navigate that carefully. We don't need another war."

Chapter 21 – Aralia

Trevan marched us the whole way back to the fae court. I could tell Rux wanted to talk with me, but he remained quiet with the fae in such close range. It felt like I was a child again, but I'd scarcely ever been in actual trouble. Not like this.

"You both are not to leave this garden except to train until further notice. Once I have discussed this situation with King Lorsan, we can talk about what further action will be needed and how he would like to handle any relocation." Trevan glared at us both until I nodded.

My life depended on being able to stay here until Ferox came up with a solution, or until I magically got better and didn't need to be here any longer.

This week I had somehow managed to break all of the rules, including the ones that I'd set for myself. Shame and guilt wrecked me internally as I weighed out each of the individual potential consequences. Would Lorsan kick us out tonight? Rux had begun to make friends, and if he'd gone out tonight, I doubt anyone would have even noticed. He could have had the good time that he so desperately needed. Instead, he was locked down with me.

"Lia, I'm so sor—"

"No. This isn't your fault." I waved him off and weighed out how I should word my own apology. We both knew exactly who had been on their worst behavior this evening. Me. As usual. "I crossed a line tonight. It's disrespectful to you, and I promise I'm going to work on it. This transition hasn't been easy. I'm really sorry."

Rux only frowned at my explanation. "I'm not sure what you are referring to. This isn't exactly how I hoped tonight would go. I . . ."

The hesitation as he rubbed the back of his head figuring out his words made me nervous. I turned to my tree so I could stare at the grooves in my bark.

"Why'd you say I shouldn't leave the court? Those people are definitely more our speed. I don't need to be here really." Briefly, I wondered if I could have avoided all of this by going to the fey pool like I was supposed to. Did I bring this ancient illness onto myself? If I'd gone there, I might have avoided Lorsan altogether. What I didn't know how to fix was this situation with Rux.

"Lia, the guards have been telling me about attacks on the fey in the wilds. They call it the yellow poisoning. It's affecting all the fey outside these walls." I nearly jumped when I felt his hand press against my lower back. "Your roots are still recovering. I don't want to put you in more danger."

"It's different from what I had already?"

221

"Very different." He sighed as he tossed a glance at his room. "Would you like to cuddle for a bit before we go to bed? I know you took a nap before we left. I'll keep you company, and we can get away from unexpected onlookers."

There were windows everywhere, and even Trevan could be watching us right now. A small pout pulled at my lips because the thought of cuddling always reminded me of my sisters. "Yeah, I'd like that. You still have that mead?"

"It was almost too tempting, but I managed to save it just in case we needed a reprise," he teased, and I was glad that he didn't seem to be holding any anger toward me. None that I could see.

I did this entirely to myself. Who fell in love with a man that they'd sworn off? A man I'd basically shoved onto Rhenei, and she saw him for everything I hadn't. He deserved to be loved unconditionally.

As soon as the door closed, I waited until he went to pass me and brushed my hands along his chiseled waist. That beautiful heat singed my fingertips the way it always did when I touched him. The mood shifted from somber reflection to desire immediately. I just couldn't kiss him like I'd almost tried to do. If sex was all I could have from him, then I would not waste an opportunity.

A playful kiss on his pectoral disarmed him, and with a quick flick of my wrist, I untied the strap of his chiton. I'd only been this forward with him once before. It was the first time I'd

222

been hungry after I finally grew into a woman. I'd been mad at him, so I'd starved myself into a frenzy. I could have taken any lover, yet he'd been the one I crashed into. My anger couldn't remove the fact that I knew I was safe in his care.

This time, I would savor him in a way he'd never let me before. I could feel his eyes watching me as I shuffled him back toward his bed. I would get lost in the way the taste of his skin and how his powerful muscles reacted to my not-so-subtle caresses.

"Lia." He tried to get my attention in that husky voice of his, but I wouldn't be deterred.

His hands roved over my shoulders and started to slide down before I dropped to my knees. I pulled the fabric out of my way, and his thick cock popped out to greet me. Who knew that there would be so much pleasure in having this control. My hands moved through the fur on his thighs before I ran my tongue along the ridged edge of him and then all the way to the base.

The way he groaned had me clenching. His grip in my hair as I traced the tip of his head, already beading with precum, filled me with self-confidence. I'd never done this before. He knew that, but I wanted to hear him call my name the way I did his.

Rux was thick, and as I slid him into my mouth, I realized very quickly just how different this had been in my mind. As he hit the back of my throat, he pressed on my gag reflex.

"Relax your throat," he offered as I slid him out and then tried it again. This time I was able to take him a little deeper, repeating the motion as I got used to the feel of him in my mouth. I was determined to memorize the silky flesh that covered this rock. He was being so still. It wasn't until I heard a soft curse that I felt a little more confident.

He really seemed to enjoy the way my tongue moved at the top of his head, or when I sucked with wild abandon, however I could when he was blocking all my airways. Oh goddess, when he accidentally thrust into my mouth, I let out a whimper.

"You're going to be the death of me, Lia," Rux said with a hungry grit to his teeth.

My eyes shot up to him innocently, but with his cock in my mouth, I couldn't reply. The way the muscle twitched; I knew I only had a moment to figure out how to keep control.

"I need to be inside of you." He attempted to pull back, but I sucked hard as he tried to slip out. "Fuck. On the bed, show yourself to me. I'm going to devour you until you beg for the pounding that you will absolutely receive."

When I tossed him a pout, he only laughed.

"Be a good girl and do as I say. I'm trying to be patient, but I don't think I can much longer."

As I rose to my feet, I bumped him with my hip so that he sat on the bed the way I wanted him to. Straddling his lap, I already knew I was soaking wet.

"Lia," he protested until I lined him up with my core. He cast his eyes to the ceiling and said what looked like a silent prayer.

The way he stretched me took my breath away, but he'd been inside me before. I could handle it. I *would* handle it as I let myself slide down. He trembled with patience as he propped himself back against the pillows and locked his hands on my hips.

"I see you want to be in charge," he groaned trying to be playful, but he tested with a soft thrust.

I didn't know what I wanted, truthfully. I wanted to explore it all with him and find out what made him succumb to pleasure like I did. He knew all of my buttons, and as I rocked my body along his cock, I realized I didn't know his the same way.

The faster I rode on him, the more our breathing increased. One of his hands slid between my legs to circle my clit, and I cried out gripping on to him to keep steady. When I slowed my pace, lost in the pleasure, his hand guided me back to the rhythm.

"You're so perfect," he praised with soft reverence, and I opened my eyes to find him watching me. Each compliment left me a mess like he knew exactly what I needed to hear.

"Rux," I whispered when I swayed again, his grip was the only thing keeping me steady.

There was no warning for the way he flipped us, his hands pushing my knees down so he could sink in. I came with a loud cry as he slammed into me repeatedly. It didn't take much longer for him to spend his release as I spun in the pleasure waves over taking every single rational thought. Would it always be like this when I was with him?

We were sweaty and panting, but I felt satisfied that we'd gotten the night back on track, avoiding those pesky intimate kisses.

With my hair braided back, I tried to look as much as possible like the other trainees in the grounds. I'd seen their uniforms enough to know exactly how it should look even down to the details on the boots. I didn't often wear pants and a plain old shirt like this, that was more Nylisa's style, but training in dresses could be difficult.

The area that had been provided for Rux to work with the guards was by the northern gardens, so it only took a few minutes of walking down the pristine white halls of the lower castle to get there. I heard Rux's voice long before I saw him. He'd taken me to my tree in the early hours of the morning so I could get some proper rest, but it didn't look like he'd returned for any additional sleep afterward.

Rux was providing one-on-one guidance to one of the few fae guards, showing him how to properly handle a sword.

"When wielded right, a sword becomes an extension of yourself in the same way your magic does. See how the grip here allows you to swing the weapon without losing your balance. Good. Now go do it again."

Rux went to move on to the next trainee, but he lifted his gaze in my direction. Well, really, he took a long appreciative glance at what I was wearing. "Good morning, Lia. Did you want to hang out with us again today?"

"I was thinking I could train with you today. If you aren't too busy." All the men had turned to look at me now, and I held my head up high to display confidence in this decision, though that confidence was becoming shaky.

"Of course we can train. What weapon?" Rux hadn't noticed the way the others gawked at my request. He'd begun to head toward the weapons to pick some out for me like he used to do.

"Sir, she's a woman," the fae man he'd been talking with before interjected.

My ryne protector took another long look at me with a knowing smile. "Yes, she is, but in Voreios, we never turn down any who want to fight for their home. That includes the nymphs who we hold as precious."

I fought the blush from my cheeks. He had a precious nymph back home that I'd ripped him away from. It didn't matter how fondly he looked at me right now. I couldn't just erase the fact that I had pushed him away for decades and that

227

wouldn't change no matter how sweetly he whispered to me when he thought I was asleep the night before.

"Swords, no magic."

"Done," Rux agreed easily. He passed me a sword and then turned back to the men gathered around. "There's a saying that we have in Voreios among our guard: 'Fight as if your cherished person's life depends on it.' Remember them when you go into battle or any situation that requires you to fight. Your strength and resolve may falter if it's just you that you lean on. Aralia is mine, you see. So that makes this type of training tricky when I see her on the other end of the blade."

"What do you do in this case?"

All of the guards were giving him their full attention. They must really respect him, and I hadn't noticed just how easily he'd slipped into his own place among them. The guards wanted to improve, and he wasn't holding anything back from them like the fae would.

"It means I have to push her even harder than I would anyone else. In the ideal world, she would never have to pick up a blade because I would always be there to protect her." Rux's hand settled on my hip, and I met his intense gaze. "But even without the shadow infernals terrorizing the lands, this world is far from perfect. I have to know that when she does fight, she is able to take on the fiercest opponent. If something happened to her, my drive to fight would be lost, and without her what happens?"

"Your resolve would falter, and you wouldn't be far behind her."

Rux nodded. "Exactly right. So, I push her until she can beat me, because then our odds are better. All right, enough talking. Aralia, go stand on the line over there. I want each of you to pay attention to how we hold our blades and the position we keep our feet in."

"Why the feet?" another guard asked as I set myself into position.

Why had I not noticed how smooth he was in a leadership role? How he effortlessly transitioned from diplomat to teacher in the blink of an eye. I'd been so blind in Voreios to just how incredible this guy actually was. Blind and cruel in some cases. Yet his smile held nothing of the lies that I'd told myself to shove him away. His touch was always gentle.

"I think we can all agree that Aralia is much smaller than I am," Rux said as he gestured in my direction. The guard took a moment to look between the two of us and nodded. "What's the goal of this again?"

"To train her so that she can beat you."

Rux nodded emphatically. "In order to counter the clear physical strength advantage that I have, her technique will need to be perfect. You can use these exact same skills to beat a stronger adversary. Now imagine if you combine physical strength and technique. The chances of going home to your loved one every night just increased dramatically. That's why

229

you are going to watch for the proper foot placement even in a dynamic fight."

The smiles on their faces warmed my heart. Rux took his place across the way from me and lifted his blade.

"Aralia, are you ready to give me everything you've got?"

In that moment, I wished that I could undo everything painful from our shared past and do just that for the rest of my life.

Chapter 22 – Lorsan

I'd not seen her since the night I'd fucked her against the wall that I currently stared at just outside my room. I could still hear her shouting my name. Her seat had been vacant at dinner every night since. There had been no response the few times I'd been able to sneak away from the contenders to visit her tree. She had to be avoiding me. I couldn't make sense of how or why? I hadn't punished her for interrupting the trials, and I didn't think I'd been too rough.

A week had passed, and I could hardly think of anything else. I was going to end up clearing my entire schedule for the day to hunt her down. I'd seen Rux with the guards, and he wouldn't likely be far from her, I just didn't know where the little nymph seemed to be hiding.

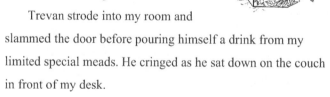

Trevan strode into my room and slammed the door before pouring himself a drink from my limited special meads. He cringed as he sat down on the couch in front of my desk.

"What happened to you?" My voice was terser than I'd intended, but my fuse had been short since she'd not come to dinner as I'd insisted.

"Oh, have I not told you the story yet?" The annoying cadence of his haughty arrogance tested my empathy, and he hadn't even elaborated. I would need to pull myself into a better alignment if I wanted everything else to smooth out.

"Clearly not. I've also been a bit preoccupied with the other things going on."

"I heard that we lost another six contenders last night."

"The magic is moving swiftly." I shot him a warning glare at his inability to answer the question I asked. I wasn't here to play games, and dodging subjects would not work. "Don't make me ask again, Trevan. What happened and why haven't you been to see the healer?"

He wet his lips and took another sip before he answered me. Still trying to keep some control over the way he dispensed information, it seemed. "Rux attacked me."

I rose from my chair and scowled at the captain of my guard. "When? How am I just hearing about this? He's not welcome here if he's going to attack court members. Even Aralia understands that. We will dismiss him immediately."

"The queen trials are more important than my scuffle with the fey." My cousin only waved me off, but I didn't miss the plural use of the word. "They will both say that it's because I got too close to Aralia."

I knew Trevan watched her closely, all of the men and some of the women in the court did. Being fey, she technically wasn't off limits to even the guards. Rux was the biggest deterrent for

232

most of the would-be suitors currently and he watched everyone a lot more closely than I suspected they knew.

"What does that mean exactly?" My tone turned cold. If she had indeed welcomed him into her bed, I'd have to deal with it. It wouldn't happen again, but I'd have to deal with it.

"I caught them out in the fauns' grounds at a party, and while they were dancing, I may have tried to grab her."

The new context changed everything. I retook my chair and leaned back to observe him as I gave my response. I wouldn't dismiss her guard for doing what he was supposed to, but fae could be boisterous when they didn't get the results they wanted.

"You know how satyrs are about other men touching the nymphs. What could have possibly possessed you to attempt such a thing?" Sure. It was the satyr's response, and not my own growing need to punch him at the mere thought of his hands on her. What was wrong with me?

"It's dangerous out there, and I needed to get their attention. I wasn't thinking, honestly. She has some intense glamour. Don't worry, I have advised them that they aren't to leave the gardens again, and if they do, then there will be punishments. The guards will alert me immediately if they leave."

Could this be why she was avoiding me? Fear of punishment after the trials and this incident? "They aren't from here. We may have to let them wander the forest if they need to. She's a nymph, and from what Celeste has told us, they don't handle even gilded cages well. As long as he is with her, she should be safe enough."

"Is that a precedent you want to argue with the other women?" he asked, but his lazy stance told me there was no bite in it.

"She isn't like the other women here. I've asked her to be an adviser on how to bring more nymphs to our lands. Observation on what she does in our kingdom to make herself comfortable would make more sense at this point than forcing her to be fae." I leveled him with a firm stare. "Do not attempt to touch her again or make any more threats. She's shy enough as it is."

"Fine, but I don't think you should be making exceptions. She's living in our land; she can't treat this like her grove. There are rules and traditions for a reason."

I could hear Aralia yelling at me about the way we treat our women and the senseless deaths she'd witnessed. The first time she'd said my name without any honorifics, and I'd liked it. Behind the quiet demeanor was a passion I couldn't get enough of.

"I think I need to make a change to the way the queen's trials are run. I don't want a harem, but I can't let any more women die for this. True fae are already rare, and with fewer women, we aren't helping our cause any."

Trevan considered my statement for a moment. "You should let other court members keep harems. I'd be more than happy to take the ones you don't get as queen."

"That will not happen." I poured myself a drink with magic and it floated over to settle in my hands. I didn't even want to think about what Aralia would say to the concept of a harem for the men in my court.

"I still advise you to dismiss Rux. He's trying to move in on my position with the guard, and he's persuading her to make decisions that aren't safe. Mages are out there. They've already attempted to take two selkies from the borders and whole isles of people are missing." His reminder settled the fact that he wasn't wrong about the dangers outside the court and the issues I still had to resolve.

"Perhaps you are right," I admitted. Just when I'd given up on Trevan as a helpful adviser, he'd pull through with some much-needed perspective. "I'll think on it."

This time when I turned my chair to watch Aralia's tree in my garden, the familiar glow of the grounds responding to her presence illuminated all the foliage. It was a radiant display when what she referred to as her spirit form manifested. Catching a glimpse of her twisting her blond hair into a braid, wearing what looked to be a feminine version of the guards' uniform, it all made sense. I'd been looking for her as she'd been attending dinner after Prinna's coaching. Of course, she wouldn't be far from Rux, and he'd been training most days.

"Tell all court members that they are required to be at dinner tonight, including Aralia. I need to be alone now."

"Prinna was going to bring the contenders by." Trevan scooted forward to the edge of his seat and frowned at me.

"Is that why you came in here?" I snarled with disapproval, even though I should have expected this behavior. This was Trevan, after all. "Get out of my chambers and relay my orders immediately. I will attend to Prinna when I am ready."

When he didn't give me any back talk as he left, I knew I was finally getting my point across that they were not to disobey me. I didn't want to be pushed into drastic measures, but the time of councilors running amok was over. I'd been a disengaged ruler for too long, and now I was ready to shape the lands how I imagined they could be.

Those blessed by Aine had a special chamber that no one else knew about but us. She'd led me there as a pastel glow that only I could see the day my father died. I'd not liked my father much, but my emotions were a torrent that day. Knowing the druwids of Voreios took his head filled me with delight, anguish, and anger. If they'd come only a few weeks sooner, they might have saved my mother.

If I'd had any suspicion that morning would have been my last with her, I might have challenged him myself. When I'd spoken those thoughts to Aine, she only told me that I would have lost without her blessing. I never asked the goddess for

236

anything, though we spoke from time to time. It would be interesting to see how this went.

A sconce on the left side of my bed with an intricately designed lantern matched its partner on the right, but this one held a secret. Pricking my finger on the metal base, slid open a secret wall. The candles inside this chamber always remained lit, and as the wall slid shut behind me, darkness descended until my eyes adjusted.

I left special vintages of ancient meads and fine offerings for the few times I came here to talk with her. I pulled out a pure silver goblet to set in the center of a basin filled with ritualized water from the fey pool.

The goosebumps across my arms indicated that she already watched me, and I wasn't alone in the space. She'd been very active since the trials compared to her usual aloofness.

"Mighty Aine, goddess of all the fae. I seek to change a long-standing tradition. Let us come to a new deal."

"Lorsan," the goddess purred in my ear, her hands sliding down my arms. What could have been very intimate was instead almost horrifying because even as a king and a proud man, she wielded powers that triggered my sense of self-preservation. "I've been hoping you would come around eventually."

"I want to discuss the queen trials." I kept my voice steady as the goddess moved to sit upon her altar, raising the chalice to her lips.

"Come to grant your favor to one of them?" she asked before she took a long sip.

"No. I will not pretend to know better than you what my destiny should entail. However, I would like to put an end to the mandatory death clause."

Her consideration of my words sent crackling tension through the room. The temperature rose dramatically, and though my clothes were light, sweat beaded down my back and chest.

"Blood is a necessary part of the trials. It is my due. What will you offer me in exchange for this request?"

To bargain with a god had to be the most difficult thing because you needed to consider all words very carefully. "What terms would you consider? I could offer you temples, acolytes, and a growth of commonplace worship among the fae. I'd like to grow the population of our people again, and to do that, I need women. We have an opportunity to reintroduce nymphs to the fey."

"As pretty as that all sounds, those exchanges won't do. Blood offerings require blood sacrifices." She paused as she placed a finger to her lips as if she thought about it.

This was a game. She already knew exactly what she wanted, but I would wait. I didn't really have a choice, even a king has to answer to someone. A cold blast of air washed over me as her smile spread, a mischievous glint in her eyes.

I moved in the liminal space, wanting to make sure that she would attend the dinner as I instructed. Her magic manifested, and the garden glowed as her spirit form emerged from the tree. Rux exited his room at exactly that moment, and I hated the bright smile she gave him.

"I can't believe he is commanding me to attend like a child." She protested my direct orders in Druidic while straightening her form-fitting green dress made of silk. I thought she'd look regal in an occasional gold or metallic dress, but so far, she'd chosen to keep to the colors of Voreios.

Rux gave her a casual shrug. "The guards said that he mandated the entire court be present. You are part of that court for now, whether you like it or not. I don't believe he is singling you out."

"That's true. With everything going on, he doesn't have any time to think about me."

What was that in her voice? Disappointment? There was a tone I couldn't place. I wasn't the one who'd started avoiding her. She knew exactly where to find me.

"Do you think he's even considered my request yet?"

"I think Trevan would have let us know if there were going to be changes. That guy has no boundaries, especially when it comes to giving orders. For your safety, I advise that you drop it for now." Rux studied her carefully before he continued speaking. "I'm ready to talk about what happened last week if you are. I'm sure we can resolve whatever it is. Otherwise, we just have to be patient and mind all their strange rules. If Ferox can figure out a stronger cure, we can return to Voreios."

"I won't fit in there again either." She frowned down at her hands. "Being able to practice with all the other women here revealed one thing: I can't avoid my magic. It's part of who I am, and I can't find that in Voreios. I miss Nylisa more than anything. Not speaking to her makes me feel like half of me is missing, and I can't do anything to restore it."

"Hey, you will see her again soon. If we are still here, then I'm sure King Lorsan won't mind letting her come visit after the seedling is rooted. Or we can meet her at the fey pool."

"Trevan said I can't leave the grounds though."

"Screw that guy." Rux caught her face in his fingers and turned her gaze up to him. "You will go where you need to in order to stay healthy. Being away from your twin has been a shock to your roots. You will need to see her and go for walks in the forest. I'm sure if you asked the king nicely, he would allow it. If not, Ferox will insist next time he is here. They haven't said that you are a prisoner."

"I'm sure Trevan has the complete backing of the king already. Face it, I'm trapped here. I may as well just live in my tree and never come out."

This conversation turned out to be more informative than I could have hoped for. The open way she displayed her deeper desires to the satyr was not common here. Everyone played the game with what they wanted most, just as she would do around us. But to him, she displayed fear, sadness, and despair so easily. They clearly didn't like Trevan, and Prinna wouldn't speak with Aralia any longer. I'd need to find a new handler if I couldn't convey messages to her directly.

The two finally turned toward the bridge that would lead them into the grand entryway. I kept close enough that I could hear but made sure not to brush her magic.

"That's no way to live, Lia." Rux slid his fingers into hers and she easily locked hands with him. Their dynamic had shifted somehow since their arrival. The fighting I'd heard initially had settled into quiet comradery. "I will bring Ferox into the conversation when he comes back. I thought Lorsan asked you to help advise him on nymphs?"

"He did, but I don't think our test run of a nymph in the court is going so well."

"There was a hiccup. You saved those women. When the dust has settled, I don't think this will be as problematic as you think. How could you have known that the deaths were expected? It's not like anyone told you that part. Veon and Zrif will find a way for you to see Nylisa. I think it would boost your mood."

"I promised her I wouldn't leave . . . and then I did. Not even a day later!" She spun to gaze up at him on the top step. I hated the sadness in her eyes. I didn't understand why I really cared, but she'd taken up so many of my thoughts recently that this sadness hit me just as deep as the way she looked during an orgasm.

"You didn't get a choice in this, Lia. You were unconscious."

Aralia's defeated sigh came with a bouncing of her blond curls as she shook her head. "Come on, we are going to be late, and I don't want to draw any more undue attention onto myself. Or give *him* any more reasons to touch me."

Rux's upper lip curled. "I will remove his hands if he touches you. I don't care what the rest of the court has to say about it."

She slipped her arm around the satyr's and pulled him along with her. "They will just say you are being a brute. You know they don't have any notions of my autonomy. It feels good to be training again because I need to be able to defend myself."

"Just say the word and I'll change the way I protect you. I will stay on you."

Aralia flushed a bright red. "I don't think that's necessary. How would Rhenei feel about that?"

"Lia—" Rux started to say but the guards opened the large door and cut off his reply.

Who was Rhenei? I knew culture in the groves was centered around mates which we didn't have here in the Feylands. Was there a chance that Rux wasn't Aralia's mate? Trevan was right that the closer she got to Rux, the more she pulled away from the court, so could I use this new information to my advantage?

I hadn't factored that Aralia would ever actually leave my gardens again to return to her home once she found out that the cure was completed. She doubted her place here enough to want to either retire to her tree entirely or find any way to leave again. What did I need to do to make sure she wouldn't consider that? It would be a shame to lose such a beautiful vision in this world and for what real purpose? I could scarcely take my eyes off her and to have that ripped away would not work.

I slipped around the hall as she took her place among the court. Perhaps what I announced tonight could change her mind. Make her feel safer here. Why did I feel like I was still missing something though?

My doors opened and the court stood to welcome me to my rightful place at the head of the table. Most of the people nodded their welcome to me. A couple continued their conversations. But I didn't care about any of them. She hadn't seen me in days after I'd tasted her, and now, she kept her eyes downcast at the table. She'd dare avoid me further.

"Have a seat." I gestured to everyone while I kept my voice level. This little dryad infuriated me. Food appeared on the

243

table, which of course I knew she wouldn't touch. "Bring in the queen contenders to the center. I have an announcement."

The final eight fae women floated into the center as the room fell into a silent hush. I could see Aralia's hand curl into a tiny fist as she counted how many women remained. All the women she'd saved from the last round, hadn't made the cut the next time.

"I'm removing the termination clause from these trials. I've come to new terms with the fey magic buried in these lands as those rules were set in times that had much different circumstances to what we find ourselves faced with today."

Murmurs rose from around the room, but again none of that mattered. The trial survivors waited cautiously as to what that meant for them. Soleil, who was currently leading the pack in her uses of our magic, didn't seem to be fazed at all, but the more nervous women appeared to be relieved. Aralia finally lifted her gaze to look at me with confusion in her pretty green eyes.

"These trials are still dangerous, so death is not guaranteed to be entirely avoided. What I can say is that we will no longer stand by while the magic runs amok. If you prove to be unable to control it, then you will be disqualified, removed from the running, and returned to your families."

"Not to a harem?" one of the women asked me.

"I will not be keeping a harem. That has not changed."

Soleil raised her gaze to meet me directly. "Then you intend to mate your queen?"

It took everything that I had to not check for Aralia's expression at this question. Why did it matter so much? "That was the plan. You are off for this evening. Relax, dance, and get ready for a renewal of the trial tomorrow. Until we have a new queen, I need every member of the court to make an appearance for dinner *every night*."

The women bowed and split up to go to mingle into the rest of the court for dinner. I needed to pay attention to where they all went when they thought no one would be watching, but instead, I looked to her. Aralia wasn't looking at me again when I glanced in her direction. She was exchanging looks with Soleil. Rux, however, was watching me from his post behind her chair. I could believe he knew every time I turned my gaze in her direction. Perhaps it would be better for him to go.

Taking the queen as my official mate had been the plan. But thinking of losing Aralia made my head spin in a different direction. I'd not wanted a harem, but I could take a consort. If she wanted a place here, I would give her one. One that would ensure no other male in this fae court could touch her again. If I had a queen and a consort, then I couldn't have a mate, but I was king. Who needed a damn mate in that case?

Chapter 23 — Aralia

I wasn't above admitting that when Lorsan announced that they would intervene in the trials to save the women, I had been skeptical. But so far, three days later, all the women were still alive.

Soleil had begun coming to my tree almost every morning in an attempt to talk with me, but once more, I just pretended to not be able to hear anything. I didn't really want to make friends with the new queen anymore. What could I say? I'd be respectful, but that didn't mean I had to watch the man mate with his future queen. Was it petty? Perhaps. But watching him dance with them all every evening had been enough torture. He was doing what I had asked though, courting them.

Rux stood diligently by his pillar that was angled enough that I could see him if I just glanced over my shoulder. That was another problem waiting to explode in my face. Being away from the grove had proven just how much I actually did care about that particular man . . . Care wasn't a strong enough word, but I couldn't admit what I truly wanted.

I was about to slip out for the evening once the dancing began, it was easier to sneak away with that as a distraction, until I felt him approach me. I could always tell when Lorsan got closer, like an unfortunate magnet drew us together.

"Already looking to escape for the evening?"

I had enough courtesy to tuck my chin and avert my eyes to the floor for being caught. "Of course not, Your Majesty. Just stretching my legs."

"Would you perhaps dance with me then? I'd love to chat with you."

I cast a glance back at Rux who rolled his eyes in annoyance but leaned back against the pillar again. He knew I couldn't refuse the request directly.

"I can't promise to be as graceful as your other partners this week, but if you are so inclined." I offered him my hand and tried to ignore the sparks that ran up my skin as we touched.

Lorsan pulled me up close into the proper position as he led us around the room in a combination of steps and twists. This was a similarity between fae and elven formal dancing. As the woman, I was led around the floor, so learning the steps had been much easier. Back home, there was nothing formal about what we did outside of rituals.

"I haven't been able to speak with you in nearly two weeks," he commented after we'd covered the room three times in relative silence. It wasn't uncomfortable, I just wasn't sure what to say.

"I didn't know that you had been hoping to speak, Your Majesty. I fear I said quite enough the last time." I let the implication sit between us, waiting for any backlash at the reminder of that night.

Instead, he didn't seem interested in that topic at all. "I see that we are back to using titles. Is that what you would like, Aralia?"

"I don't understand what you are asking," I replied softly, but he now held my full attention.

"I'm saying that between us, you should keep calling me Lorsan. You didn't use my title the last time, and I think you should keep doing that."

"Do the rest of your advisers use only your name?" I asked even though the way his fingers stroked into my skin told me the answer before he did.

"No, this is just for you. I like the way you say my name, even in fury." The huskiness in this voice sent shivers down my body that I couldn't hide when he held me this close.

"K— Lorsan." I corrected myself quickly before I continued, "I don't think I can drop these barriers. You are looking for your queen right now and this feels . . . wrong."

"Come to my quarters with me. I want to talk with you. I think I can put your mind at ease once we sort out all the details."

Oh, how I wanted that, but I had to stay firm as he twirled me around again. I would not be second fiddle to anyone else's destiny. "I can't. I won't."

I flinched waiting for him to be angry, but instead he pulled me closer with an amused chuckle. "Going to make me play the long game, I see."

He held me so close that I actually relaxed as he wove us around the floor. The world seemed to vanish except for the two of us.

"I really should have met you at the fey pool when you used to travel there while you lived in Voreios," he mused as I followed his steps. "Or gone to improve the dynamic we had with Voreios. I knew you were there, but after your parents rejected my offers to have you trained at the court, it slipped through the cracks. I regret that missed opportunity."

"I stopped going to the pool a few years ago," I admitted, not knowing how he'd respond. "I really tried to limit using my magic at all, because it doesn't quite fit into grove life. When my mom was there, it seemed to flow naturally with how she blurred elemental and fey magics, but now that she's gone . . . I just felt so out of place even in my own home."

"It's because you belong here," he insisted. "I think you were meant to come here."

"To what end, Lorsan?" At my question, his hold tightened. "Look at me. I'm an imitation here as well. I'm not fae. I won't fit in the pristine little box that you all want to put me in either. Did you even consider my request?"

"What request?" There was genuine interest in his response that made me think he truly might not know, but one can never be sure with the fae.

"I asked Trevan if I could relocate my tree outside of the court. It would still be on Feylands, but I know there are concerns about what I might bring back with me through the roots. I'll tell Ferox that it was my request to connect with the land so there would be no concern to the relationship with Voreios. He said it would be your decision and that he'd let me know. I don't want to hurt any of the fae, but we all know that I don't belong."

Charges of lightning and fury raced through the magic around us, and I frowned at the sudden tension between us both. Only a moment later, the energy was replaced with something like a masked calm that could only be felt by the cloudless sky before a storm.

"I had not been advised of that request; however, I will tell you now that it is denied. I need my advisers close, and the Feylands are not safe for you. How would your twin feel if I let you go out there into the wilds and something happened? Even if you were the one who decided to move. I can't, in all good conscience, let you out of our sights."

250

Lorsan leaned in closer, making sure that only I could hear him. "Talk to me about Rux. Is he your mate?"

I stumbled in my step, but Lorsan caught me easily, and his eyes studied my face, waiting for a response. I really didn't like this question, and I wasn't sure where it had come from. Was he angry that Rux hit Trevan? The fae weren't always direct, and this could be part of what he wanted to talk with me about privately.

"No. He's not my mate. Why do you ask?"

"Well, it's pretty clear to most of us how unhappy he is to be here. If he was your mate, then I figured it might have just been the relocation. However, if he's not . . . some of the guard think from their conversations that he might be looking for a way to go home."

I risked taking a peek at where I knew he stood. Rux looked uncomfortable leaning against the marble column, out of place in the elegance of the court. If I decided to play the game with the fae, they'd make a space for me. That wasn't true for Rux. They'd already decided he was nothing more than the help. He had a lover who might be his mate, he had routines and a life beyond me. As Veon's second, he could have the whole world open to him.

"Oh. That makes sense. I didn't know that the others had heard him mentioning some of these things. I've just never been without him. Sounds pretty selfish, I guess."

"Not at all. I don't fully understand how these things work in the groves, but if it's protection you are looking for, we can cover that. You can let him return home. It's obvious that you care for him and his well-being."

"I do," I whispered as if trying to prove it to myself. I needed to show that I genuinely cared about letting him achieve the best things in life. I couldn't be scared to be alone here. This was my fate, not his. "I am safe enough in the court to not need other protection. Thank you, Lorsan. I will think on what you have said."

"I'm glad you feel safe here," Lorsan replied earnestly, then he lowered his voice again. "Please come with me to my quarters. I want to chat with you privately for a while."

If Rux wasn't what he wanted to discuss privately, I knew that we would not be talking much. I pushed my glamour call back down as I thought about his invitation. "I cannot. I'm sorry, but I will not disrespect you, the new queen, or myself any further, and being alone with you puts me on a path of temptation I do not wish to travel down."

Again, he only seemed amused. The fae king stroked my cheek the way that Rux usually did, and I leaned into his touch. "Why fight destiny? I will chase and I will win, Aralia. At my side, you will want for nothing. Everything will be yours."

"I want to find my mates, Lorsan. I want to be cherished completely by my partners. You can't offer me that. I'm beginning to think that no one can." I curtsied to him low as the song ended and spun on my heels to leave him in the center of the dance floor.

I would hold my ground against even the fae king's advances. Now I had to also do what was right for the man who'd done his best to protect me all his life. I needed to set him free.

Chapter 24 — Rux

It had been a rough night. Lorsan moved like a predator with his eyes on his favorite prey, and she'd responded with glamour. I'd always known that she had a crush on him, but I thought it would play out and dissipate the more time she spent in his court. None of the guards seemed to catch her attention, and a tryst with the king would only end in Aralia getting her heart broken. I could do absolutely nothing as she radiated light under his affection. In a way that recently she'd begun to do with me.

The conversation must not have gone down the way that Lorsan had expected based on the look on his face. Aralia only seemed to be mildly distracted as she made for her tree. Her shoulders were straight, her posture confident as she embraced the earth of the garden.

Once more, however, she still wouldn't talk to me about the exchange. At least she wasn't crying this time.

Sleep did not come for me. Something was off. It wasn't the fact that she'd not joined me in bed, though I missed having her in my arms. I didn't question it when the change led to her coming to me every night after our failed outing. I couldn't stop as her hands roamed over me with an eagerness I'd never seen before. I knew she'd sleep in her tree occasionally, but there was something in the air that didn't feel right. I just couldn't put my finger on exactly what it was. The magic was not any more charged than usual.

Everything centered around Aralia, but when I checked her tree for any signs of the illness, there were only some curious red spots, but the black ooze had faded from the bark.

"Rux." Aralia's soft voice sounded almost apologetic as her spirit form manifested from the tree to stand beside me. The lights of the garden responded to her presence and then slowly returned to their natural state.

"Good morning. I know you don't like it when I ask, but I'm going to anyway. How are you feeling?" I'd get to the bottom of whatever this was. I stepped up closer so I could brush my fingers down her arm, just needing to touch her somehow.

Instead of giving me an attitude, as she often would when I pried about her health, she did something worse. She bit her lip as she considered her next words. My Aralia never thought before she poured her soul out with whatever words she believed would get her point across.

"What's wrong? Are you feeling ill? Homesick? I'm going to send a message to Voreios to see if we can find a way for you to talk with your sister." *Why is your expression so sad? It wasn't like that yesterday.*

"No. I mean, that sounds wonderful. Perhaps you can just take that message back with you."

"I'm not going back to Voreios until you are well enough to travel," I told her firmly. I wouldn't leave her exposed to things that terrified her again, which is why I went to every single one of those stupid dinners.

"I think that you should. I'm rooted here now, so there shouldn't be any more surprises. Why delay the inevitable?"

"I'm not sure what you are trying to say." She didn't fight against my touch as I wrapped an arm around her waist, but her eyes wouldn't meet mine any longer.

"I'm telling you to go home."

"Aralia . . ." I groaned as I realized she'd reverted back to her original thought pattern. We'd made such progress. I'd planned to tell her how I felt the night at the faun's party, but then after we'd been interrupted, she'd been inseparable from me. I assumed she knew. Now we were back to this.

"Rux. Go home. Start your new life. I don't need you here any longer. I haven't needed you to follow me for decades. I'm not going to be a vasilissa, and I haven't been a true contessa since the day I emerged. I do not need a ryne." Her green eyes fought with tears as these words came, but were they for me or for what she had lost in the last few weeks? "Think about what's best for Voreios."

"I'm not leaving you here alone."

She wiped frustratedly at the tears that fell then. "Let me put it this way then. I will never go back to grove life, and you don't belong here. I don't want you here. If you care at all about me, then you will leave me alone and never look back."

"What did he say to you?" I growled as she pulled out of my arms. I hated the tone I'd used, but I was having to fight against the fury. Everything had changed last night after they danced.

"He didn't say anything. He shouldn't have to. You delivered me here safely, made sure I properly rooted, and trained the guards to keep me safe. Your role here is done." She listed off each of these items on her little fingers.

My hands shook. I wanted to hold her, to beg her to reconsider what she was asking for. But even with the tears streaming down her face, I saw the determination in her expression. I could always tell when she tried to play games with me or responded from irrational emotion. There wasn't any hint of that now. She truly didn't want me to be anywhere near her.

"Can we talk about it?" I tried one last attempt.

"I'd rather not. I think we have said everything that needs to be said." Aralia turned from me to return to her tree.

"What if I don't want to go?" I really couldn't let her go without trying everything.

She let out a muffled sob but refused to turn around. "Do you care about me, Rux?"

"Of course, I do."

"Then please go home. I can't see you ever again."

There are so many words that I haven't said to you, and now I will never get a chance to.

"As you wish." That was the only reply I could think of. Had a ryne ever fucked up as egregiously as I had? Not even Rhiap and Lilise's relationship had ended this poorly. I'd have to talk to the grounds keeper to make sure he had the right information to take care of her, but then I would leave the court. Could I even go home? I guess I would have to go to update them on my failure.

"Oh, Rux," she said as I walked in the opposite direction.

Maybe a little too eagerly, I turned, hoping she'd changed her mind. But when a few more rapid tears fell from her eyes, I knew that wasn't it.

"Thank you for protecting me while I grew up. I know you saved my life more than a handful of times, all while I continued to behave like a brat. You were a finer ryne than I could have ever hoped for."

All I could do was nod as words failed me. I'd thought we had turned a corner, that she could see what she really meant to me. Even as she tried to comfort me with the words that she thought would ease my distress, she couldn't even begin to understand the true pain. In the end, this was still my fault. I knew it. I was the coward who had not told her how I felt, and now she was closing that door.

Lia, I would give you my life even as my heart bled out for you.

Don't tell me to go. Let me stay by your side forever.

Chapter 25 — Aralia

I couldn't feel the world beyond the gardens here in the Feylands like I could back in Voreios, but I felt every step that Rux took after I told him to leave. One day, he'd look back on this and know that I'd done it for him. As he held his children and loved his mate, he'd see that I was right. That this was the best decision we could have made.

I just hadn't expected it to hurt as much as it did. He'd been my anchor even when I refused to admit it. The feelings blooming in my heart would only become the weapon that I used on myself, knowing that this couldn't be anything more. I'd done this, and it wasn't as if I could ask him to pick me now. Eighty years of pushing him away, only to beg for him to still have some piece of hope for us? No. That chance was dead, and he deserved better.

To heal I needed to put all of Voreios behind me. I knew the truth, though. I wasn't here to get better, even the Feylands couldn't save me. The dark patches across my skin and my tree grew every day, no matter how many times the scientist came to add new soil meant to aid my recovery. Everyone told me I was getting better, and I went along with it. This illness went far further than Ferox or the fae could see. The very magic that ran through my veins was going to shred me to pieces.

I held my breath, struggling with the part of me that hoped he would come back to fight one more time. He never listened to me, why would he start now? As he hesitated at the edge of the garden on the bridge that would exit the seelie court, I knew I would crack and tell him not to go. That for the first time in our relationship, I would tell him I was sorry for everything I had ever put him through.

But then Rux didn't turn around and he was gone.

And just like that, my whole world had changed. If I somehow survived this illness, I would rise or fail in this new life on my own. I sat along the base of my own tree and let a few more tears fall while I had the privacy of the garden to myself. My throat burned before I chided myself for getting overly emotional. I covered the cough that came next with my hand, but I couldn't stop coughing. When I pulled my hand back, more blood coated my skin.

This new part of my story might be the shortest chapter, but I could still walk with dignity until my number was called.

Hours passed as I cried silently in my tree, ignoring everyone who came by to see me. Prinna shot a curious glance my way, as if she could hear my sniffles buried under the layers of the trees screaming outside the garden, but she didn't care and soon left me alone. Perhaps heartbreak was why they spoke

261

the way they did too. They never really would explain why they did it when I asked. Maybe they'd just been screaming for so long that they didn't know how to do anything different.

Ferox had told me to look around for the support network I had here. My mind had only gone to Rux, but as I thought about what he said again, another very important group of people came to mind. New determination filled me, and in a moment, I'd manifested into my spirit form.

My bare feet slid across the soil, picking up on the movement in the gardens.

The guard on the bridge eyed me warily as most of them did when I moved around the court without Rux. I wasn't like the other women here, and I was okay with that, but they didn't know what to do with me.

"I am going to see Macendil," I advised him politely as I stepped off the bridge onto the main Feylands.

He tried to step into my path and block my way. Even though his expression was apologetic, he kept his voice firm. "Members of the court are not permitted to leave the grounds at this time."

"Look, Aodh, right?" I asked and waited for him to nod before I continued. "I wasn't really asking. I was giving you the courtesy of letting you know in case someone asks. I want to see the dru."

With a wave, I continued on my journey, and my vines knocked his hands away from touching my arm. As soon as I crossed the threshold of the court grounds, my roots sang again with the knowledge of the Feylands beyond. The trees whispered about the cold that had settled and the snow coming as we approached the winter solstice.

Voreios would be preparing for the annual gathering. Would they tell the others about me? Could I hope to have some visitors from Anatoli? I'd not missed a ritual since I'd matured, one of the small rules I'd always broken. I would have memorized every little detail if I had known it was going to be my last.

My roots immediately located Macendil in the land before me. I took off in a sprint toward him. The roots also pointed out all the other dru and their relative proximity. One of the elder dru had passed away recently; their numbers continued to decline. It always made us sad when they would leave for the great energy.

"Little tree," Macendil greeted me as soon as I came into view. The dru were tree folk like dryads were, but unlike us, they did not manifest into spirit forms. Instead, they appeared as thick oak trees that rooted firmly into the ground. The hollows of their mouths and eyes pierced into the darkness of the ether. The small bell chime rang in the wind as he summoned the magic my mother had gifted him.

"Macendil," I called as I jogged the remainder of the way. They moved much slower than dryads did, but many of the dru would skirt the border with Voreios and Anatoli to connect with the magic found there every few decades. "I've come to join you in the Feylands. Isn't that wonderful?"

"Little seedling is in danger in these lands."

"I'm not a seedling any longer," I reminded him as I had to do every time he saw any of the dryads from Voreios. "Sadly, I'm in danger no matter where I go now. I cannot go home."

He didn't say anything for a moment, but as I felt his roots brush mine, an understanding settled in his connection. He could tell what I hid from all of them. "Haven't seen this in many years."

"You've seen this before? Ferox said it hadn't been seen since before his era. I won't make you sick, will I?" That could derail all of my new plans, but I would never risk them no matter what it would cost me.

"Only impact your species."

"My tree is in the court now, but I'm trying to get Lorsan to approve moving my tree out here. Maybe I can move in with you all. We could become a grove together." I had family here, I just needed to look beyond my immediate surroundings. The dru often came to play with us all as children, and I had many fond memories with the old trees.

"A new grove." He sounded almost thoughtful at that. "These lands would welcome you, but there are shadows that run in the night."

"Shadows? But isn't the old god dead? I think you are telling me scary stories again." I laughed as I sat against his roots like we would all do in years past. "You know I used to not sleep for days after you would come visit us."

"Fond memories. Little seedlings grow so quickly." He sighed in the way that an ancient tree who had seen too much and was exhausted would do. "These are not stories. They hunt peculiar things."

My skin chilled with what his warning could mean, but it would be best not to assume. "Like what?"

"Mostly selkies. Alone, you would be a target too. You carry a power not seen in the days of this place."

"I wouldn't be alone. I'd have you. What do you mean about my power? My mom has this magic." I knew they were old, but they couldn't have forgotten about her already. My fathers both always said that trees remember everything.

"Not the same," he replied immediately, and through our root sync sent me images of a world that didn't look like this one. "Once upon a time, elemental magic did not run across the lands the way it does now in the groves."

The group of women I looked upon in the images he sent through the roots were dryads. I could tell that they were, but they didn't look like our kind does now. There weren't lines all over their skin like mine or my sisters', they had more leaves in their hair. Their eyes were wild like a beast, and in an instant, they could blend into the surrounding forest.

"They did not move the world freely as you do. Only a few feet from their roots."

Now I had a lot more questions. Was it the lines on our skin here that allowed us to travel the way that we did or something more? Where could I find these women?

"Look," he encouraged as the vision continued to move and the woman closest to me lit up her hands. White magic glowed out to encompass her entire being. Like the magic I had seen since I was a little girl coming from the well in my heart. The ground began to grow and flower from the snowy coverings.

"What magic is she using?" I asked with a hushed breath, but my heart already knew.

"Fey magic," he replied, and I gasped audibly when all the other women joined her, and their magic poured out onto the field like mine. I wasn't a weird anomaly after all.

Dryads with fey magic were a thing of the past, and now they might be the only way to unlock my future.

I headed straight into the library after I'd returned from my conversation with Macendil. Of course, Trevan found me as I crossed back over the bridge. I twisted sideways to avoid him grabbing my arm.

"Where have you been?"

"I went for a stroll in the forest. Is there a problem?" I gave him a shrug as if it wasn't any big deal.

"I gave you explicit orders," he spat at me with a hole searing into my back from his gaze, and I felt the breeze warning me of his fingers coming closer to my skin.

The vines in my hair pushed his hand away before any touch was completed. "I am going to have to insist that you do not touch me as though we are familiar. We are not, and I have not given you any consent. I am a dryad. I need connection with the ground, and as you have the court entirely isolated from the world around it, I will need to occasionally be out for a walk. I am more than capable of protecting myself. His Majesty has asked me to advise him on the groves and nymph culture, so please have him discuss this with me if he does not feel it is necessary. Otherwise, do not lecture me. Thank you."

"Where is your sense of gratitude for the fact that we have opened our home to you, endangering our safety."

I wanted to laugh out loud. Did he actually think that the one tonic they gave my roots cured me? Perhaps they did because I glamoured away all the other signs, but the arrogance was unnerving. "Did you have something else that you were looking for, or are you just meaning to bully the newest member of the court?"

"I have my eyes on you. Anything suspicious and you will be dragged before the rest of the council." He stared down at me, willing for me to fight back. When I said nothing to him, Trevan shifted topics. "The king has requested your presence in his chambers."

Not this again. "Tell him that I politely decline. He may join me in the library if he wishes to speak with me."

"You . . . what?" For once, he was stunned into silence. Goddess, it was a beautiful moment.

I batted my eyelashes at Trevan and turned back to continue my journey into the library. With Rux gone, I had no desire to go to the garden, and I knew exactly what Lorsan wanted in his chambers, so instead I would stay right here. Out in the public eye where I couldn't get into any more trouble for the time being.

It didn't take long before the sensation of that familiar gaze sent shivers up my skin while I pulled a few books off the shelf. I involuntarily coughed a few times. Summoning leaves, I cleaned up my hand to remove the blood and wiped the corner of my mouth to make sure that I looked presentable.

"Aralia?" Lorsan dropped his voice to match the space that we stood in. I loved the way he said my name. I just couldn't help it.

"King Lorsan." I gave him my best smile as I turned with a handful of books in my arms.

"I told you to call me Lorsan. Why will you not come to my chambers?" he asked, going straight to the point. He really didn't seem like the kind to waste time if he could avoid it.

"I believe we discussed that last night, and I was quite clear on my position. I have come across some wonderful new information though, and I think it could be helpful in bridging the gap between your people and mine." I lifted the books a little bit to show him what I referred to, but he only frowned at me.

"Did you really go to visit Macendil?"

"Yes," I replied as I set the books down on the table, trying to hide from the intensity that I found in his gaze. "The dru have always been part of my life. They each made trips to see us every few years. Macendil gave me some glimpses into the past, and I know it has to be a key of some kind. I can't imagine the things they must share with you. Each time I talk to them, I feel like I've gone through root shock."

I'd hoped my attempt to be casual would ease that frown, but Lorsan only shook his head. His light hair framed his face perfectly, and I had to fight against all of my instincts in order to push down my glamour call. Being near him, my entire body vibrated with the need to be closer.

"Have you been crying?" He strode closer and rubbed his thumb across my cheek. The touch startled me from my thoughts, I'd not heard him move at all.

Yes, I felt as if I had ripped out my own heart and smashed it into the floor, but it was my fault for getting involved with men who had other destinies. "I asked Rux to go home after I thought about what you said. I feel like I've lost my last link to Voreios and my sister. I will be okay though. It is for the best."

Was I telling him or trying to convince myself? I couldn't be sure. The reality that he wasn't with me anymore hadn't fully set in. Tomorrow morning, when he didn't come to check on me first thing like he had for a century . . . Well, I wasn't ready for that experience.

"Ah." Lorsan faltered. "I bet you do miss Nylisa. I've heard twins have a bond that is stronger than even mate connections in the groves."

I did miss my sister but leaving kept her safe. This was the king of the fae. I couldn't show any weakness in even simple conversations, or it could impact later negotiations. Every word always mattered. "We were very close, but it's time I let her lead. She's amazing for Voreios."

"I know that the seelie court and Voreios have a history that is rocky at best, but with you here now, perhaps that can change. Once you are adjusted, we can see how you feel about being our ambassador."

So many things weren't being said between us. I wasn't used to having to monitor everything that I said, and he only knew how to do that.

"I don't think that's a good idea." My mind went immediately to Rux. He and Veon had also grown close, and once he arrived back in the grove, he'd likely end up being Veon's second-in-command officially. I'd have to see him all the time. I wanted him to have all the best things in life, but that didn't mean I wanted to watch him any more with Rhenei.

"That's okay. I'd love to talk with you privately about something much more advantageous, but I need to be away from being overheard."

And just like that, my guard went back up. "Your Majesty, I cannot have any further engagements with you. You should be courting your queens. I hear how the court whispers about the timing of my arrival."

"I don't care what they say. Every day with you here makes me wish that I'd visited you in Voreios, that I'd tried harder to acquaint myself with who you became." His golden eyes were full of heat, but something else I couldn't quite place. It wasn't the soft affection I'd seen in Rux. More like an intense focus that I'd be unable to deter.

"You don't know me, Lorsan. Prinna mentioned that I may be an exotic distraction. Now, unless you would like to read up on nymphs before the great migration, I really must get to work. I'd like to be a good advisor to you and your queen, and I can't do that if I don't have the right information."

"Your glamour call tells me that you want this."

I blushed at the way he called out my evident attraction, but when I tried to turn away again, he snatched my wrist.

"Aralia, you will drive me to madness. Why are you fighting against what this could be?" His gravelly plea did things to my insides I would not admit.

"Do you understand what you are asking from me?" I whispered in disbelief that this continued to happen with him regardless of how the last time went. I just couldn't turn off my glamour when he was so close. "Nothing good can come from this."

"You haven't heard my plan yet." He sounded so sure, so confident.

I pursed my lips into a tight line as he leaned in closer.

"One meeting. I will not touch you if you do not want me to, though I will say that I have thought of nothing else in weeks."

"Fine, I will come to your meeting. I have a few conditions though."

Lorsan stroked my cheek again with the back of his fingers. "Anything."

"One. You will allow me to use a fey ring straight to you so no one will see me enter or exit. Two. You will give me two days before this meeting occurs and two after to consider your terms and the situation. Three. I will not be stalked by your cousin around the grounds, and if I decide to leave the court to see the dru, then I am allowed to do it without fear of retribution." I counted off each item on my right hand, and he watched me closely.

"You negotiate like the fae." Lorsan hummed as if he were impressed. "If I may counter?" He paused, twisting a piece of my hair in his fingers waiting for a response from me.

"Okay, I'm listening," I conceded. There was something enjoyable about discussing terms this way.

"First. During our meeting, you will actually consider what I am proposing and not interrupt me while I explain my idea." He paused again here to make sure I was agreeable to that. This point seemed to matter to him, and I knew that I could be quite stubborn once I'd decided on a matter. When I nodded, he continued, "Second. If you leave the court to see Macendil or any of the others, then you will advise me by note with an approximate return time into said fey ring straight to my room."

"I can see this might be problematic if I am entering your rooms every time I wish to leave the grounds."

"I'm inclined to not let you leave my rooms ever."

273

"Well, that's just not practical. I am a tree, and you are about to have a queen," I snarked, but before I could protest again, his lips pressed against mine. Softer than our first kisses, but still containing that undercurrent of hunger.

He couldn't seriously be doing this in the public library. But as my fingers curled into his shirt, he chuckled and pulled back. "You have two days. When you wake up in the morning, come to me and we will discuss my plan."

"What time do you wake up?" I asked him quietly as he stepped away.

"I doubt I will be sleeping in anticipation of your arrival."

"Don't say things like that," I protested without any true fight in my words, but he only gave me an amused shrug.

"See you at dinner tonight, Aralia."

Chapter 26 — Aralia

After what was a fairly typical dinner, I wandered back to my tree. Lorsan had been respectful of my wishes to have two days. He danced with the queens he should have been courting and kept his heated glances to a minimum. I didn't know if I was grateful or confused at the way he could play a part in front of a crowd.

The dark room across the way glared at me with accusations. Taking a few steps to the empty room, I pushed open the door with my knuckles. Everything was left exactly as it had been when he'd left me yesterday. I could still feel his warmth, smell his familiar scent. The tiny room had barely contained the bulky satyr, and yet I always had known there was just enough space for me here too. I didn't know how he did that.

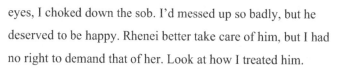

Tears collected at the corner of my eyes as I lay down in his bed, in the indent he'd left. So much larger than me. As the water leaked from my eyes, I choked down the sob. I'd messed up so badly, but he deserved to be happy. Rhenei better take care of him, but I had no right to demand that of her. Look at how I treated him.

With Rux gone, I didn't hold back any of the coughing. I didn't have to. No one was watching me in here, and the longer

275

I held it back, the more it burned my throat. How bad was this going to get before the end? I should have asked Macendil more about it, but when he showed me the women, I just thought maybe, somehow, I could figure out a way to save myself with my magic. I might not have the time though. Should I just try to enjoy whatever this was with Lorsan to pass the last of my days? I'd be out of his new queen's hair in no time anyway.

"You always knew what to do." I spoke out loud to the energy in the room. I could feel his arm around me as I settled into his blankets. Maybe for tonight, I could just pretend he was still here.

A charge ran through the magic of the lands as my eyelids fluttered shut, almost too heavy to stay open another moment longer. The screaming of the trees beyond fell eerily silent. That was when the guards to the north began to shout.

With quiet precision, I opened Rux's door and immediately my eyes were drawn to the bright flashes of light across the sky. The court was surrounded on all sides by a moat, so whatever attacked had to be flying, not uncommon for fae. My protector also left a stash of weapons in his room. He would always say that he could never be too prepared.

With a short sword strapped to my waist, daggers in the boots I manifested, and a traditional sword that was lighter in my hand, I charged to get up onto the stone wall. Vines crawled up the structure, encouraged to grow by my nature, so that I could climb up the stone as easily as if I used a ladder. On the top, I could hear the guards' coordinated calls as they fought off the attackers.

The fastest way for me to travel was to tree step, but on this court island, I was the only true tree. I had to settle for running, which I did immediately. My heart skipped a beat when I saw a dark-haired mage land on the back of a scrawny blond fae guard. The young man shouted in terror, his whole body was trembling.

Leaning into my run, I twisted my body so that I could ram the assailant with my shoulder, knocking him off the guard. I followed the mage with confident footwork as I jabbed my blade into his fleshy side.

"Aralia!" the boy behind me called, but I would not be distracted right now.

The mage's dark eyes latched onto me as blood poured down from the corners of his mouth before he spat. "This is the time when nature sleeps."

A haze of magic wrapped around him as he drained what appeared to be life energy into the spell that he'd just cast. I leaped back to get away from the tainted air as it swarmed directly toward me like a pack of furious bees.

"Cirro! Aralia is up here!" the young guard called again as he tossed me out of the way of the magic, his arm disintegrating at the bare touch of the energy.

Oh my god. His flesh was gone. The horror spread down my body as the spell lunged for me again, avoiding the guard entirely. I couldn't move back fast enough before the magic whispered that another mage approached from behind.

Pulling from the well of my magic, I slipped the dagger out of my boot as vines shot me into the air. Using the momentum from my twist, I landed the blade in his throat before he could mutter any spells. Summoning fey magic, I felt the familiar burn in my throat, but I pushed out an imitation of wind magic to direct the swarming charge out back over the moat.

Cirro tossed the body of the mage I'd killed off the edge onto the pathway in the gardens below. The flora turned carnivorous and shredded him to pieces. The faun summoned the bits of magic he could to aid with my efforts to keep the twisting magic away. As he took in the injuries on the other guard, I landed softly beside him.

"I'm going to head into the wilds. I think it's after me," I shouted so that he knew not to follow me. Instead, he grabbed my wrist and shook his head.

"We stick together. We will fight to keep you safe too," Cirro insisted, and he slid me behind him as a mage lunged at us from somewhere in the cloudy skies. Cirro's footwork was perfect as he tore the sword across the mage's throat. "We need to stop that spell!"

"I got it." Anchoring myself into the stonework, I felt my roots grow from the bottom of my feet pulling at the fey magic in the world surrounding us.

My body hummed with the white light from my well. I could feel the other six mages that were farther up the way. I could see the swarm moving in the sky through the magic. Pain burned through my body, but I tugged the magic toward me. It would bend to my will, and if I had control, then they couldn't use it anymore.

"Come to me," I encouraged, my vision going blank as I could only focus on the sensations racing against my skin. I felt light-headed but whole as the Feylands sang. I focused my intention on the spell in the air, polarizing the fragments with a heavy mass that I tugged in on itself, so it fell as a tiny sphere on the ground between us all.

With the mages not able to access their magic as easily, the guards snuffed out their lights. I swayed on my feet, my roots pulling back as exhaustion washed over me. Cirro caught my arm.

"I need to go back to my tree." Those were the last words I said before I passed out.

Chapter 27 — Lorsan

I'd been deep in the lower levels of the court with the contenders when I'd heard the news of another attack on our perimeter. Trevan had insisted that I stay put, to not alarm the potential queens, but my mind was on her. It was always on her now.

Once we'd been given the all clear that the mages had been dispatched, I called Trevan and the commanders to my quarters immediately. That came with a check to make sure her tree was still in my garden. The tension in my chest cleared as I watched her leaves blowing in the chilly winter night beyond.

"What the fuck is happening? Spare no details," I snapped at the five men gathered in my room.

"This was a coordinated attack with a much larger group of mages. We can confirm that they are all fae from the way that they were flying." The faun commander on the far right seemed to be the only one with information, based on the expressions on the other's faces.

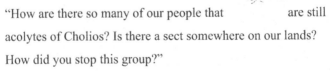

My head ached already, but I leaned back to study each of them. "How are there so many of our people that are still acolytes of Cholios? Is there a sect somewhere on our lands? How did you stop this group?"

I'd turned to look at Trevan because he was their leader, but he gave me a wide-eyed look, indicating that he didn't know the answers. Not a great start.

"Sir, if I may," the faun said, then waited for me to grant him permission to speak. "Aralia took the power from them, allowing us the opportunity to get them under our control. I have reason to suspect that they may be targeting her."

"No one would waste time on a little dryad." Trevan shook his head as if he didn't like the notion. "Her skills with our magic are sporadic at best. The mages have to be targeting us because of the trials."

Though the faun commander didn't seem to agree, he said nothing else. Now I was curious, however. "The selection of a queen can be a problem for those attempting to wield power from the well. I want all of their bodies thoroughly examined by our laboratory. Was Aralia debriefed after the attack about what she saw?" I was bound to give her two days, but if it became a security issue, I could likely find a work-around.

Trevan shrugged at me and took a long drink from a glass I'd not seen him pour.

"Aralia passed out after the attack. I took her back to her tree as she requested, but she remained unresponsive afterward. I will debrief her as soon as she wakes up."

"Fine," I conceded so that I could stay in line with my agreement with her. "I need an update on the selkies. How many have you located?"

"None, Your Majesty. But so far, we have only checked the Feylands." Trevan finally had an answer for me, and it was not one that I liked. "I have to go through the treaty process with Voreios and the merqueen to look for the others."

"Have those requests already been made?"

"Not yet. I'll get to it tomorrow." He didn't look as if this bothered him at all.

"You will do it tonight. You have three days to locate the rest of the living selkies. They will be brought to us here or left in a secure location with the other leaders. Do you understand me?"

"It's rather difficult to locate random women, especially when they don't want to be found right now."

"If you'd been looking for the last month like I asked, this wouldn't be a problem," I snarled quietly and noticed the faun raised his hand. "Did you have something to add?"

"This is the first we are hearing about the selkies. I can spread it around the fey that you are asking for the selkies to seek shelter. Most of them will likely head for Voreios or Dytika so they have a mother tree's protection, but at least we can get a count on them there."

I glared at Trevan again. The fact that his commanders didn't know anything about this infuriated me, but we'd have that fight by ourselves. "Yes, please send the message. The sooner we bring them to safety, the better it is for all of us. I want an update from all of you in three days. Commanders, you are dismissed."

I waited for them to clear the room and the faun commander stood outside in the dark by Aralia's tree, likely checking on her again. I'd have to see her in the morning if she would talk to me early.

"Why were they not aware of the search for the selkies?" I asked him, masking my fury in a bland statement. "This issue with the mages does not seem to be a one off."

"I thought we had discussed keeping this quiet so as to not tip off the mages. I didn't mean to show any aloofness, I just wasn't sure we wanted the fey knowing how bad this situation actually was." Trevan looked thoroughly chastised as he rose to stand by my desk. "It won't happen again."

That did make sense. If the fey knew that Cholios' acolytes were rising to power, we could have some dissention among our ranks. A fey uprising would not be ideal in the middle of the trials and the attacks from the mages.

"I understand your reasoning. Next time run it by me first, that way I don't look like we are not on the same page." I gestured for him to sit again now that the stickiness was out of the way. With a snap of my fingers, the fireplace on the wall roared to life. The warmth lifted the cool night off my skin. "We need to keep the women safe, obviously. I'd like to increase the number of guards around their quarters. Include the two with the highest marks in magical tactics."

"Done. Or you can let them take up my quarters. I'll keep them safe." He smirked at me, begging me to take the bait.

"No. I said no harems. Who is the faun commander? He seemed to be keenly aware of the details from tonight." Careful interest. I couldn't play my hand over my concern about Aralia. At least not until I officially declared her as mine. Then all the restrictions were off.

"That's Cirro. He's been on the guard for about three decades. He's the one who invited Rux and Aralia out to the fire night. I think he's moving in on our guest now that the satyr has gone." Trevan stuck out his tongue in disgust. "He'd be good to place in charge of the queen's defense once she's been selected though. For a faun, he's fairly respectful of women. I think that's why Rux liked him."

Part of me wanted to respond with a tinge of possessiveness, but I was the king and emotions were beneath me to display. I knew he was trying to see if I'd respond. Aralia was beautiful, and with Rux gone, I knew most of the people around her would begin to move in. Soon, it wouldn't matter.

"Cirro. Keep an eye on him, he may be up for a promotion if he continues the good work."

In a few days, I needed to have a team I could trust to protect my little consort, so she'd stop running off to fight mages by herself. I could barely wait. Once she signed the deal, Aralia would never be able to discuss leaving this court ever again.

She would be mine.

Chapter 28 – Rux

I must have wallowed on the edge of Voreios and the Feylands for more than a handful of hours. There had never been a moment where I assumed I'd be returning to Voreios without Aralia.

A sleek dark wolf sat on the edge of the border waiting for me when I finally decided to approach. Arbane shifted back into his usual skin and greeted me with a warm smile.

"I wasn't sure if I was going to have to come get you." The wild elf looked a little shaggy with his growing facial hair. Being a new father seemed to be getting to the alpha of Voreios's pack. "Come and get some food. Zrif is waiting for you in the main grounds."

"How is everything going here?" I asked hesitantly as I followed Arbane's enthusiastic steps.

"I'm sure Veon will want to update you more, but the last few weeks have been rough. Nylisa—" He hesitated and then changed his mind. "I'll let them explain."

I'd been so wrapped up in taking care of Aralia that I'd really not given her twin too much thought. "How is the seedling?"

As a vasilissa, she was often expecting seedlings. Veon and Nylisa had already welcomed seven beautiful daughters to the grove in the last few decades together. Part of me had hoped Aralia's increased feistiness might mean she would be flowering soon. Now that she'd sent me away, that possibility sat like a pit in my stomach.

"Healthy. I think it will be good for you to be able to talk with Nylisa."

Voreios was quick to get snow this time of year, even before the official change of the seasons. The scents of the pine and forest brought me back to my entire life. Yet I couldn't shake the wrong feelings. I'd not ever known another home before, yet this didn't call me back the way it used to.

Every portal we passed, every landmark, only reminded me of her. Her absence rang through the soil. I wouldn't hear her laughing with her twin as I watched her from a distance. With a glance to the mountain, I could see her favorite place to hide from here. I'd never find her there again after we had a fight, practicing her magic when she thought no one else would know. I'd never hear her sing off pitch in her joy as she helped plant the flower seedlings.

How could I ever hope to get over the fact that the only person who mattered in my world would haunt me as a ghost from my past?

"Welcome home, Rux." Zrif's voice called from the main grounds. The fires were being built for the gathering this

287

evening as the satyr expertly moved the snow piles out of the way. Arbane leaned in to kiss his mate before tossing a few of the logs into their place with the kindling. "Ferox gave us a brief update, but how is Aralia's recovery going?"

"Ah . . ." I faltered, looking for the best way to respond. Zrif was the oldest brother of all of the dryads in our grove. Of course, he would go straight to the well-being of his sisters. "They say that she is on the path to recovery, and from our talks, she seems to be feeling better."

"Did the healers have a timeframe on when she would be able to return?" The satyr took a seat to give me his full attention.

"So far, the only information has been that she will not be able to leave the Feylands. The cure won't hold."

Zrif frowned and cast a glance back at Arbane before he responded. "That's troubling news. Nylisa has not been herself since the separation. She's distraught, and with our less-than-ideal relationship with the fae, well, we've feared the worst. How do you feel about being able to open up negotiations between our people? You can bring a message with you when you return to the court."

"That's the thing. I'm here to stay, it seems." When Zrif's eyes narrowed at that response, I got nervous in a way I hadn't been since I was a child. "Aralia has dismissed me from her service."

"Has she found her mates?" Arbane asked, and I took in the posture of the usually quiet wild elf.

"No." I wanted to shout, *I am her mate*, but what good would it do?

"Then I believe Kelan was quite clear on the boundaries put in place to both of you." Even with the druwid gone for almost five years, Zrif and Arbane continued to follow through with his orders. I should have expected this.

"This isn't just a tiff we had. We didn't even fight." I hoped I could articulate the details that I could tell just from the way she'd behaved. They knew her, but not like I did. "She outlined it very clearly and told me that if I cared about her, I would leave and never return. I don't know how to fight against that."

Zrif pinched the bridge of his nose before letting out an exhausted sigh. "I told you this would happen. Did you tell her how you feel about her?"

"No, but after the last few weeks, I thought it was becoming obvious," I confessed, but hearing the words out of my own mouth, I knew I sounded dumb.

"How are you being this dense? It's not that hard to tell someone you love them." Zrif sank back on his hooves against the trees next to them.

"I think you are being too tough." Arbane tossed a knowing look at his mate. "These feelings can be some of the most difficult to articulate. Especially when you aren't sure that you will hear them back. You know that."

289

"Rux."

I instantly recognized the soft voice that called me as the vasilissa's. Nylisa's tanned skin lit up the night around the main grounds as the sun fell silently behind the trees. Nature responded to all nymphs, but the experience was more intense when a mother tree was nearby.

"I thought I felt you come into the grove. Please, I must hear about my sister. You didn't bring her with you. Is she all right? Has the illness faded? I—"

"My star, you must take a breath." Veon consoled her as he appeared from the path behind her. My old friend looked as if he hadn't slept in weeks.

She only nodded at him as she took a few slow breaths before she turned to me with expectant bright green eyes.

"Lia is getting better. She can't leave the Feylands just yet, but she's up and causing trouble as always." I offered my hand for her to take, and as her fingers settled in mine, I gave them a gentle squeeze. "She misses you immensely. There's an unfounded fear she carries that you may feel abandoned by her, but please know that this is not the case. If she could come home, she would."

"Oh, of course I know that." Nylisa's eyes filled with tears, and she rubbed them away quickly. "Why is she not with you? Who is protecting her over there?"

Veon met my gaze and shook his head subtly. We were able to communicate almost as effectively as the twins we watched over from the amount of time we spent together. He wanted me to gauge what I said so it didn't further stress out his mate and her growing seedling.

"I have the entire fey guard watching her for me right now." That part wasn't a lie. I'd asked Cirro to keep an eye on my little dryad, and he swore an oath on his clan to do it. "She needed to check on you and insisted I must go personally. She'd not accept it any other way."

This excuse would only hold for a few days, but that would be enough time for me to talk with Veon. He'd need to be the one to break any unfortunate news to her.

"Are the fae behaving themselves?" Nylisa seemed to be pacified with that answer, and the tension evaporated from the group. "I have no qualms about going over there to straighten Lorsan out if he is mistreating her."

"Aralia is being treated with the utmost care. King Lorsan has asked her to advise him on behalf of the nymphs, and she's been welcomed into the court."

"You are not going anywhere right now regardless of the situation, my love." Veon wrapped his arms around her and rubbed the small curve of her belly. "Let Rux rest for the evening, and then you can grill him again in the morning. All right?"

"I know you are just sending me away so you can drink with your buddy," she chided Veon, who kissed her forehead.

"Fine, I will go see Ov. I know you have missed Rux as much as I have missed Lia."

I waited until she strolled down the path toward the dryad grove before I raised my brow at Veon. "Was she referring to Ovgim?"

"Yeah." He gave me a rueful smile. "She spent so much time on the eastern border after you'd left. Well, seems we have found our newest bond. He's still learning the ropes, so I'm letting him settle in with our seedlings."

I let out an amused huff. "We'd always said that as soon as they separated for a week, they'd likely find their other mates."

Veon nodded his agreement and clapped a hand on my shoulder. "Why are you really here without Aralia?"

"I don't know where I went so wrong, Veon." I took the mead that Zrif offered me and contemplated the bare future in front of me. "Away from the distractions of Voreios, we were . . . connecting. Everything was changing, and then all of a sudden, she told me to go."

"She's told you to go every single day of her life since she turned twenty."

He wasn't wrong about that, and it had never felt great.

"I took that as more of a banter, a challenge. This was different. She wasn't angry or frustrated at me. I've never seen her cry like that, and I couldn't comfort her at all."

"You are in love with her." Veon cut straight to the point before taking a drink for himself.

292

"She's my mate, literally my everything. I don't know what to do." The confession spilled out of me like a searing flame tearing through my throat.

Arbane locked his gaze on Zrif, but I knew what he said next was for me. "You won't find that answer here. Until you've been honest about what you really need to say, the conversation isn't over."

I slept hard that night in a way I hadn't since I left the grove. Part of the perks of having a bond mate, especially when your shared lover was a nymph, was that you had another set of eyes and ears to watch over them. Between the copious amounts of mead, and weeks of not sleeping, I could barely rise the next morning. Lia's tree wasn't safe in the Feylands like it was here behind her sister's barrier. They were right. I couldn't leave her there by herself.

Raised voices echoed down my cavern from just outside the entrance, so I splashed some water on my face quickly before going to make an appearance. It only took a handful of steps to cross into the morning light.

"I'm telling you that Edina should have been home last night. Something happened," Elura said with a furious look on her face to Arbane who looked to be trying to placate her.

Sweet Elura never raised her voice in front of anyone, though Zrif commented a few times that she could be very particular about things in their shared cavern. Even now as she saw me approach, she began to lock inward on herself.

"She may have just decided to stay another day with your cousins. Neither of you leave very often, so they may have been caught up enjoying the company." Arbane tried to soothe her, but she wouldn't have it, the instant refusal displayed in her head shake.

"I'm going to go look for her now. You can either come with me or stay here. I don't care."

There was still a heavy amount of sass in the tone, even if she was being much quieter now.

"Is there something I can help with?" I offered.

Arbane tossed a glance over his shoulder at me as his hands squeezed his tiny mate's arms. "Looks like we are going out to the ocean to search for Edina, would you like to come with?"

Elura frowned but didn't complain out loud. One mission for old time's sake couldn't hurt. How much trouble could it be? "Yeah, I'd be happy to—"

"Rux?"

I tensed as I processed Rhenei's voice before she sprinted to my side.

"I had a feeling you would come back." She offered up a soft smile.

Her touch on my arm brought back the years of rejection when I'd pretended to not have feelings for the mate who wouldn't acknowledge me.

"I've missed you."

"Rhenei." I shifted my body away from her caress.

She picked up on the change in my body language and frowned. "Oh, I see. Well, that sucks."

"I'm sorry." It was the only thing I could think to say. I needed to be a man and take ownership that there would be a second nymph getting hurt because I hadn't been entirely honest.

The nereid blew out a disappointed huff but then gave me a weak smile. "I guess at least she came to her senses. I always thought she was insane for dismissing you so quickly, but you can't tell dryads anything."

"I know your mates are going to cherish you in the way I couldn't." I opened my arms to offer her a friendly hug, which she took. In the groves, it wasn't uncommon for partners to split when they found their mates. She and I had never been true lovers, but that didn't make her feelings any less real. I just had never been able to truly reciprocate them.

"Rux." Arbane tapped me on the shoulder as Rhenei let me go to continue about her day. "Elura's about to charge off on her own. If you are coming, we've got to leave now."

The more I interacted with this triad, the more I realized that the frail selkie seemed to be the one calling the shots.

Arbane was the leader of the wild elf pack and Zrif was a senior adviser to Veon and Nylisa now that they'd taken over, but both of them seemed to have no control over the fey woman.

"Where is Nineve?" I inquired as to their little selkie pup. Elura never let the baby out of her sights.

"Elura took her to Nylisa. She won't trust anyone else. Zrif has been trying to get her to leave Nineve with the river nymphs so we can have some time, but so far that hasn't gone so well." Arbane rubbed his stubbled chin in exhaustion. "If it wasn't Edina missing, I don't think she'd even consider parting from our pup."

I followed along behind Arbane down to the shores of the northern coast. Zrif was guiding a boat along the ocean waves toward a dock they'd recently added. Before I was born, Voreios had been isolated for some time, so there hadn't been a need for such things. Now we were frequently welcoming visitors, and sometimes it was easier for the elves to come over by boat instead of land.

The satyr draped an extra blanket over Elura's shoulders that she promptly shook off as she climbed aboard the tiny vessel. "Sweetheart, you are going to get cold out there. It's already winter here."

"My sister is missing! Something is happening, I tell you. I can feel it like I did the day they attacked us the first time." Then Elura turned to face the ocean, her dark hair blowing in the breeze with her white dress. Her next words were almost lost on the ocean winds in a whisper. "I told them that they should find a mother tree to live under. No one wants to listen to me."

Zrif gestured for the rest of us to jump aboard the boat before he took his place beside the woman. Once out on the water, she put out an echo of a song in a tongue only selkies could understand. Supposedly, it sounded different underwater, but I wasn't about to dunk my head into the ocean to find out.

"Where are we headed first?" I asked Arbane quietly, so I didn't distract Elura.

"The isles. That's where Edina mentioned she was going before she left Voreios." The wild elf frowned at the ocean. "It's oddly quiet today."

I'd never spent much time out here on the water. My elemental magic was earth, and Aralia had fey gifts, so the only water I went around was the fey pool. Honestly, I really didn't enjoy having wet fur, so I could never find the draw, but Arbane didn't have that luxury with a selkie mate and even his satyr lover being gifted with water magic. They spent almost all of their time on the coast.

An explosion on the horizon caught all of our attention. A dark trail of smoke bled into the sky, whether as a warning or a call for help was anyone's guess.

"Go faster," Elura cried at Zrif with clear despair in her face.

Somehow, he pushed the waters to surge at a speed that shouldn't have been possible. The wind itself felt like it would either peel my skin off my face or slice me into tiny shreds from the salty tears of the ocean.

As the isles came into view, the smoke blocked out half of the island. It didn't shield us from the blood-covered sands and the screaming. Elura's furious screech tore across the water in ice shards that punctured through the sky before she dove in the water followed by Zrif before the boat slammed into the wet sands throwing us all into action.

Arbane half shifted to a form with an elongated jaw, fur, and nine-inch claws. He howled to the sky as the winds blew the smoke out of our way to show the fae mages taking measure of our arrival. As soon as my hooves met the earth, I could sense the locations of the bodies along the sand. It appeared there were seven people currently on the isle, most of them clustered together in a small cavern. As I rounded the corner of the cave, I took note of the gray cape blowing in the wind around a dark-haired fae male struggling with a woman whom he tugged by her brunette hair.

"Drop her!" I growled. Shards of earth protruded through the ground to stab at him as I drew my blade. He barely avoided one of the projectiles but twisted just enough that she could pull free. She immediately changed into a seal and waded to hide under the shadows of the earth that I had disturbed.

I bounced off the new stones to gain momentum to slice my blade down at the man, who struggled with which of us to deal with. My blade dragged in a diagonal line across his chest and then through his arm.

Blood hit me as it sputtered from the clean cut before he screamed in delayed pain, his mind catching up with what had just happened. Before I hit the peak of the arc, I twisted my blade around to puncture holes through both of his wings. He fell to the ground with a thud, and I ducked under Zrif's daggers flying above me and straight into the back of another mage.

I kicked over my target with my hoof, and he scrambled to try and get away from me. I pressed my blade into his shoulder, then transformed the sand into stone, trapping my sword and his body in place. Sliding another dagger out from my belt, I leaned closer to him.

"Your god is dead. What is the point of all of this?"

"He will rise again . . . and he's going to slaughter . . . you all." The man tried to sound brave, but he knew what was coming for him. "Once we take over the fae, you won't be able to stop us."

"Lorsan will never let that happen."

"The new fae king will never see it coming." The mage laughed before he popped something into his mouth.

I didn't have time to react before his mouth began to foam and his skin boiled and sizzled over as if he were cooking from the inside out.

Elura stood protectively over her younger sister, Edina, who sat on the sands sobbing over the body of a woman whom we'd clearly been too late to save. Zrif was talking with the remaining sisters and a few merfolk who had been in the fray since before we arrived.

"Please return with us immediately to the grove. It's not safe for you out here right now. Where is the rest of your clan?"

"Some are in the merkingdom, and some are in Dytika," the woman answered shakily.

"We will send out an escort to find the ones in the ocean and bring them to Voreios," the merman insisted and used a few gestures to pass the message along to the dolphins.

"Why are they attacking us?" A younger selkie trembled beside her sister, and my heart broke for them.

"There are rumors that the mages are clearing the isles. You are easy targets, unfortunately. You will be safer inland until we can get this under control." The merman brushed his hands along her cheek with affection, and she threw her arms around him to cry against his chest.

I knew it was more than that, but I'd had the insight from the original incidents after years of serving under Graak and Kelan. Selkies were a crucial part of the rituals associated with the mirror magic needed to enhance the shadow god's power. All the more reason to protect them, but much like nymphs, they needed to come willingly.

Elura's eyes met mine directly for the first time, and I almost shivered from the intensity of it. "I believe you have somewhere else you need to be. If they are coming for us, they will come for her, and you can't do anything about it if you are a thousand miles away."

She was right, of course. I'd never listened when Aralia had told me to go before. I wasn't going to start now. Even if she fully rejected me, I'd protect her until the day I took my final breath.

Chapter 29 — Aralia

I awoke before dawn, but my roots advised me that I had missed a whole solar cycle. The illness seemed to be dramatically slowing my typical recovery time, or it could be the ridiculous amount of fey magic I'd used. Either way, I had better things to do with my limited time than sleep in my tree.

My roots provided me with a quick play-by-play of the events I'd missed, how many people had stopped by to see me, and an update on the weather with the marginal chance of precipitation for the next few days. I needed to find the soil nutrients that Rux had made at some point, or I was going to starve, but that would have to wait for a bit longer.

My stomach twisted into knots as my first item of the day hovered in my thoughts. It was time to meet Lorsan. He'd personally stopped by several times with scientists, healers, and Cirro throughout the day. Without being conscious, I couldn't recall what they had been saying, but the expression on his face hadn't been pleased. Hopefully, he was in a better mood today.

Fey rings were fun things to use. They were pretty inconspicuous to most people, appearing as just a ring of flowers or mushrooms that could be easily masked as something else. Being a dryad, I could actually put this ring straight on my tree, so when I manifested, I would be in the space that I wished to be in. I liked mine to look like little green flowers that were tattooed along my bark.

Pushing my energy against this marking, my spirit form slipped into a dark room that had regal curtains blocking out the slow-rising sun. He must still be asleep. I should come back later. I knew how tiring running a grove was from what Nylisa experienced. The Feylands didn't seem like it would be any easier.

A snap jolted me, and I bumped into his desk as candles flickered to life around the room to reveal him sitting in the center in a massive chair. Lorsan's face was stern, but as he rose to his feet, my eyes swept down his bare chest to the low-riding pants he wore, which hung just above where that defined V came to a close. Oh, my goddess, what had I gotten myself into?

"I was concerned you might not awaken in time for our meeting." His voice was smooth, but a visceral fury sat between us.

"You accepted my terms, so I told you that I would be here." If he was going to play this way, then I could too. He didn't know how truly stubborn I could be.

"That's not what I meant. As a member of my court and my adviser, you should not be out there fighting with the guard! You could have been hurt." His fierce yellow eyes drank me in slowly, but still he kept his distance. "When you didn't wake up yesterday, I didn't know what to do."

Something in his tone cracked my tough exterior. He'd been concerned about me. That's why he'd come to visit so many times.

"I'm sorry to have worried you . . . Lorsan. I just needed rest. Look." I took a little twirl and then held my hands out to him, encouraging him to come closer to me. He didn't move, but the tension in his shoulders settled after I said his name. "I'm perfectly healthy." Okay that was a little white lie, but the incident yesterday didn't have anything to do with the underlying illness. I thought.

"Come here," he commanded, and his eyes scorched me like he didn't believe a word I'd said. I liked the forceful tone, but I'd always been a bit of a brat, and that wouldn't change today.

I took a few steps in his direction, and as soon as I stopped moving forward, his eyes flashed with something akin to annoyance. One of his hands caught my wrist and the other snagged my waist, pulling me until my body pressed against his.

"Hey . . ." I protested, if only to break up the tense silence between us. He didn't seem to be paying attention from the way he scanned my face. I'd forgotten to hide my dryad lines, I realized, as he traced over each one with his gaze.

"I don't know what you have done to me, or even how it is possible, but a day without you is too much. You've become an obsession that I cannot shake. I think about you constantly." He kissed the inside of my wrist, and if he'd just turn in my direction, our lips would meet instead. "I see why kings used to lock certain women away."

"That's not why you wanted to talk to me, is it?" I said hopefully even as my breath hitched with his next kiss against my skin.

"No, but I can't promise it won't come to that if you keep putting yourself in danger."

My body instantly stiffened at the thought. Being in the court garden surrounded by this moat was difficult enough. How much more isolated could I become? Perhaps I should have thought about this a little harder before playing these games with the king. "I will not be locked up, by you or anyone."

I hoped I sounded convincing to him. His proximity made my brain fuzzy, but I would not spend my time trapped.

Lorsan let out an agitated breath and regrettably released me. The absence of his warmth played its own game on my mind. He took a glass of something he had on the desk and paced for a moment before he looked at me again.

"This is harder than I thought it would be."

"What is?"

"Rationally outlining my plans to you. I've had this conversation over and over again in my head, and I'm still not sure where to start." He gestured to a seat across from his. I sank into the rather large chair, enjoying the plush cushions. "I have refused to take a harem. I haven't wanted one. But it was my intent originally to make the queen my mate. My father didn't do that with my mother, though he should have. No, instead he was promised an elven princess, made Calla his consort, and then was driven to the brink of insanity by a dryad. He killed my mother in his madness, and as such I had decided that I would never take a consort on that principle alone."

When I opened my mouth to comment about the shared history of our parents, he shook his finger at me.

"You agreed to listen. Those were my terms."

I frowned at him but didn't follow through with my thoughts. If he was comparing us to the past, I would have to wait to disillusion him from those errant connections. My mother and I weren't in the same league, and she had already been bonded to her mates. Not even a fae king could have overridden her destiny.

"In order to maintain the balance of the fae kingdom and the fey magic, I must produce a fae heir. I have to take a fae queen as the law decrees or this world will fall apart.

But I do not want them. I haven't ever wanted them or to be part of this tradition. Your arrival has thrown everything on its head and forced me to face the reality that I cannot mate the fae queen." He paused as the words settled between us. A new tension filled the silence that we shared that spread goosebumps of need over my skin. "I cannot be without you. So here is my proposal, be my consort. I will publicly declare you as mine, no one in this kingdom will touch you. Everything that is mine will be available to you."

My jaw dropped before I could pull my features back into calm composure. I'd not expected that offer. Maybe I should have, but I had to think carefully over every word.

"I cannot be with you if you take another as your queen." I shook my head, all of my loose curls bouncing around my face.

"She will be queen in title only. I will do what I have to do in order to produce a son, and then she will be set aside." Lorsan strode to my chair and sank to his knees beside me, gazing up. I wasn't oblivious to the message he was sending by allowing me to look down upon him with that raw persuasion in his voice. "There would be no connection between her and me. Only duty. Aralia, I wish with everything I am that you were born fae, but you were not. This is a work-around. Perhaps the only one."

"If we do this, then neither of us can find our mates." I tried to sound reasonable. Of course, I'd always had a crush on him, but was that worth sacrificing my dreams of perfect matches? As the illness scratched up my throat before I could glamour it away, I realized that I might not have the chance to find mates anyway. A little piece of my heart felt crushed by this new realization.

The way he tilted his head to the side as if he was amused by my statement caught my attention again. "You won't find mates here. Mates are not really a thing in the fae culture. Never have been. It's more for show than anything else."

"You said you would take your queen for your mate. I heard it in front of everyone. Now you are just changing your mind? If it's not really a thing here, then why bother?"

"The original plan was to do it for a show of unification that hasn't happened in many generations of fae kings. Then I met you. I can't have a mate and also have a consort who isn't. It defeats the purpose of the whole show." Lorsan watched me closely as if he wanted to make sure I was understanding the explanation. "I cannot abide by anything that removes the option for something more permanent between us."

When I shifted to sit up straight in front of him, separating my knees to lean closer to where he knelt on the floor, I increased my glamour and heat danced in his eyes. For me. His dark wings unfolded behind him, and his skin took on the glow that made me weak. There was something intoxicating about having a reciprocated glamour call.

Because only nymphs had this gift in Voreios, I'd never seen the magic that unfolded when there were two going.

"I'll ask you again, be my consort. I don't do this lightly but give me your terms."

Lorsan waited patiently, not pushing me for an immediate response.

There was a problem that I hadn't fully considered when I'd sent Rux home: I was going to need to feed. At least, until the illness made it so that I'd not be able to leave my tree. The last thing I wanted was to get so hungry that I lost all sense of boundaries in a kingdom that revolved around word play and actions. Could I play this game with him? Even if just for a few weeks to buy myself some more time?

"I won't pretend I haven't wanted you. I can't even try to lie about it. Now seeing you look at me this way, I want nothing more than to give in to your request and see where it goes."

Lorsan slid his hands up the outside of my thighs, rising on his knees to graze his lips against mine. My chest tightened with the need to taste him and experience everything this slight touch promised. It would kill me to outline the rest of my counter, but I needed to make my own proposal, or he would take this as my acceptance.

"However, if this is just a fanciful obsession on our parts, it could derail a lot of well-thought-out, important phases for your kingdom. So, while I still have clarity, I'd like to present a new option."

"Aralia, I don't—"

"Hear me, Lorsan, please," I purred as I placed a finger to his lips. To have the power to silence a king sent a thrill through my body. "Have me. As often as you want until the day the queen is selected. Let's ride this wave out, and then I will step back to allow you to meet your destiny. That way I'm not putting aside a poor woman who should be your mate, and you won't feel as though you missed out on what is here."

"A few weeks will not be enough," he protested even as he slid me toward the edge of the seat.

"Let's just see. Can you agree to these terms?"

When dealing with the fae, I needed to hear his confirmation to seal any contract. His powerful wings fluttered while the tips of his fingers caressed my legs. I could see the decision warring in his eyes. I'd circumvented his plan, but our glamour calls sang to one another. A simple agreement would dissolve this last barrier between us in a temporary truce. He knew he asked for what I couldn't give him. It didn't matter that the fae didn't believe in mates, I did.

"For now."

I fell into his lap and his lips crashed into mine. I kissed him like he was the air that I needed to survive. For a few weeks I could pretend he was mine, in the way I had with Rux before I sent him back to his true calling. Lorsan

lifted me up and carried me over to his bed as banging rang
from his door.

"King Lorsan." It was his cousin. "It's time to wake up. We
have protocols to discuss with the wild hunt coming up."

Lorsan waved his hand and the door vanished.

I guess that's one way to send a message.

Chapter 30 — Aralia

"I'm not having this conversation again. We already came to an agreement on your compensation," Lorsan replied, not bothering to mask his irritation. The large arched windows along the back wall gave the fae king an ethereal glow that was blinding.

"Yes, but those terms came from before the contenders were present. We are having to work harder in the evenings now. New negotiations are needed to keep us happy, or we will all leave." Tuimac wagged his finger.

It was my first meeting as an official adviser to the king and his council, and I'd already learned an awful lot. The fae had contracts for everything down to the food that the court animals would eat. I couldn't help but compare the situation to the only one I knew: Voreios. Grove life was a foreign language out here. It seemed as though all my training on the efficiency of running a kingdom would be absolutely pointless. So far, I'd not even been able to get a word in anyway.

A fae adviser who I wasn't familiar with tapped me on the shoulder to show me a sketch he'd made of the broonie currently talking, and I politely covered my mouth not to laugh aloud as his amateur work clearly intended to mock the poor man. Being the only woman in the room, I drew a lot of looks as they tried to figure out what angle the king was taking with my presence here.

I'd made Lorsan swear to not tell a soul about our temporary contract, and for the past few days, he'd been quiet about it. He hadn't been willing to make a contract on that particular point, so it would still be at his discretion, but the fae liked secrets almost as much as they liked shiny things, so I felt relatively safe.

"Most of the women will not be staying in the court after the trial is complete. What would you consider fair trade for these few extra days of work?" Lorsan leaned back in his chair, keeping his eyes level on the adviser. Even dressed, I could often catch glimpses of his muscled chest, and I ogled him secretly every chance I could.

"It's hardly a few extra days. We could start with five hundred apples with seventeen additional cream dispensaries for the remainder of the time they are present."

Broonies haggled in food items from what I gathered at this meeting. Tuimac had mentioned fruit and sweets mostly, and from the stern look on my lover's face, he didn't like these terms.

"Two hundred and the cream will be available every three days only until the winter solstice." Lorsan's terms were very specific, as with the fae you had to be. He was definitely a

313

master negotiator, which made me proud of myself for the contract I'd worked up between us.

"Aralia," the fae man on my right whispered, and he waited for me to acknowledge him before he continued. "Would you like to go see my kelpie pond after this meeting? I've got quite a variety of new steeds that are marvelous to watch."

"Ah." I smiled at him politely but didn't know what to say. Kelpies weren't exactly the magical equivalent to the unicorns I'd grown up with. They could transform their hind legs into a tail and had rows of gruesome teeth in their mouths.

"Your father was the elf druwid, correct? I even have a bottle of elven wine I can open for us. I'd been looking for an opportunity to try it out." He seemed to only be half waiting for a response from me.

Subconsciously, I checked my glamour to make sure I'd reduced my ears to a more appropriate size for the fey, but I kept my face neutral. In the groves, we didn't bother with who was my exact father, because it had never mattered. While odds were that Kelan was indeed where I got my genes from, Graak was just as much my father as he was. Parentage mattered a lot more to the fey cultures.

"I appreciate the offer, but—"

"Any attempts to court Aralia will need to be run by me first," Lorsan interrupted, drawing our attention back to him. There was fury in his gaze, and the man beside me straightened his back and nodded his understanding. "I will stress this to all

314

of you: she is our guest and the twin sister of a neighboring vasilissa. The protocols that apply to my sister are the ones we will use for Aralia. Do you all understand?"

Sister? I didn't know that Lorsan even had a sister. I knew he likely had a few half sisters and brothers sired by Helio, but how had I never heard about this before in all of our lessons about the other leaders? I quirked my eyebrow at him to let Lorsan know that I knew exactly what he was doing. Technically, while we were seeing each other I'd planned to stay off the hunt for my mates, but he was laying the groundwork to have all the others avoid me entirely.

"Great, now that the rest of those items are out of the way. Aralia, let's discuss your first impressions and what we could do to enhance nymph relocation."

The entire room shifted to me, and I wanted to slide down my seat to hide under the table. I managed to keep myself firmly planted in my chair somehow and cleared my throat. "Well, first, thank you all for welcoming me. It's only been a few weeks, and I think that there will be a lot of changes with the new queen settling in place, but once she's ready, I think we should invite Celeste and her druwids back to the court. Anatoli would be the easiest grove to arrange more frequent meetings with."

"Yes, the queen will likely have opinions on how to arrange the gathering. We'll circle back to that after the solstice," Lorsan agreed, but his face looked unmoved about the prospect of having his queen's opinion. I'd thought that part of his initial discussion on the proposal had been overblown, but he continued to give me this exact look when I broached the subject. "What about your impressions? Any thoughts as to why they wouldn't want to relocate here currently?"

This was a double-edged sword. If I lied, then I wouldn't be behaving as an effective adviser. If I were truthful, I risked offending everyone. I was also dying, so I was going to go for it. "Everything here is beautiful, deadly, and full of misdirection. I'm not sure exactly what to be watching out for, whether it's the dangers of the monsters and mages outside the walls or the smiles inside."

The fae king merely looked amused, and he waited for me to continue. The tension grew in the room from the others around me as I guessed people weren't used to running the risk of angering the king.

"Let's think about this from another angle. Your people who have left as a result of the mate bond with nymphs left for a reason. I believe that it has to do with perception. Outside of the mother trees' barriers, we don't feel as though we could be safe, including when we travel through the Feylands." The room was silent enough that I could almost hear the conversations in a hall beyond. I'd never commanded this much attention before, and it was thrilling. "I have wandered these forests by myself a few times since Rux has left, and while I felt more secure with him beside me, I do not fear these lands anymore."

"There are dangerous things that do lurk in those woods," Tuimac said warily as if caught up in his own notions.

"The world is a dangerous place, but it's the narrative we have to change. And there are some elements of culture that may need some reconsideration."

"What do you mean by that?" Trevan raised his voice and slammed his fist on the table. If I'd not seen his movement in my peripheral view I would have been startled, which I believed was his exact intention. "Who do you think you are to talk about a culture you've barely scratched the surface of?"

"I'm answering the question I have been asked." I kept my voice down and tried to keep any expression off my face as I smoothed my dress on my lap. "Nymphs are nearly one hundred percent female with very few exceptions. The Feylands do not have a great reputation inside Voreios for how women are treated, and while I have had a good experience, it's not enough to change the perception. Time and dedication to the work would need to be put in to change the conversation."

Lorsan raised his hand to keep Trevan from responding. "Is it just your sister's barrier that makes your kind feel safe?"

I couldn't help the frown that came across my face, because the answer would likely genuinely upset him. "No. I grew up surrounded by a community that I knew would protect me and my other form with everything they had. I did my best to make sure that I could defend myself, but I could be whatever version of myself, and they had my back. Even on the craziest, sex-

317

charged party nights, I knew I was safe no matter what. I knew that they respected me enough to hear a 'no' if I gave one."

"You don't think we have that here?" Trevan asked incredulously and tossed a pointed glance at the king, whom I couldn't look at anymore.

"My initial perception is that this is not the way it is in the wilds, but it's too early for my own experience to inform my decision. I have already been advised that I should find a match to 'keep' me on more than one occasion, however, and that does come with its own implications."

Ambassadors cleared the room quickly when the king dismissed us, and yet I stalled in my chair as I felt Lorsan's magic brush mine in his intimate gesture. The only way he could touch me secretly while we were outside of his chambers. When the final door shut, he was at my side, pulling me to my feet.

"Let me escort you to the library." Lorsan hesitated before adjusting a piece of my hair behind my ear. "That is where you are going now, correct?"

"We really shouldn't be seen together," I pressed, but he leaned in to take an inhale of my glamour which raged immediately at his proximity.

"The advisers believe I am going to treat you as my sister, so it should be fine." His eyes danced with playful amusement. "You were more honest than I expected you to be in a room full of critics."

"You asked for an adviser. I intend to do my job to the best of my ability. Even if I get into trouble with the king." Everyone was going to figure out exactly what was going on if I couldn't keep my attraction for him under control. "I didn't even know you had a sister. I hope you don't behave the same way with her as you do with me."

Lorsan laughed against my neck. "Definitely not. I thought I was going to lose my mind seeing you smile at them so freely. I'm going to fuck you until you submit for each smile I counted earlier. You are absolutely in trouble."

"That won't leave any room for sleep tonight then. A smile can also be appropriate for just saying hello. But I will have to find my mates eventually, and I can't do that if you are scaring off any potential lovers." I put a tiny pout in my voice, and his finger rubbed gently over my bottom lip.

"I could just have them executed."

For a moment, I was taken aback by the subtle ferocity layered in his voice. "You will not do anything of the sort."

"I think you forget that I'm the king and can do whatever I would like to." His hand slid down to my lower back, twisting my body into his. "Since this seems to be the roadblock preventing your decision to be mine, I have to ask. How would you know if you've run into one of your mates in the groves?"

"Since I'm not a mother tree, it's mostly just suspicion until I find intimacy with the right combination. All the mates have to be together to set the bond. It's like nothing in the world matters more than they do. You just want to touch them, hold them. Your heart feels like it will explode from your chest at the sight, and then there is a peace that comes from being in their presence." With a deep sigh, I turned my head back up to meet his gaze.

"Have you felt that way here?"

Yes, but I can't feel this. Not truly with the men who seem to be wrecking my mind. Perhaps the gods just knew there was no hope, so I got skipped over. "It's complicated, I think. Since I'm only going off of what others have said, I don't know if I have or not. Rux mentioned once that one of my mates might be in the Feylands, and I think that's part of the reason I was so nervous to come here."

Maybe this was too much honesty, but what did I have to lose? He couldn't be mine anyway. Maybe he had a brother hiding somewhere who would be the explanation for this feeling in my heart. Lorsan tilted my chin up toward him, and his eyes roamed my face in that way he loved to do before he kissed me.

Not here. We shouldn't do this here. I tried to lecture myself to back away from him, but instead I surged forward. My fingers gripped into the front of his shirt and pulled him straight

320

down to my lips. My hands sought whatever skin they could find as his tongue caressed mine. He always tasted like winter mint, so addictively cool. His grip rounded my ass, so he could grind his hard cock against me.

He'd been a dream I'd lost myself in as I ignored the growing pain in my heart and the weakness in my tree. Lorsan was a place where I could forget everything else, for just a few weeks. A golden vision of a passionate love that could only be a taste in a lifetime wasted.

"King Lorsan!" a voice called from the hall beyond, and I pushed away from him as the door creaked open. "Are you still in here?"

"Soleil." Lorsan didn't miss a beat. He turned away from me to face her, but I didn't miss the way she took note of where I stood. "What can I help you with?"

"I'm assisting Prinna with some of her assignments. It seems she spends a lot of time tracking you down." Soleil offered him a playful smile. Her skin began to shimmer, and I rooted my feet in place to resist the urge to claw at her pretty face. She was well within her right to glamour the man she might marry, no matter how much I claimed him as mine in the evenings.

"Yes, she does spend a lot of time filling my schedule with things."

I couldn't see his expression, and I really didn't want to, so with a low curtsy to them both, I would make my exit. "I shall see you both at dinner this evening."

They made a beautiful match as they stood together this way. With my shoulders straight and tall, I kept my pace casual so that there wouldn't be any indication that my heart raced with the need to run far away from this.

As she placed her hand on his arm while I opened the door to make my way out, my heart twisted. If this had been in Voreios and he had been anyone else, I would have fought for him. But for them, there are no mates. The magic picked who he ended up with, and it would never be me. We'd made no contract of exclusivity, even if he actively worked to remove any potential suitors from me. I knew that he was looking for his queen, and with that came talk of heirs. This could never be anything more, and I had to accept that.

Chapter 31 – Aralia

"I know you are in there." Soleil stormed across my garden. It felt as if her feet were made of lead from the vibrations in the ground.

"Good morning, Soleil," I muttered in my sweetest voice. This wasn't my favorite way to wake up, but I wasn't deep enough into rest to ignore her. "I never thought I'd see the day I'd find the contenders seeking me out."

"As you are an adviser to the king, I think I should be aware of all interactions you have with him."

"I believe all of our interactions are highly supervised by a room full of other advisers. Is there anything in particular you are looking for?" The lie fell easily, and I topped it off with an easy shrug of my shoulders.

I had to leave Lorsan earlier than usual this morning to get a few hours of rest in my tree. Leaving his warm embrace had been so difficult, but I had a routine to maintain for regular health. He'd ended up making me promise to slip out of the evening dancing early to make up for the lost time.

"As future queen, I like to be privy to all the contracts that are being negotiated with the fey. Do you currently have any contracts with the court?" She raised her slim eyebrow, and that piercing gaze would have been fierce if I had any fear of her or her magic.

"I believe the only one I have currently is the favor from Voreios that my presence and cure triggered. I have not committed to any other outstanding contracts with the court or any other advisers. Does that answer your question?" I leaned back against my tree trunk, fighting against the urge to curse the heels I was forced to wear. "Also, are you sure that you are going to be the queen? You have some stiff competition, and the magic whispers."

If I hadn't been watching her so closely, I might have missed the way her face paled for only a second. It might have been cruel to say, but I didn't feel bad about the remark.

When she shook off the initial reaction, she glared at me. "What have you heard?"

I raised my hands up as a sign that I didn't want to get in the middle of this. "All I'm saying is that some of the fey are pulling for the other contenders. Tasi and Dalila are pretty impressive as well."

She paused and then rubbed her hand across her chin, her eyes focused on something I couldn't see. "He did almost respond to Dalila's glamour. I may need to watch her more closely. Tasi won't be an issue. She can never be queen."

The news about Lorsan's response to Dalila took me by surprise. He'd been so insistent that he didn't want any of them.

But if he had chemistry with her now, and I agreed to be his consort, how long would it be before I was the one set aside? All of the contenders were beautiful, and he would have to make his peace with one of them at some point.

"Why can't I ever be queen?" Tasi's voice broke me out of my thoughts, and I offered her a genuine smile.

"Two contenders in one day? This is quite a treat."

Tasi's eyes twinkled with mischief and elation at my playful statement. "Now that the death clause has been lifted, I don't see why we can't all be friends. Now, Soleil, why can't I be queen?"

Soleil's upper lip curled in a snarl. "You know Lorsan would never agree to it."

"If I win, he has to. He's accepted the same contract that we did. His signature was on each of our scrolls," Tasi retorted, but there had to be something I was missing.

"I think your family took a deal too big for you to handle. I think you'd be just the person for him to bet with the magic against. Could you really see him tying himself to you as a mate?" Soleil laughed this time, and I could only frown.

"I don't think he's like Helio. If I win, I think he will honor his word."

"You dare speak ill of the last king?" Soleil sounded shocked, but even I could pick up on the false pitch.

"*King* Helio cost a lot of fae everything. My father made his bed, but it doesn't mean my family deserves to suffer for it."

Tasi practically growled the words, but then she turned her gaze to meet mine as if remembering they still stood by my tree. "I should thank your father for getting rid of mine before he could assist with any further stupid choices."

My father? For how big this world could be at times, everything seemed to weave back together time and again. "Who was your father?"

"The late general, Ellisar. He served as Helio's war general in the elven conflict, and then in our battle against Voreios, from which he thankfully didn't return home." Tasi waved her hand in dismissal of the thought.

None of this explains why Lorsan wouldn't have her as queen, but if I had to lose him to anyone, I still couldn't help but hope it was her.

My normal walk to Macendil filled me with peace that I'd only associated with the trails of Voreios. The trees of the Feylands begged me to explore beyond my usual scope, but I needed to talk with my friends. I'd left my note to Lorsan while he'd been talking with another adviser in his chambers, and I'd taken notice of his frown.

I could feel the weight on his shoulders when I caressed his skin each night, and some part of me knew that my visits outside of the court only served to stress him further. But how could I show him that this connection to the world beyond was necessary for me to fully embrace my nature? Rux knew all the ins and outs of my nature, but he also knew me . . .

My former ryne had looked so defeated when I'd told him to go this last time. Had he found his joy now? I left a prayer to our earth god, Montibus, that wherever he was now he could heal. I'd hoped that my resolve to release him would strengthen each day we were apart, but for me, the longing only grew worse. I'd kept him at arm's length, but he was always in my shadow. I knew he was there, always close enough to be at my side in a few moments' notice. The absence of him was a loneliness that I didn't know how I would ever recover from.

"Little tree," Macendil greeted me before the tree line cleared to give me a straight view of him.

"How are you today?" I gave him a bright smile as I jogged the short distance over to him.

"The king's energy marks you."

"Ah . . ." I stumbled on what to say to that as my cheeks burned. "It's only temporary, no mate marks for me at this time."

"Old fae kings used to mark the dryads," he said as he sent me images from the old world again. A woman stood behind what appeared to be a fae king and queen in front of a regal court.

"Were they mates?" Triads could be any combination of lovers. Perhaps the queen was this dryad's mate, too.

"'Consort' was the term the fae would use. The marks didn't come from the gods, they came from a blade." He sighed as more flashes revealed dryads marked and bleeding from fresh cuts on their chests, cuts in the shape of what I'd learned were signs and sigils of fae families. Though their faces were full of resignation, their magic poured from their hands, displaying strength.

Was I playing a much more dangerous game than I realized? "Would the kings have other types of consorts?"

"Not after the pact was made. Dryads, like the vasilissas in the groves, bring community, and they are natural hosts and leaders. Many of the fey would follow the guidance of the great trees, so it was advantageous to have a dryad tied to the king."

I would have to unpack all of this later. Had this been part of the reason that the past king desired my mother so badly? Were Lorsan's declarations of a need to be with me nothing more than just pretty words as he moved toward bringing the fey in line? Could I even trust him to be honest with me? I didn't know, and I wasn't even sure how I could find the answers.

"If I had to move my tree in a hurry, what would I need to make that happen?"

He hummed for a long minute before he replied, "First, you will need a large quartz."

Chapter 32 – Lorsan

Aralia danced on the edge of a passion and an obsession for me. Each day it only burned brighter, even down into the well of the magic within my soul. As the end of the trials drew nearer, I knew we needed to renegotiate, but she continued to distract me with her body and another day would pass. I wasn't quite sure how she did that.

During the day, she faded the dryad marks that ran down the length of her skin so she would blend in better with the fae in the court, as if that could make anyone miss her. Now in her sleep, I enjoyed teasing my fingers down the lines and finding the sensitive places.

The sun poured in from the small slivers in the blackout curtains I'd begun to use. Before Aralia, I awoke before the sun and had no reason to linger in this room. Now, I'd do whatever I needed to in order to keep her in my bed.

She hummed loudly as I kissed her neck and pressed my body to the length of hers. She was softer than the silk sheets we lay between, and each night she slept a little closer, tangling her limbs in mine. Fae were used to sleeping with one eye open, but nymphs weren't like that. Once she'd decided I was safe, she slept with no concern of danger. In my arms, she'd never need to do anything other than that.

"Again?" Her soft laughter danced around the room, warming the space. I loved the way she laughed when we were together.

"If I recall your exact words, they were that I could have you as often as I wanted." I continued to place kisses up in a trail to her mouth as I turned her face back toward me.

"I believe you have trial stuff to do today, Your Majesty." The tease of my title out of her mouth made me hard.

"You will say my name," I growled in her ear and slid my hand down her stomach, twisting her so I could grind against her perfect ass. "What spell is it that you have cast?"

"Lorsan," she purred as she caught my hand tight against her, playfully trying in vain to stop my movements. She knew when I heard my name that I always followed it up with reward. Then she froze in my arms.

"What's wrong?" I shifted so that I could roll her onto her back. Her eyes had gone glossy as if she gazed far away. Was she having a stroke? Did that happen to nymphs? I still had so much to learn about her, and yet we didn't spend much time talking when we were alone. "Aralia."

"One of your queens is at my tree." She sighed with pure resignation and gave me an apologetic smile as her bright green eyes returned to normal. "This must end for this morning, I'm afraid."

"You can tell when someone is by your tree?" I asked as she slid out of my grip, leaves wrapping around her form to cover her bare body in a beautiful dress of blues and golds that left her back exposed.

"Yes," she admitted shyly.

"So, you have been ignoring me when I come by your tree and call for you." I eyed her, unsure about whether I should be angry or not. On one hand, no one should ignore a king, on the other, we both knew any punishment I attempted to give her would end up in a pleasure romp. Mostly because, even now, my cock ached with the need to sink into her, even as this new truth twisted what I thought I knew.

"Not every time," Aralia replied as she fidgeted with her fingers. "I have to be conscious to respond, otherwise my tree will fill me in later with vague details that the soil can remember. After the experience in the hall, I was overthinking what had happened between us. Before you, I'd only been with Rux. Sex is supposed to be casual, like what we have now."

"You wanted it to mean more?" When she blushed and turned away so that I couldn't see her face, I knew this was the perfect opportunity. "I want to talk about our contract."

"Do we really have time to get into that now?"

A knock on my door seemed to emphasize her point, but to hell with all of them. I wouldn't delay this any longer. "The trial is coming to an end. We don't have much more time to talk about it. Become my consort. Stay with me."

331

The pause that followed my request strained even my tough nerves. I wouldn't pretend I didn't understand that she was holding on to her last card of independence in a world where leverage was everything. The mate thing mattered to her, Rux mattered to her. She talked about these things in her sleep, revealing a side of herself that I wanted to experience when she was awake. Even now, I could watch her expressive features having a struggle that I just wanted her to vocalize freely.

"I can't, Lorsan." Her shoulders fell in defeat, and this was the part I didn't understand. I knew she wanted to say yes from the way she responded, but something else was holding her back. Something new. "Your relationship with the queen chosen needs to be allowed to blossom. You can't do that if I am shading your garden."

"Aralia." My voice took on the husky quality she always reacted to, and she turned back to give me her full attention. "You know I don't want anyone but you, right? I don't care if you are the only one getting the sun. Allowing you to leave my side will not grow affection where there is none."

"I . . . It doesn't matter, Lorsan. We both know this can't continue after the trials are complete." She grabbed her head and stumbled before I got to her side and caught her. "Oh, that was a strange rush. You've made me light-headed, my king."

That was classic misdirection, but she genuinely appeared to be feeling unwell from the paleness in her face. Her glamour wafted over me as she responded to my touch. At first, I'd thought it was a controlled thing, but the more time I'd spent with her the more I realized she didn't seem to be able to control it at all when I was too close to her. Talk about an ego boost, but it also made her awfully shy in the grand hall. I wouldn't mind if everyone knew that I turned her on to this degree, but she demanded that we keep this a secret.

"Did I bruise you?" I asked as I noticed the black marks across the skin on her arms.

"Oh, no." She shook her head and they vanished instantly. Aralia took a step away from me with a renewed energy, and the color returned to her cheeks. Something wasn't right about this situation. "See, I'm fine."

"What was that th—" I tried to question her before another loud bang on my door interrupted me. I would absolutely murder everyone who was disturbing me right now.

"Why is this locked?" Trevan shouted from the other side, and Aralia's frown only fueled my fury.

"I'm busy! I will come to the meeting hall shortly."

"You should go." She gave me one of those radiant smiles before she kissed my cheek. There was a subtle sadness in her expression, but knowing that others were this close, she wouldn't talk anymore.

"Tonight, no sex until we renegotiate. I want to talk about our contract and whatever is going on with those marks," I demanded in a low growl to make sure she knew I was serious.

"Mm-hmm. We'll see who caves first." Those beautiful green eyes lit up as she slipped out of my arms and vanished into her fey ring.

I dressed quickly before using magic to rip open the drapery covering the windows to let the light in. Her tree blew in the strong breezes this final autumn day brought, and for a moment, I had to question that I still didn't know anything about caring for her tree. Not like Rux did. He'd been right that day, and in arrogance, I'd not considered that I would need to have that expertise. Would she get cold as the nights brought snow and blustery winds? Would he know what was going on with her now?

She visited Rux's old room often, but I wasn't sure what she was looking for. I didn't know whom they'd discussed the night before she'd dismissed him, but I did know that whoever that was, Rux didn't love them. The man loved her, and I'd used that to separate them. As a king, I shouldn't have to share, but I was in the dark about the true Aralia, and Rux might be the only counterbalance to keep her safe.

If only I'd met her again before the trials, one of the times at the fey pool after she'd become a woman. Now, the prospect of a queen didn't only threaten to diminish my peace, but my sanity as well. If I had to give up Aralia because she wouldn't negotiate, I would lose my mind.

Under the cover of her branches, Aralia looked to be having a heated conversation with Soleil. The contender hadn't taken

334

her eyes off my dryad all through dinner last night. If Soleil had picked up on our arrangement, then this would be all the more reason to make it public. She'd won the favor to become queen from most of the court, which meant she'd have to make her peace with being second to the nymph if she did win. Now I just had to find the words to persuade Aralia to believe and accept my new offer.

"What do you want coming to my room at this hour in the morning?" I snarled at Trevan as I opened my doors with magic in order to allow him entry.

"It's almost afternoon. You have been uncharacteristically late for the last two weeks. Are you playing with the contenders without me?" He raised a playful eyebrow. It wasn't uncommon as younger men for us to share the limited available women, but I had no interest in sharing with him as of late.

"It is none of your concern what I am doing. You do know that once one of them is my queen, she will be off limits."

"Yes, yes but by then I will be on to something new. Perhaps this evening, we can discuss my intention to court the dryad."

I raised an eyebrow at him. Every possessive fiber in my being disliked the sentence that came out of his mouth. He'd not even used her name as he'd thrown in the request to follow the protocol I'd put in place. "I didn't think you liked Aralia very much. Not from your very public attempts to humiliate or intimidate her."

"It's not a matter of liking her, she's powerful. She will only be second to your queen, which means that she's ideal for me as your captain of the guard. Aralia is stubborn and needs to learn that her opinion on the way things work here doesn't have a space. She'll need to be taught to obey." Trevan took a seat on my couch and lounged back. "Plus, as a nymph, she will have fae children or dryads. Their race doesn't create half species. You know I have the resources to care for her as I would if I made a move to match with the fae princess. I'm willing to negotiate, though."

There was a lot of information in his brief summary of his intention to court Aralia. Contracts for marrying into royalty among the fae could take weeks because of the sensitive nature of the potential breeding. The part about nymph children though, snagged my interest above everything else. Why had I not heard that before? "So, you could have full fae children with a nymph mother?"

"Well, yeah. That's why they tend to mix well into the world no matter where they go. Most of the court is watching her for that purpose now that the satyr is gone."

The mention of Aralia's ryne didn't raise my ire any further. Perhaps because she'd spoken of him quite a bit in the times that we'd shared. I wished someone had mentioned that about nymphs earlier. Not like any of the fae would be happy about an official union between the king and a nymph. Some of my father's actions were beginning to make a bit more sense now, however. Was I falling into the same madness?

"We can discuss that later. Like I said, I'm willing to negotiate fair terms. I just want to put in my intention before Roso can. He's obsessed with elven women and can't stop talking about her now, even if she glamours away her ears. That's such a freaky ability," Trevan commented underhandedly, again emphasizing that he really didn't care much for her. "Anyway, there was another sighting of the mages on the other side of the labyrinth. Most of the wild fey are fleeing to sanctuary locations. They are requesting that we open up the liminal spaces again."

"How is it that you always start with the thoughts of your cock and not the actual important things?" I pinched the bridge of my nose and counted to three to calm my fury. "Just how many mages are there? Send the guard out to deal with them and be done with this."

"Then who would protect us here?" He looked genuinely shocked that I would even dare to command such a thing.

"Are you telling me as captain of the guard that we don't have enough men to fight a handful of mages and also protect the court?" I asked, unable to contain my anger at his laziness. "Wasn't Rux training them?"

"Yes, but that wasn't with the intention of them leaving to protect the masses."

"Is that what Rux thought? If I'd even slightly hinted that Aralia might be in danger from this mage threat, he would have marched off to deal with it single-handedly. Where is that courage in our men?" Being diplomatic, I'd included all of my guard in the statement, but I knew this was solely Trevan's own lack of initiative.

"Sir, we aren't brutes."

"Yet here we are." I sent out a summons to the commanders who would appear in just a moment. No one except Aralia made me wait for very long. "I will go and deal with the mages."

"You're the . . . you're the king!" Trevan stammered as he rose to his feet, trying to understand my actions.

"I'm aware." I glanced out the window at Aralia who was remulching her tree. The closer these mages got to the court, the more danger she would be in. Cirro may have been correct in his observations from the last fight, and it was a chance I couldn't take. Now I really felt stupid for asking her to send away her protector. If he wasn't here, then I would have to make sure that I took up that task.

"The wild hunt is coming. You should be . . ."

"Taking my job seriously so that those women don't get too hurt or stolen away while we are hunting. It's one thing if we are the monsters in the woods, it's another thing if it is the mages. Don't you agree?"

"I see that you can't be talked down from this."

"No," I snarled as the four commanders appeared in the doorway to my rooms. "We are taking two units of six men out with us into the woods. You and you will come with us." I pointed to the two that I wanted, not giving Trevan a chance to take command of this situation. "I need you to move the court indoors and keep them there until we return. Cirro, you are in charge of the grounds. Does everyone understand their assignments?"

When they all nodded, I locked eyes with the faun to make sure he clearly received my message. The stern determination in his expression told me he knew I was specifically referencing a particular dryad who would be in danger if the court was left unprotected.

With that taken care of, now I needed to go clean the lands of this recent pest and take my kingdom back, by force if that was what it called for.

Chapter 33 — Aralia

Lorsan, wearing battle armor I hadn't seen before, strode by on the walkway heading toward the bridge to cross the moat. His dark wings exuded the land's magic, and even without glamour, I was swept away by his beautiful form. A group of seven people were with him, including Trevan all dressed in similar armor, and I realized that something must be happening elsewhere in his kingdom. Their wings reflected the sun back at the gathered crowd as they lifted off the ground.

I wiped the mulch from my hands onto my pant legs as I rose to my feet. I struggled to keep the frown from my face, it would reveal too many emotions in the crowd. If it was bad enough for this type of wardrobe, why would they send their king? I'd seen what he could do with the magic, but what if they attacked him with a curse like they'd tried to hit me with?

He waved back at the onlookers as they left, his eyes lingering on mine for just a moment longer. His commanders began giving orders to get the people back inside the court. As Cirro headed my direction, I knew what task he'd been given.

"There was that look again," Soleil snapped at me, and I remembered that she'd never left this morning. I just decided to start ignoring her after her tirade about the fact that fey shouldn't be so close to the king for any reason. I wanted to retort that he'd been so close that he was inside me repeatedly the night before, but what could be won from that fight, really? "What have you done to him?"

What hadn't I done with him was the better question. "I don't know what you are talking about. He just waved in the general area. I don't even know where he's going."

"I heard there are mages in the woods from the broonies." Soleil provided the answer as if to prove she knew more than I did. Congratulations to her. I was often out of the loop, and she might be queen, but good for her, one-upping the "fey."

"King Lorsan is going out to fight the mages?" I heard my own shock before I could cover it up. If it had been Rux, I wouldn't have even batted an eye. My ryne . . . former ryne . . . could handle any threat, but Lorsan? What if the magic glitched like it had been. I wasn't sure I'd seen him carry any weapons.

"Lady Soleil, I'm going to need you to return to your chambers in the court until the king returns," Cirro advised once he'd reached the boundaries of my tree.

"Oh, it's wonderful that he's so concerned about my safety." She tossed me a smile that I mockingly returned as her wings fluttered to lift her up onto the bridge into the court.

Once she cleared the area, the faun returned his gaze to me. "I've been assigned to protect you here until the rest of the guard returns."

341

"Is the situation that dangerous?" I asked him cautiously, not sure if I could handle the honest answer.

"The mages must have been given some impressive gifts of persuasion to pull so many from the worship of Aine. It's better to clear them out so we don't have to deal with as many conversions. If they keep expanding this way, we may end up in another war before the end of the next season."

That did make sense, but I was still concerned about my lover. I knew I shouldn't have involved my heart in our transactional agreement, but it was hard not to. So, I decided to do what any nymph would. I was going to follow them. Trailing behind the men as they flew would be difficult when I was in the root network moving through the trees, but I'd make it work.

"Okay, well since you have everything covered here. I'll be back." I slipped past him and ran toward the bridge so I could get over the moat.

"Aralia!" Cirro shouted, but I could see his hesitancy to grab me, which was the only help I needed to escape.

"Thank you for looking after my tree!" I called back to him as I merged with the tree line to travel the roots.

As I moved quickly to catch up with their group, the trees nudged me in the right direction. Out here in the Feylands, my presence would create a glowing effect on any tree that I traveled through, so I couldn't remain still for any true length of time. It wasn't too long before bright flashes of light ripped

342

through the sky and the sounds of swords clanking caught my attention.

I moved around the group slowly, keeping my eyes on Lorsan as he fought with a blade made of pure fey magic. Instead of the silver I was used to seeing, it was black and reflected the light just as his wings did. His footwork and stance were beautifully poised. Perhaps I really didn't have anything to worry about after all. But now that I was with him, I wouldn't return to the court. Just in case.

Four mages died in the first round of encounters, six in the next. This group with the king seemed to be taking everything in stride, and with each fight my concern only lessened. They would be fine.

Instead of ogling the king, I used the time to explore areas of the Feylands that I hadn't seen before. Hours passed and the sun sank in the horizon, crossing the sky with beautiful oranges, purples, and pinks along the cloudy evening.

The guards looked tested and tried, but Lorsan's determination continued to push them forward. He really wanted this forest to be cleared, it seemed. The trees alerted me to the largest group of mages they'd encountered yet today. There were twelve individuals on the other side of the tiny creek that ran across the dirt trail in the forest they'd been walking along.

Lorsan turned to his group and put a finger to his mouth. He must have noticed them too from the sounds traveling across the opening. I felt his magic tug on mine indirectly, and for a moment he seemed distracted by picking up on my traces. He was pulling their magic away from them, but I could see him scouting the area for a sign of me. His ability to snuff out other's access to fey magic wouldn't work on me, but it didn't mean that we wouldn't recognize one another in the pool.

Shouts and screams came from across the water's surface as the mages charged in to fight the king and his men. It was pure chaos for a moment as explosions of magic went off and then reversed, depending on whose will was stronger at the time. Lorsan ran his blade through the gut of one of the mages and tossed his body to the side.

Whispers through the trees began to crawl across my being. Something dark had been cast, and it tore away at healthy limbs of the trees a few feet away. Everything on those trees disintegrated down to the roots. The path headed straight for Lorsan. I dashed through the roots again to find the casters and found four people walking slowly toward the king from the opposite direction of this curse.

The men were so engaged with the mages directly attacking them that this new group would come out of nowhere. Mages and guards screamed before their bodies shredded apart, and I knew I couldn't wait any longer.

I stepped out of the tree, manifesting my spirit form, and my magic poured out at the approaching mages. Vines grew out of the trees behind them and wrapped around all the closest body parts before drilling their way through their flesh. The spell faltered with the concentration of the casters broken as one by one I reduced them to chunks of flesh, bone, and blood.

"What are you doing out here?" Lorsan arms wrapped around my body from behind, and I was distracted from my assault on the last two mages.

"Saving you is what it looks like to me," I teased him quietly, hoping none of the others could hear, but I felt all eyes on us.

One of the mages took his dying breath anyway from the injuries he'd sustained, and as I shifted to focus on finishing the last one, the fae king whispered in my ear, "Leave him barely alive. I'll bring him in for questioning. I went today to make sure you were safe, not to put you in danger."

"Rux would have brought me along because he would have known that I was going to cause trouble." I frowned as Rux raced through my mind. I had to let him go, but part of my chest hurt knowing that I had to lose them both.

"Lesson learned then." He tilted my chin up before he kissed me.

Trevan charged by us in a blind rage, shouting like a madman, and slashed through the chest of the last mage. His eyes were crazed as he turned back to our gathering.

"Trevan! I'd just asked Aralia not to kill him, so you went and did it?" Lorsan growled at the captain, who still appeared to be dazed.

"We can't leave any of them alive. They will just report back to the rest."

"Yes, now you see why I asked her to leave that one. We need to know where they are gathering."

I could tell the king hated having to explain himself, but there was none of that tension in his gaze on me as he pressed another kiss to my lips.

"Sir!" Trevan shouted as the adrenaline crashed from his system and he took in Lorsan's behavior. "She's glamouring you. I can smell it from here. She should not be out of the court, and after this display, we may need to have her locked up."

I tried to shy away from him, but Lorsan's grip only got tighter. He scooped me up to hold me under the knees and against his chest. I felt my furious blush scorch my cheeks. "Lor— Your Majesty, you shouldn't carry me this way."

"I won't have *no* for an answer, Aralia. New terms. Today," Lorsan demanded before he turned to scowl at his cousin. "She can't be that dangerous if you were intending to court her, and I believe she just saved all of our lives. While she is not from the Feylands, she has proven her loyalty to me. We will resume this search tomorrow in the morning. Get some rest, it's going to be a long day."

I nearly gagged at the sentiments of his cousin courting me. Fae may not mate the way we did back home, but it didn't mean I was ready to settle. If time was limited, then I wanted to be right where I was. Even that though, drew to a close. Maybe a

346

week longer in the trials? I felt my heart would shatter my soul long before the illness took my body.

I clung to Lorsan as he lifted up into the sky. Dryads weren't meant to fly, our roots needed the ground, but my magic hummed in his presence. Though we had been traveling for hours, the return flight was much faster than I'd anticipated. Lorsan landed on his balcony ledge and strode straight into his rooms, dismissing the others with an easy wave.

"Lorsan," I said as he set me down on his bed. "My answer has not changed since this morning, no matter what we just went through. I cannot be yours while you have a queen."

When he didn't reply, I gazed up at him to find his eyes closed and his mouth set in a firm, thin line. Was he angry with me?

Then his eyes snapped open, dancing with a golden fury, and for the first time since I'd arrived, I knew I was in trouble.

Chapter 34 — Lorsan

At first, I'd been elated to see her. Her very presence lit up my world, and as the mages fell one by one, the danger passed. As I flew back home with her in my arms, however, rapid unwelcome thoughts came to me. What purpose did she have in the woods, following us in the shadows?

Now she looked up at me with that stubborn resolve to tell me that nothing was going to change. Her eyes were a forest green in reflection of the magic she'd used, and I'd learned that the darker they were, the more hungry she would become. My fingers trailed her cheek, past her ear, and slowly down until I gripped the back of her neck.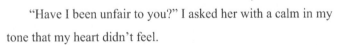

A gasp escaped from Aralia, and though her eyes were slightly wider from being startled, she didn't attempt to push me away as I pulled her to her feet.

"Have I been unfair to you?" I asked her with a calm in my tone that my heart didn't feel.

"What . . . ? No," she replied, and her hands pressed against my chest. My fingers tangled in her hair, securing my control.

"Have I been unkind?"

"Lorsan, no. I don't know why you would ask me these things." Finally, she tried to pull free of my grip, but she wasn't able to gain any ground.

"Why were you in the woods? I'd left you at the court with Cirro." Slowly, I began to wrap my magic in threads around her wrists. She might realize what I was up to, but it was already too late for her.

"I was worried for you," she muttered softly as she attempted to turn her head, testing my grip again.

"I am the king. There is nothing in *my* woods that can hurt me. Not mages, or druwids, or an uprising of fey," I snarled at her. The bands on her arms dragged her hands together, bound with a tight knot.

She whimpered, but kept her gaze on me, confusion clouding her clear eyes. The fact that her beautiful scent still permeated the space between us told me everything.

"Did you think that I couldn't handle myself?"

Immediately, she wouldn't meet my eyes any longer.

"You will look at me!" My shout made her jump, and she wiggled against my hold. "You doubted my capability?"

"Only for a moment. I'm sorry. I just . . . I couldn't lose you. Everything has changed and I . . ."

I didn't reply to her confession, but it soothed the anger. With her hands secured, she couldn't fight me as the blindfold flew over and settled across her eyes.

"Lorsan . . . what are you doing?" she asked sweetly, but I wouldn't be deterred.

She followed me easily when I tugged her arms toward the head of my bed before I secured her fey-rope ties to the center of the headboard. Still so trusting. Aralia shivered when I ripped her dress as she straightened up on her knees trying to shake the blindfold off. When I made a second rip, her dress vanished in a gentle whirlwind of leaves.

A moan fell from her lips, my hands grazing the inside of her thighs as I pulled her from behind to spread her out for me. She was just as hungry as I was, but this wasn't going to end quickly for her. I was a bit older and didn't have to feed quite as often, so I could hold out. Weaving more fey rope around her ankles, I locked her into the place that I wanted.

"Lorsan?" she called for me again as I stepped back to marvel at her beautiful curves and glistening slit. There was need and heat in the way she said my name, but I wouldn't cave.

Two stones appeared in my hands, and I leaned forward to press the smooth black stone in my left hand up against her clit. I couldn't stop myself from dragging my fingers through her exposed lips, moisture coating my fingers. Another whimper slipped from her as I traced her pussy and then held them to my mouth for a taste.

My chair dragged itself into place at the end of the bed where I took a seat, a drink manifesting in my hand. Then I rubbed my thumb against the white stone in my right palm.

A beautiful hum took over the room as both stones vibrated, and Aralia's body immediately jolted. She couldn't escape because of how I'd secured her. Her breathing sped up to pants of need and pleasure. Words, perhaps in Druidic, came out, but they were not coherent as she struggled against the bonds.

Her shouts only increased, and I loved the way I could enjoy her body moving. Her dripping pussy made a mess that I wanted to sink into repeatedly. And I would. Just not yet. As she tensed up, I pushed the vibrations a few more seconds before I ran my thumb the opposite way and the room fell silent except for her strangled sob.

"Why?" Aralia cried and tried to glance back over her shoulder to see me, but the blindfold prevented that from happening.

I took a long drink from the ambrosia in my goblet while she muttered frustrated curses in her native tongue and struggled against her bindings.

"I know you are th—" She bit into her pillow when I rubbed the white stone in my hand to turn the vibrations back on but at a slower setting.

After the initial shock wore off a second time, she mewled in the most beautiful, frustrated way and used the angles she was tied in to chase her release.

"Lorsan, please," Aralia tried again, and the use of my name repeatedly was almost enough for me to stop her torture, but I wasn't quite ready to give in. The heady buzz from the ambrosia and the view I currently enjoyed made my cock painfully hard. But for her, I would wait.

I turned it off again, and she let out a sob with her head hung down between her tied arms. My magic brushed her and was met with charged electricity. If I untied her, there was a good chance she'd pounce on me, but I was in control now.

With barely more than a thought, I flipped her over with the magic and set her legs free. Her arms twisted tightly, pressing in against her ears. Her beautiful features were trapped in between pain and relief as my hands glided up her legs. That was until I turned the white stone back on and placed the black one into position again.

Now she fought, her hips thrusting until I dug my fingers into her thighs, stretching her against the ties that bound her. Keeping her spread for me.

"Be good for me. You know that you misbehaved today, and I can't reward that with orgasms." I wasn't sure she could hear me, but her rapid panting resumed as her legs settled.

"I helped you . . ." Aralia's voice was strained as if each word hurt her to say.

"Yes, you did, but I went out there to keep you safe. I left Cirro here to protect you." I leaned down across the bed as I trailed kisses up one of her thighs. "If something happened to you . . ."

"But it didn't! I was careful. I stayed in the trees," she reasoned before another moan ripped from her.

She trembled, and I turned the stone off with a quick flick of my thumb.

"Please, Lorsan."

"Will you stop putting yourself in dangerous positions and leaving to follow the guard when you haven't been asked?"

Her silence spoke volumes. While this wasn't exactly a fae contract, she was stubborn and independent. Perhaps Trevan had been right in some of his assessments. She'd need a firm hand if she would be my consort.

Her lower lip pulled into a pout with an adorable quiver. "Just . . . It doesn't matter."

I moved the black rock with my nose and ran my tongue up her slit to latch on to that pearl I knew had to be oversensitive by now. Her legs clamped around my head as she moaned my name. I loved how soft her skin was under my fingertips as she gyrated against my sucking.

When my tongue penetrated her, she let out a strangled whimper. My little nymph was a live wire right now, ready to explode, but I couldn't let her have it just yet. Slowing my exploration, I drank her at a torturous pace. It was only a matter of time before I lost my sanity to the woman in my arms.

Shredding my clothes, I climbed up to join her on the bed once she'd finally given in to trails of silent tears down her cheeks from under the blindfolds. I fisted my cock a few times as I trailed the other hand with a feather light touch up her stomach. Had she finally broken in some of that stubborn

353

determination for independence? I doubted it, but I was ready to find my release.

Aralia was soaking my bed. Pulling out another stone toy, I slowly pushed it inside of her. My eyes remained locked on it as it penetrated her repeatedly, watching how her body responded to each sensation.

"Lorsan. . . please, I want you. Not the stone."

A slight laugh escaped from me at her appeal, but I continued to work her. "How about you have both?"

I slid the stone out and down, pressing against her back entrance and she tensed up immediately. With a little manipulation of magic, I pinched her nipples to distract her and the moment she gasped, I pushed the stone in, using her still dripping pussy to coat the way.

"You keep talking to me about mates as in plural, consider this warm up for when your partners all want to be inside you at the same time." I leaned down and kissed on her neck as she panted, adjusting to the new situation while I softly continued thrusting. While she seemed turned on by the idea I'd presented her, a new rage coursed through me. There wouldn't be a group of others bringing her to this pleasure.

I used magic to continue the stone's movement as I leaned back to line the head of my cock to her core. Her breasts bounced, but the need to mark her somehow grew in me. As I pressed my head into her, I manifested a dagger made of dark fae shadow and controlled the blade to scratch a line between her breasts. How would a king write mine on the body of a stubborn woman when she wouldn't let herself be adorned by jewels?

The knife dragged over her skin again as I thrusted fast into her. Aralia cried out and her hands struggled against the restraints each time I made a cut. Tiny streams of blood ran down towards her belly button, but the glow from the cuts drew my attention. Without meaning to, I'd carved my mother's family sigil on her. It felt right. Aralia's magic tangled with mine as I picked up the thrusting, chasing that beautiful tightening that threatened to strangle my cock as she greedily begged for my seed.

Her head rolled back against the restraints, and she moaned my name in a beautiful chant as I let her drag us both under into the pits of ecstasy.

Aralia's fingers stroked my chest in a way that I found soothing. Her presence calmed all the chaos that happened outside these doors. I didn't understand why she wouldn't give me her terms. From the way she melted into my side and curled herself around me, she had to be comfortable here too.

Ever since I'd removed the blindfold and cleaned her, she'd been watching me with these fond, soft eyes. No calculation, no secrets, just unmasked, unbridled, dare I say . . . affection? She could be good at acting, but I'd watched her when she'd not noticed me. I'd seen these looks before when she thought Rux wasn't watching.

I stroked along her hair and vines to cup her cheek before I settled back to get some actual sleep. Tomorrow would be more mage hunting in the morning, and I needed to be at my best.

"Is there a contender you favor to win?"

My mind jolted awake and every bit of peace I had prior shattered. "I do not want to discuss that with you."

She shifted away from me, and as I glanced at her to see why she was moving, I could see the hurt in her eyes even as she wouldn't meet my gaze again. I needed to be more tactful in my replies to her.

"My sweet nymph." I pulled her back into my side with a tight arm around her. "That's not how I meant it. My cock is still warm from being inside you. They are the last thing on my mind right now. I don't want to think about them when I am with you."

This seemed to settle her again, and her nails brushed against my skin. "I understand. I just thought that maybe if I knew who you were leaning toward, I could put in my favor for them too. That way the one that you liked most would be even more likely. I think I may have chosen one that you don't like very much."

With her here, I didn't want any of them, but she didn't seem to grasp that, even when I'd told her repeatedly. However,

356

the fact that she leaned toward one could offer some interesting information about my dryad. "Who did you pick?"

"I don't want to say."

"I haven't made a choice, and as you are one of my advisers, your insight is invaluable to me."

She chewed on her lip for a moment and then let out a huff as if she expected this conversation to go poorly. "I picked Tasi. She was the only contender who was friendly to me at first when I was in the classes with your other potential queens. She offered me an olive branch, so I thought that if any queen could make up with the groves, it'd be her. There was nothing for her to gain in friendship with me at the time, but she did it anyway. Then I overheard something about how you'd never pick her, and I feel like I messed up. I just want to be on the same page with you."

I rubbed my face with the hand not wrapped around Aralia. This was a lot more complicated than I'd expected. Of course she'd pick Tasi. Tasi's family had been banished from court as soon as I became king for one reason. Her father had suggested that Helio execute Calla because dryads don't share, and he'd risk the nymph never accepting him. My mother died that night. Had the general been wrong? I had a dryad in my bed refusing to be my consort essentially because she wouldn't share.

"So, I was thinking that maybe you are leaning more toward Soleil or Dalila."

357

When she mentioned Dalila, there was an inquisitive look on her face. I had found the fae woman attractive, and she was fertile, but I hadn't thought about her since the day I'd watched Rux and my nymph. "I'm not leaning toward any of them. I am letting the magic and Aine sort that out."

She hesitated for a moment. "Even if she picks Tasi?"

I'd never truly considered that Tasi would win, though she could. I wasn't sure I could look at her every day without thinking about my mother, and that would not bode well for heirs.

"I will make my peace with whoever wins, however, while I have this arrangement with you, I'd rather keep this talk outside of my chambers when you are in my bed. Do you understand?"

"I do," she whispered and laid her head against my shoulder, resuming her calming strokes until I fell asleep.

Chapter 35 – Aralia

I awoke the next morning cocooned against the fae king amongst his sheets. He was typing with one hand on some kind of device. The arm keeping me secured in place, it wasn't uncommon for me to find myself mostly on his chest, or if I turned at night, with Lorsan spooning me, practically engulfing me with his lithe body.

"Good morning," I scratched his chest a few times gently and tried to turn to get out of bed. "I know you have important things to do. You know you can wake me, right?"

"I don't see a reason to ever do that." His eyes turned from the device and Lorsan leaned in to kiss me on the forehead before he let me go. "I'll have to learn to use the tools around me anyway. I'm also thinking that I need to make some changes to my chambers."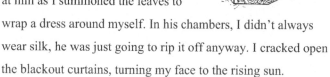

"Why?" I raised my eyebrow at him as I summoned the leaves to wrap a dress around myself. In his chambers, I didn't always wear silk, he was just going to rip it off anyway. I cracked open the blackout curtains, turning my face to the rising sun.

"I don't need anybody coming in to accidentally catch a glimpse of what is mine as she sleeps so trustingly in my bed."

With that, I looked over my shoulder back at him. Lorsan sat on his bed watching me with that intensity again. After the rough play last night, along with his shallow marking on my skin, I knew that this game had turned more dangerous than I'd intended. Could he mark me permanently somehow? Right now, he's still asking for permission to claim me, but could I stop him if he marked me again?

"I want you to know you are safe in here and if people have access while I'm not around, then that doesn't work," he continued before he stretched out his defined muscles before throwing on some pants.

"I shouldn't be in your chambers if you are not around to begin with," I reminded him as he strolled past me to sit at his large desk. Walking up behind him, I kneaded the tension in his bare shoulders, and he closed his eyes to enjoy the feeling of my hands working out some of that pressure.

"As my consort, you have access to everything whenever you want it. There won't be any space that is off limits to you."

I sighed and moved so I could sit on the desk in front of him. "Lorsan. . . you know I am not your consort. I am just a nymph you happen to be sleeping with before you take a queen. I know you are going out to hunt mages again today, so I really don't want to fight with you before you leave."

"I'm not intending to fight. I told you that I will chase you and win, this isn't over if you are still trying to escape." He leaned in closer and pressed a teasing kiss to my lips. "There is

360

no other way out of this for you. I can smell how badly you want me. I just don't understand the stubbornness here. You want freedom to walk in the forest? Done. Just tell me where you are going. You want protection from the other fae? Done. You'll have my seal until everyone in the kingdom recognizes you. You want to see your sister every other week? Done. I just need to know what you want."

"I won't pretend to be able to negotiate against you long term, my king," I tried to soothe his ego. I knew that he'd never been told no this many times about something he desired, but it really was for the best. "Things can change in time."

"Am I?" he asked, seriousness etched in his eyebrows.

"Are you what?"

"Your king?" For the first time in a while, I was stunned into silence before he spoke again. "I don't want an adviser's answer that is perfectly polished. I want the truth."

I didn't know when the answer had become an affirmative, but I offered him a gentle smile. "Yes, you are."

"You will drive me to madness, I swear." Lorsan cupped my cheeks on both sides and kissed me gently again. "If you don't want to negotiate forever terms then just give me the ones that will make you feel comfortable saying yes to being mine. Do you not feel this the way I do?"

"Of course, I do," I protested. "We are trapped in this place. I want nothing more than to claim you as my own, but I cannot be second to another. I know you say that it will be fine to set

361

her aside, but what if your first born is not your heir? You were your father's third. It would tear my heart to go through this repeatedly."

"You will not be second to anyone else. The queen will know her ranking and it will be beneath you. If you agree now, then they will know it even before the trials have completed. Give me your terms. That is all I am asking for," he pressed. Then, when I didn't answer, he leaned back in his massive chair to study me. "I heard something about nymphs yesterday that could change everything. Would you truly give birth to fae children if you carried my child?"

"Lorsan, it's not that simple. There's a chance that I may have fae children, but it's the same chance as having a seedling instead." *If I would even ever flower.* I kept that part to myself for now. "You need to think about your people, your lineage."

"Then we will keep trying until we have a fae child. There'd be no harm in adding more dryads to the garden. Our daughters would be beautiful. If I don't select a fae queen, would you allow yourself to become my consort?"

I tossed him a sad face at his willingness to toss away Aine's terms. "That is not a good idea. The magic demands it. Please do not toss that away for me. Who knows what is awaiting you on the other side of your destiny? It could be a love that shines so brightly this will pale in comparison. Allow yourself the opportunity to find that."

"Give me the terms that allow us to make this permanent. The ones that make sure I wake up to you every morning, hold you in my arms every night. Kiss you in front of everyone just because I feel called to do so. Give me those terms, Aralia. After that, you will never have to negotiate a need with me ever again. I will give you the world for the rest of your life."

"I can't." I couldn't stop the stray tear that fell down my face.

"Let's try something." Lorsan wiped the tear away and held up his hand to mine. His magic covered the surface of his hand. "Pull your magic out and place your palm against mine."

I raised an eyebrow at him, but curiosity won me over. "This isn't some type of nonverbal contract, is it?"

"No, though in your case I wish it were. All fae contracts need to be in written or spoken word."

My magic danced like lightning along the surface of my hand, and I felt the charge as our hands met before my mind was transported to someplace else. The sun was setting, and the stars shot across the sky like a radiant display. I could see myself standing beside Lorsan, gazing up at him with all the affection in my heart out on open display.

A woman's laughter rang in my ears. I'd heard her voice before when I'd visited the pool, but I didn't know who she was. The Lorsan I watched caressed my cheek, and a heartbreaking reality set in.

Perhaps in a different life, one where he wasn't the king and I wasn't a sick nymph, he might have been my mate. It crushed my heart to think about him with a queen, because he should only be mine. If he were my mate, unbonded or not, it would devastate me to know he had to be with another even once after the time we'd shared. I couldn't keep up this ruse any longer.

"That vision told me everything I needed to know, Aralia," Lorsan stated, and it shook me out of my trance. There was a new fire in his eyes even as my heart was breaking. Did he see what I'd seen? It didn't matter. "I just need your terms. I will give you anything. After what Aine has shared with me, this is what I want."

"I need to think about it. Give me the two days I didn't take when we started this," I said with resignation. He didn't have all the facts, and while that was the case, there wouldn't be any change in my answer.

"As long as you will genuinely consider what I am saying. I want new terms. If you can have fae children, then that changes everything. I will tell the magic that we don't need a queen. We can figure everything out together."

"If that is what you are getting excited about, please don't. Lorsan, I should have had at least ten children by now. I have not flowered once. I do not have any running around in Voreios, I've had none with Rux. I cannot promise you an heir because I may be incapable." I ducked under his arm and stood up, spinning on my heel to face him. I knew he could see the hurt on my face as I confessed this. It wasn't a secret in Voreios, but here. . . here I could hide it and not feel so different. "Take your queen, have your legacy and your heir, I want all of this for you. It just can't be with me."

His hesitation gave me the only opening I needed to flee the room through the ring to my tree.

Chapter 36 — Aralia

I'd spent the next night in Rux's bed. His scent had begun to fade slowly as time had passed, but every once in a while, I could turn a pillow and catch it just long enough to find comfort. The weeks had passed, and without even an update from Ferox, I wasn't sure what to do anymore. For some reason I couldn't guess, I must like the pain associated with imagining Rux happily reunited with Rhenei.

The black spots under my skin had continued to spread. My energy was beginning to ebb from using my glamour to vanish them and the blood. How much longer could I keep this up? I couldn't leave my tree behind, but I just wanted to find a quiet place to dissolve into nonexistence.

For the first time since they'd left, I wanted to call my parents. My mom would know what to do, but she was off saving another world. Maybe my father Graak could heal me, since Lilise no longer had the ability. I wasn't sure if the call would even go through, however. There were a lot of factors that depended on what planet they were on.

I needed to find a way to save myself somehow, but even in that case, where would I go next? The land of the dragons?

Would I also ask my parents to drop me off on some other planet where I could truly be whoever it was that I wanted to be? That would be nice. I could put Rux and his mate, and Lorsan and his queen, far behind me.

I found the bottles of mead that I had brought to Rux, one unopened still. I could drown away this misery tonight.

Lorsan had kept his distance, and with room to breathe, I was coming up with a plan. I would have to gather a few things, but for now, I needed to make it look as though nothing had changed.

The queen contenders wandered around, mingling with the crowd. My seat beside the advisers remained open, and I slid into it with easy precision. They'd stopped presenting me with grandiose plates, knowing that I really would only sample the food anyway. As King Lorsan walked into the room, everything fell silent. He was regal as always. His gold-accented wardrobe highlighted his lighter hair. He swept around the room, taking note of me but not lingering. At least there wasn't dismissal in his expression.

Honesty would go a long way, I hoped. He'd see the reason I needed to let him go.

"The second full moon after the trials began is upon us, do you know what this means?" Lorsan's deep timbre filled the hall and there was a hint of mischief in his words.

The court went wild with cheers and excitement at the question he had posed. I folded my hands in my lap, hoping that he would elaborate as I seemed to be the only one who did not know. Soleil looked downright radiant reflecting the king's glow, triumph in her features after the last few days of trials came to a close. I briefly wondered whether he'd taken her to his rooms in the days that I'd been gone, but honestly, what could I expect? By all accounts, even Lorsan thought she would be queen. I just tried to avoid her now.

"That's right, the wild hunt begins tomorrow at sunset. Everyone in the court is to attend in your assigned roles."

I didn't have a role; he'd never even mentioned this event to me at all. I guess it didn't matter anyway. If I could make it happen, I would be gone before the festivities even started. All I needed was to find a stone, and I was pretty sure that Macendil could procure one for me.

The dancing began, and from the corner of my eye, I could see Lorsan moving toward one of his contenders. Good. I could sneak off to the library now. Perhaps I'd cleared the way for him to forget about me entirely.

Instead, I walked straight into him, not quite sure how he moved that quickly. "There's a look of trouble on your face, Aralia."

"I don't know if that's the right word for it, Your Majesty." I curtsied formally as the others would expect. "I was hoping to get some air, or would you still like me to leave you a note?"

"I believe the note was our terms, if I remember properly." He stroked my face gently, like I'd seen him do in the vision.

"Lorsan," I whispered urgently, making sure he noted my distress at the public setting. "Not here. You promised."

"I did, but that wasn't specified in our contract. I am still the king, and I can engage with anyone I desire. I crave the feel of your skin on mine. You need time to think this all through? Fine. I will give you that, but tomorrow there will be no more avoiding this. I am over playing these games in the shadows. Do you understand?"

"Because of the hunt?" I asked him for clarification. I wish I understood more about the significance of the wild hunt, but people were already staring at us.

"Yes. I'm out of time and I will have your terms before we begin."

I took his hand in both of mine and kissed his palm while making sure I kept eye contact with him as I did. "I understand, then. Till tomorrow, my king. I will leave you a note on my way out."

"Will you return this evening?"

We both knew that he wasn't referring to my trip out into the forest. "Don't have the guard wait up for me."

Chapter 37 — Lorsan

I didn't think she actually meant to take the two days. I honored her wishes, mostly because I was contractually bound to. I just wished she had taken them before we began this. I couldn't think about anything else, and my room was cold without her presence.

"I really think the magic is going to select Soleil. Don't you?" My aunt prattled on as I stared out the window.

Aralia didn't come back last night. It was just now as the sun rose over the castle walls that she slipped on by the guards with a soft smile and bare feet. When she did this, I was left wondering how Rux would have handled her. The forests were dangerous, but her ability to disappear into the trees made walking safer for her. I didn't have the luxury of time to shadow her jaunts in the woods, but I still wasn't quite sure how to keep her in the garden. Long-term, that wouldn't work either.

She moved much more naturally without all the fancy fae regalia that she wore to the dinners that I'd forced her to attend. If Aralia agreed to be my consort, I'd have to change some of our customs to welcome in the other groves. Even our other neighboring vasilissa didn't often frequent the court like her mother used to. Allowing Aralia to be herself would likely make them feel more welcome, though she was beautiful in everything that she wore.

"Perhaps." I finally conceded as I realized Prinna actually stopped speaking to wait for an answer from me.

My aunt studied me closely after my nonchalance, and I cursed internally, knowing this would now be a broader conversation. "Are you not excited about her? She would make a good match for you. Powerful, commanding, intelligent."

I twisted Aralia's last note between my fingers. Was there something wrong with me? I couldn't get the words from Aine out of my head. A life with Aralia offered me something so simple. One word. Happiness. The imagery played into everything. I'd never seen the stars so bright and clear. It didn't matter that she hadn't carried a child before, the goddess would clear the way. I knew it. I wished Aralia could see the vision too, then she wouldn't fight so hard against what I was trying to offer her.

"What's the real reason my father went mad?"

"Why are you bringing up Helio now?" My aunt sat up straight from the comfy couch she'd been lounging on. "You are not like him in the least. I think you got more of your mother's genes if I'm being honest. Let's not talk about him so close to your triumphant day."

Yes, because accepting a woman to lock in the fate of the magic's power is a triumph for me, I scoffed internally. "Power and madness go hand in hand, don't they?"

"Only once you start trying to take things that aren't being offered to you. There's no war in our kingdom from your need to pursue foreign women and land." Concern layered her tone and the space between us. "Where is this coming from?"

"If I'm king, should I really ever have to deal with *no* being the answer?" I'd let the little nymph control most of our interactions, but now as the big event closed in, I didn't have time to mess around with this anymore.

"Depends on the question you are asking." Her hand brushed my arm before I realized Prinna had moved to my side.

I finally tore my gaze from Aralia to meet my aunt's worried brow. "This is all hypothetical, of course. I have everything I could ever want and look at all the potential in the future."

"There's my sweet boy. Your mother would be so proud. Yes. If you don't like Soleil, you can always ask for the magic to pick another one of the contenders. There are so many wonderful choices this time around."

"I trust the magic and the goddess's judgment. What I'm not sure of is if I trust my own." I turned to the window again and caught Aralia looking up at me. Why was there such sorrow in her face? *What have you decided without me?*

"You have a final breakfast with the contenders before the events this evening. It will be a great time for you to lock in your own selection. Make sure you ask them all the questions." Prinna fixed the collar on my loose shirt before she started heading back toward the door.

Aine had already shown me what they all would provide me, and in return I'd experienced a glimpse of their own goals and shortcomings. I didn't really need or want to discuss the situation any further, but this breakfast was also tradition. After the wild hunt, no one would be in the dining hall for days.

"I'll be down shortly. I have to get some work done." I waited until Aralia vanished into her tree before I took a seat at my desk. I still had about half a day before I could approach her for an answer. Fae contracts were very literal, and I was not a patient man. It would be cutting it close to the start of the wild hunt, but it would be enough time as long as she didn't make me chase her.

Her answer couldn't be no or that she couldn't. I wouldn't survive it knowing that she could be something that none of my predecessors had ever truly experienced. Wealth, power, prestige, and legacy were all things they had already accomplished. But none of them had been happy when their time was called. Everything had been for duty or the fae.

Even just these two days away from her had taken everything from me. I was the king, damn it. She wasn't allowed to do this to me. She could have the next few hours, but then she would come here and give me the right answer. The one we both wanted. If not, well, then she'd learn what it meant to say no to a king.

"It's so nice to have some time together with you. Any hints you'd like to give us for the hunt?" Soleil leaned in from my left and winked at me. Her placement beside me as the six remaining contenders gathered for this meal spoke volumes. They were beginning to fall in line behind the presumed queen, and my fate was taking shape.

The only problem was with the vision that Soleil's magic provided me. She'd have made an excellent match for my father, not that he would have noticed her at all, but I was not Helio. I didn't want to suppress and abuse the fey beneath me. There was only one I was interested in conquering, and that was in a completely different context.

All of her assets were covered but still out on display for me, her wings fluttering with graceful distinction. By all normal senses, she should have this in the bag. She was beautiful, and the fey magic responded to her call with authority.

"If you are selected, what's the first thing you would want to do as queen?" I trailed my finger down the side of her arm to her elbow. Her skin didn't warm under my touch the way Aralia's did, but I had to weigh the chances that Voreios could have been playing a very long game with me just to upset the balance of our kingdom.

Her smile turned seductive as she leaned into my touch, those golden eyes meeting mine as if I were the mission. I guess in this sense I was. I hadn't touched any of them since they arrived, which had been one break from tradition that no one had seen coming. Her fae glamour made her appear brighter in an attempt to draw me closer.

"I would have to say that it depends on the tasks that you would like for me to assist you with. During the day, I could manage the schedule for the court and our annual festivities. At night, I'd like to work toward securing our lineage."

Straight and to the point. We were a sexual people, but an heir would unbind my hands so I could make decisions that would further the fae agendas. My deeper goal had been to transform the fae lands into something untainted by centuries of history, either by relocating to a new world or making a major transition. No one really knew this yet, of course. One never revealed their plans until the time it was necessary.

"Is there anything in the court that you would want to change immediately?" I continued to ask her questions. This would be important because I needed to know what systems she would interrupt within the next lunar cycle. The other women looked positively bored, but they kept their expressions polite.

"Hmm, well, there is one thing." She lowered her voice, using a seductive drawl. "I'd like to move the events back to being fae exclusive. The fey ambassadors need to be limited in access to both of us and the other members of the council. I think we could even set up a proxy to handle their requests and negotiations. Someone like Prinna, so we don't need to deal with them."

My lips split into an amused smile. She'd been to see my dryad quite a few times over the last few weeks since Rux had left. "You don't wish to see them at all? There really aren't that many of them in the court."

"The few that I have encountered are mostly a drain on our time and resources. They can't truly understand our ways and shouldn't be given such honor in our society. I'd make sure there was never an interruption again during one of our sacred rituals."

She *was* referring to Aralia specifically. "You weren't worried about the magic choosing you to sacrifice? What happened that night shifted the conversation so that more of you would survive, isn't that a good thing? Why does it matter that a fey is the one who instigated it?"

The silence in the room from the others was deafening as they waited for her reply to my question. Tasi's expression was full of fury, though she sat without speaking a word. She had an independent streak like nymphs did, and though the magic responded to her with a powerful current, she didn't even pretend that she wanted to win these challenges. I was grateful

376

to not have to spar with that one about potential futures neither of us wanted.

I was still curious about why she entered the trials to begin with but knowing that Aralia had favored her for queen from the beginning, held back the part of my fury reserved for her family. My dryad would need community to feel at home here, and if she was friends with Tasi, then I would just have to deal with it.

"Let's just say that I have given my due to Aine. I'm willing to provide the goddess with whatever she needs to let me embrace my power. A true queen wouldn't have anything to worry about. Together we will be unstoppable." She climbed up into my lap and her hand rolled down my chest between us as if we were alone, not that it mattered. My father had had his rounds with women, and it hadn't mattered that my small sister had been in the room to see the exchange. "There would only be two of us here tonight if that hadn't happened."

"Things change. There's four women who are still here today because of one fey woman standing up for them." I knew there would be outrage over my declaration about Aralia after I claimed her as mine. Ideally these four women would take it to heart to remember who was looking out for them when no one else had. "We can discuss it more if you are chosen to be queen."

"But it's better than even being queen if I have the chance to be your mate. A fae king hasn't had a mate since before the split of our worlds. I would make sure to keep you so happy that none of the rest of it will matter."

I wanted to laugh at the difference between her and the woman I wanted. I knew that a king hadn't taken a mate since before the split. My mother talked about it all the time as she was relegated to consort when she should have truly been the queen in her own right. But I was a damn fool trying to appear to be different when it all fell down to a pair of green eyes I refused to live without. Before I knew it, Soleil's lips pressed to mine. My body froze in response, a wall forming between the future I thought I could force and the one I chased with a wayward dryad.

"I can't wait to do that forever," she purred and kissed my lips again. "I will do anything for you, and as your mate, I will shoulder all the burdens you don't want to deal with. I will be the best queen, you will see."

The bell chimed, indicating that her time was up, and she rose up to stand in front of me. "I am looking forward to tonight, King Lorsan."

I wiped my mouth, cursing myself internally for going along with this stupid idea.

Chapter 38 — Aralia

Just as I expected, Macendil had been able to get the piece of quartz with relative ease. He knew exactly where they were, and his powerful roots had been able to move it with only a thought and a few hours. It was larger than a melon and kind of heavy, but that was the size I needed to contain my tree.

The dru were slowly gathering in a field closer to the garden at the center of the labyrinth beside the fey pool. That was where I'd gone to meet them today.

"I don't understand why you are all gathering like this," I said as I studied the quartz. I didn't understand what made this one a moonstone quartz versus a clear quartz, but apparently there was marbling that told the differences. My particular stone just didn't have very many extra marks.

"Macendil advised us that you might leave the court to form a grove," Lesius said as the trees in the distance began to scream.

"We will be seedling's grove," another dru in the back volunteered. Maybe once we were officially rooted together, they'd stop calling me a seedling. My mom carrying seedlings of her own hadn't erased the nickname, so I didn't hold much hope that I would ever shake it either.

"But you can tell that I am sick," I protested. The large treks took a lot of energy from them, and I really didn't want to see any more of them pass into the great energy. "I'm not sure it's worth the effort."

"Then we will stay together for as long as we have," Macendil agreed with the others.

Tears pulled at the corners of my eyes, and I took a deep breath to keep them from falling. "I need to be hidden from Lorsan; he may come after me once I leave. We should go to the garden of the fey pool. That's shared with Voreios, and I know a corner where we can fade into the forest. Could that work?"

"We will follow you. It will take three of us to mask your signature in the magic, but it can be done. How soon?"

"I'm going to do this spell now and leave before the hunt, so he's distracted for a few hours with the large event," I advised them, and the dru all fell silent. "What is the wild hunt, anyway?"

"It's an event that used to happen every year, but now has not happened in centuries."

I wanted to laugh at that response. The dru were just being practical, but it still told me absolutely nothing about what to expect. "There seems to be a lot of things from the past coming back into being. Not sure I'm a fan of this trend."

"Some things repeat, and some things are lost forever," Lesius replied somberly.

I set the stone down carefully onto my central root. The dru had been able to pass me the spell, but I had to admit, I was nervous. I'd seen enough dryads move their trees to other groves to know that it didn't feel great, and usually they couldn't do it by themselves.

Carefully, I cast an illusion around myself and my tree, so no one else would see what I was doing, before pulling both of my halves into the liminal realm. I only came here sparingly, even while my mom and Ferox trained me. It was easy to get lost in here if the magic shifted, and then who knew when I would be returned?

"From roots to the leaf, my grounding here has been brief, unbind me from the soil to settle in the stone, so that I may move about in the unknown."

Bright magic wrapped around my form, twisting three times, and then repeated the motion around my tree in the same way. My roots sizzled as they vanished, the quartz started to etch an image of my tree as it disappeared. Planting my spirit form's feet in the ground, I leaned into the pain. If this is what I had to do, then so be it. Everything felt as if fire were incinerating every inch of both my halves.

Coughs tore from my throat, and blood coated my fingers, my skin turning pale as the black bruises spread farther until they expanded beneath my clothes. The amount of magic this spell used was going to shorten my life considerably.

As much as I struggled to keep my eyes open, the ground called me in closer, and I fell unconscious, cradling the stone of my tree.

Night had already set in by the time my eyes opened. They would have already gone for the hunt. I'd have to sneak around whatever happened in the world beyond. I'd not gotten to say goodbye to him. But perhaps it was for the best because I couldn't know how he would respond to my answer on the eve of selecting his queen. How could I hope to leave if I had to tell him no again? He just might actually lock me up.

I'd gone on some hunts early on with Zrif and Arbane, but as dryads didn't need to eat, I found I didn't like watching what happened during them. The fae seemed to be very excited about this wild hunt, but I'd never seen them do anything related to catching their own food before.

As much as I preferred to run around barefoot, the glow of my presence on the land would be lessened by the additional damper of shoes. Rux would tell me to wear boots that covered up to my ankles if I needed to be stealthy. I hated that I thought of him tonight, but I needed to be gentle. He had literally been with me every day up until this phase of my life. He could be the good advice sitting on my shoulder as I made my way to whatever new journey awaited me beyond all this.

Matching the shoes with the jeans my mom was always fond of and a long-sleeved shirt and gloves. I felt pretty ready for whatever would come my way. Leaves wrapped around as I tied my hair into a braided bun at the top of my head. The rock of my tree sat heavily in my carrying bag, which I threw over my shoulder.

The trees began to whisper as the night fell, and they got louder with each step I took into the forest. I'd studied Fae all my life. My father Graak had been proficient in every language, and my mother thought we all should be as well. But these words felt ancient. Something called, and I hated the goosebumps that formed across my skin even under my clothes.

"Aralia. There you are. Enter the forest. I have been searching everywhere for you."

That was Lorsan's voice, brushing my mind with his magic. So, I wouldn't be able to sneak past him after all. Might as well get it over with so he could pursue Soleil in whatever this event was. I strode out to the bridge over the water that separated the seelie court from the rest of the Feylands.

"Where are you?" I called back, and the trees' whispering fell hush again, more of a murmur, as though to not draw too much attention. I'd asked not to live in her shadow, perhaps life was giving me the opportunity to rise up. What would she have done if she stood in my shoes now?

I shook off the chills and strode with confidence that I did not feel out to where the tree line broke. Once I'd passed the water, I could sense the world around me. It wasn't the entirety of the Feylands where the roots didn't flow like Voreios's did. Perhaps I could straighten that out now that I was here.

Macendil had moved closer to the court again, and I could feel the exhaustion through his roots as he'd pushed many miles in such a short time.

"Why are you here?" I pleaded with him. "You were supposed to go the opposite way."

"Little dryad wasn't moving in time. Came to warn you. It's too late to leave for tonight." He started, but thankfully, he halted his forward movement. "You meant to leave earlier, now you must turn back."

"You know I have to go, Macendil. The ritual took more than I expected, but I think Lorsan knows I am out here. Do you know where they went? I can't fly like they can, but I need to avoid them as much as possible."

"The hunt has begun. Must return home."

"Macendil, I can't. That isn't home, and I have to leave before he returns. My new home needs to be with you." I tugged on the emotional heart strings, but he needed to understand. "Please help me."

A woman screamed in the distance as an eerie howl drowned out the sound of the trees whispering. Her shrill cries awoke a new fear at my core. This didn't always happen in the night around the Feylands.

"What exactly are the fae hunting tonight?" I asked him as I replayed all of the fae's excitement for this gathering.

"I cannot protect you, though I will try."

"What do you mean?" Why wouldn't anyone just answer my questions?

"Run, little dryad. They come."

Wind picked up around the dru and blasted out to the east, and the new screams were clearly not natural. A blast to the left, so loud that I couldn't think clearly anymore, startled me.

Snarls and howls took me rapidly in the opposite direction, toward the east around the walls of the labyrinth. I could hide in the trees. That was what I would do. They wouldn't be able to find me. But as I placed my hand on the bark, a force pushed my energy back out. Why wouldn't it let me in? Was this some type of fey magic? But I *had* fey magic. I didn't have time.

"Why is this happening?" Why couldn't I enter the tree? It might have to do with the current spell I'd bound my own tree in or the fact that I was startled. Either way, I was on my own for now.

A roar behind me was met with a shiver of fear down my spine, and whatever these beasts were closed in on me. I couldn't hide and I couldn't run any faster. Where could I even go? My chest heaved, and I coughed up more blood onto my sleeve.

There were two options that I could see now. I was one of the oldest daughters of the guardian, and I'd not been raised to cower or flee. That only left the option to fight. Rux had been my protector, but they'd made sure I could use my magic all of my life. I was from proud Voreios, and they would learn not to fuck with me.

Catching the ledge of a rock, I somersaulted myself up for higher ground. Another small coughing fit came as I brought my magic in around me, pulling from the air. Being so surrounded by fey magic was its own boon that I would use to my advantage.

I'd been prepared to fight, but the monsters that charged at me were unlike anything I'd seen before. They moved like animals but were uninhibited by the natural structures of trees and rocks, as if they were shadows. Too bad for them, they'd underestimated the wrong dryad. These beasts must not know who my fathers were. Beneath me, my fey powers imitated earth magic to make golem guards and replicated fire magic ripped across the sky as lightning.

Some of the two-legged creatures began to halt in their steps, and I couldn't help but smirk.

"Not prepared for the prey to fight back, I see. Well, come and get me." My golems charged and chaos broke out in the trees.

Right now, I felt pretty badass. I'd never had a reason to use my combat training like this. Directing the lightning, I struck out at the snarling beasts that weren't engaged with my golems. I needed to find something I could use as a rod to avoid hand-to-hand combat as much as I could. Their mouths and talons had a larger range than I did, and I'd hate to work at that disadvantage.

Where were the rest of the fae? Where was Lorsan? Was he being attacked too? I could help him. Had this fae event gone terribly wrong? I could only keep repeating the words that Macendil had spoken. This was the hunt, and I had been tricked somehow.

The more fey magic I used, the more I coughed up blood. Black spots appeared in my vision as more of these beasts showed up replacing the ones that I killed rapidly. Even with the golems restoring life energy to me with each victim they tore to shreds, I couldn't keep up the power indefinitely. I used fake wind to shift farther up on the rocky ledge, but I could only take on so many at a time.

The beasts parted and a shadowy man walked through them. His glowing red eyes landed on me. There was no way that he'd come back after all this time. The nightmare that my family had always chased. If the shadow god lived, then we were all doomed unless I could somehow get away. I screamed, and my fey magic exploded all around.

Chapter 39 — Lorsan

Aralia was magnificent. I'd never seen anything like her before. At first, I'd only wanted to see what her fear tasted like because we'd never dabbled in that area of fae hunger before. But then she'd turned around and rose to face the unknown, displaying not only her ability to imitate all forms of elemental magic but also her mastery against nearly unbeatable odds. After all, I was her opponent. When I'd called off the attack and my hunters split for me, her eyes stared at me, but she did not see me.

I had to summon every ounce of power I had to shield my lands from her terror-stricken attack. I had to release every single one of my illusions to contain her blast, but even that impressed me beyond words.

It wasn't until she fell from the ledge that she'd perched on that I considered the risk of fey insanity on her mind. I could see the blood on her sleeves, but none of my creatures should have actually touched her. Nothing in this forest should have been able to touch her, she hadn't been out here long enough.

My wings grew rapidly from my back, and I flew to catch her before she could hit the ground only to be gutchecked by a hoof. Rux landed with Aralia in his arms instead as I caught myself from being thrown into a tree.

"Lia." He cradled her in his grasp. In his urgency, the rest of his words came out in Druidic. "Lia, I need you to open your eyes and tell me you are here. Remember our word? Pixies. Come on, my sweet dryad, I need to hear you say it."

I should have known that the satyr hadn't gone very far from her, regardless of her dismissal. I wouldn't listen to her either if she told me to go. The only thing I needed to confirm was whether she knew he'd been following her or not. "Did you ever actually leave?"

"Fuck off, Lorsan," Rux spat in Fae and turned his fierce dark eyes on me. "What the hell is all of this?"

I couldn't answer him before I heard her small voice. "Rux? Pixies. . . How—"

She couldn't even finish her sentence before she began coughing violently, her whole body shaking in his arms as blood splattered against his chest.

"I'm going to rip off a limb of yours for each of those monsters that touched her," Rux snarled at me, and she grabbed his arm, shaking her head. I wanted to hold her, but the way he shifted his weight indicated he was ready to make good on his threat despite her distress.

390

"No, Lia. You can't tell me no. He should be protecting you!" he said as if trying to make her see reason. "This needs to be a line."

"She doesn't need protection from either of us after that display," I offered, and Rux turned his glare to me as if begging me to talk again. I just needed to touch her, so I slowly hovered a few steps closer.

"None of them touched me," Aralia said weakly, though she shrank away from my approach. My magic brushed against hers and was met only with wariness. "I still couldn't fight them off on my own."

There was no world that any warrior could have handled that many hunters on their own. I watched as defeat clouded her eyes while she sank against the satyr with a trust that I may just have broken in our growing affection.

"Aralia, the hunt isn't a challenge that's meant to be won by any but the hunters. It's a fae king's way to claim a prize."

Sure, her satyr complicated things, but I still intended to collect. Her sharp green eyes turned back in my direction as she caught the meaning of what I was saying. A small hint of her delightful glamour scent moved between the three of us. Rux glowered at me but didn't say anything. The groves functioned differently than most places in the world. If she wanted me still, he wouldn't stand in the way.

With an easy flick of my wrist the world around us transformed to a dark room in the liminal space. When I offered my hand, she wouldn't take it. Instead, she clung on tighter to Rux, but the tension in her eyes eased as she took in the room I'd created.

"Nothing will harm you here, Aralia," I coaxed. I loved saying her name. It rolled off my tongue with a seductive purr that the nymph perked up to.

I could fix what happened tonight. While the fae could feed on all intense emotions, I didn't like the smell of her fear the same way I'd hoped to. Pleasure it was, then. After tonight, she'd not be able to say no to me ever again.

Chapter 40 — Rux

I'd returned to her side a few days after the fight in the ocean, and this was exactly why. I couldn't stay near the court because she could sense me, but I'd taken up residency in the faun's glade. Cirro kept me updated on her, and Macendil's warning came through the ground straight to me this evening. The magic felt different than it had ever been before, so of course tonight would be trouble.

She could handle herself *mostly*, but that last scream came from a place she'd only go when fey magic messed with her mind. Most of fey magic was illusions, and even the most skilled wielder could drive themselves mad when pushed to an extreme. I'd only seen this happen to her twice, but I was glad that I could make it in time.

Being that she returned to us within a few moments, she'd likely be really hungry, but there wouldn't be any permanent mental damage.

The blood that covered her wasn't from a wound that I could see, and she'd not engaged any of the beasts physically, so something more was going on here. I could figure it out later when she wasn't so defensive. For now, she eyed Lorsan cautiously as I begrudgingly set her back down on her feet.

Even standing on her own, I felt her hand searching to make sure I was still beside her. I'd take it. I'd watched her sleep in my old room quite a few times after I'd "left." Being unable to touch her had driven me crazy for those weeks, but she needed this. Now her fingers gripped into the skin of my arm; it scorched my being.

Lia glanced up at me, and her dark green eyes gave me two pieces of information. She was nervous, and she was starving. The intensity of the experience had left her needing, which I had expected. From Lorsan's posturing, I could see that he was innately aware of her situation as well.

Her scent of honey and wildflowers danced openly between us here as her racing heart slowed. I took a seat on the edge of the bed in this room that Lorsan had brought us to. I could feel the fey magic, but I'd spent most of my early adulthood training with Aurinia and Ferox and dealing with the fallout of Aralia's practicing. I was more in tune with it than most other non-fey creatures, so it didn't bother me at all.

Aralia turned to face me, clearly deciding that she needed to address the situation between us first.

"I'm so sorry, Rux."

I caught her wrist and pulled her into my lap as her face crumpled up in the adorable way it did when she was truly sad. Wet tears hit my chest as I closed my arms

394

around her in a tight hug. Finally, she was back in my arms, and I'd never let this slip away from me again. The apology was nice, but her presence meant everything.

"Hey, you're okay," I crooned softly to her. My fingers spread out to rub down as much of her back as possible. I didn't love these jeans between us, but one thing at a time. "This has been a hard adjustment for all of us."

"That's no excuse for what I said to you. I didn't mean it. Any of it." She pulled away from me just enough to watch my expression.

"Lia. There is no world that exists where I will leave you behind, even if you command me to." I needed to tell her everything, but for now, I could start here. "I love you, and there is no home for me without you."

I should have been ready for it, but I wasn't. Her lips pressed to mine. Tears still fell freely against my face as she sorted through her own emotions. I'd wanted to kiss her forever, but this wasn't like any kiss I'd ever experienced before. Her lips parted for me, and as my tongue brushed hers, my whole body sang with the overwhelming sense that this was what sunshine felt like after living in the dark my whole life.

This was a claim, and my heart knew it for what it was.

Chapter 41 — Aralia

Just kissing him felt like the world tilted back on the right axis. I'd fought this for so long; I'd been a brat for years, making his job harder just because I could.

I needed the truth from Rux. When I pulled back from him, I felt my fond smile as he kept his eyes closed, lost in the last moment of our shared passion. "What about your mate?"

He opened his dark eyes slowly and stroked my face. "What about her?"

"I . . . Just . . ." I couldn't find the right words to say. I needed him, but at what cost?

Then he chuckled. He actually laughed at me. But when I tried to lean back away from him, his strong grip stopped

me. "Hey, I'm sorry, okay? I didn't mean to laugh. Aralia, I've only ever loved you. I told Rhenei that. You come first. Always. I will follow you from Voreios to anywhere, and I will be there to protect you. You have not been and will never be alone."

He pressed a soft kiss to my lips after I nodded. My glamour mixed with the pull from Lorsan's. His skin appeared brighter and heavenly, making it so that I couldn't turn away from him. Slowly, I pivoted my body to face him while still making sure I kept in contact with Rux.

Sitting on my protector gave me renewed strength and clarity, knowing he would catch me. Lorsan frightened and thrilled everything inside of me, but Rux gave me courage again. As soon as my eyes met his, Lorsan shifted forward to catch my shaking hand.

"Do I scare you?" he asked me, eyes stern.

"Yes." Perhaps it wasn't as much being afraid of Lorsan but of what my magic would push me to if I had to fight against him. The trauma of my younger years came back when I went to that place, and once I was stuck in the illusion, I might not ever return to sanity.

"Would I scare you if you were at your full strength?"

"I don't want to be afraid of you at all."

"Never again. The hunt brings out the true nature of those running, but you shone so radiantly. It's an important tradition, but much like the other things you have already altered, I do not want to chase you away from fear or doubt."

Something unreadable passed through his expression before his hand grabbed the back of my head to pull my mouth to his. Rux's hands felt up the curves of my pants, and I moaned, allowing Lorsan to slip his tongue in my mouth. There was something electric about feeling both of them touching me this way, something I could get lost in. Given their relationship to one another, I'd never imagined this even being possible.

"Lose the clothes, Lia," Rux coaxed as his grip on my hips guided me down to his trapped erection. "Let us feed and pleasure you."

The leaves wrap around my body to remove my hiking attire, but I wouldn't make it that easy for him. A light, see-through chiffon robe appeared in the place of my jeans and shirt.

"Fuck," Rux cursed softly as he reverently caressed my skin through the new material. He'd seen me naked before, but as my mind went back through our history, I could replay the looks he'd given me. Oh, how much I'd tortured him while he took care of our needs in the past. I went for Lorsan's pants while I had clarity. His tongue brushing against mine would make me lose my sanity quickly.

Lorsan had also changed, and his loose-hanging pants fell easily once my fingers brushed against the top of his hip. His long cock popped right out to greet me, so I wrapped my fingers around his length as he hissed against my lips.

"I won't do two days ever again in our future negotiations." Lorsan groaned between kisses as Rux's hand came up to cup my breast.

"I thought you said any terms I wanted," I teased, unable to help myself even if I would never be negotiating with him again. "Not off to a very good start, Lorsan."

"I think *Lorsan* should watch as I bury myself in you repeatedly, since he enjoys watching so much," Rux said easily as a challenge that seemed to be directed at the king, and I was a little surprised when Lorsan stepped back. I wasn't quite sure what Rux meant by the comment, but I also didn't care to dive into the clarification at the moment.

Rux moved quickly to toss me back on the bed, his hands parting the robe to hook his fingers through the straps of my lacy panties. He kissed a trail straight down from my stomach to the top of my covered mound. His hot breath stirring me into a near frenzy. He pressed his nose against the fabric and took a deep inhale.

"I agree with him. I'm not going along with anything that keeps you away from me again," he said huskily before tearing the thin fabric out of his way and burying his face between my legs. "I need to be able to taste you whenever I want."

I whimpered at the way his hands dug into my thighs, spreading them for his tongue to traipse through my slit. He started with slow laps that went the entire length from my clit to my back hole, and after the first few, I was writhing in growing need for him to pick up the pace. When I opened my eyes, Lorsan only smiled at me as he stroked his cock.

"Looks like we both enjoy torturing you," Lorsan mused as Rux's tongue penetrated me, caressing every inch of my core his long tongue could reach.

I crooked my finger at him, needing him to come closer. When he obliged, my hand replaced his in a fluid motion that made him growl. The velvety flesh of his penis glided through my enclosed fingers, and I dragged his precum down his length before I leaned forward to pop his head into my mouth and suck. If Rux was going to torture me, then I could give as good as I got.

Lorsan's fingers threaded into my hair. He coaxed my throat to take more of him just as Rux's mouth locked onto my clit and two of his fingers pushed inside. I sobbed as his tongue flicked me over and over again, but the sound came out muffled.

"You look so beautiful submitting to Rux and taking my cock down your throat," Lorsan praised, and he thrust gently to gauge my reflex from this angle.

I worked my tongue along his cock as he slid back out, then latched on to suck and swipe my tongue over the top of his head, chasing as much of his flavor as possible. Lorsan cursed in Fae and pulled my hair to rein me back under his control. Below, my clit vibrated under one of Rux's smaller toys, and his tongue worked faster than my mind could keep up, sending me straight toward the building orgasm. My entire body shuddered as he dragged his fingers in and out in a tempo meant to drive me mad.

Stars danced in my eyes, and Lorsan removed his cock from my mouth just in time for me to cry out. I didn't even have enough time to recover before Rux flipped me over and dragged my ass back toward him at the end of the bed.

"Look at how she glistens," Rux purred and spread me wide in front of him, assumedly showing Lorsan what he was marveling at. I should perhaps feel self-conscious, but instead I was on to the next ride as Rux pressed his cock to my entrance.

"Rux," I whispered into the pillow as he pressed slowly forward, filling me with every inch that I didn't think I'd ever have enough of.

His hands gripped my hips as he went from half in to slamming his way home. "Every time I'm in you I think, this is it. This is heaven. And then the next time I sink into you this way, it's still better than the last. Do you feel me?"

"Yes," I let out, but I wasn't sure it was coherent as he picked up his tempo. Lorsan's magic rubbed circles on my clit, and I met Rux's thrusts in my pure inability to not grind back on him.

He alternated the tempo by slamming in and slowly pulling back out. I lost myself in the rhythm. I was lost in the energy of these two men who shouldn't be mine. I didn't know where Lorsan was, but as the rubbing on my clit turned into pinching, I screamed into the pillow on Rux's next thrust. They were going to kill me with orgasms.

My satyr hesitated, and his cock twitched in the very tight space in my core. He was trying not to release himself in me, and it came with some sexy grunting as he pulled me up to sitting on my knees while he was still buried to the hilt.

I felt Lorsan move, and when I managed to open my eyes, Rux had my body completely bared to Lorsan as he continued to fuck me, keeping me propped up against him by my shoulders. The fae king drew his hand down the front of my form, following the path with his tongue. When he got to my clit, he licked and licked until I shattered again all over Rux's cock.

"I don't think I can . . ."

"Oh, you will," Rux growled in my ear, and I was shaking. "I'm doing my best to hold off so that we can both be inside of you, but all I want is to release so much cum in you that you'll be dripping my seed for a week. Can you be a good girl and take us both at the same time?"

Oh, sweet Montibus. I'm fucked. Literally. I could only nod.

Rux walked my body back with him, so that he could prop himself up against the headboard. Lorsan climbed on the bed in front of me, and with the size of his hard cock and Rux's already filling me to the brim, I wasn't quite sure how this was going to work. However, I wanted to be a good girl. I wanted to find out just how far I could go to please them.

Lorsan lifted my hips, and my hand grabbed onto his shoulder for support as Rux slid out just enough to only keep his head sheathed inside.

"Goddess damn, you are so tight, Lia. You are going to have to relax. Let me support your weight. Just hold on to Lorsan," Rux coached, and Lorsan caught my mouth for a few heated kisses. His dick glided against my sensitive clit before he pressed at my entrance with Rux.

There weren't enough words in any of the many languages I could speak that would describe the intensity of feeling both of them penetrating me at the same time. My body felt like I would explode from the amount of cock inside my core. I wasn't sure it was pleasurable just yet, but as they began to alternate thrusting, gently at first, my breath came on rapidly and my nails dug into Lorsan's skin for a hold on anything as they used my body. From one thrust to the next, I could feel the storm coming, and I was ready to unleash it. As my body constricted around them, I knew I wanted it all. Exhausted and messy, I would never be able to let go of the fireworks going off in my brain.

Rux came first and bit into my shoulder, making me orgasm harder than I ever had in my life, dragging Lorsan along with me. Fey magic poured from me as I couldn't contain the well in my heart any longer. They were mine, and I wasn't sure how I'd be able to correct the destiny we currently walked on. But for tonight, everything could be how it should have been.

Chapter 42 — Rux

I couldn't stop kissing on her, even as she'd finally given in to sleep. Newly bonded couples could go for days, and she'd handled quite a few rounds with us both already. The pain from the etched markings all over my skin was the greatest blessing I had ever received. Aralia was mine. She was Lorsan's too, but I didn't care. She was mine. Now there could be no denying it.

Her blond hair fanned out around her on the pillow. As she slept on her stomach, I couldn't see the marking on her chest, but she now had four new, clear wings with green designs that looked like a dragonfly's, long and rounded at the tip. They currently folded back and down her beautiful frame. I was very careful not to touch them, but as I massaged the place where they connected with her skin, she let out a sleepy moan.

Lorsan had gotten up from bed a few moments prior, but he responded much as I did to the beautiful sounds she made. His eyes turned back to observe her still sleeping. We were both trying our hardest to let her sleep, but those sounds made it even more difficult. He pulled on some pants and studied his own markings with a tight grimace on his face.

"I've seen these but couldn't have imagined what they felt like. I can feel her in my chest, feel how peaceful she is right now. At least this means she can't leave me now, right?"

"Was she trying to leave?" I asked him casually and massaged down her spine again to evoke the pleasure sounds, even if she also protested my continued attempts to arouse her.

"I have to take a queen in a few days. Aralia wouldn't agree to be my consort, no matter how many ways I tried to negotiate terms with her. But this means that she is mine, correct?"

"Well, technically it means that the gods have blessed our match, and that we are hers," I corrected because he seemed to be confused about the way that it actually worked. "But yes, I enjoy thinking that she is just as much mine, even if I have to share with you."

"Yes, you do complicate things," he agreed thoughtfully. "Typically, consorts don't have their own consort, but I guess exceptions will have to be made."

"She's not your consort. This means Lia's your mate." The fae king had always frustrated me, but now we'd have to be practically inseparable. I couldn't take my sweet nymph away from her other partner any more than he could try to do with me.

"I can't have a queen and a mate. That's not how it works in fae society. I can only have a mate if she is the queen, and

Aralia is fey." He tried to explain, but it sounded like he was trying to convince himself more than he was me.

"Sounds like you are giving up your queen then," I growled at him. Lia would be distraught if he took a queen now.

"I have to take a queen. I have to have an heir for the throne. Aralia said that she might not be able to have children, so I cannot avoid whomever the fey magic chooses, even if I didn't claim them at the wild hunt."

I rolled my eyes before I stroked her hair, allowing her presence to soothe me. "You will break her heart if she even thinks about you with another, especially now. It'd be different if they were part of our bond, but I don't see any of your potential queens with us now."

"I don't wish to break her heart, but I don't know what else to do. The magic demands an heir. Why do you call her Lia?" he asked, and I'd allow him to change the subject for now. She'd have to stress to him how important it was that he didn't take a queen, because the chances of Lorsan listening to me were marginally small.

I couldn't help but smile at the question. "When she was really young, she couldn't pronounce her full name in Druidic. She could only say it in what we call tree speak. That's when seedlings chirp or sing. Aurinia knew what she was saying, but the rest of us didn't. So, when they first started talking, we called the twins Nye and Lia. I've just called her that since. Well, that or princess, because that used to really set her off."

He looked thoughtful for a moment. "You called her princess to make her angry?"

"Yeah. She's feisty on even the best days, but I enjoyed our verbal sparring. It meant that she was being honest with me. What can you tell me about her wings? I've never seen these before." I ran my fingers over the smooth surface of the wing on the left.

"Honestly, I haven't either," Lorsan admitted with a frown. "I've never seen wings that fold down this way, though where they meet with the skin is a pleasure point for her like it is for the fae. Our wings tell us what court a fae's lineage is from and how powerful they are. She's not fae though, so she shouldn't have wings."

"Well unless you put some strong mushrooms in the food we had earlier and we both are tripping, I can't argue with what I'm seeing. I just wish she'd stop hiding her dryad lines." I leaned closer to her and whispered in her ear, "Revelare te."

"Rux," she murmured in protest, rubbing my cheek but not opening her eyes. The green lines drew themselves out along her skin, and I traced them gently.

A black spot under her skin spread out across her shoulder and grew down her back.

"What is this? I tried not to hurt her when I caught her fall last night."

"This looks just like the marring on her arms last week." Lorsan slid closer and turned her wrists around to reveal more of the bruising.

"I'm going to turn her around," I said urgently as I shifted up to my knees. I cupped my hands under her gently, Lorsan assisted by laying her up against me, and she stretched.

"You both are insatiable, I swear. Let me sleep half an hour more." She leaned forward to kiss Lorsan before she settled back against me, her eyes already closed again.

I was in a stupefied horror as I stared beyond the beautiful marking of our match between her breasts. The bruise consumed most of her body. Lorsan looked at me as if I would have the answer, and a pit grew in my stomach.

"Lia, my love, can you wake up for me?" I asked quietly, trying to keep my tone neutral.

"Rux . . . I mean it, just a little bit longer," she protested, but she must have seen Lorsan's expression because she immediately covered herself.

"Oh, don't worry about this." Then her eyes caught on the mark on her chest as she tried to glamour away the dark marks. Her eyes widened as she looked between us both. "No. No, no, no, no. This can't be right."

"Aralia, we are marked by your gods, why do you sound so distressed? This should be a good thing, right?"

Lorsan asked her gently, though the concern hadn't faded from his face.

She dressed with the leaves quickly and slid out of my arms. Her wings were folded neatly behind her, but she hadn't seemed to notice those yet. The bruises vanished along with her dryad lines as if there was nothing wrong with her at all. Lia's frantic pacing began as she looked for a way out of the room.

"The gods have made a horrible mistake. You have a queen to take, and you are supposed to be back in Voreios with your mate."

"Lia, you are my mate. You always have been. That's what these marks are." I tried not to growl at her because I did not want to go back through this fight. "What is going on with your spirit form? Are you hurt?"

"It's just my dryad lines." The lie rolled off her tongue so easily that I raised my eyebrow at her. It would never work on me though. I knew all of her vocal tones.

"That was not your usual markings. Did the medicine they gave you not work? Why didn't you say anything to me?"

"Rux . . ."

"Don't lie to me again. What is going on?" I asked her as gently as I could. I sat on the end of the bed and pulled her back to me. Lorsan watched cautiously, unsure what to do. He wasn't as familiar with her tricks to get out of hard conversations.

Aralia picked at her nails, refusing to meet my gaze. "I can't be your mate. I'm . . . dying."

"That's not possible." Lorsan shook his head and took her hand, so she'd stop fidgeting. "Even now you are radiant. Full of life. The medicine should have weeded out the initial illness."

"It didn't," she confessed, and my vision of the future began to crack immediately. "I can't stop coughing when I'm alone. I try to mask it, but each day it becomes more difficult. I glamoured the effects away from both of my forms as long as I could."

"That was the blood on your sleeve last night." It wasn't a question. Now all the pieces are beginning to make sense.

"Yes. The more fey magic I use, the faster the darkness spreads." Her eyes flashed as if she remembered something, and she began to pace the room again frantically. "No, it should be here. I need to go back. Lorsan take me back to where you found me."

"What's happening now?" I asked, not understanding this new panic. "We can go back to the court, and I'll examine your tree."

"That's just it, my tree isn't there anymore. Lorsan, I need to go back to where you found me right now."

"What do you mean?" I caught her waist and spun her around to face me. "What did you do, Lia?"

"I . . . put my tree in a stone and it was in the bag I was carrying when I came into the woods. It's not here. I have to go find it."

"You didn't come out here for the hunt, did you?" Lorsan asked her quietly. There was hurt in his question that I hadn't expected from the man, not that I didn't understand just how deeply this woman could wound.

"No," she admitted so softly that I almost missed it.

"You were trying to leave me."

"Lorsan . . . I had . . . I have to. I can't be your consort. I don't have long left, and I can't spend the last of it watching you with your queen. Even knowing what I mean to you." She turned to look at me. "And you were supposed to have long forgotten me."

The fae king looked torn between sadness and fury as he weighed out what happened. "You are mine, and you will not leave. I am a king, and you cannot keep telling me no. You will negotiate new terms with me, and we will do it now." His wings flickered with emphasis to this point and hers responded subtly.

"That's not how this works. I will not give you any new terms, you cannot keep me. There is a way to reject the mate bond. That is the only way that we can move forward from here. But first I have to find my tree. If it . . ." Her eyes grew wide again. "Rux. Someone else is touching my tree."

Her magic blasted against Lorsan's liminal wall before she cried out in pain. Her spirit form began to flicker and before I could get to her, she vanished.

An echo of "help" was all that remained.

Chapter 43 — Aralia

Every part of my body hurt. Whether it was the illness or whatever it was they were doing to the stone that carried my tree, I couldn't tell. My spirit form continued to flicker in and out of existence so often that I hadn't been able to get my bearings on the room at all. It was just dark, with sketchy lighting and what appeared to be a doorway on the other side of the space.

"It looks like it's working. She should be ready for the ritual," a male voice said in the darkness, breaking the tense silence.

"The stone is going to make it easier to sever the magic."

This was a new male voice, but I still didn't recognize it. Were they trying to split me from my fey magic? I didn't want that, but I couldn't figure out how to use my voice just yet.

"This is something that we will have to advise the mage council of."

Of course, it was shadow mages who had discovered my moonstone quartz. It'd be easier to just vanish back inside of my tree and remain there, but then I'd have to worry about what would happen if they smashed the stone.

When my form settled, I went to rub my face when a shadow chain tugged at my wrist. How could they do this while I wasn't solid?

"She's awake." The two mages cast their gazes in my direction, and I gave them both my best glower. My stone was trapped in a vise on the table in front of them, shadows engulfing the entire surface.

"What are you doing to me?" My throat felt dry as if I hadn't had a sip of water in days, and considering my time in the stone, I wasn't getting the proper light and water recommendations.

"Oh, didn't you know?" The man I recognized as voice number one was a shrill man with glasses and a strange curve to his back. "The king has asked us to make you feel better. It will be quite painful at first, but it will be transitory pain."

Lorsan asked them to help me? Were they able to find me after I vanished? "Where is . . ." What should I call him? He was my mate, but the world didn't know that yet. "King Lorsan? Rux?"

"Only healers are allowed in this space, I'm afraid. You are quite ill, and it could be contagious."

The way he smirked while he said this to me raised all the red flags. They weren't wearing healers' garb at all, but the robes I'd seen the mages use just a few days back. They must really think I was stupid.

"I'm glad they are safe then. Can you tell me what is wrong with me?" I tugged at my secured wrists. "Why am I bound?"

"Until the procedure is complete, you must remain in place. We can't touch you or your illness could spread to us," the second man responded. He had a tall and lanky form with dark brown hair that fell to his knees, and he peered at me with hollowed eyes.

"If you can be this close, please send King Lorsan into the room. Even if he stands by the door." I would try any piece of bargaining. My new fate mark told me that unfortunately neither of my mates were nearby, and they were concerned and furious.

My mates. What a strange thought to have, but a beautiful one. I'd never known it could feel like this. Even in this strange place far away from them, it was as if our hearts could still beat in unison. I didn't feel so alone. For a brief moment, I focused on my affection for them, and almost immediately it was returned.

"He is busy attending his trial for a queen. As a guest of the court, you don't get to demand to see him."

Hmm. How much did they know? Clearly, they hadn't spoken to him at all if they were still referring to me as a guest. "I am his consort. It was official after the hunt. He will always make time for me even if he is dealing with the new queen."

I'd never agree to be his consort, but that was between us. Lorsan was all but demanding a renegotiation the last time I saw him. It was a bold lie, but I was willing to bet these mages didn't know either of us well enough to call it out.

"He has taken you as a consort?" The one mage glanced nervously back at the other.

"He said he was going to mate the queen. Repeatedly, even when she asked him." The second mage looked toward the door as if this news would bring someone crashing in. "She's not going to be happy about this."

Who was this *she* they kept referring to? I groaned as a new wave of pain rippled down my flesh.

"It won't matter in the end," the lanky fae man commented as he turned back to the table between us all. "We must stay focused on our role."

"Why won't it matter?" I asked when they both fell quiet again while they avoided making eye contact. "I need to see the king, or I do not consent to this treatment."

"I'm afraid, you've misunderstood, little tree. You'll never see Lorsan again." I knew this new voice almost too well. I glanced at the door as it swung on its hinges. Trevan stepped through and gave me the most chilling smile. "The moon is about to ascend to its highest point. Let us begin the ritual."

Chapter 44 — Lorsan

"What the fuck just happened?" I yelled at the satyr as he leaped to his feet. The markings on my chest relayed that Aralia was flustered and in pain, but I couldn't tell where she was.

"Get us back on the usual plane immediately," he barked, scouring the room for his clothing and weapons. "Aralia is in danger. Nymphs only flicker out like that when their element, in her case her tree, is going through something painful. It's a forced reunification of the two halves. Whoever has her tree is going to die a very gruesome death."

I snapped my fingers, and the world returned to the forest we had been in before. Rux hunted around for a few minutes in the pitch darkness before he found a random bag that had been cast aside in the brush.

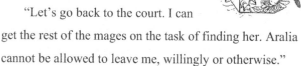

"This must be what she put the stone in. Her tree is gone." He tracked the area, but as was to be expected, there was no telling which direction this person had gone.

"Let's go back to the court. I can get the rest of the mages on the task of finding her. Aralia cannot be allowed to leave me, willingly or otherwise."

"That is hardly the point." Rux glowered at me as if I was dense, like he didn't believe I would just as easily cut the person who currently held her into tiny pieces. "She's a nymph. If she wants to run from you, then you will have to let her until she changes her mind. That's fine. I can get the rest of the guard rallied up."

"The guard? Do you mean my guard?"

"Sure. What else could I mean?" he snarked back as if I'd asked a stupid question. "I have no say with Voreios's guard anymore, and it would take them way too long to get here."

"Mine don't take orders from you, though," I remarked, not fully understanding the bold confidence in his claims to run the fae guard. "Trevan can get them in line."

"You cousin is incompetent. I have continued to train them these past few weeks, and he didn't even notice. They listen well enough to my orders because they actually want to be capable."

"Hmm, that could work. I'll let him know you are taking over as captain of the guard. He really was shitty at that job; I just didn't have anyone else to put in there."

"Who says I want that role?" Rux snarled at me as I opened up a fey ring to the court. We stepped straight through to my quarters. "We are getting farther away from her. Damn it. How are we going to find her if we don't even know where to start looking?"

Aralia did feel farther away now that we'd left the forest. "I don't care how many fey rings I have to put up, we will keep jumping until we find her. These markings will be quite useful if they can tell us whether we are getting closer or not."

I strode to the door to find a puffy-faced Soleil standing there about to knock. I'd forgotten entirely about the queen trials, and in hindsight, I really should have known that claiming Aralia during the wild hunt would derail absolutely everything else. I just genuinely hadn't cared. Even if she had been a few hours late, I'd never even considered hunting the other women.

"Your Majesty. I just . . . I don't understand. I was supposed to be the one. There is no one else the magic has pushed forward. All signs are pointing to me." She sniffled and straightened her shoulders to demonstrate a return to her pride. "To slight me this way mere days before the magic makes its selection is foolish. What a bad place to start our relationship."

We were never going to have a relationship, but that was hardly the thing to say right now if I wanted to avoid a much bigger conversation. "I'm sure you have thoughts on all of this. At some point, perhaps I will make time to listen, but right now I have something to do urgently. Step aside."

"Who did you claim?" She wouldn't move out of my way.

"Who I take to my bed is not, and shall never be, any of your concern." I guided her body to move to the side so that I could walk around her, but she seemed to be made of stone.

"You promised to take the queen as your mate. I demand to know." She had the audacity to shout at me. "If you have a mate, you shall not have another. That's what it means to take a mate. It's the dryad, isn't it? Is she in there now? I will not allow this. Not in my court. She needs to be removed immediately."

"It is not your court yet, and you would do well to mind your tongue and tone in my presence." The words poured out, and I heard my father in them. "Get out of my way."

The glare she gave was venomous, but she stepped to the side as I leaned over the rail and called for Trevan. He may have caught his own prize last night, and the sun wouldn't come up for many hours yet. The hunt wasn't only good for the king, and I also hadn't intended to leave the liminal plane this early. Typically, all the hunters would find a catch once they knew which the king had marked.

Rux stepped out behind me, and I noticed he had covered his markings on his usually bare chest. He didn't want anything to delay us in the search for Aralia, and that included court politics. I could appreciate his urgency even if I hadn't hidden mine as effectively with my fashion sense. Soleil noticed him and although her eyes revealed calculations, she kept her mouth shut. I stormed down the wing to Trevan's room and pounded on the door. No reply.

"She's not wrong about mates. That's why you can't have a queen now." Rux said quietly so only I could hear him.

"With the severity of this situation. I'm going to have to tackle one thing at a time. Let's find her first. Then you really should take the role."

"The only thing I care about is Lia," he retorted easily, reminding me of the only real thing that mattered to him as if I could have forgotten.

"And how would Aralia feel if something happened to me?"

"I see what you are trying to do, but it won't work. I've hit you enough times to know that you are pretty sturdy." Rux cracked an amused smile as he presumably thought about our numerous encounters with one another while Aralia was a sapling.

"That would have to come to an end if you became the captain of the guard."

He rolled his shoulders with an annoyed sigh. "You know what? Once we find her, I'll consider it. She can't be your consort, though. Oh, and if you hurt her in any way, I will hit you again until I feel satisfied."

"You negotiate a hard bargain, but I think we might be able to make your terms work."

After a few more knocks, Rux grew impatient and kicked in the door. The bedroom was undisturbed with the curtains drawn tight to prevent the light from entering.

"Where is that lazy sack of shit?" Rux growled at me.

"He could be in the liminal realm like we were last night. It's fine. Call the guard to attention and then meet me at the courtyard in five minutes. I will be ready to go. We can find her ourselves."

"Fine by me," Rux replied and leaped off the edge of the balcony to the ground floor.

I did a quick search across his room to see if he'd left anything out. He'd been acting a bit strange when it came to Aralia the past week. As I opened each drawer, I only became more confused. Everything was empty and there were shelves layered with dust as if he hadn't stayed here in a very long time.

I met Rux in the courtyard as he was delivering final orders to the guard, splitting up units to scout the forest and the labyrinth. He also included a few units to stay and protect the court. If he became captain of the guard, this just might work out between the three of us. Knowing that Aralia would be loyal to me, and Rux would always be loyal to her meant that I could trust him.

Chapter 45 — Aralia

"What do you know about wisps, Aralia?" Trevan stalked around the table in front of me as he messed with an old book in his hands, flipping the pages with an easy disregard.

"Not much. I've never seen one before." Where was he going with this?

"No one has seen them in quite some time. A new one hasn't been born in centuries."

I didn't want to talk about this anymore. I struggled against my cuffed bindings and tried to pull up my magic. "Why can't I see Lorsan? He didn't ask you to do this, did he?"

It wasn't a question. I was calling them out on their bullshit, and we all knew it.

"No, he didn't. I thought it was going to be a bit more difficult to sneak you out of the court with the size of your tree and all. You did all the hard work for us by putting it in this stone. Where were you going?"

"I'm not telling you anything."

"It really does matter. I need the story to be believable. The fact that you willingly unattached yourself from the grounds helps quite a bit. Where were you going?"

I glowered at him. "Are you the one who made me sick?"

"Not initially. We were able to cure you of vitium sacer almost immediately. Giving you the mors cavium though, that was much harder. I hadn't expected Lorsan to let Rux stay. I also hadn't expected that you would tough out being sick and cover it up for us. Your satyr was problematic, so I had to make sure he vanished long enough for you to pass the point of no return."

"So, this is to kill me. To what end though? Surely there have to be easier ways."

"And now we circle back to my original question. This isn't to kill you . . . Well, that's not quite right. You will die, but it is so much more than that. This is a ritual to separate a nymph from their element to create a wraith." He picked up the quartz holding my tree and turned it over in his hands. "Where were you heading, Aralia? I'm very curious."

A cold sweat broke out on my forehead. "But . . . why would you do this?"

"There are only a few ways that a wisp can be born. The one that produces the most energy and can leave the most destruction in its wake is the one we are going to perform here today. A nymph when pulled from their other half is left as a wraith on the land. You will do what we say when we say it."

I tugged against the restraints, but the shadows latched on to my skin. "I absolutely will not. You will release me right now. Look, I'm sure Rux could fill you in on this. I'm a real brat when anyone tries to give me orders."

Trevan lifted a knife off the table. The old, rusted blade looked to be stained with years of use, and to have never been cleaned from the way the grime caked on. He read over the page he'd left the book open to again, before he headed in my direction.

"No. Do not do this."

"Is that an order or are you going to start begging?" He dragged the blade against my jawline slowly. "I would love to hear what your pleas sound like. Lorsan wouldn't let me have a go before we got here. After though, you'll be pleading to play with everyone, hungry bitch."

"Maybe everyone but you," I snarked back, unable to help myself, and he backhanded me with the knife. I felt the thin slice across my cheek before a drizzle of warm blood ran down my chin.

"Elouan, light the candles." Trevan gestured behind him, and a fourth man came in the open door before it slammed shut and vanished. Apparently, we were all present for whatever was coming next.

Fire poured out from Elouan's mouth, but it didn't feel like either elemental or fey magic. The stream of flames split into more individual balls of light than I could count, which spread out across the room, lighting all the candles around the room.

"We summon Crom Dubh to be present in the ground tonight." Trevan spoke, lifting his hands with his palms turned up toward the roof. "Cleanse the space of earth."

Shards shot up from the slab that I rested against and sliced thin cuts all over my skin. The movements were so quick that I didn't feel the initial pain, only the lingering burn all over my body as tiny trails of blood ran down from each of them.

"We summon Crom Dubh to be present in the wind tonight." The shrill man came up on my right and lifted his hands in the same way that Trevan had. "Cleanse this space of wind."

My lungs compressed as if the breath would tear itself from within me. Fighting to keep the air in my lungs wouldn't help, but my body was in shock now.

"We summon Crom Dubh to be present in the flames tonight." Elouan said from above my head. I couldn't see him, but I could barely see the room as a fire lit in my gut, burning me from the inside out. As a tree, fire was a natural fear and I let out a small cry as I fought for control of my mind in the flames. "Cleanse the space of fire."

"We summon Crom Dubh to be present in the water tonight." The final man came up to my left and sweat poured over my skin. It steamed from the flame's heat and sizzled away threatening to dry my flesh out. "Cleanse the space of water."

Trevan took a candle and poured the hot wax in a design on the tops of each of my feet. The scalding pain seared up from the pathways my root system would normally use, and the pressure in my head built into a headache I'd not soon forget.

"We bind this creature of nature to walk with the wraiths, leaving no physical marking of her existence."

The stone containing my tree lit up like a beacon, and waves of pain rolled inside from my feet to my head back down to my feet, like the ocean's waves crashing on the shore. Trevan lifted the blade again and pinched at the shadows coming off my toes from where the candle wax seared my skin. Slicing up, I felt a rip through my soul as my spirit form flickered again.

"Hold her on this plane. Everyone needs to focus!" Trevan roared at the other three, and the slicing continued.

"Mama." The sob ripped from my throat as tears poured from my eyes. The pain was on a level that I had never experienced before. I should have found a way to call them. I knew she couldn't help me now, but it was the last strand of hope I had left. "Mama!"

"She's calling for Aurinia."

"The guardian won't make it in time. Stand your ground, the split is almost complete."

A blinding white light burst out from my chest, and I screamed into the brightness that consumed us all.

Chapter 46 — Rux

Lorsan appeared at the top of the steps with a scroll in his hand. "Let's go back to the forest first. She was closer there than she is here."

A fey ring popped up in front of me, and I walked through it, followed quickly by the king of the fae. "What is the scroll for?"

"It's the shortcut through the labyrinth." He answered succinctly as he unwound it to read over the transforming chart.

"You think she is in there?"

"Call it a hunch. It's where we found the selkie. Things go in there to avoid being found, and we know she is not in the court. If the mages took her, then that has to be where they are hiding in my kingdom." His steps didn't slow as he headed toward the labyrinth, but he grew quiet for a moment.  "She was going to leave me, but she also thought you were back in Voreios. Where would she have gone if it wasn't back to Voreios?"

"Likely the fey pool to plan her next step. Then she'd probably ask her parents to take her off world if she was really trying to escape," I reasoned, as if I understood anything about how Aralia thought.

"She'd leave the planet to get away from me?"

"Lorsan," I chided as I followed him to the next ring. "It's not for lack of affection. She's had her heart set on you for a long time. Her mother used to say that her crush developed because she likely enjoyed the sound of your voice when you were negotiating the contract with Voreios. Dryads are hard to sway when they set their mind on something, even as seedlings. Trust me, when I fucked up with her as a sapling, she did not let it go."

"You seemed quite comfortable here together," Lorsan commented, and that warmth filled my being as I thought over the few weeks before she'd ended things between us.

"The Feylands helped heal some of the fracturing. I really wish I'd been honest with her before you convinced her to send me away," I prodded, but Lorsan only nodded his head in acceptance of his role in that.

Pain tore through my chest like a meteor ripping its way free, and both of us flinched.

"What was that?"

"Aralia is in trouble," I said through gritted teeth. "The bond allows us to experience her emotions and each other's. We need to move faster."

The ground was torn up in trails in the brush across the entrance to the labyrinth. Lorsan also seemed to take note of that fact. "I've never seen them move this frequently and with such speed."

"Those dru love Ferox's kin. Every single one of Aurinia's children grew up with them as extended grandfathers."

"She was going to visit Macendil regularly. Where would they all go?" The fae king's wings fluttered, and I realized with my new bond mates I'd have to adjust to wings all around.

"I bet we are about to find out."

The hedges of the labyrinth stood another foot over both Lorsan's and my head. Through my connection to the magic of the earth, my hooves could pick up on the shifting of the hedges from the root levels. They were constantly shifting. With Lorsan's map, we took the right turns, but we both pushed the pace.

"Why can't you just fly through the portal or make a fey ring to skip all of this?" I finally asked him as the ground hummed in the familiar patterns that I'd always associated with the fey pool.

"Most fae can fly and powerful fae can create rings. It wouldn't be a punishment if they could just fly out."

Well, that made sense. It sucked for us right now.

"I feel like she's close . . . but I can't see her anywhere." I gestured around the empty garden and even toward the pastel waters. "She has to be right here."

"They must be in the liminal plane." Magic spilled off Lorsan's wings and twirled out in spirals into the world around us, shaking up some of the illusions.

"Can't you take us there?"

"Most times, but there are some private ones that can be tricky to dispel and locate." He met my gaze. "But nothing will stop me from finding our mate."

Aralia screamed again, and my heart shattered. I wouldn't be able to make it in time.

Chapter 47 — Aralia

I could feel my lovers closing in despite the pain that echoed through my being. I had to eliminate the chanting. I had to do something. I would not just sit back and let this happen to me. The fey magic poured out from my body, filling the room with an electric charge. I needed my tree. If I could just touch the stone, I'd be able to catch my breath and escape these chains.

Another scream tore from my chest. It just hurt so damn bad as he sliced the knife farther down my soul. If he made it to the bottom, I'd be parted from my other half forever. Luckily for me, this was a slow process. My insides felt like they were being shredded into tiny slivers of all that I was. Simultaneously, I pushed the mages back away from me with the pure force of the element leaking from my body while I pulled the quartz stone on the table 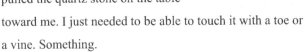 toward me. I just needed to be able to touch it with a toe or a vine. Something.

"There is no way out of here! Stop fighting this!" Trevan snarled and stopped cutting to pull my hair back against the wood of the chair. "I should have added more restraints, but you should be unconscious by now."

I ignored him and focused only on pulling the whole table over. It fell, throwing everything in my direction. The stone clanked and chipped as it skittered down on the floor.

It still wasn't close enough as I pushed my toe out to touch it. Darkness clouded my vision before a piercing pain sliced into my gut. All the wind was knocked out of me and, in shock, I glanced down to see the knife he'd been using sticking out of my stomach. Blood pooled in my lap before dripping onto the floor.

"There, now you will stop fighting. Just a bit more to go, but it would probably be better if you passed out here. I can promise the pain will only increase." He pulled the knife out roughly, and my vines grew from my hair to try in vain to put pressure on the hole. This was it. I was going to die. Each deep breath felt as though there was liquid in my lungs.

He bent over to retrieve the old crusty book, and I used what little magic I could to pull the stone one more time. At first it wouldn't budge, but thankfully he ignored me as I cried in pain at the exertion of calling more magic. The stone rolled over itself once . . . twice . . . a final time until it touched my toe.

"Fuck you." I spat the blood out of my mouth as my spirit form vanished back inside my tree stuck in the stone.

Chapter 48 — Lorsan

Aralia kept flickering in and out as I felt for her in the garden around the pool. I wanted to curse and rip everything to shreds. How could we be this close and still unable to find her? The pool currently whipped around violently, whether in response to my plight or the lands I couldn't begin to guess.

Rux stood on one of the boulders, examining the toxin that leaked out of the stones into the pool.

"What is going on here? This wasn't here a few years ago."

"No," I admitted. It wasn't a time for secrets. "This is the cause of the venenatio luteus affecting the fey population. The mages love to contaminate our magical sources so they can wipe out the other users. This is where a queen was supposed to be helpful."

"Lia!" Rux shouted as he accepted my explanation. "Tell us where you are!"

My wings carried me up over the center of the pool so that I could observe the toxin. Only three of the stones leaked from their center. That had to mean something, and it could be part of what prevented us from seeing her.

A warm liquid drop hit my face from above. It didn't rain on these lands since they danced in their own magical world. I wiped the water off, then pulled my hand back to see that my fingers were coated in red. I glanced up to see another drop before it hit my nose. A small crack in the world above dropped this down on me, and as my magic met it, a blind fury took over my body.

That was my mate's blood. My queen's blood.

"Found you." I reached forward, lifting up toward the crack, and with a violent rage, I split the door to the liminal realm wide open.

Rux didn't waste any time, though I wasn't sure how he got up there, and he went straight for the first mage on the left. I recognized the man with his back to me instantly.

"Trevan!" I roared and the men turned to us, full of shock and awe. The table they stood around was covered in blood, but I didn't see Aralia.

The magic in this room didn't come from the usual fey sources, so pulling on the power didn't work, but good old battling would. Rux landed a few punches into the gut of the tiny mage before he bashed his head on the wall behind them.

Summoning my dark dagger, I sidestepped around the oncoming attack from the guy on the right and stabbed the blade back, straight into his gut, using his momentum to rip a hole that dropped his intestines to the floor.

"You're too late! You figured it all out too late and now we will take over your kingdom," Trevan spat at me, and I raised my blade to block his strike. It was on. "Your court is already being overrun now. Face it, you have failed."

He'd always striven to be my equal even when he wouldn't put in the work or the time. I'd never asked to be king, but that didn't mean that it wasn't who I was supposed to be. I'd wanted a mate, and that was what the gods had provided to me. I wouldn't lose either of those things. Not to this piece of shit.

We exchanged blows as Rux moved onto the fire-breather in the back of the room.

My power crackled all around me as I picked up a tease of my sweet lover's scent. "Where is she?!"

Chapter 49 — Aralia

I hadn't expected to get so much time to recover, but so far no one had touched the stone. It was cramped in this space, and my magic felt stifled, but I took a few long moments to count to ten and heal the tear in my soul. I would have to rest for days to repair the entirety of the damage. Days I didn't have as the rot still spread through my veins.

As I pushed out of the additional containment of my tree, I knew the fight must go on, but unbound, I would be far more trouble than these mages were prepared for.

"Lia?" Rux grunted as something roughly hit the wall to the far left. I turned and let out a relieved breath. They'd found me.

With two of the four mages dead, my lovers were tearing into the final two with an enraged focus so pointed that I didn't want to distract them further. Rux and Lorsan radiated their fury through our bond, and all I could feel was grateful to see them. My tree flashed out an alert again as someone picked up the stone. I turned to find Soleil turning my moonstone in her beautifully pampered hands.

"How do men always manage to fuck this shit up?" she snarled as our gazes met. "How are you not a wisp yet! You end

437

up in my way at every single turn. I knew you were the real problem, not the other contenders. I don't care that the rest of these morons can't finish the task. The magic can."

She tossed my tree out the huge hole that revealed the regular world through the liminal barrier. It fell straight toward the fey pool, which had begun to boil.

"No!" I shouted and flung myself over the table, but Rux ran to the edge faster and attempted to catch it with earth magic.

I felt each twist of the stone as it hurtled down. I could go after it with my powers, or I could deal with her. Spinning on my heels, I tightened my hand into a ball where all of my fingers touched, trapping the magic within my grasp. I willed the fey gifts to be sucked from her body. I didn't know how I knew it would work, but as she grabbed her chest and stumbled back to the ground, I knew it was. When I crushed the energy trapped in the ball of my fist, she screamed in pain. Blood ran down from the corners of her eyes and lips, marring her once-perfect face.

"You will never be safe again. He will rise and then he's coming for you." She panted, and there was a tug on my power as she attempted to regain control. I wouldn't have it.

"Let him come. I'm not afraid." My voice reverberated, and I opened my palm up to face her.

Tiny cracks appeared in the center of her body, ripping across skin as if replicating a dry earth. Roots burst out from her chest, splitting her in half and burying the pieces in the layers of dirt in the liminal realm.

By the time I had enough mind to look for my mates, the silence was deafening. Lorsan stood over his cousin's dead body. The once-ceremonial sword protruded from his chest in proud victory, despite the turmoil on the king's face.

Rux. Where was Rux? I glanced around for my satyr protector to find him standing in the middle of the boiling fey pool. He held the stone with my tree in his grasp and looked for a way to leap back to shore, but the distance was too great for him without the opportunity to gain some momentum before the jump. He appeared to be manipulating the stones so that he could make his way to the shore.

"Are you all right?" Lorsan said in a voice that was too soft for his position in life.

"I think so. I got to my tree just in time. They almost split my . . . soul." I choked on the last word, and Lorsan pulled me into his arms. I tried so hard not to break down. The exhaustion from the past few days was overwhelming.

"You are safe now. We won't let you or your tree out of our sights again. Let's go home, and once you've rested, we need to talk." He held my body so tight against him that I wanted nothing more than to let go and lean into the support he was offering. The mark of our fated bond hummed with relief from the embrace.

I nodded against his chest. We would need to discuss the ramifications of our bond, but I wasn't ready to remove it. I knew I had to let Lorsan go, but if Rux also wanted it, then I knew that I would die of heartbreak.

I wiped the rogue tear off my cheek as I slowly began to process everything and turned to the waters of the fey pool. Rux had made it to the other side, but the boiling waters contrasted with all of my memories. This wasn't natural. Shutting my eyes, I willed them to cool, to cease their fury. A gust drifted by, and the chill in the air aided my message. It was winter after all.

"No need to be angry," I said gently, and with each breath, the tension in this isolated garden slipped away.

When I opened my eyes, I could feel Rux watching me from below. Lorsan stroked his fingers down my spine with a sweet caress. He lifted with his wings out of the hole he'd ripped in the liminal realm and took my hand. When I looked back at the pool, all the stones were lit up, and I noticed that Rux had left the quartz with my tree on the new island.

"Rux, my tree," I called to him.

"I know, Lia. I think this is where your tree should stay," he shouted back at me. He gestured to me to come down to him.

"With the fey pool?"

"And with the court," Lorsan added, and he pulled me toward the edge gently. "I agree with Rux. Some changes are necessary."

"But I can't be at both. My tree can only be in one place." I summoned the winds with a little bit of magic since the fae king didn't seem to remember that I couldn't fly.

"I'm going to move the court so that this is the garden, my sweet nymph."

"Release your tree, Lia. Take root. We can discuss the rest after." Rux encouraged again, and I looked back at the stone.

They seemed to have a plan. For once, it would be okay if I went along with things.

"Reset radices quercu." The fey magic pulled on the final strands of my energy. I'd exerted more power today than I even thought was possible. The white glow in the center let me know that the spell had been cast, but even more important than that? I saw the reflection of a woman looking at me through the water, and from her smile, I could tell that the fae goddess Aine had accepted those plans as well.

My tree's roots hummed in contentment as they mixed with the water of the fey pool. Light pastel bubbles rose from the water's surface. Wings fluttered behind me, but Lorsan still hovered in front me. I turned my back to the reflective light of the pool, and my jaw dropped.

"I have wings?" I asked breathlessly as they fluttered again in response. I trusted them to work, especially with Lorsan so close to me that I stepped off the cliff of the liminal realm back to our reality. The flight was gentle and smooth, and then I set my feet on the ground. "How is this possible?"

441

"They showed up last night," Rux replied as he appeared at my side. It only took half a second for him to rove my body for injuries. He brushed his fingers over the deep wound in my stomach that I hadn't had enough time to fully repair. "At the same time that we received our mate marks."

"I'm not fae though." I twisted to see my reflection in the fey pool to study them closer.

"Maybe not." Lorsan spoke up and wrapped an arm around my waist, drawing my face to him. "But I don't think that matters anymore."

I gaped at him, and he only gave me a warm smile. "You can't do this, Lorsan. The trials haven't been completed yet and I wasn't competing in them."

"I'm beginning to suspect that Aine brought you here to compete. We just didn't know it. The rules stipulate that the only way to adjust Aine's will is to make her an offer of something more than what she intended to give you, but I don't think even that applies here." Lorsan's hand trailed down my back where my wings met my skin, sending a chill across my body. We'd been interrupted from our days of mate bonding, and need rose in my being, but this was hardly the time. "When the trials started, I'd intended to mate the queen. Your gods have blessed our union to create the mate bond you needed. Aine created conditions that you

442

couldn't avoid in order to bring you both here, and I bet she has healed you too. Drop your glamour and let's see."

He waited as I fidgeted with my fingers not wanting to destroy this pretty illusion that he was painting for me before I realized I wasn't hiding anything. This was my true form, lines and all. I also hadn't coughed up any blood since the horrifying ritual began.

"I'm not covering it up." The words were so soft I almost couldn't hear them.

Rux leaned in and whispered in my ear the Latin phrase he loved to use on me. "She's telling the truth. Look, Lia. There's no more signs of the vitium sacer or bruising under your skin. You don't need to run anymore. Though you never should have to begin with."

I easily ignored the rebuff; I'd figured that both of them would give me a lecture about my half-baked plan to run away. "What are we going to do? There's no way that the fae would accept me, let alone Rux. You are both my mates. This is such a complicated situation. If Trevan and Soleil were both part of the mages' plan, where do we go from here?"

"They will accept both of you because our magic demands it. We will make it work. Even now, I can feel your roots settling into the grounds of the pool. Your presence is going to change the land." Lorsan lifted his hands and the illusionary boundary of the eternal garden around the pool dispersed. My roots relayed to me that I was beginning to receive signals from the Feylands. "None of this happens without Rux with the nature of these bonds, so they have no choice."

"I'll be the new captain of the guard, seeing as the position is vacant." Rux kissed the tips of my fingers. "I don't want to be a king, Aralia. The only thing I want is to stay by your side and keep you *both* safe."

The look that passed between my two lovers was one I couldn't believe. They were making space for each other. Rux had been Veon's support and he now offered that to Lorsan. Given all the double play in fae culture, I wasn't sure why Lorsan so readily accepted it, except that I could feel through our mate marks that this was sincere. The healing cut in my stomach ached and drew me out of my thoughts as I winced at the pain.

"We need to get you to a healer." Concern filled Lorsan's eyes as he took in the size of the injury. "Let me take you back to our quarters and then I will go handle the court. I just need to know you are being taken care of first."

"I will heal in my tree," I reminded him as my senses continued to pick up on changes happening in the world beyond. My magic brushed Lorsan's for insight, but the signals still weren't making sense. "What are you doing?"

"Moving things. There's so much about caring for you that I don't understand, but I want to learn. I'm pulling the fey pool back into the main world so it will be on the same plane, dispelling the labyrinth, and moving the court off of

444

the island moat to settle where the labyrinth was." He kept his information brief as he appeared to be distracted by the tasks he'd mentioned. I'd not even thought it was possible to do any of those things, but my roots continued to provide data that it was happening as he said.

"Why?" I asked him softly, even as I slid my hand into his and offered up what I could of my own gifts. My wings fluttered again and took on a pale green glow.

"I need to be able to see you from every window in our court at all times. Leaving you here to heal in your tree is not an option. I also want you to be close enough to talk with your twin anytime you want to *without* having to leave our home."

On hearing Lorsan's words, both Rux and I turned to the east and the familiar mountains of Voreios came into view. I wasn't sure how to feel at the sight of my old home, but the changes didn't end there. The dru began to appear in the area around the pool and instantly connected with my root network strengthening my ties to the land.

"Won't this be too close to Voreios? I know you've always liked your privacy." As much as I loved what he was doing, it needed to work for all of us.

Rux also turned to the fae king with a look I could imagine echoed mine. "I agree. It means a lot that you would be willing to do this for us, but I think I speak for us both when I say we are committed to what we can do for the fae and for you. I don't want your people to feel like we are persuading you to remove the proud lineage your people have."

I nodded my agreement and Lorsan lifted our joint hands up to kiss my knuckles.

"This is all my decision. With you and Rux at my side, I have a feeling that the relationship with Voreios is about to change. I can tell the fey are already migrating to be closer to my beautiful queen and the proximity will allow nymphs to wander the borders to test our transition. The fae will have to understand that change is needed, not just for a dynamic with the world, but with the fey in our society. None of this has occurred in centuries, and I want the Feylands to be an option if bonds occur. I'd like to explore all of this first, but, if needed, we can move the court again."

The open field shifted as the court appeared from the smoke in the early morning light. My king was determined to make all the changes and he'd barely even broken a sweat.

Rux again brushed his hand over the wound on my stomach and knelt down beside me to take a closer look. "I think you need to rest a bit, Lia."

I ran my free hand through his hair, but before I could reply an explosion shook the grounds. My eyes shot up to the court as it finished the transition to its new home.

Mages flew all around it, pillars were on fire, and the fae were in a massive panic.

"Fuck," Lorsan cursed and slid around us as his wings burst out of his back, shimmering of black fire, and leaving a trail of golden magic with each step he took. "Protect her. I need to deal with this."

I could feel him manipulating the magic and the entire land moved in the sky as his fury lashed out at the individuals, striking them down with pure magic. This version of Lorsan would burn down the world if he had to, and we would be right there beside him.

My wings fluttered as magic pooled on the tips of my fingers. A flowery fey ring opened in front of Lorsan leading straight to the center of the court gardens. "We will do this together."

Chapter 50 — Aralia

Rux charged through before Lorsan and I entered the ring. The earth tore up from the ground, seizing the group of mages by their feet and flinging them outside of the walls. "Guards! Fall in line, clear the center first."

The people gathered in the court displayed various forms of relief seeing their king coming through my fey ring as Rux took charge of leading the attack on the perimeter. A grey cloak charged out from the depths of the court halls straight towards him, but Lorsan moved so quickly I'd not noticed him. Snapping his neck, the body fell discarded to the side. Then the form began to bubble. This was the only warning before the flesh exploded.

Rooting into the ground, I caught the flames and absorbed them into the land. Tiny green balls of light rose from the soil as my magic pressed to soothe the chaos of the ongoing attack. The power of the newly released fey pool was cleansing the land from the filth and poison that had been stuck here for centuries. The contamination ran deep, and I was determined to have it all removed.

More explosions rippled around the court as Lorsan, Rux, and the guards silenced each life of the tainted fae. I just couldn't focus on that; I knew they could handle that. The dark energy that coursed through our kingdom wasn't Aine's, but it was just as old.

"You are not welcome here, Crom Dubh." I growled out the words as the name from the ritual came back to me. "With the spilling of your acolyte's blood, your invitation has been revoked. These lands belong to Aine."

Dark laughter echoed in my mind, and at first, I thought it was only his, but then I felt the goddess brush my power. Chills swept down my bare skin as the charge picked up along the earth.

"You heard her." The goddess purred with words that fell like a poison drip. "Get the fuck out."

"This isn't over." The deep voice replied ominously before the energy dispersed.

Lorsan's magic sent a ripple out that knocked all of the rest of the mages from the sky as Rux tore them apart with the earth and buried them deep in one final offering to the goddess.

When I opened my eyes, Lorsan stood over me, and I nearly startled from how close he was without touching me. On hearing my slight gasp, his gaze turned down to trail his eyes over my face with so much affection that my cheeks burned before I couldn't help but glance the opposite way.

The fae in the court naturally gathered around us in order to be closer to their king for their new directions after all the changes over the course of the evening. Almost everyone looked to be roughed up from the scratches, blood, and torn clothing. Tasi met my eyes as she approached the gathered crowd and understanding dawned on her face. The rising balls of light that came from my presence shifted from green to gold to match the ones that radiated from Lorsan's wings. The fight was over for now.

It took the remaining part of the next few hours to coordinate the healers and recovery efforts. Rux kept coming to check on me as I wrapped lesser wounds, because I'd still not taken care of the wound in my stomach. I continued to promise him I would rest, but I wouldn't leave him and Lorsan to handle all the heavy lifting.

A pulse in the magic tugged towards Lorsan, who stood at the edge of the old gate that would have crossed the moat before he'd moved it. I headed in his direction and couldn't help the smile that passed as I saw my tree behind him by the glistening waters of the fey pool with the mountains of my childhood in the background. The others gathered had given him some space, but I didn't miss their glances as I approached him.

The king kissed my forehead and then slid his hand into mine before he turned to the others. "Clearly, there have been a lot of changes this evening. Transformation will come swiftly, and we will work through the next steps after we have all rested. Before we part ways though, I have an announcement. The magic has made its selection, and it lines up with my choice. We will do all the grand celebrating another time, but Aralia, will you sign one final contract with me?"

My smile widened as I replied, "Lorsan, I can't be your consort."

"Good," he whispered in my ear with a hot breath that only served to turn me on and gestured for Rux to come join us from behind the gathered fae. "The only role that is right for you is as my mated queen."

A scroll unfurled in front of us. Lorsan signed it without even reading it with a quill that hovered beside it. Electricity ran between us as his fingers brushed mine to give me the instrument.

Still not taking my eyes off of him, I leaned up to brush my lips against his. "What am I agreeing to?"

"You are welcome to review it. I'll wait. Essentially, it's a promise to spend a lifetime together. . ."

"Done," I cut off his explanation with an easy flick of my wrist to sign the document and then, in front of everyone, I kissed my mate. My wings fluttered in sync with his and our bond hummed in that pure joy in my inner soul.

Rux's proximity as he finally came up behind me caused my heart to swell like it would burst out of my heart. Carefully, he wrapped an arm around me from behind and rested his head on top of mine.

Lorsan passed him the quill. "You also have to sign, for our bond is not complete without you."

I heard Rux release an amused huff of air, but again our bond hummed with the respect that Lorsan had given him. He leaned forward against me, pulling me in closer, as he signed the contract.

As soon as he signed, the fae around us starting with Tasi took a knee and bowed their heads in respect. The sun rose on the horizon and beautiful pastel colors rippled out from the beams of light. I'd never seen anything so beautiful. What better indication of the bright new future ahead of us?

"She who paints the sunrise," Rux murmured in awe as he watched the same skyline. "That's what the pixies said the day that I brought you here. Now, no more avoiding rest. Let's go back to your tree so that you can heal."

Lorsan scooped me up in his arms and opened up a fey portal straight to my tree that the three of us used. Rux's trailing commands to the guards were the last things I heard before it shut. Lorsan set me down on the roots for my tree, but I wasn't ready to leave them yet.

My protector picked up on my hesitation and moved to lean back against my trunk. He settled up against my bark in a way that I'd not known that I needed. Graak used to sit like that beside my mother's tree while he watched over us all. When Lorsan joined him, I sat on Rux's lap and rested my legs against Lorsan. Feeling them both and my tree settled my heart for the rest I so desperately needed.

His arms wrapped around me to keep me cocooned in his warmth as gentle strokes pet my skin. I'd fought this for so long, yet the love I was dying for had been there all along, if only I'd opened my eyes and seen it.

The sun continued traveling up over the court revealing just how many changes Lorsan had made. My roots in the fertile soil of the fey pool spoke of the magic spreading to touch every corner of the lands that we claimed as ours. The power would be available to those with the heart to use it. The dru and their wind chimes sang a beautiful melody to the shifts and a tiny hum drew my attention to the small seedling breaking through the surface. The first of their kind in almost a millennia.

Today would be a new day, one where I would be beside Lorsan and Rux as the queen of the fae. Nothing was out of reach, and together we would change the world with the union that defies the past and makes the future whole. The dark god might return, but it was a fight we would be ready for. For where there is happiness, there will always be hope.

The End

Thank you for reading!

About the Author:

Callie Pey is the steamy fantasy romance author responsible for The Dryad Chronicles. She loves fantastical worlds and epic stakes that embrace love in all its forms with a heavy dose of adventure. A current Austinite, she enjoys reading almost as much as writing, painting, and finding even the smallest moments to capture joy. With one completed series behind her, Callie is now embarking on two brand new series to come: A dark fantasy not for the faint of heart and a paranormal romance that will feature parts of Texas!

Keep up with her at:

www.calliepey.com

Made in the USA
Monee, IL
20 September 2023